BOLD CONQUEST

Bekah splashed the refreshing water about herself, reveling in this cool luxury. A startled gasp escaped her lips as a shadow fell across her. She twisted around in the water where before her stood a man of strong build. His wide shoulders, lightly furred chest and arms were deeply bronzed.

Bekah knew true terror as the stranger splashed down into the water. Trancelike he reached out, catching her in his grasp. She struggled to free herself, kicking and twisting within his hold. Cupping the back of her head in his hand, he pulled her reluctant mouth to his own, bringing their lips together. She pushed against him with her hands, trying to pull her lips away. His encircling arms were like bands of steel as he lifted her and carried her onto the sand.

The reality hit her with a blow as she saw the glazed determination in his eyes. The shock of what was to come paralyzed her with fear . . .

Other Avon Books by
Katherine Myers

DARK SOLDIER

Winter Flame

Katherine Myers

AVON
PUBLISHERS OF BARD, CAMELOT, DISCUS AND FLARE BOOKS

WINTER FLAME is an original publication of Avon Books.
This work has never before appeared in book form.

AVON BOOKS
A division of
The Hearst Corporation
1790 Broadway
New York, New York 10019

First Avon Printing, April, 1984

AVON TRADEMARK REG. U. S. PAT. OFF. AND IN
OTHER COUNTRIES, MARCA REGISTRADA, HECHO EN
U. S. A.

Printed in the U. S. A.

WFH 10 9 8 7 6 5 4 3 2 1

To
Pamela Transtrum

Without whose help **WINTER FLAME**
would not have been possible

WINTER FLAME

Fragile flame,
Trembling in the breath of snow.
Thy light glints off ice,
Expanded in reflection.

Yet which face does
My mind glimpse,
Frozen in this orb of light?
'Tis it golden king
Or black-haired knight?

Snow encircled flame,
My love is likened unto thee:
A glow of amber in
Winter's bleakest season,
A contrast of heat and ice.

Yea, 'tis fate's cruel twist
It was lit twice.

PROLOGUE

REMEMBRANCE

WHAT LOVE IS THIS, SO LIKE A BRIAR ROSE?
IT BLOOMS IN SPRING, YET IN THE SNOWS.

THE WIND HOWLED MUCH THE SAME THEN AS IT has through all the ages since. Its moaning would increase to a wail of sobbing voices, then die down into stillness until the next crescendo. Bekah, listening to its fearful cry, wondered if the tales from her childhood were true—if the winds were in fact the voices of restless souls. Yet here she was, safe, with firm walls of stone and timber surrounding her, and many tapestries woven in threads of scarlet, blue and gold to keep the cold from her. The fire in the hearth burned brightly, filling the room with warm orange light by which she precisely moved her needle up and down, embroidering a design which she had created. The finished cloth would depict a scene of heathered hillside, a rainbow and clouded heaven on the horizon.

With her needle poised to enter the material, she stopped, her face a sculpture of concentration. Her features were beautiful, but in her pensive expression was a past that held secrets. Bekah remembered back to the time of her beginning. It was truly not so long ago, and yet so much had happened since her childhood that some of her memories were foggy. Still, she could recall running freely through fields where wild wheat grew, both she and the green grain in the new growth of life. Rugged emerald hills, spotted with black rocks and bordered by jagged coastline, came to her mind. As if seeing herself through clear glass, she remembered her past. Bekah now recalled exactly how it had been.

The stone walls of castle turned to the turf and stone walls of the Nordic farmhouse of her childhood. The coarse walls of that earlier dwelling once again surrounded her.

PART I

SOGN, NORWAY

IT WAS A HOT DAY. BEKAH LEANED AGAINST ONE of the parallel posts which helped to support the roof, trying to avoid the smoke which rose upwards from the long, stone-paved fireplace in the center of the floor. Fresh fish, scaled and cleaned by her earlier, now cooked in the coals of the fireplace, the smoke ever-rising through the hole in the roof. Through the winter Bekah had had difficulty finding a comfortable place by the fire-pit, yet now, during the fleet days of summer heat, she was forced to tend to the uncomfortable warmth of the fire.

She had lived along the Scandinavian coast from birth, yet still she felt a stranger to its angry surroundings, and a stranger in this house. Helg, her father's wife, sat in a corner of the room, weaving on the wooden loom. Bekah watched as Helg released the warp yarns that were tied around heavy stones and proceeded to run the shuttle through the yarns while deftly packing them with a bone tool. Bekah would have liked to try the loom, but Helg never allowed her to, for Bekah's duty (as her stepmother made clear) was to perform the more menial chores. To avoid further scolding this day, she bent over the fire to examine the cooking fish.

Bekah's sigh drew the attention of Jorgen, who looked up from his game of *Hnefatafl*. He had been feigning interest in the wooden board with its pieces of stone and bone chips. Bekah kept her eyes averted from his direction, not wanting to draw his attention further.

Jorgen was Helg's son and the resemblance was clear. Like his mother, Jorgen had dull yellow hair and small, close-set eyes. Bekah felt uncomfortable in his presence.

A shaft of light came down through the smoke hole and illuminated Bekah's thick golden hair that lay in twin braids down her back. Jorgen's burning gaze engulfed her as she removed the fish from the coals and peeled away the

7

leaves that kept in the juices. She took up the meal onto large wooden platters, discarding the charred leaves. Jorgen watched her movements, thinking what a pretty manner she had. Her hands, blistered by hard work, still retained a delicacy. Her mouth, innocently appealing, seldom smiled, for she had little reason to. Still, he found her beautifully disquieting. It was obvious to Jorgen that his mother hated his stepsister, and that she took pleasure in punishing the girl. That would change, he reflected, when Bekah became his wife and he became a true man. He would head the farm in time, keeping Bekah occupied with bearing his sons. It would be then that he would tame her defiant attitude and rid her of the foolish notions of her mother's people. It would take time, however, for her father still thought of her as little more than a child. Sometimes Jorgen wondered if Lars were blind. Many men at the farm and also in the village were well aware of Bekah's blossoming womanhood. He must be patient, he thought, continuing his study of her.

Helg looked up from her loom and noticed Jorgen's gaze directed at that skinny child who grew to look more and more like her Saxon mother as the days passed. Helg's mouth drew into a tight line. She admitted to herself that the girl was growing more comely. She felt threatened, for how could she protect her son from the scheming of the girl?

"Bekah!" Helg fairly yelled in her near-masculine voice. "Hurry with those fish. It is well past the meal hour, you worthless piece."

Bekah looked up with that combination of defiance and fear that Helg so despised. It seemed to Bekah that her stepmother did nothing but scold her now. Helg would sit at the loom, weaving and surveying the kingdom of her kitchen, constantly finding fault with Bekah but never helping.

The men were called in from the fields, where their crude wooden ploughs were left at rest, and assumed their places around the plates of fish, bread and bowls of goat milk. Helg left the weaving and seated her bulk. Jorgen, unable to work now because of a leg wound received from a scythe, found a place next to Bekah. How she wished Jorgen would leave her alone! What had overcome him this last year, that he stared at her so?

She wiped the perspiration from her brow and reached for the bread, then chewed thoughtfully on a crust. Her father looked up from the noon meal to gaze at her with a mixture of love and pain and sorrowful pride. Helg noticed her husband's look, and a ruddy flush spread across the roughness of her cheek. Bekah looked up and recognized the glint of bitter jealousy in Helg's eyes. The jealousy was for her mother, Bekah knew, even if she must bear its brunt. It made her own life miserable. Her plight was the worst of the three in this unhappy circle, she knew, and cast her eyes down. She remembered her mother's sweet, finely featured face and slender form. Those had been the happiest days of her young life, when Mary, her mother, was still alive.

She looked at the unhappy lines of her father's face and remembered when he had been handsome and the light had still been in his eyes.

Lars had been a Viking warrior, raiding Brittany and the Saxon coast for slaves and loot, when he had found Mary terrified and hiding in an abandoned mill. She had desperately tried to fight him, but to no avail. He had carried her aboard his ship and brought her back with him to the Nordic coast.

Bekah remembered hearing her mother tell of her terror of the Norsemen. They were barbaric and cruel, yet Lars had fought for her and had brought her to his homeland. Gentle, quiet Mary had soon accepted the demanding ways of the handsome Norseman and had become his wife, but the Norse winters were cruel, the land dark and unyielding. Mary had been homesick for the green lands of Angland. Very soon Bekah was born, and although Lars was disappointed at not having a son, he came to realize that the daughter was a comfort to his wife. Color returned to her face, and often Lars would enter their small house to hear Mary's pleasant voice singing Saxon songs to her child.

Lars loved Mary deeply, often fascinated by her foreign ways. Patiently he waited until Mary learned to view him with affection. Now, with happiness that was almost pain, Bekah remembered how her mother used to sing songs or tell stories of her homeland. On wintry nights, before the cozy fire in their cottage, Mary would weave stories like entwining ribbons of lore for her daughter. To this day Bekah dreamed about the fine manors, the knights on prancing horses or the festivals on hallowed days. In her mind she could see the green forests and blue skies that her mother so vividly described. Bekah had grown to love the unseen Angland, and she spoke both tongues with a native adeptness.

Mary and Bekah had been more than mother and daughter. They had been friends. But four years ago during a terrible, freezing winter storm, Mary had come down with a fever, and her frail body had not been strong enough to throw off the illness. She had died, leaving Lars broken and Bekah lost. Until then neither had realized that Mary had been the backbone of their small family.

How could Lars look at Bekah, so much resembling her mother, and not feel a pang of sorrow? It wrenched his heart to look upon his daughter as she grew more beautiful each day.

"Oh, Mary, Mary!" Bekah had heard him say one time when he thought no one was near. Her father now found himself uneasy in Bekah's presence, and sometimes even seemed angry at the sight of her. All Bekah could understand was that she had lost not only her mother but her father as well.

Two years after Mary's death, Lars had remarried. Helg was a widow with one son, Jorgen. Her husband had been a wealthy man whose farm supplied the fort with the grain and flour it needed. The farm was half a day's ride from the Sogn village, much of its lands extending between farm and fort.

Bekah glanced up at Helg's square face with its small, pale eyes, so in contrast to her mother's delicate features. There was nothing feminine or loving about her stepmother's bulky form, and her straight yellow hair held no resemblance to Bekah's honey-golden braids. In fact, the two shared nothing in common, except their concern for Lars's welfare. Bekah did not understand her father's decision to marry Helg any more now than she had before. Still, she reflected, her father was from this country and he had

10

grown up with Helg. They had been children on adjoining farms and they had been childhood friends.

Bekah had heard a rumor once that Helg had waited for Lars to return from an ocean voyage, and when he had arrived with the beautiful Saxon girl she had been furious. Later she had taken her dowry and married someone else, an older man who had been a prominent farmer. Bekah did not know if the story were true, but she did know that when Helg's husband died, Helg had become owner of the farm and all its benefits. Under poor management, it had rapidly declined in production.

It was at this time that Lars had offered marriage. They had become wealthy under his new ownership, and the farm once again returned to its state of production. Helg did not blind herself to Lars's motives in marrying her, but since she once again lived on a productive farm and her son, Jorgen, did not object, she was satisfied.

Helg glanced up at Lars as he emptied his bowl of milk, wiping his mouth on his sleeve. He was a man of fine stature, as he had always been. And he was not unaffectionate, always treating herself and Jorgen with kindness. Yet in Lars's daughter she could see the Saxon mother and she could not suppress her hatred. Why could they not live in peace without this constant reminder of the past living within their home?

Bekah caught Helg's contemptuous glance and thought that life would be so much better without this unending circle of unhappiness. Her father still missed and longer for Mary, and Helg knew it. Bekah felt frustrated and often bitter, and guilty as well. Helg's cruelty brought out many of her own hateful passions, and Bekah struggled to suppress them, for her mother had taught her the ways of a Christian in this land of pagans. She sometimes felt anger at herself for failing—or worse, for not caring if she failed.

When Lars had first divulged his plan to marry Helg, Bekah had cried out, "Nay! How can you marry her and say that you loved my mother?" The look of hurt in her father's eyes had made her wish she had bitten her tongue. He had tried to explain why this was best for them, but Bekah had not been able to understand his reasoning because

11

she was young and had loved her mother so. Instead she had felt betrayed, and whatever argument she brought forward against the approaching marriage was dismissed. Finally she had become resigned. She had been afraid to challenge her father's temper any further, for he was the head of the family; his word was law.

She remembered arriving at the huge farm dwelling, feeling shy and frightened. They had moved into the large communal house, leaving behind the grave on the hill where her mother lay. They were far from the cottage where Bekah had spent many hours sitting in the warmth of sunlight on the floor by her mother's knee. She could still picture the roughly carved wooden furniture made by her father's own hand. Above the hearth, on the shelf which held the pots of fat burned for light, had been a wooden bowl filled with yellow flowers. A braided rug had covered the floor and fur pelts had been cast upon the carved wooden beds. Their home had often smelled of hot bread and freshly churned butter. Sunlight had spilled in through the oiled skins that covered the windows. There had been nothing cold or hard about their cottage, and Bekah could not bear to leave it. Even though her mother was gone, the wonderful memories remained, and tales of Christmas feasts, summer festivals and simple moral plays had seemed to echo through the cottage.

In the doorway of Helg's big farmhouse, Bekah, her clothing tied in the quilt she had brought, had stood shyly behind her father, hoping for an instant that she might find friendship here and the mothering she so sorely missed. Helg had stood looking grimly down at her, stating she would take the child in hand and teach her. With a sinking in the pit of her stomach, Bekah had realized that the loving she so desired was not here. The stark farm was large and cold, spiritually cold, even in summertime.

That seemed like a lifetime ago, Bekah reflected. Since then she had slipped more and more often into the worlds of daydreaming her mother had created for her. While she scrubbed dirty shirts against a board to make them clean, she would think of the homeland her mother had described. In every menial chore she would let her mind wander to better places among the castles of her mind. This

12

daydreaming often brought reprimands or a sharp awakening pinch. Helg called her worthless and lazy. And the more Bekah was chided, the more she longed to travel away to the land of her mother.

This time she was drawn from her reverie by the feeling of eyes upon her. She looked up to meet Jorgen's fixed stare, which he reluctantly diverted to his now empty plate. She had come to dislike his constant scrutiny. Jorgen had always watched Bekah, invading her privacy and often rebuking her, but his reprimands had lessened during the last year. Now he often endeavored to gain her attention. This was even more confusing to her, since she had reason to be distrustful of him, and she tried to avoid such awkward confrontations. Many times Jorgen would force her into conversations, trapping her with sly words, and she felt uneasy over his attentions. His few attempts at kindness were baffling. There were, as Helg repeatedly pointed out, so many pretty maids in the village to thrust his attentions on that Bekah prayed one of them might quickly catch Jorgen's eye so that she could be left to her own thoughts. Helg, amazingly, accused Bekah of encouraging Jorgen's affections, but Bekah was sure Jorgen saw her as nothing more than a bothersome child.

The meal was soon over, and slowly the men left to return to their work. Jorgen went out, also, while Bekah removed the eating utensils. The dogs eagerly snapped up what scraps were left while the bread was stored away for the later meal. She moved a yellow and brown spotted mongrel aside with her foot when it blocked her way. The animal bared its foul teeth, growling as it slunk off. Even the dogs, it seemed, were at a superior position in this household.

The midday heat was becoming stifling, and as Bekah leaned against a shelf to wipe the perspiration from her forehead the shelf tipped, sending the wooden plates to the floor with a clatter. Instantly Helg, provoked even further by the heat of new summer, scolded her for such clumsiness.

"I am sorry!" Bekah exclaimed in Anglian before realizing her mistake.

"I have told you before not to use that wicked language

13

of your evil mother! She was a witch, and I will not have her devil's tongue in my house!"

A spark of anger ignited Bekah's pride. "My mother was not a witch! She was good and kind and beautiful, all things that you are not!"

Helg stared at her stepdaughter, mouth agape. Never had the child dared to speak so, and she felt hot with fury. "Speak to me so, will you, chit! Your mother was an evil witch and you grow more like her each day. I will teach you to hold your tongue!"

Helg grabbed the rod used to turn the coals, hitting hard across Bekah's thigh, feeling the insolent girl deserved worse. But before she could strike again, there was an angry roar from Lars, who was standing in the doorway. Too late, Helg realized that her husband had not immediately returned to the fields, but had entered the house again in time to hear and see everything. She had grown careless in her punishment of the girl. What had started out as a reprimanding word or a secret pinch that could make Bekah's eyes smart with tears had now become more obvious.

Lars strode forward angrily, wrenching the rod from Helg's grasp. She raised her arms in flinching protection but he did not strike her. He flung the weapon across the room, where it noisily hit against a bench. Fearfully Helg stared at Lars's impassioned face and clenched fists. The tense silence was broken when he spoke without looking at his daughter.

"Bekah, get out."

"But where will I go, Father?" she asked quietly.

"For a walk. Leave for the rest of the day if you like. Your mother and I will talk."

Bekah thought, she is not my mother, but she dared not speak the words. Quickly she slipped outside, taking a deep breath of the heavy summer air.

Although the pain in her thigh had diminished very little, the prospect of escaping the house and having a free afternoon lifted Bekah's spirits, and she left without hesitation. Wondering what was going to happen and which upset her father more, her own bruised condition or Helg's unkind reference to her mother, she hurried out.

Once outside she felt an easing of tension and moved

14

away from the large building. She glanced back at it, seeing the drifts of smoke which issued from its high roof. Its mouth yawned open to her and she still saw it as a fearsome abode, threatening to swallow her. It had become familiar but no more welcome. She had one corner to herself, with a straw mat for her bed. In winter she had a coverlet of wolf skins, in summer the comfort of cold earth against her face.

She sat down by the well, dipping the dented tin cup into the crude wooden bucket that was smeared with pitch. She drank deeply, the cool water quenching her thirst. She lifted her skirt, examining the red welt, fingering it gingerly. Ah, well, it would heal soon enough.

Her father's gruff voice rumbled from the building, pierced occasionally by Helg's protestations. Bekah could not hear what they were saying, and she had no desire to. She hurried away, kicking the squawking chickens from her path. A large white goose spread wide its beak, hissing at her as it chased its fuzzy goslings to safety. Bekah brushed a stray lock from her forehead and sighed. She had no true friend here, no one she could confide in and laugh with.

Moving past the fields she saw the dry brown earth, men and beasts leaning their sweat-shiny backs to the toil. Sunlight glinted off tanned shoulders and wet hides, and she thought that there was little difference between worker and beast. Each toiled, each sweated and ate dust in an attempt to gain sustenance from the unyielding earth. She headed down the path to the animal stalls, the stench of the pig barn already reaching her nostrils. Beside the path grew some wild flowers, the only scraggly plants to grow within the confines of the dwellings. She bent and picked a sprig, tucking it behind her ear as she moved along. Her mind was many miles away in daydreams, and she hurried down the twisting pathway that led past the stables. As she rounded the corner and passed a darkened doorway, two hands suddenly reached out and grabbed her. Stifling a cry, she looked up into the grinning face of Jorgen and felt her own cheeks go hot.

"Do not ever scare me like that again, Jorgen!" she cried.

"I just wanted to talk," he said, pushing her against the wall and blocking her progress with his arm.

"Well?" she asked impatiently, wishing to be free.

"Why do you always scurry away from me like a frightened rabbit?" he asked, giving her no time to reply. "I wanted to know if you want to go to the fort with me on the morrow." This drew her attention. Seldom was she allowed to go to the fort, and it sounded exciting.

"Why are you going there?" she asked guardedly, afraid to show interest lest he snatch the prize away. She cast her eyes aside, not wanting to look at him. He had a perfect setting here against the barn—his dull yellow hair, washed-out features and dirty clothes blended with the bland gray of the building's wooden planks. Bekah's dainty bare feet were burning as she stood in the dry dust, brushing the flies away. Her golden hair seemed alive as the breeze tossed loose strands against her ivory skin. Her blue eyes, cast down, were hidden by dark lashes that lay against her rosy cheeks, and her full red mouth glistened in the sunlight.

"Bekah, are you listening?" He had been rambling on while her mind had been swirling with visions of an excursion to the village.

She looked up at him, her blue eyes flashing. "What is it you wish to say, Jorgen? I have little enough time on my own as it is without spending it standing in the blazing sun."

He stared at her, his pride pricked. Despite his hulking size, she made him feel insignificant as he said, "Have you forgotten? Tomorrow is Odin's festival, to give thanks to him for allowing the warm days to come."

"Odin!" she scoffed, feeling unusually brave. "What does he have to do with summer coming? It comes every year without any help from him."

"Quiet!" Jorgen said, hunching his shoulders a bit and glancing skyward. "Do you want to bring his vengeance down on us all?"

She could not help but smile at his simple fears when there were so many real things to fear: wolves and famine, fire and draught. "I do not believe in Odin or the other barbaric Norse gods."

16

He looked at her in disbelief, unable to comprehend her denouncement of the gods. She would rue the day she had laughed at Odin, god of sea and sky. The fearful black-eyed god had been known to walk upon the lands, granting bountiful harvests or causing dry, withered grain. He had even taken a few beautiful maidens, stealing them away and casting them aside when they grew old or tiresome. Bekah's flippancy would bring ruin upon her own fair head. " 'Tis foolhardy to speak so, Bekah."

She laughed. "I am not afraid of him."

"You should be," Jorgen warned, sliding his hand loosely down one thick braid until it came to rest on her shoulder. " 'Tis not wise to speak so. Come with me on the morrow to the festival."

Not caring for his touch she stammered, "But Father might not . . ."

"Lars says that you have never been to one of the celebrations."

She nodded, wanting to go, yet knowing that Jorgen was no brother of hers. She had no desire to be indebted to him or burdened by his presence while she tried to enjoy the festivities. "Nay, I have not. I must ask my father first."

She tried to go but he stopped her.

"Stay here and talk to me for a while," he pleaded, unable to refrain from touching her hair again.

"But I . . . was going for a walk. Father told me to," she hastily added.

He pulled back, his mouth in a grim line as he glared down at her. "You think you are too good for me."

"Nay, 'tis not that! I just explained."

He tightened his grip on her arm. "I am a man who deserves respect. In time I will oversee our entire farm."

"Let me go, Jorgen."

"Nay!" he said stupidly, glaring down into her face. She looked at his large jaw and stiff yellow hair that stood in disarray. His complexion was ruddy, splotched here and there with chaffed blotches of white. He was large and heavyset, reminding her of the oxen he tended. His breath was hot and unpleasant as his face loomed menacingly near. "There will be changes here, and you would do best

17

to learn your true place. It will be easier when we are finally married if you mind your place now."

"Married?" she gasped.

"Yea, married. What do you think is going to happen? I have already asked your father."

"You have asked Father?" she said in stunned surprise, her hand going to her throat. "What did he say?"

A quick plan formed in Jorgen's mind. He would show her. "What do you think he said?"

"Well, surely he said nay."

He smiled and shook his head. "He says that you are not old enough, that I must give you a little time. How old are you anyway, seven and ten or more? All the girls I know of your age are already wed. Our parents cannot keep us apart much longer, and your father cannot keep you a child forever."

"How much longer then—a year? Perhaps two?"

Jorgen snorted in disdain. "A month or two, certainly not past harvest."

She was so startled by this horrid revelation that she could think of nothing to say, and could only stare at his repulsively smug face.

"I will own this farm. I will provide for you. And then we will have sons and they will carry on the traditions."

"Nay," she whispered, wrenching away from him. "To be forever under the ruling fist of your mother and you? Never! I will not let it be so!"

He grabbed her wrist, leering down at her. "Oh, but it will be so."

She jerked her wrist free, stumbling from him and then, lifting her skirt, ran down the hill until she was out of sight behind the trees, where at last she slowed to a walk. A muffled sob escaped her as she imagined the terrible fate of being Jorgen's wife. Almost hysterically she laughed, realizing she was free of him for the moment and that the wound on his leg kept him from following her. She despised him and could not stand the thought of his touch. What would it mean to be his wife, to share his pallet and sleep by his side? She did not understand the marriage intimacy, really, but if Jorgen were to touch her like that she would die. She could not marry him, for she could not tolerate him, and she knew he would rule over her with an even more brutal temper than his mother's. Her situation, already miserable, was destined to become even worse. How she wished that she could throw herself upon the warm earth of her mother's grave and cry until the terrible ache in her heart ceased. Instead she sat upon a nearby log spilling her tears and worries and frustrations into its gnarled bark. Finally she wiped her eyes with the edge of her skirt and looked up as she heard a scurrying sound. There on the dark log sat a squirrel, fluffing up his furry tail. His eyes were like two shiny black beads, and he tilted his head to the side, clucking his tongue like an old woman. She picked up an acorn, holding it out to him. He hesitated for only a moment, then, his tiny paws brushing her palm, he took it from her, clicking his teeth. The little animal chattered happily, finally hopping away. Bekah sighed, feeling better now.

The warm weather that had finally settled upon the land, bringing out green leaves, wild flowers and the mingled chatter of birds, raised her spirits. Where could she go to spend a pleasant afternoon away from them all? Instantly she thought of the cove. It was a secret place she had discovered while exploring the coastline on another of her outings. It was about an hour's walk from the farm, and she happily headed in that direction.

In time her problems receded as she walked the difficult distance to the shore, and her heart was greatly lifted when she reached the gray waves pounding the sands. She traveled along the water's edge for a while until a steep cliff with many rocks stopped her progress. It looked impassable, yet she knew that if she waited until the next wave moved out, there was a small opening at the base of the jutting rock. When the ocean receded, she hurried through the hole on hands and knees, then back onto the shore before getting caught by the fierce, cold water. Once inside the large cove, she viewed its emptiness.

Another cliff on the opposite side stopped the wind also, and it was warm and still inside. Above her were ledges that led back into shadowed half-caves and dens. Beyond the reach of the waves were deep tidal pools left by the last high tide; these had warmed many hours in the sun and were good for bathing in. At one far corner, a small stream splashed over the steep cliff from the highlands and fell in a filmy waterfall to a large rivulet running to the ocean. Even though it was an icy cold runoff from the snows, it was a good way to wash off salt water.

Bekah sat near the largest of the tidal pools and began to unplait her braids, brushing out her hair with a bone comb which she had concealed in her pocket. As she smoothed out her hair into a wave of glistening silk, she thought back over the day. Unhappily she remembered Jorgen's words. What if she were forced to marry him? She recoiled from the thought. Certainly her father would not insist upon the marriage. But Jorgen had said that Lars had only postponed it for a while. Harvesttime would be here all too soon. There certainly was no happy solution to this problem, and no deliverance from either Jorgen or his mother. If only she could talk to her mother just once more and relieve the lonely ache within her breast! A feeling of total aloneness engulfed her.

Yet she was not alone. Unknown to Bekah, a man was sitting on the large ledge several heights above her. He sat looking out at the gray-blue ocean, its waves crashing on the sands. Kenric of Kartney viewed the rocky landscape of sea and earth, the pounding of water and frothy spray of foam never-ending. He saw the lacy edge of water tease the sand like the gentle fingers of a lover. He was startled from his reverie by a sweet voice half-sobbing, "Oh, Mother, Mother. What shall I do?" It sounded as if it were in his own language of Anglian, but he could not be certain of what he heard, and after a while he thought it might have been only the sighing of waves. Still, he carefully moved to the edge of the overhang and peered down. Close below him on a piece of black driftwood sat a girl. He could hardly believe his eyes; she was dazzlingly beautiful; even her rough Nordic clothing could not disguise it. Her smooth, creamy skin and delicate features were like a finely carved piece of ivory, set with large blue-violet eyes the shade of the flowers that grew on the hills of his own homeland and edged by long, thick lashes of a sooty color. Sweetly curved lips parted as she sighed. Adeptly she wound her thick hair the color of sunlight and honey upon

20

her head. Had he been of Nordic descend he might have believed the tales of beautiful Valkyries that come to guide the dead noble warriors to Valhalla. Unbelieving, he watched as she slowly removed the rough clothing, casting aside the garments with disdain. He could not tear his gaze away as she stepped into the cool refreshment of the tidal pools. He sucked in a deep breath.

An instant awareness flooded him at this invasion of her privacy, but it was not enough to turn him away from the scene below. He knew the girl believed herself to be alone, but an irresistible force prevented him from announcing his presence. He was overcome by her beauty. A dream could not be this real, this believable. He rubbed the back of his hand across his eyes. Sunlight glinted off her silken shoulders, and he stared as she then submerged herself in the waters, washing the perspiration from her skin. As she rose up out of the pool, sending out a spray of water drops like hundreds of diamonds, she appeared like some splendid wood nymph. He was mesmerized by the vision before his eyes. As if sleepwalking, he silently descended the craggy cliff.

Bekah splashed the refreshing water about herself, reveling in this cool luxury. Her tensions lessened in her solitude, and she began to hum a melancholy strain. Suddenly a shadow fell across her, and she gasped. She twisted around in the water. Before her stood a man of strong build—a stranger. His wide shoulders, lightly furred chest and arms were deeply bronzed. He was a man of the sea, as apparent as if she had seen the water spew him onto the bleached sands. She saw a face of well-chiseled features and piercing gray eyes. A mane of soft black hair fell in disarray. Had she seen him in other circumstances she would have been entranced by his rugged appearance, but now she stared up at him in horror. Had she believed in Odin, she would have thought this stranger was one of his warriors—or Odin himself. A puzzled expression was etched upon his features.

Bekah knew true terror as the stranger splashed down into the water. Trancelike he reached out, catching her in his grasp. She struggled to free herself, kicking and twisting within his hold. He could not resist pulling her to him, meaning to take a kiss from her. Cupping the back of her head in his hand, he pulled her reluctant mouth to his own, bringing their lips together. She pushed against him with her hands, trying to pull away. His encircling arms were like bands of steel as he lifted her and carried her from the water. He knew he should free her, for she was not his. But here she was. He pushed her down against the white sand.

The reality hit her with a blow as she saw the glazed determination in his eyes. The shock of what was to come paralyzed her with fear, and she realized her struggles and cries were useless. A foggy blackness clouded her eyes as she felt herself sinking into oblivion.

He overwhelmed her.

The screech of an overhead gull brought his senses reeling back to him. What had he done? The folly of his mistake was full upon him as Kenric looked down at the lifeless form. Had this act caused her death? Frantically he shook her, relief flooding him as a moan escaped her lips. He was ashamed. She had been an innocent, that was apparent to him, making his shame doubly strong.

Her eyes fluttered open and she rose up on an elbow, wildly looking about her. He hovered over her and she recoiled as if he were some devilish vision. Drawing herself away from him, she pulled her knees into her body, hugging herself with her arms. She began to experience intense feelings of shame and wretched embarrassment as the numbness wore off. How could she ever return home? Could she pretend that nothing had happened? How could she stop from throwing herself into her father's arms and sobbing out the whole horrid incident? Even if she were able to hide her shame, it would only be temporary, for when she married her lost virtue would be discovered. No one would want her now.

Her accusing gaze fell upon the man who had so unthinkingly changed her life. "Why?" she managed to ask. "Why did you do this to me?"

He shook his head in dismay. He had no answer. She was trembling and turned her head away, unable to stop her quiet sobs. She quaked like a frightened child, and

22

guilt coursed his veins where fire had just been. His desire had blinded his logic. He cursed himself, and as he watched her he was overwhelmed by a sudden desire to protect this frail maid.

Hurriedly he gathered up her clothing, bringing it to her as a peace offering. He held her rough garments out to her, and she looked scornfully at him until he dropped them at her feet. He turned away, his mind working frantically. How great would be the fury of her kinfolk, should they discover his deed? Was she the fairest flower in all this land? Would angry brothers come to slay he who had brought her harm?

Even though it was late afternoon, the sun would not set until after midnight, and the dark would never be more than a twilight. Gray and white gulls daintily stepped along the lacy edges of the tide as the first foam crept closer. Sand ferns whipped their slender leaves in the breeze, and the waterfall splashed and gurgled, unaware of Bekah's plight. Overhead, blue-black clouds slowly gathered in a barbaric rain dance in the Viking skies that had been blue an hour ago. It grew dark, and the cool wind made Bekah shiver. She quickly put on her clothes, noting that the tide was coming in. She wrapped her arms about herself, her eyes taking in the seabirds, the filmy waterfall dashing itself upon the rocks before running out to sea and the clouds moving in overhead. The surf still crashed upon the sand, sending out its frothy fingers, and she was surprised to realize that her cove was still the same. In truth, the whole world appeared the same, yet how could it be when she herself had changed so?

The tide was now so high that the opening through which Bekah had planned her escape was submerged in water. She knew she could not go back the way she had come, so she turned to gaze at the high cliffs. If she must climb the cliffs to escape, then she would. She reached the cliffs, trying for a handhold, but he was by her side, stopping her.

"Where do you think you are going?" he asked. Receiving no response, he repeated the question in Nordic.

"I am leaving before the tide drowns me," she spat, not bothering to look at him.

23

"I cannot allow you to leave and warn your countrymen against me. What would become of me?"

"Become of you?" she cried, turning astonished blue eyes on him. "What will become of *me?*"

"I have no intention of letting you drown, nor do I plan to let you escape me," he said.

Cold fear gripped her as she realized he was planning to keep her here. "You must let me go! I cannot stay here longer!"

"You are not going," he said with new command. "I admit responsibility for my actions, but I will not sacrifice my life as penalty! I cannot release you until later. When my ship is ready to set sail I will release you, but not before."

Angrily she viewed him; he stood so sure of himself. Facing him bravely she spoke. "Do you think I would lower myself to divulge this horrid secret? I will take this to my grave. Do you realize that now I can never marry? My life is ruined and my death lies in your hands."

Kenric tried to stay calm before this beautiful woman. She was no lowly serf, rather some high chieftain's daughter, no doubt. Her presence could easily grace King Alfred's court, yet here she stood looking at him with disdain and anger. He was not used to that from women. His pride was stung. "I had no idea at all of your innocence. What could I think when you so willingly removed your clothing before my eyes?"

"You knew I had no idea you sat hiding up there, spying on me!"

Large drops of rain began to fall, chilling their skin, and she shivered. He realized their position and started to scale the cliff. With one hand secure, he turned to give her assistance. "Do you have a name? I am known as Kenric."

She did not answer him. The water began to lap about her ankles and she felt trapped, yet he withdrew his arm as if he had all day to wait her answer. "I am Bekah," she said hesitantly, unwilling to give him any further part of herself.

"All right, Bekah, let us get out of here before we drown." He was already climbing up to the ledge from which he had descended. "Here, give me your hand."

She did not want him to help her, but even less did she want to be engulfed in the water and perhaps swept into the sea. Reluctantly she accepted his assistance. He pulled her up easily.

It was starting to rain in torrents, and the wind howled mournfully. A cave-den was at the back of the ledge, and Kenric guided her into it. They were both drenched. Once inside, Bekah grabbed a corner of her skirt and began to wring the water from it. Kenric's eyes scanned her slender body, noticing the red welt and bruises on her thigh. Miserably she sat down against the black rock wall, huddling with her arms about her knees. She ached all over, her muscles still tense with the shock from this ordeal. If only she could remain calm, lasting out the storm, she could then make her way back to her people. He had said he would release her when his ship was ready to leave. He was a foreigner, then. She had heard him speak clearly in the tongue of her mother, although they had only conversed in Nordic. She had always envisioned her mother's people as genteel, as Mary had been, but this man was a barbarian. Without the least concern he had harmed her and now acted as if nothing had happened. She clenched her teeth together to still their chattering, working to control her shaking. If she could just bide her time, he would release her and she could return home. The home which she had despised only this morning seemed now to be a welcome haven.

He reached for a heavy cape lined with fur that had been tossed carelessly to the back of the cave, then tucked it around the shivering girl, glad that he had brought it along.

The warmth of the cape was comforting, even though she resented it for being his. Just endure, she thought. Soon the storm will end and I will go home. I will forget this man, and this day. Father will believe that I was caught in the storm; perhaps he need not know. She pulled the cape in around her, calming a bit as it hid all but her face.

Kenric gathered a pile of dried leaves, bark and debris from the floor of the cave. Taking out a flint he struck sparks at the dried leaves until the pile ignited, and he

25

carefully blew a fire to life. The flickering flames grew and sent out warmth and eerie light; the smoke was sucked out into the rain.

He seated himself, rubbing his hands together before the fire. "Do you live far from here?"

"Nay."

"Will your father come looking for you?"

She nodded. "If you value your life you had best let me go."

He raised an eyebrow. "I see. If I let you go now you would drown in this rain." It was true. The wind was howling and the rain was coming down in sheets.

"He could be looking for me now. If he finds you, he will kill you."

"Certainly he will try. He must love you very much, and prize a daughter so very fair. One thing puzzles me, though. If he loves you so, then why does he beat you?"

She looked up startled, but said nothing. He continued, "I know a welt when I see one, and there is one on your thigh. Strange, that your father loves you, yet hurts you."

She did not want to talk to this hated man, but she must not dishonor her father by not defending him. "What you did to me hurts far more and in many more ways than that," she said. His face took on a stormy look and she cast down her eyes. "My father has never touched me. It was my stepmother, Helg."

"Stepmother? I see." The cave echoed quietly, the fire lending its warmth. Her shuddering diminished. He studied her beautiful face in the orange light. "Your mother is dead."

She did not answer for a long moment, then decided that it did not matter. She would be free of him soon. She must bide her time, and incur none of his wrath. "My real mother died four years ago, and then my father married Helg. She punished me for knocking over some wooden plates."

"Severe punishment. But then she is perhaps a strict mother."

"She is not my mother. Mary was my mother."

"Mary?" he said. "Is that not an Anglian name? I have never heard it as a Viking name."

26

She was quiet for a moment more, lulled by the growing warmth. "Viking she was not. She was Saxon." There was a glimmer of pride in her voice.

"How did she come to be in this forsaken land?"

"Father was a Viking warrior. When they raided the Saxons he was struck by my mother's beauty. He stole her away, bringing her here."

He laughed softly, chilling her to the bone. "So, history repeats itself."

Her eyes widened, and she fought to control her voice. "You said you would let me go. Are you not a man of your word?"

Declining to answer, he blew on the coals to stir them up, adding the last remains of dried bark. "Then when your mother died, your father remarried this woman Helg. And Helg is not all that a good stepmother should be?"

She sighed. "If you must know, she dislikes me."

"I cannot see why anyone would dislike you," he said softly.

"I think she is jealous of my mother, even though she is dead, because Father loved her so. He fought for her, as he would fight for me. Your life is in peril with each minute that passes."

"Then I must be careful," he said with a smile that irritated her. "I will keep a sharp lookout for him and your many brothers who are no doubt scouring the hillsides."

Exhaustion was overcoming her, and she felt irritated at having to explain further. "I have no brothers, unless you count Jorgen, who is Helg's son."

"Something in your voice leads me to think that you dislike him."

"He is a stupid ox. He thinks that I will be his wife, but I will not."

Kenric nodded, thoughtfully digesting this information.

Within the warmth of the cape she became somewhat dry. The rain did not touch them, yet out to sea bolts of lightning seared into the water, crackling, while the roar of thunder competed with the sound of smashing waves. The sea roiled blackly, the clouds hiding the midnight sun. The raging storm outside was a reflection of the battle of emotions that was raging within her. She felt as if the crashing storm were within her own breast, the black clouds of emotional pain descending on her. Kenric, too, was stirred by emotions with which he was not familiar and which he disliked.

Although they were safe from the crashing sea below and the bellowing storm without, Bekah became increasingly uncomfortable. It was not the bruise on her thigh or her other physical aches but the renewed awareness of her situation that made her restless.

Why had she been such a fool as to tell no one of her secret cove? How would her father ever rescue her if he could not find her? She would have welcomed even Jorgen's help in saving her from this fierce Anglian man. By now they would probably only think she was upset by the events of the day and had stayed away longer than expected. Perhaps they would think she was waylaid by the storm—but never, never would they guess her true fate and be able to save her. What would become of her? Though crying was useless, she could not help the muffled sob which escaped her.

Kenric was startled from his own reverie by the sound of her crying. He looked up to see the small figure engulfed in his cape shaking with tears. He softly cursed. Now he must put up with the bother of a female's tears. Because he knew the fault to be his own he searched for some word of comfort.

"Bekah," he said quietly, "the hurt will pass."

She shook her head. "It will never pass. You do not understand." How differently she had envisioned this prelude to womanhood! The man of her choice coming softly to her as she lay within the security of their marriage bed . . . the excitement almost overwhelming as she awaited the tenderest of all moments. She had thought of it as a love scene, a quiet time where only lovers could dwell. But her dreams were now destroyed. How quickly this black devil had come and taken from her the only perfect gem she had to give. "How can I go home? They will know when they look at me. What can I tell my father?" Her eyes pleaded with him and he thoughtfully considered the situation. He could well understand the accusation she would feel from her people. Who would believe her story? The actions of this day would be revealed in time to her humiliation and shame. He could not give back that which he had taken, so what recourse was open to him? If he returned her to her people, her life would be full of censure. It seemed there was no one she could turn to for comfort.

He looked up, warming his hands over the coals. "There is one solution to your problem," he said.

She looked at the stranger with a mixture of surprise and wonder. Who was he to carry her burdens, even if they were burdens he created?

"You will come with me."

"Nay," she gasped. "I will never go with you! That is no solution, for you are the very cause of my sorrows!"

"Oh? I am surprised that you would wish to return to a future in which you must marry your oxlike stepbrother, a home where your stepmother beats you, and to a life which you yourself have said will be worsened. You may not want to leave now, but in time you will see it is for the best."

"To be put into the hands of a man such as yourself?" she cried, panic welling up inside her. "I will fight you to the death. In truth I would rather die than go with you!"

"Do not speak of death. That is the coward's way out. I know you are afraid of me for what I have done, but that will never happen to you again, I give my word. In this way I shall make amends for what I have done: I will take care of you. You are young, and in time you will come to see that it is best."

A groan of misery escaped her lips. "If you wish to make amends then let me return to my home!"

He seemed to pay no attention to these last words, standing with his back to her, peering out at the beautiful violence of the storm, rain spattering him.

She bit her lower lip, thinking that her own words of misery had woven a net to trap her. There was no arguing with this gray-eyed devil. She must wait cautiously and then escape him. Pushed into even deeper despair, Bekah felt sparks of angry determination. Neither he nor Jorgen would possess her. Somehow she would get away and no one would ever hurt her again. There must be some corner, some small part of the world where she could live away from pain and frustration.

She felt exhausted. The roar of the ocean and the warmth of the fire lulled her, in time, into a half-waking sleep. Finally total slumber enveloped her. Her rhythmic breathing soon reached Kenric's ears. He forced himself to lie down, but sleep would not come. His mind was a turmoil of confusion as he watched her sleep. Her beauty awed him, and he was flooded by a sudden understanding of why he had done what he had. It was a very long time before he, too, slept.

The piercing scream of a sea gull awakened Bekah, and she realized it was very early morning. The storm had broken; the wind was sweeping away the last tirade of rain and thunder. The sky was turning pale blue edged with scarlet, the clouds of gray dawning with summer light. She remembered exactly how the events of yesterday had moved, the recollection like a black ribbon wrapping itself about her. The stranger, Kenric, was sleeping beside her. There was just a chance that she might escape him if she moved very cautiously. However, he had rolled next to her in the chill of night, seeking warmth from her. His face rested on her hair, her silken tresses providing him with a pillow. Carefully she tried to pull her hair from beneath him; in restless sleep he moved and she held her breath. He did not awaken, and slowly she exhaled. Finally she was able to pull her hair free. She moved slowly, hardly daring to stir. Finally she gained courage; she would have to cross over the top of him and then make her escape. Cautiously she poised herself above him. Just as she thought she would be free of him, she felt warm hands encircling her waist. She let out a cry, staring down into his gray eyes as he pulled her down against him.

"I am afraid I cannot let you go." He smiled and shook his head. "You would no doubt run crying for your father, and he would have my head, most likely." His hands tightened about her waist as she tried to move.

"Let me go!" she cried, struggling until he released her.

He studied her silently, then rose, pulling her to her feet. "It is time to get out of here—before your father comes after us with the whole village."

"Then leave me here," she said, hoping that during the night he had abandoned his wild plans. "It will take me hours to return to my home, and by then you can be gone. I have no knowledge from where you came and can be no threat!"

She was like a lustrous pearl wrapped in a piece of rough cloth, he thought, as she handed him his cape. He slung it across his arm and stepped out on the ledge. He did not descend the cliff as she had expected but pulled himself up to the ledge above.

"Here, Bekah, give me your hand. We will leave by the way I came."

She gazed down, seeing the wet sand far beneath her and wondering if she could make a run for it.

"Do not try it, Bekah, for we do not have the time for me to chase after you. Now give me your hand!" he commanded.

She looked up into his piercing gray eyes, knowing that in a clash of wills he would be the victor. She allowed him to help her up, and slowly they proceeded to the top of the cliff. With Kenric's help it was not as difficult as she feared. With his hand at her back he guided her along the cliff's edge. Unhappily she realized that they were traveling away from the farmhouse where by now her father certainly would be worried about her. They traveled far along the cliffside with which Bekah grew less familiar.

Jasmine, wild berries, poppies and pale green ferns grew in profusion among gray moss. The storm had left the new day clean and sparkling, and the brilliant blue sky changed the usually gray water to azure. But despite the dew-glistening beauty of summer and the mingled chirping of forest birds, Bekah's spirits were still as grim as the darkest skies.

They made their way down to a beach and after they had followed the water's edge for a while a Viking ship came into view. Its sleek lines and wide sail crackling in the morning breeze made Bekah take a deep breath.

"There she is. I suppose my crew is already back from Sogn, wondering what has happened to me."

"That is your ship? But it is a Viking ship!"

He chuckled softly. "Yea, and since we are turning

31

homeward today, I do not mind telling you that I am a special courier on a voyage for King Alfred."

"Who?" she asked, her curiosity getting the better of her.

"King Alfred. He is the ruler of Angland. I am here to see exactly where old Guthrum's sympathies really lie."

Her brow was knit in a puzzled expression. "I do not understand. Who is Guthrum?"

"A pompous Dane heathen and current ruler of Danelaw, which used to belong to Angland. You see, Alfred was ruler of Angland, so when Guthrum took over Northumberland, they decided to rule in peace, after a terrible amount of slaughter. However, Alfred does not wholly trust Guthrum. Therefore, I was commissioned by King Alfred to see if Guthrum was getting battleships together to take over Angland entirely. The King supplied me with a crew which speaks some Nordic—which was a difficult task—and sent me on this mission. I have spent these past many months searching out the truth, and I am happy to say that I can return with the report that Guthrum has no such plans."

He pointed to his ship. "Looks like they have her rigged to go." It was a plain, small ship of a kind with which Bekah was familiar.

"But that is a merchant ship."

"Only in appearance. That is just a disguise. Now we are ready to return home. It has been interesting visiting the Norse coast again, but I will gladly return to Wessex."

"You have been here before and that is why you speak our language," she deduced smartly, hoping that their conversation would slow their progress towards the ship. She could feel a desperate fear welling up inside her as she realized there was no help for her here.

"That is true. You see, ten years ago when I was about your age, I was taken from an Anglian ship by Guthrum himself, as a slave. In time, though, he took a liking to me, and we had many long and interesting discussions. Although Alfred has insisted that Guthrum become a Christian, Guthrum has tended toward that direction because of my influence. Therefore he has abandoned your god, Odin."

"Odin is not my god," she said scornfully, and he laughed.

"I had forgotten your mother's influence in your up-bringing."

"I had thought my mother's people were honorable, yet I see you have come to spy on us, even having been this Guthrum's friend."

"I am no friend of his. After a year as his slave I escaped my bondage. You see, freedom has always run strong in my blood."

"Oh. Freedom for you, but none for me."

"There are many types of freedom," he responded enig-matically.

"The exact kind of freedom you sought is also that which I desire," she said, arguing her case in the hope of chang-ing his mind.

"You desire to return. I thought you preferred death to living the dismal life that is planned for you."

"I only want to rule over myself."

"Certainly you cannot do that in the household from which you just came," he said seriously.

Bekah leveled dark blue eyes on him. "Certainly I can-not do so with you."

"Milady, I am a knight of King Alfred's army who has traveled far and abroad. I know of what I speak."

She realized that there was no arguing with him. They were getting closer to the ship, and her spirits sank. What could she, a mere girl, do against this man? She knelt down, picking up a few sand-smoothed stones, and a flicker of hope came to mind. She could throw a stone far and with good aim; indeed, she could skip a stone four or five times on a pond. Even Jorgen admitted she was better at it than most boys. Perhaps these rocks were not much of a weap-on, but she had heard her mother tell the story of a young boy who slew a giant with a sling and a stone.

"What are you doing?" he asked.

"I thought I saw some amber," she lied cooly. " 'Tis a stone prized highly by my people, a sign of good omen. I did not, though."

"Come, then. We need to get aboard and be off." He had walked several paces before realizing that she was not following. Angrily he turned, only to find her running down the gravelly beach.

"Get back here!" he shouted hotly, then, seeing she gave no heed, he gave a curse to the winds and started after her. Bekah could hear his pounding feet behind her; he must not catch her! She turned briefly and he was brought up short by a rock hitting his shoulder. A look of surprise came over his face, but Bekah saw that the blow had not even slowed his pace. Perhaps one placed squarely between the eyes would stop him. She pulled her arm back and let a stone fly with all her might. Kenric, seeing her intent, managed to dodge to the side barely in time. The projectile whistled by his ear as another glanced off his chest. Bekah, down to her last stone, stopped and threw it hard, then turned to run. The stone struck Kenric's thigh, and he growled a curse. Bekah dared not slow down enough to glance back, but with a sinking feeling of despair she realized that he was close upon her. Suddenly she felt a force hit her from behind, knocking her to the ground, and she was barely able to gasp for breath. Her hands and knees were skinned by the rough sand but she paid them no heed. She was quick to get back on her feet, but immediately he had her in his grasp. No matter how she fought and pulled she could not break it. When she gave his knee a sharp kick, he let out a yell, then wrapped his arms around her, holding her tight against him until she stopped her struggling.

"You little hellcat! Did you think you could escape me?"

"Yea, and I will!" she shouted back as he dodged a swift kick to the shin and placed a resounding whack upon her backside.

She turned indignant blue eyes on him, and he spoke. "If you insist on acting like a child then I shall treat you as one. Now settle down, for you are going with me and there is no escaping it."

"I shall escape you if it takes the last breath I have to give!"

Angrily he gave her wrist a jerk, pulling her along behind him, ignoring her struggles and protests as she wreathed his head in names both foreign and familiar. About the time she was comparing his attributes to those of a mule, he wheeled around and picked her up, slinging her across his shoulder as if she were a sack of grain. The air was knocked out of her and her cursing was brought to a sudden halt by his steady jaunt.

"Does your father let you speak like this at home? It will take much effort to make a lady out of you, but perhaps it can be done."

She was pummeling him with her small fists, and he smiled to himself as he thought that this wench had a temper. He was nearing the ship when he felt her teeth sink into the flesh of his shoulder blade, and with a yell he dropped her to the ground. The men of his ship watched with curiosity as he pulled her, still struggling, into the water after him.

She screamed furiously in the last hope for rescue as he placed her within the partially beached boat. There was a flurry of slender legs as she pulled down her skirt, aware that the crewmen had ceased their labors to gawk.

"What treasures be ye bringing aboard, Cap'n Kenric?" one grizzled old man named Goudwin finally asked as he tightened the forward ropes.

"Why, one of this country's fairest flowers, 'tis all, Goudwin." Kenric grinned. "If all the men are back, then rig the sail before this fair wench's menfolk come in search. I will settle her below."

The men laughed over this, and marveled at the nerve of their captain who was kidnapping a local wench. Often their womenfolk had been ravaged by the barbaric Norsemen, and they thought this reversal was a good jest.

"What a tasty bit of tart. I would not mind having her for myself," a nervous-eyed seaman said.

"Dinnot, ye be a fool to talk so, for the cap'n does not give up easily what is his." Goudwin was a trusted sailor who had long served on King Alfred's ships.

"A wench like that would be worth a fight, Goudwin," the seaman surmised.

"Only if ye were the victor. But the cap'n, although he has an amiable enough way about him, is hard as flint. I saw two men jump him in the dark once for a bag of gold.

Neither one of them walked away with it. Be no fool, Din-not."

Bekah could hear the voices above as Kenric took her into the gloomy depths of the boat. Shame and indignation filled her breast as she experienced a more intense despair than she had ever known in the whole of her life. He guided her down inside the hull, past boxes and bundles of cargo, until they reached an enclosure, which he illuminated with a flame from a small iron bowl filled with fat. It was nothing more than a little room with thick furs on the floor and bed, two chairs and a table.

"This is my room. We will stay here."

Her spine stiffened at the thought of a long journey alone with him. He guided her inside the room and then left, bolting the door. For a long time she stood there in the flickering flame-light, staring at the bolted door. Horror grew within her until finally she threw herself against the door, screaming and pounding her fists against it. She was being stolen away from all that was familiar and precious. Her mother's grave and her father's face both came to mind; the cottage of her childhood and the ragged Nordic hills. How could this be happening to her? The sharp sting of reality was compounded by the lurch of the ocean-bound vessel. She sank to the floor, hopelessness washing over her. How desperately she wanted her father's comforting arms about her, the safety of his protection. She could imagine him standing on the cliff's edge calling her name, fearfully looking out to sea, waiting for her frail form to be cast ashore. There would be no way to let him know what had become of her, for no body would ever be washed ashore. Her heart ached, yet no tears came, and she felt empty inside. The farther they moved from shore the more miserable she became.

It was not long before she heard the door unbolt, and Kenric entered carrying a large plate laden with bread, cheese and salted meat.

He grinned and set down the food.

She said nothing, only scowled at him and moved to a corner of the room. "Ah, I see you are still unwilling to make peace. Well, I thought you might be starving so I brought you this."

36

The meat smelled delicious, and she realized how hungry she was, for she had not eaten since the previous day's noon meal. Still, she did not want to accept any favors from her captor.

"I do not want anything from you," she said icily. "I would rather starve."

He shrugged. "Suit yourself." He picked up the platter of food and went to the table, sitting down in an oversized chair covered with fur pelts. He placed the plate before him and began eating.

She caught her lower lip between her teeth, watching him pensively and reflecting that pride was a singular comfort, though it did not fill one's stomach. She casually walked about the small chamber and examined the few articles she found. Kenric devoured the food, and she began to fear it would be entirely gone before she could get a morsel. She manipulated her way nearer to the table, and Kenric pretended to be unaware of her. She sat down opposite him, and he pushed the plate to her. They both knew he had won, but what victory with hunger his ally? They ate silently.

Soon Bekah became increasingly aware of the movement of the boat. With each swell that lifted it, she felt uncomfortably more than just a loss of balance. She finished the meal and felt worse with a full stomach. She could not account for the sensation of queasiness.

Kenric, well accustomed to writing within the sway of the craft, took out his log and pen, and pushed the plate aside. He began to update his journal. Bekah managed her way to the bed where she sat down but immediately stood again. A moan escaped her, drawing his attention, and she looked frantically around the room for some escape. Kenric, seeing her predicament, quickly led her out of the room, and she promptly lost her dinner through a side hatch in the vessel. She felt both sick and embarrassed, fearing he would laugh at her, but to her surprise he was gentle as he led her back to the small room and laid her down on the soft furs.

"I am afraid that you do not have your sea legs yet."

"I never will," she moaned, turning her head away.

He chuckled. "You will be better. It just takes time."

She lay still, her eyelids closed. An exhausted stupor overcame her. She slept under his gaze, and he pulled a pelt over her before ascending to the upper deck.

The oars were abandoned and the sail bellied out with the stiff wind which had come up. The sound of the waves and whispering cries of wind were audible to Bekah when she awoke, and she felt lonely and afraid. She did not know how much time had passed, or whether it was night or day.

Dark thoughts, like flies infesting brown-bruised fruit, nagged at her. Did her father grieve for her, and was he torn apart by her disappearance? She dreamed that he would come in a boat and find her and she would return home to her mother. But then, nay, her mother was dead. Bitterly she thought it was for the best. Mary would not have survived the terror of her disappearance. How she appreciated what her mother must have suffered! She, too, had been taken captive in the primitive ritual forced upon her because she was a woman. But Lars, Bekah knew, had adored her mother; Kenric appeared to her to be stormy and fearful.

Did Jorgen miss her? She shuddered and admitted that she did not care one whit. What of Helg? No doubt she was elated that Bekah had not returned. She could picture the villagers, their torches glowing like many burning fireflies in the night as they scoured the forests and hillsides for her. She would not be found, not even her remains. The mystery would be even worse than her death, and she grieved for her father. Better to have died in her homeland than to be taken to a foreign shore where her fate would be uncertain. Plans for escape filled her mind, and she sorted through them, saving some and discarding many. Once she was free of him, then what? She anticipated and dreaded the moment. If only she were brave, she would slit her own throat, letting her life forces ebb away. He would be sorry then, once he found her still warm yet no longer breathing! But she had no knife, not even a sharp tool— and even if she had, she did not know if she could use it. She was a coward and she despised herself for it. Even so, she felt it was a sin to take one's life, even the life of a defiled maiden with grievances enough.

For as long as she could remember she had yearned to

see her mother's homeland, yet never in her wildest dreams had she expected to be taken there in this manner. Now, in a ship which was being tossed about on the great seas, she realized there was no hope of escape.

Bekah's seasickness grew worse, her health also hampered by fearful misgivings about what would become of her. Her terror and her sorrow plunged her into a deep melancholia of which she could not rid herself. It hovered over her like a black storm cloud, descending periodically in a shower of pain and self-sorrow.

Bekah's memory of the voyage was a blur of long hours of sleep, the inability to eat and the presence of Kenric. He brought her food which she was unable to keep down. The most she could eat was dry bread, and her only relief from the illness was in sleep. Days passed, unknown to her.

Kenric returned once again to find her asleep, curled up like a kitten on the soft furs. For a long time he stood looking at her delicate form beneath the rough clothing. The innocence of her face held his attention, and he was hit by the realization that it would be easy for him to love her. He, who had never loved a woman before, was now pleased by the idea. She was lovely and sweet. But how was it possible for him to feel this way? She had given so little—how had she gained this power over him? Indeed, it was a power she had held from that very first moment. He scoffed at the idea. No woman reigned over him, and was she not his prisoner?

He removed his outer clothing and doused the light. He glanced at the unyielding chair in the corner where he had spent so many restless and uncomfortable nights and grimaced at the thought. He cast a lingering look at his already occupied bed. It looked so inviting, yet he knew he could never venture near. He grabbed some blankets, seating himself. He threw his long legs over one arm and bunched up a blanket for a pillow. Soon his legs were aching and he twisted and turned, trying to settle his bulk comfortably within the confines of the wooden furniture. His body was already sore from nights of this abuse, but tonight it was worse than ever, and he glanced over at the warmth of his bed again. Muttering a curse, he threw a blanket on the floor, then stretched out upon the planks to sleep. He knew how he would feel in the morning after a night spent rolling around upon the hard floor.

Kenric was awakened in the morning by a soft sigh coming from his bed. He looked over to see Bekah curled up in sleep; she was so childlike. Her sooty lashes lay upon creamy cheeks tinged with coral. Small curly tendrils clung to her brow and traveled down to her perfect neck, moist with the warmth of dreamless sleep. She gently stirred and opened deep blue eyes that came to focus on him. She rolled over, then stretched and let her arm trail over the bed, her fingers brushing the hardness of the floor as she looked at him. When he scowled at her she giggled and stretched in her comfort. "I see that you woke up on the wrong side of the floor," she said, bursting into laughter.

"Well," he responded as he arose and massaged the aching parts which had been pressed into contact with the floor, "were it not for you I should be sleeping comfortably in my own bed." In a better mood he would have enjoyed her laughter, first time heard. He pulled on his chausses and cloak.

" 'Tis not my fault you brought me here, and I would gladly vacate your bed if I could return to my homeland."

"You should only be thankful that I do not share it with you." He turned on his heel and flung over his shoulder, "Be back with breakfast." It was a grumble more than a sentence, and she laughed, feeling a little better for the first time.

Outside he heard the last refrain of her mirth. Why, she was a temptress, one minute innocence itself and the next moment laughing at him! Surely she must have some knowledge of the spell she cast over men. Would he never learn that a female is not to be trusted?

Breakfast was a much more sober occasion. She had almost enjoyed the exchange with her captor and now sat primly across from him at the table. She had caught herself in time and would not allow any friendship to form between them.

"We will be reaching land before long."

She did not answer him, and Kenric reflected that she had taken on his own poor mood. Was she feeling sadness and homesickness again now that the seasickness had abandoned her for the moment? He looked up from his crust and fish to find himself pierced by sea-colored eyes.

"You have something to say?"

She nodded. "What is to become of me when we reach land?"

He looked at her in surprise, for it was a question he had put off asking himself. "I suppose you will stay with me," he said, noting the gentle down-curve of that pretty mouth. "I have not given it much thought."

"Why did you bring me in the first place?" she asked, the softness of her accusation barely audible.

"That," he stated, finishing his breakfast, "I have given thought to, and can find no intelligent answer—except, of course, that my life was in danger." He smiled ruefully, turning away from her forlorn look, and went up onto the deck, where he found comfort in the sting of sea air and sharp breezes.

Bekah felt no comfort. It had become a stranger to her.

Later in the day she, too, slipped up to the deck of the craft, standing discreetly in a corner behind some lowered sailcloth. She gulped in lungfuls of the briny sea air, and it stung and revitalized her senses. The blue-gray water churned beneath her, its depths almost inviting. She could end it here, she thought to herself. And he would not be the wiser until it was too late.

"Would not do that if I was ye," a raspy voice grated. She reeled about to face Goudwin. "Ye would not die easy. Before ye could drown, one of those great fishes would bite ye in two. Saw a man lose an arm once, cut clean through the bone it was. He died from losing too much blood, I remember. Saw another man, caught in the grips of a slimy sea devil with the stringy feelers that wrapped round him, burning him with liquid fire. Horrible sight to see, him all blistered and screaming for days 'til he died."

Bekah stepped back in horror. The waters were cursed, and what dwelt in them she did not know. The thought of that watery grave began to terrify her. She turned her head away, looking about at the vast sea. There was a total circumference of water-horizon, their boat but a tiny leaf following the sun. She shuddered.

41

"No need to fear, missy. Long as ye watch your step this ship is a fit one, fit as an old spring bow, and there's none better than this crew either. The new Anglian boats I worry about, but the Norsemen, barbarians though they be, still build a seaworthy ship." Remembering her Nordic ancestry he hastily threw in, "No harm meant, miss. Old Goudwin here ain't nothing but looking out for ye."

A light mist began to fall, the sun still shining. "Look yonder," Goudwin said, pointing to the east where there arose a full rainbow, a perfect arc of color.

" 'Tis beautiful," she breathed, eyeing its splendor against the blackening sky. She did not notice when the mist turned to fine drops.

"The waters is a harsh mistress, but like any true woman she has her beauty too. And yours be all too visible in that wet clothing." He coughed, averting his eyes in embarrassment. "Ye'd best get below now. Old Goudwin here ain't got no mind to see ye harmed, but the others on the crew . . . well, they's a lusty lot."

Her face flushed. She descended into the yawning opening of the hold. Behind her she could hear his voice rasp after her.

"Fear not, miss, the worst be over. Cap'n's not so cruel as he seems, and ye've a friend in old Goudwin."

She turned back to him and smiled gratefully, laughing within herself because he looked so embarrassed, as if he had said too much.

For the present moment her depression had lifted, and she brushed out her wet hair, cast off her clothing and wrapped herself in a heavy knitted blanket. She had made a friend in Goudwin, and he might prove to be a great friend. She felt that if any man would have influence on Kenric, it might be this loyal sailor. Perhaps she could convince Goudwin to persuade Kenric to release her or send her back to her father. She knew she must tread softly, for Goudwin's loyalties certainly lay with his captain. Still, time would be her ally—ally and also enemy.

All in all, she did not seem so alone now. She snuggled down into her warm coverlet, napping, for the moment free of her fears. She survived this day of her voyage better than any of the others.

Her depression returned on the morrow, and she spent what time she could up on deck. She had one special corner in which she sat behind a large crate and a pile of hemp. The miles of water, gray or green or blue, the small circling seabirds hoping for scraps, the ever-changing sky all freed her mind. She wrapped a blanket about her to keep her safe from both the chill air and the stares of the seamen—especially the one called Dinnot.

He was a young seaman, perhaps her own age, but ugly in appearance and manner. Often he wore only frayed breeches, his sinewy muscles scrawny compared to the captain's. His hair was scraggly and brown, shooting out in straight tufts like ruffled feathers on a duck's neck. His eyes were pale, small and deep-set, giving his face a blank look that made Bekah uncomfortable. He was not much larger than she, yet she thought him a dangerous man, though she did not know why.

Often, especially when Captain Kenric was busy with other duties, Dinnot would try to engage Bekah in conversation. In her innocent way she tried to be polite, but she could hardly tolerate him or his broken Nordic. His sneaking suggestions that seemed to be slight insults, his habit of looking at her sideways, made her think of a dangerous badger. Finally she simply began to ignore him when he tried to catch her eye. She would casually gaze out to sea, pretending not to hear his remarks, crude or otherwise.

The more she ignored Dinnot the more he tried to gain her attention, often making crude jests she did not understand. When Bekah could not stand Dinnot's company any further, she reluctantly went below. As evening drew near she heard footsteps approaching. She looked up, expecting to see Kenric. Instead she saw Dinnot, who ducked his head and entered her chamber with a grin. He carried a tray sloppily laden with food.

"Here is your dinner, miss. The cap'n sent me down with it."

"You may set it down there," she said, pointing to the small table nailed to the floor. He did so, pausing to look at her, his hands rubbing together. Would he never leave?

"Thank you," she bit out, trying to get him to depart.

"Need not thank me, Bekah," he said, glancing at her

43

sideways. "A man does not mind doing for a pretty miss if she be willing, know what I mean?"

"Kindly leave, Dinnot," she said, leveling a burning stare at him.

"Is that any way to return a kindness? The cap'n sent me down here, waiting on ye like royalty, and ye answer back like that. Do ye think ye are too good for Dinnot? Maybe," he said, smiling slyly, "ye just be playing as a fox tricking the hounds."

She became alarmed at his leering manner, pulling the blanket tightly about her. "If your captain heard you speak to me this way he would toss you into the ocean," she said, gathering what bravery she could summon.

"Seems to me he is about ready to grow tired of ye, for we have been days at sea and there will be others for him when he lands. Maybe I can do him a favor." He grinned, lunging at her before she could move.

She tried to scream, but his slobbering lips were on her mouth, his nails digging into the flesh of her arms. She caught her fingers in his hair, pulling it from its roots, and a small guttural sound came from his grotesque mouth. He forced his lips onto hers, and she was so reviled that she bit down with all her might. She tasted blood, and he pulled back with a howl, allowing her time to bolt. She tried to escape out the door but he grabbed her, knocking her down and forcing her back onto the bed. He was incredibly strong for his size, and with a terrible sinking feeling she realized she was helpless beneath him. She tried to scream again but she could hardly breathe. She felt that she would suffocate under the weight of his body. If this filthy swine defiled her she would surely plunge a dagger into her heart!

Kenric, on deck, had just finished writing in his log, its crisp ecru pages neatly covered by his bold script. He put the quill and small container of ink away, then glanced up, looking about his ship, its sturdy planks beneath his feet, rolling water surging by.

The crisp snap of wind applied to sail, the creaking ropes and slap of water on wood were familiar to him. The salty spray was in his nostrils, the wind whipping the soft black

44

hair about his face. He was aware of his crew busying itself with menial chores, the men throwing themselves into their work with unusual vigor. Vernie, a young fellow in charge of the crew's food, stood nervously in the shadows looking down at his feet. Goudwin scurried towards the captain, his wizened face looking worried.

"What is wrong, Goudwin?" Kenric queried.

"Vernie just told me that Dinnot was in the cookhouse putting food on a platter. He said 'twas for the lady. Vernie saw him take it down."

Kenric bolted upright, shoving the log into Goudwin's hands. He hurried forward, scurrying down the ladder and into the hold shouting, "Dinnot!"

"Dinnot!" He burst into his room just in time to see Dinnot struggling with the desperate Bekah. Dinnot jumped to his feet, fear glinting in his pale eyes. Bekah desperately pulled the blanket about her, her body shaking.

"Sir! I brought the miss some dinner. She provoked me, she did. She's a naughty bit, this one. No decent man is safe around such!"

"You filthy liar!" Kenric bellowed, pulling his knife. "Defend yourself!"

"Cap'n!" Dinnot faltered. "Ye got it wrong. It was her, I tell ye!"

"Draw your knife," Kenric repeated through clenched teeth.

Reluctantly, a shadow of fear flickering across his face, Dinnot drew his shiny blade. He circled his captain, his knife gleaming wickedly. Bekah took in a deep breath, retreating to the corner. She no longer underestimated Dinnot, knowing that he might very well slip the blade into Kenric's back. She had wanted Kenric to die for his deeds, but somehow she had not envisioned it like this, and she had no desire to witness it.

Dinnot thrust out, but Kenric turned; neatly he parried the blow. Then Dinnot became more frustrated, flashing his knife here and there as Kenric expertly turned the blows aside. The tension within Bekah eased as she realized that not only did Kenric know what he was doing but he was superior at it.

Kenric did not strike out as Dinnot was doing but waited

45

calmly, playing with the foolish sailor, who became more terrified with each passing minute. Dinnot began to regret his hasty actions. After all, Captain Kenric was a knight of King Alfred's realm. Out of the corner of his eye he saw Goudwin and appealed to him, beginning to fear for his life.

"Talk to him, Goudwin! He is crazed!"

"Ye are the one who is attacking him. Stop your blows, Dinnot, ye fool."

"Stop! He'll kill me, he will! Look at the blood in his eyes!"

It was then that Kenric began his attack. His hand slashed out and nicked the sailor's arm, and Dinnot howled in fearful protest. As Kenric brought down his knife, Dinnot stabbed at him. When Kenric moved to avoid the blade, his knife came in direct contact with Dinnot's ear. It sliced off the top, leaving the lobe and middle portion still intact.

The sorry Dinnot dropped his knife, screaming in pain and horror as he stared down at the piece of his ear lying on the floor.

"Ye've cut off my ear!" he screamed. Goudwin handed him a rag to hold to the cut while the sailor cried, "Ye've ruined my good looks. What will become of me?" He shed actual tears. They were tears of relief as well as pain, for he realized that the fight was over and he still retained his life. Kenric stood quietly, surveying the situation as Dinnot scurried from the room.

Kenric tried to comprehend his emotions. He would have killed Dinnot had the seaman done more to Bekah. He was amazed at his own rage. Never would he have wasted the time of day on Dinnot, yet now he could have cut him down in anger for touching Bekah. He also felt intense relief that nothing had happened to her. Who was this woman, to make him care so much for her safety and protection as he had for no other?

He turned to Goudwin and said in such a quiet voice that it chilled Bekah to the bone, "Let this be a lesson to the crew. What is mine, is mine, and is to be touched by no man. When we arrive at Jarlshof, Dinnot is to find other employment. I will not have him on my ship."

46

"Are you all right, Bekah?" Kenric asked softly as Goudwin wiped up the last of the blood and then departed.

"All right! How could you expect me to be?" she snapped angrily.

Kenric was taken aback. He had expected her to priase his use of the knife in defending her. Instead she lowered accusing eyes on him. "This is all your fault!"

"I did not send him here, Bekah. When I heard he was here I came as fast as I could. What more do you expect of me? I did defend your honor," he added.

"You are the one who brought me on board as if I were a common strumpet! And now I see that your entire crew thinks of me as such. How my mother must be turning in her grave at this!" she cried out, her eyes burning with anger.

"Your anger is unwarranted. I fought the man for you and he has been punished. However, if you truly desire he be punished further, then I will order him thrown overboard. He will be ready bait for sharks with his bleeding ear. I will give the order at your word."

She looked up in surprise. "Nay! As much as I despise the man, I could not order another's death."

"Ah, the lady is indeed virtuous. You have mercy for him but none for me, I take it," he said, his voice tinged with sarcasm.

"You deserve none."

"And Dinnot does?"

"Nay," she replied. "But Dinnot is what he is, and I should not have expected higher of him. But you, sir, are a knight of King Alfred's realm; you know how to treat a lady." She sighed. "Neither of you deserve mercy and I have none to give."

Kenric smiled sadly. "Your perception cuts me like my own blade. I believe I will be a long time winning your favor. I hope your heart has not become too hardened. I do not know how long I will have to wait for you to grant me absolution."

With that, he left. She gazed after him. She was alone with her own thoughts, which became more melancholy as time passed. Would this voyage never end, would the turmoil within her breast never cease? In anger she grabbed

47

the tray, smashing it against the wall. Then she threw herself upon the comforting furs and wept.

In the days that followed her ordeal with Dinnot, Bekah again fell ill. There was no wind to fill the sail, and the small ship lurched with each swell and wave. The unbearable misery of her motion sickness stilled only in sleep. A warm wind finally rose to fill the sail, and the oars were put to rest.

A faint mist of perspiration kissed Bekah's forehead, her fingers limp in the curled relaxation of sleep when Kenric entered the chamber to find her so pale upon the bed. He worried for her health. She had been so sick and had lost weight as well as the pale glow of youthful health he had first seen. He, in part, was responsible. He hoped that once on land she would regain her vigor.

He gently shook her shoulder. "Get up, Bekah."

"What is wrong?" she asked, stifling a yawn.

"Just get up and come along," he said quietly, pulling her to her feet and wrapping a blanket about her. She had no idea where he was taking her or why and was exasperated that he should wake her for no reason. Would she ever understand him?

He guided her to the deck of the ship and seated her in a solitary corner, sitting behind her. She chastised herself for leaning against him, but she felt too weak to support herself. He held her with an encircling arm, hoping that the fresh air would help to bring life back into the sick girl. She needed some sun, too, but Jarlshof was not too far away and there she could bask in the warm healing rays.

The course was smooth. The wind against Bekah's face and the stars peering brightly out of the black velvet sky, like scattered diamonds within a jewel box, made her feel at ease. Her stomach was no longer upset as it had been, and her old self returned.

"I am hungry, Kenric," she said simply. He left and shortly returned with salted meat and water, which Bekah ate eagerly. She was surprised at how little she could eat and how quickly she became satisfied. For a long time they sat watching the men control the sail, observing the pattern of the stars, each very aware of the other. Bekah could not account for the half-pleasant tingling of her skin where his hand supported her, and she felt her senses heighten at his nearness. He smelled of earth and sea, his raven locks brushing against her cheek as he bent close to tell her of the stars they used to chart their course. He pointed out the morning star and the moon's terrestrial path. Kenric was so close to her silken hair that he could smell its mild fragrance, and his words faltered for a moment before he continued on. In the east a faint light appeared, turning the sky from black to gray. Soon it became a rosy color, and then the heavens filled with flaming pinks and oranges. With the coming of light, land was sighted and the shout went up. Kenric told her that this was the island Jarlshof where they would stay for a while before traveling down to Wessex. Suddenly the small craft was alive with men pulling ropes, guiding the slant of the sail and estimating the time it would take to reach shore.

Bekah watched the activity with interest and felt mild excitement that soon they would be reaching land. Kenric left her to attend to his tasks about the ship. From time to time he glanced to where Bekah sat. The wind blew the tresses away from her face, displaying its tender oval to the morning sun. Color touched her cheeks, and light was in her eyes.

He could hardly keep his eyes from her, and found that it was the same with most of his men—excepting Dinnot, who kept his eyes averted. He had lost his desire for this particular maiden, spending his time creating stories with which to intrigue other maidens about his wounded ear. Currently it was a tale in which he took on an entire group of Vikings, slaying the leader who had cut off part of his ear.

Tawny backs with muscles bulging were put into the task of turning the sail; the wind teased them twice before blowing strong. With luck the oars would not be needed. Bekah saw old Goudwin test the wind with an expertise that only he had. Their eyes met and he smiled, his eyes twinkling.

Kenric felt a twinge of possessiveness. He enjoyed her presence on deck but had no desire to allow the other men to do so. He helped her to her feet and guided her below.

"But I want to stay up there and watch the approach of land," she protested.

"Are you aware that every man on deck is watching you, and that they cannot do their work or even pay proper attention to it?"

"I did not think I was in the way," she stammered.

" 'Twas not a matter of being in the way. Do you know nothing?"

"You do not need to raise your voice with me, sir," she stated cooly. "I did nothing wrong and do not see what your grievance is."

"The fairness of a woman is very tempting to men who have spent months at sea. Perhaps it is time that you learned this, so that you can act correctly. You cry for your lost virtue, yet what fate do you expect when you sit and flirt with my entire crew?"

She looked at him in amazement. " 'Twas not flirting! That was Goudwin. He is an old man, yea, as old as my father or more! Do you find cause for jealousy in him?" She began to laugh.

"You cannot now parade your charms as if they were for the taking, as you did that day on the beach when you tempted me," he retorted sourly.

Her mirth died instantly. "How dare you chastise me for something which is your fault, trying to place the guilt onto me!" She burned with indignation.

"I bear my burden of guilt and place none on you, for your were innocent of the act itself. However, you do not realize just how your actions are interpreted by men. My men know you are my woman, yea, but certainly you have not forgotten your encounter with Dinnot?"

"You state that I am your woman," she scoffed. "But I see no evidence of it. Where are the banns of marriage? I cannot belong to any man until given to him by the hands of my father, and since he is miles away I see no way of that ever being possible."

"You eat my food, do you not?"

"Little of it!"

"And sleep upon my ship."

"Would that I had never been forced to come aboard this vessel and that I were free of it now!"

"That could be arranged," he bit out.

She looked at him in surprise. "Oh?" she said, wondering if he was going to allow her her freedom once they landed. "Then by all means do so!"

He nodded, then grabbed her up and slung her across his shoulder. She gasped, and her hair fell in a mass as she squirmed beneath his grasp. After his last experience of carrying her in such a position he was careful to keep his shoulder blades out of the reach of her teeth. "Very well, my pretty little Northern wench, if that is your attitude, then into the sea with you. I have had enough of your biting words."

"The sea!" she cried, struggling desperately to free herself. She could see herself being plunged into icy water too far from shore ever to make it to safety. Wildly she envisioned strange slimy creatures with sharp teeth and clinging tendrils; they came vividly into mind like beasts from childhood nightmares. She beat her fists against his back, struggling with all her might to free herself. After all her kicking and hitting she found herself still prisoner to him. Certainly he jested and would not throw her out to drown. But even now he was going to the ladder and stepping upon the first rung!

Her efforts weakened her and she lay limply against him. Immediately he lowered her down into his arms, staring into her pale face. Her eyes were closed tight. He lifted her face to his and, on an impulse, pressed his lips to hers. Her eyes flew open and stared into the deep pools of his dark gaze. Reluctantly he pulled his mouth from hers. "You are mine. I have just put my mark on you." Abruptly he released her, turned and vaulted up the ladder.

She ran back to the cabin and slammed the door, then threw herself across the bed and balled her hands into fists. She screamed in frustration, then vowed, "Just let me reach that shore and I will escape him, even if it means dying in the wilderness!"

She would teach him his lesson. She would bring him to his knees if it was the last thing she did and took her last breath! Every time she thought of that handsome face studded with glinting moonstone eyes and framed by that black mane of hair, every time she thought of his hard-muscled body and the steel-strength of his encircling arms, she became more determined to escape him. It was her fiercest moment of determination.

The distant outline of land upon water, a focal point toward which to guide the sea vessel, was merely a smudge of dark color against the cloudless horizon. Kenric recalled the warmth of those lips moments ago, and he looked towards that distant shore. He thought to himself, She did not fight me or pull away, and even her look was not one of disdain. He mulled this over and then smiled to himself.

Goudwin was mystified as he watched his captain who now smiled, when only moments ago Goudwin had heard the poor girl scream. What had happened to the captain he had come to admire, a man who treated his men justly and was a knight under King Alfred? And what of the maiden? Goudwin had heard her crying and throwing things, but then she had appeared submissive. She had been very ill, though today she had looked better and had even smiled at him. What had Kenric done to her to put her in this stormy mood? In truth, she had virtually been a prisoner here. Goudwin had witnessed the couple's fights and had begun to side with Bekah more and more. After all, she was but a mere girl, while the captain was a man of stature. At that moment Kenric turned and bade Goudwin take her breakfast.

Within a half hour's time a knock came at her door. It startled Bekah from her black reverie, for she knew it was not Kenric. Since when did that black-haired devil ever have the consideration to knock? When she reprimanded him he had reminded her that this was, after all, his chamber.

The knock came again, this time more insistent. Fear crept into her as she realized it might be Dinnot. No one had ever come here before when Kenric was gone except him. She shuddered to think of that scene being reenacted, maybe with different results. Quickly she searched the room for a weapon, settling on an earthen water jug. She clutched the jug close to herself, readying for a possible battle. She made her way nearer the door before recalling

that the bolt was on the outside in order to keep her impris-
oned.

Her voice, barely a whisper from fright, called out, "Who
is there?"

" 'Tis I, milady, Goudwin."

"Oh, Goudwin," she laughed. "Come in." As he entered,
she continued, "I was terrified. You should have announced yourself."

"Sorry, miss," he began, as he wondered at the fright
shown by the girl, the jug she held so closely to her. What
had Kenric done to cause this maid to fear him so? "Kenric
is detained, but wished your breakfast not be. He sent me
down."

He placed the tray of food beside her intended weapon on
the table and turned to go. Bekah reached out her hand
and touched his sleeve hesitantly.

"Yea, miss?" He turned again. His eyes closely scrutinized her face. She paused, then with eyes cast down she
murmured in a voice barely audible, "Who do you think I
am?"

The question, so direct, startled him. How could he possibly know who she was? In fact, he was not even sure he had
quite understood her intent in asking. Was he supposed to
answer her name? Did she inquire as to her station in re-
gard to Kenric; was she a great lady from a great kingdom
and now a kidnapped victim upon this ship?

"Milady?" he questioned.

"Perhaps, sir, I should rephrase. What do you think I
am? Or better still, what do you think of me?" She looked
up now, defiance showing clearly in her exquisitely blue
eyes, though a slight tremor crossed that ever-sensual
lower lip.

"Milady, ye are who ye are. Bekah. A beautiful young
woman. What ye are is what ye make of yourself from the
varying experiences through which ye pass. No one can
make ye be or do anything."

He saw the hurt in her eyes and wondered what he had
said to cause it. He stood quietly, waiting for her to evalu-
ate the words he had just spoken. It was a while before she
answered.

"You are wrong, Goudwin. Before that fateful day when

53

Kenric first laid eyes on me, I was, as yet, a girl who had known no man. Yet he took me with force and there was no stopping him."

Here she paused, and he saw the burden she carried as she tightly shut her eyes. Softly she went on, "Therefore I am not what I was, but it is not of my doing or of my choice."

Goudwin saw the tears in her eyes, the paleness of her cheeks, her clasped hands still and lifeless upon her lap. Like a fallen flower, he thought. Golden tresses fell around her in a silky covering. It seemed to him that the very effort of speaking about her plight had almost broken her. He saw the tears drop on her coarse skirt, leaving small round stains, mirroring the stains she felt upon her soul. She, a pure angel, wore guilt in her heart where only love and joy belonged.

"I am sorry, Goudwin. My troubles are my own. Please forgive me . . ."

"Oh, nay, Bekah! The forgiveness is not mine to give but yours to give. For no one has been injured but ye." He spoke with such earnestness that she was touched. She stood there, staring down at her clasped hands as if in prayer, he thought. Why must she suffer for Kenric's act? It was apparent that she had done nothing to deserve this. Goudwin felt a flush of anger upon his face. Nay, his captain had gone too far this time! He had done irreparable damage to this young girl. And he, Goudwin, would not let it pass. Angrily he slammed his fist down on the rough table. Bekah's head shot up, a look of fear and apprehension on her face.

"I will speak to the cap'n in your behalf. We'll see what sense I can talk into that thick skull of his. I will return for the tray and tell ye of the consequences." Goudwin stormed out the door. Bekah, still standing, was mute with surprise and alarmed by Goudwin's fury. What would Kenric think when Goudwin approached him to let her go? Worse still, what would Kenric do? For his rage would be far greater than that of old Goudwin. Even if she could physically endure his wrath, could her senses possibly live through his verbal wrath? Her terror mounted. He had threatened to throw her overboard; surely now he would make his threat good. She crept into a dark corner of the room, waiting with pounding heart for Kenric's appearance and the onslaught that would follow. The creaking of the ship's old wood made her start, for each time she thought it was Kenric's step outside the door. Inside and out she trembled as she huddled in the corner, praying for safety in this unsafe situation. As she sat there, waiting, and nothing happened, her intense fear lessened slightly.

A tiny glimmer of hope in the darkest recesses of her mind began to grow like light in the predawn grayness. Kenric had often spoken fondly of Goudwin, for the man had been with him several years. He found the man's dry wit, able seamanship and courage to be appealing. Perhaps, with the help of Providence, Goudwin could convince Kenric to let her go. She pulled her knees to her, resting her chin on them, and began to pray fervently for deliverance.

Kenric heard, rather than saw, Goudwin's presence as the older man breathlessly approached him. He turned to Goudwin and saw, amazed, the fury in the older man's eyes.

"Goudwin, what is the—"

"Cap'n, I've never spoken to ye like this before, but then ye've never given me a reason. But now I feel I must speak my piece, as I can no longer hold inside these angry feelings." He paused for breath and courage, too, for though he knew he spoke for a good cause, he also knew that Kenric would be furious at him for so doing. Maybe there was a chance, slight though it might be. He had to try.

"Ye must let the girl go, sir. Better still, turn the ship around and see her to her homeland. She cannot possibly fend for herself, especially in a foreign land—and such a young miss, too. Cap'n, ye've gone too far and I cannot stand the suffering ye be bringing onto this child."

Kenric stood amazed as the realization of what Goudwin was saying slowly spread over him. Then, as Goudwin had expected, his whole countenance blackened, his voice boomed. "Nay! She is mine and she will remain mine! What sorcery has the wench used on you, old man, to make you turn against me? What spell has she cast upon your feeble mind? Yea, she is young, but youth does her a favor,

55

for it gives her time, and in time she will be glad that I have seen fit to put her in my care. I will not take her back, nor will I release her—and you would do well to keep that in mind. Do not ever approach me on the subject again. I have decided."

Kenric waited for Goudwin to weaken and meekly excuse himself, but he did not. He straightened his age-old body to its tallest height and glared back at Kenric with accusing eyes. He spoke quietly and evenly. "Then I will have no part in this wicked treachery. Your servant I am, willingly, but I'll do nothing to harm that girl below." With that he turned and walked away, feeling Kenric's burning gaze sear his back.

As Goudwin stood outside the door he tried to summon the courage to tell Bekah the heartbreaking news. He had failed! Kenric had been most stern and adamant. Now, more than ever, Goudwin knew that Kenric would retain his possession of the girl caged within this ship. Yea, she was like a small trapped animal, and if the sting of her captor did not hurt her then surely the imprisonment would. Wearily he knocked on the door and, remembering her fright, called out his name before opening it.

He stood for a moment looking down at the planks of wood beneath his feet. Finally he looked up, and poured out the entire story of his encounter, and failure, with Kenric. " 'Tis so, Bekah. I did my best."

Quietly he closed the door, shutting from view her forlorn face. The look of utter aloneness, shock and sadness written on every beautiful feature was frozen before his eyes. Although it was no longer in his sight, he felt that his mind would never forget that expression as long as he lived.

PART II
JARLSHOF

JARLSHOF WAS A SIGHT WELCOME TO ALL. BY
late afternoon the small ship, its sleek hull rising with the
crests of water as its sail lay slack, was anchored in the
green water. The sun lay near the horizon as if ready to
submerge in the wet green coolness. Bekah was aware of a
delicious feeling of firmly packed wet sand beneath her
feet. She was filled with the insatiable desire to run free
along the white-bleached shore, filling her lungs with the
fresh air.

The clouds were like thick velvet ribbons strewn across
a bright blue sky. The gentle breeze caressed her face. In
the distance another ship could be seen, its dark brown
hull rocking gently in the push of waves. No dragon head
decorated its bow; the sail shimmered white with no Nordic stripes upon it. The cliffs rose before Bekah, black rock
and earth, sea ferns finding root wherever seed had taken
hold.

Kenric took hold of Bekah's arm guiding her up a
winding path that twisted its way to the top of the cliff. By
the time they reached the summit Bekah was out of
breath, surprised at her weakened condition. At the top of
the cliff, a village came into view.

There were buildings and cottages, the stone walls and
wood aged by sea air. The roadways which snaked between
the houses were of hard-packed earth. The marketplace
was filled with people, the air vibrant with gaiety and the
busy noise of buying and selling. Brightly colored awnings
were spread out, giving shade to the merchants and craftsmen who displayed their wares. A few horses passed by,
prancing nervously and snorting at the commotion. A slender, gray-haired matron showed off her finely woven fabrics and yarns, and on the table next to hers were skillfully
carved figurines. The old man who displayed them sat
carving, a pile of curled shavings at his feet. There were

beautiful tattings and laces, candles and vases. Earthen pots were being created under the skilled potter's hands while another man presented his wooden platters and bowls. A rotund tinsmith had women flocking about his goods while an elderly woman with a kindly face watched over headdresses of garlands woven with colored ribbons.

There was every kind of useful item or foolish trinket. Carts piled high with green and gold vegetables or glowing fruits were guarded by cheerful farmers good-naturedly arguing their prices. There were fish and meat markets and one large shop from which arose a sweet aroma of pastries. A brawny man passed by, his back laden with furs for trade, while a young juggler aroused cheers of delight from the children. The sounds of creaking wooden wheels, tinkling chimes and indistinguishable voices rising in various pitches were threaded through by the haunting sound of a flute.

The huge stone well, overgrown by furry-textured moss, was in constant use. The smell of fish and sweetmeats, pungent strawberries and leather mingled in the unique spicy-sweet aroma of the market. There were people of every shape and size, and women dressed in the loveliest clothes Bekah had ever seen. Their woven goods were exceedingly fine, and she felt garishly uncomfortable in her rough, soiled clothes. People gave her little notice, though, caught up in their own affairs.

She was amazed by all she saw, finally turning to Kenric as they wove their way past the tinker's stand. "Is it always so?"

He turned and smiled down at her. "Today they have all come out in their brightest because the ships have arrived. Also, this is Saturn's day when the market is its fullest. Soon the summer festival will be here, and everyone readies for it."

Odin's festival in the Nordic village came to mind. Compared to the common Anglian marketplace, the village of Bekah's childhood seemed shoddy. Her eye was caught by a young family examining the small metal mirrors and other wares at a bright outside shop. The handsome man, his arm encircling his wife's dainty waist, nodded his head in approval. The young woman was lovely, her dark eyes flashing, and a plump baby boy cooed happily within the protection of his mother's arms. Love emanated from their faces, sheer joy in living within their newly created family; a pang of loneliness plucked at Bekah's heartstrings. Was that what true love was, this tenderest of all creations? Even as she acknowledged this truth, a slow spreading ache grew within her, leaving her feeling empty and hollow. She would never know it. Suddenly the marketplace lost its magic aura for her, and she felt weary and travel-stained.

They found themselves in a deserted part of the village, the din in the marketplace left behind. They walked along the main road as it led away from town, each content to remain silent. They passed by low-roofed, thatched cottages where naked brown children played, their distant squeals barely audible. The land was like an old comforter, its patchwork farmlands of greens and yellows quilted together by threads of brown road. There were beautiful meadows dotted here and there with clusters of wild flowers; cattle and horses grazed within the confines of a rickety, timeworn fence. In the distance a great two-story house came into view. Kenric smiled proudly, pointing at it.

"I would guess that it must seem grand, after your rough homeland, eh, Bekah?"

She instantly suppressed any excitement she felt, saying flatly, "It is not so grand."

Oh, but it was! It all but took her breath away! The wood and stone were dark with bright green ivy upon the walls. The slanting shingled roof supported a stone chimney, and the front double wooden doors were heavily carved. A huge weeping willow, its pale green tendrils stirred in the breeze, stood to one side. Fruit trees in full bloom surrounded the house, clover growing wild about the lawns. A small stream, cool and clear over smooth stones, chortled by in front of the house, rushing down to the sea. Kenric led her across a stone bridge that arched over the brook, and up the steps. He pushed open the double doors and stepped inside.

If the house had appeared grand without, then it was doubly so within. The narrow hall opened into a beautiful chamber. The stairway was to the left, while on the right was a large room. Perhaps in winter the stone and brown wood might be too dark, but not now, with all the glorious sunshine of summer.

The many arched windows were open, the outer shutters cast wide. Slanting pillars of sunlight came through the latticed, ironwork windows, dancing in a merry pattern on the smooth wooden floor. A huge rectangular dining table stood majestically in the center, a beautiful white table-covering upon it. In the middle was a blue vase filled with pink and white blossoms. On one wall was a shield, depicting the Kartney lion in black, silver and blue; behind it were crossed a lance and long sword. On either side hung banners in the same colors depicting battle and victory. Through three huge archways to the right was a great room, empty save for tapestries on the wall, banners and garlands.

Near Bekah and Kenric was the stone fireplace, cool now, and clean of all ash. Upon the mantle were finely carved figurines of Christ and Mary, and a yellow and white vase filled with poppies and marigolds. Before the hearth was a rug, expertly woven in black and varying shades of blue, sunlight resting upon it. To the side of the fireplace was a sturdy wicker basket, now empty of fire-wood and instead holding a furry white cat, two kittens greedily sucking her milk. A third kitten, gold and white, its eyes still shut, mewed pitifully at the loss of its mother. Seeing that no one was about, Bekah moved forward, picking it up and helping it to find its mother's nipple. She stroked the soft creatures, listening to their purring. Kenric thought to himself that at times she seemed to be merely a girl, just now stepping out of childhood. Once again he felt that wash of guilt which had been present far too often. He steeled himself against it, a frown flickering across his rugged features. He viewed her from the back, her hair cascading down to the floor where she knelt.

Glancing up she could see down into the kitchen, its brick floors polished and clean. A heavyset woman, her back to them, hummed a tune off-key as her fingers adeptly cleaned and prepared beets and beet greens, her hands stained red. She wore a clean white apron, the ties barely reaching about her waist.

In the center of the kitchen was a large block table, the thick wood sturdy under the use of a cleaver; fresh strawberries sat on it in a large wooden bowl. An open kitchen hearth glowed with red-hot coals cooking a pot of stew; the walls next to it were hung with knives and other utensils. Copper and tin pots hung from the ceiling; a small brick oven was in the south wall. Open shelves held earthen jugs, wooden platters and bowls, large tin mugs and thick-rimmed goblets. A stream ran beneath a portion of the kitchen, and a trap door led down into the cooler. The walls had long ago absorbed the scents of onion, meat and oily spices, giving the kitchen its own culinary aroma.

Bekah stood up, tearing her gaze away and letting Kenric guide her from the room. As he led her up the stairway, she caught one last glimpse of the beautifully carved chairs and tapered candles in oaken holders. The stairs had been worn shiny, the wooden railing smooth beneath her grasp. Once upstairs, the banister continued on, leaving a balcony on the right to look down over the dining area. To the left were rooms, their open doorways letting her catch but glimpses of luxury and beauty. The balcony ended, coming into an enclosed hallway. The walls were decorated with beautiful stitcheries on fine white and blue linen. They came to one archway, the door snugly closed. In its center was a round grille through which one could see. Kenric slid back the bolt and threw open the door.

Inside there was a cheery gold and crimson carpet upon the shiny floor. Three high, arched windows gazed out towards the village and sea, curtained by white lace turned ivory with age. An oaken cabinet for holding clothes was covered by an embroidered linen runner. Atop it sat a glossy black vase filled with white and yellow daisies interspersed with bluebells. There was also a sunny pitcher sitting within a bowl; it held clear water fresh from the stream.

Late afternoon sunlight slanted in from the window, casting itself with abandon about the room. There was an elegantly carved bed with a foot bench. One wall was covered by a tapestry depicting children running through a field of flowers, the ocean and ships visible in the distance. There was a small, three-legged table waxed brightly; on it

63

were fluffy linen towels. On another wall was a finely polished copper mirror, framed on either side by two pictures of dainty needlework flowers. This room would have been right for her mother, Bekah decided.

Kenric lit a thick white candle in a heavily carved oaken holder. She thought that it was the finest lighting tool she had ever seen, and suddenly she understood why her mother had despised not only the crude fat pots, but everything of the Norse culture. She dared not show too much interest in the beauty of the room; she felt oddly worried that Kenric might think her the daughter of a barbaric culture. Still, she knew at once it was his room.

"Perhaps you will not need this, but the sun will set soon and I do not want to leave you in the dark. I am going now. I trust this will suit your tastes and you will be comfortable."

"Where are you going?" she asked as casually as she could. She felt uncomfortable at the idea of being left alone.

"To celebrate my return, of course," he said, smiling.

"Must I stay here?"

"You wish to come with me?" he asked quietly, studying her face.

"Yea, I am so tired of being locked up," she sighed wearily.

"Well, another time I would enjoy your company, but I am afraid that tonight I have other things I must get done."

She turned her back to him, disappointment obvious in the gesture. She crossed the room and pulled back the curtain to look out the window. She saw the distant sea and in her mind's eye envisioned her homeland across that expanse of water.

"I want to go home."

He looked at her in surprise at this simple statement. "Why can you not resign yourself to the fact that you are not going back, Bekah? I have told you time and again that you are mine. Is not your being here the final proof? Now I have not the time to sit here and argue with you. Why do you not get some rest?"

He left her, shutting the door. The sound of the bolt sliding into place made her flinch as if he had literally locked her in chains.

A deep feeling of despair overcame her and she fell against the door. She heard footsteps and again noticed the small wrought iron grille in the door. Standing on tiptoe she peered out and saw Kenric walk away from the door. They were both startled by the sound of his name being called out.

"Kenric! Oh, Kenric, I wondered when I would see you again!" Suddenly there was a dark girl in his arms and he laughed aloud with his jesting voice, swinging her around.

"Why, Meg! It is good to see you." He spoke in Anglian. "Let me look at you. You are still as pretty as ever and no doubt breaking the hearts of every swain on the island."

Bekah strained to look through the grille, seeing Meg's pink mouth upturned in a smile. She was pretty and she looked lovely in a finely woven pale green tunic. How Bekah wished she had a lovely dress like that. She felt in awe of the girl whose hair was neatly wound on her head in dark braids and whose expression was coquettish.

"I have been waiting so long to be with you again, Kenric," Meg said in a throaty voice. Bekah, watching them walk down the passageway, Meg's arm linked in Kenric's, was unable to hear the rest of what was said. Her feeling of despair was now coupled with something Bekah would never have interpreted as jealousy. However, Kenric was the only person she had in this strange country, and unknowingly she clung to him. She had no one else and how could she fend for herself in this land? Ah, but she did know its language! The realization slowly hit her that Kenric knew nothing of this, for they had conversed solely in Nordic. The fact might be useful in plotting her escape.

She began to examine the interesting aspects of the room, coming at length to the polished copper mirror with which she was totally fascinated. Never before had she seen so clear a reflection of herself. The face that looked back at her was smudged with dirt, her hair a tangled mass, honey strands down her back. The clothing she wore was roughly coarse and could not compare to the dress Meg had worn. But her eyes were a woman's, and where she had expected to see a young girl she saw instead a maturity she had never known she had.

Outside she could hear laughter and music floating up towards her from the village, and she peered out one of the windows to see flickering lights and distant shadowy figures passing each other in the twilight.

She began to wonder if she could have done things differently, and a nagging thought like an unwelcome fly buzzed through her mind. All who had seen her had no doubt thought her a willing guest instead of a prisoner. If she had fought him, kicking and screaming as he dragged her through the streets of the village, then all would have known her plight and perhaps offered assistance. Now, however, it was too late.

Why had she gone so meekly? What was the hold this man had over her; what was it about him? Undeniably she felt an unusual attraction for him. She hated herself for it. Perhaps it was all those years of living under Helg's iron-fisted dominance which made her weak and passive. Perhaps it was because she had been raised in a land where woman was always submissive to man. She realized she had come to accept Kenric's powerful dominance, and guilt screamed at her—guilt and shame at her lack of resolve in fighting him. She grew more determined to be free of this tyrant.

She had no idea how long he was gone or how long she was agitated to the point of being unable to sleep or even rest. Soon it grew very dark, the flickering orange flame of the candle her only light. The stifling quiet of the late evening was pierced now and then by distant shouts of laughter or the haunting sound of a lyre. Finally she thought she discerned footsteps in the hall and rose from the bed, quietly standing before the closed door. She was surprised to hear Meg's voice again.

"I am just going in to make sure that all is ready in Kenric's room. It is already late and no doubt King Alfred's messenger has received his report."

"I have cleaned this room earlier today, milady, but have your way. Shall I help you?"

"Nay, Violet. You have enough to do already. It will take but a minute."

Bekah heard the other girl's footsteps retreating, and realized that Meg was planning to enter her room. A strange fear, like that of a thief caught prowling, filled her. How could she explain her presence here and maintain any last shred of dignity? She froze as hinges creaked and the room was flooded with flickering torchlight. For a long still moment, Bekah's eyes reflected the light. The two women stood facing each other, one slender and golden-haired, the other amply endowed with darker locks.

"Who are you?" Meg demanded, studying Bekah's slender form and rough clothing.

"Bekah," she answered, using her most cultured Anglian, unspoken for weeks.

Meg could not conceal her surprise. "Oh? And just what are you doing here?"

"I am here because Kenric brought me here."

"Are you to be Kenric's woman for this night?" Meg smiled with sweet insincerity.

Bekah's mind was racing. Kenric was not out partying after all. He was on business and truly could not have taken her with him. She gazed back at Meg, lifting her chin.

"I am Kenric's wife." Her lips quivered in a delicate smile and she herself was astounded at the words.

Meg sucked in her breath. Caught totally off guard, she dumbly repeated, "Kenric's wife?" Her eyes narrowed into twin yellow slits. "I do not believe you!"

Studying the beautiful ivory features of the girl's face, Meg scoffed, "Kenric would never marry! He has been free all his life. If he should marry it would be to me; I have known him since we were children."

With a shock Bekah realized that most likely Meg was right. Why should Kenric ever marry someone of such an unrefined past as herself? She realized that her words had sounded ridiculous. Besides, what did she care if he married or not?

With startled surprise, Bekah realized that this was her chance to escape him forever. With the bolt unlocked and the door open, this was her perfect moment to flee. She stared at the open door, and the smell of freedom enticed her. Abruptly she strode out of the room and past Meg and cautiously hurried through the house.

The abode which had earlier appeared warm and pleasant had changed with the coming of night. Eerie torchlights cast shadows about, and her light footfalls softly echoed through the corridor. She held her breath as she hurried down the stairs, luckily finding the dining hall empty. As she reached the front doors there was a distant clattering sound that made her jump for a shadowy corner. There was a curse, a mumble of voices and the sound of wooden platters being retrieved from a stone floor. Her heart was pounding within her ears as she peered down into the kitchen, where a warm glow issued from the cooking hearth. Slowly she pushed open the heavily carved wooden door, fearful that the old hinges might cry out and warn the household of her escape. Her eyes searched the outer darkened landscape, seeing no one about. She slipped outside into the cool night air which acted as a soothing balm to her tingling nerves.

She hurried across the stone bridge and began to run down the road. The wind blew her hair into a tangled mass, but she did not notice it; she was aware only of the brown road skimming by beneath her bare feet, and an exultant sense of victory.

Free at last! This small victory was like a jewel within her palm. She would show Kenric! He had underestimated her, and it was her fondest hope that they never meet again. If their paths did cross in the future, then she hoped it would be at a time when she could face him on his own level and rebuke him with disdain. If she must run and hide, then she would do it; it was so important that he never find her again! The selfish rogue would rue the day he had thought her simple enough to be locked away. Her pace increased and she ran wildly and without direction. Eventually she found herself nearing the village, its few lights flickering in the blackness of night.

Her lungs felt close to bursting. Too tired to run anymore, she slowed to a walk. The darkened streets, filled with colorful tents and awnings earlier today, were now virtually deserted. A stray cat quickly ran into the night ahead of her and she startled from it. She saw that the merchants had simply packed up their wares and gone home. Only the litter of the day's transactions remained to tell the story of the afternoon's scenes. She caught the faded scents of the marketplace which mingled with the cooking smells from the nearby houses. The distinct aroma of beef roasting over a flame made her mouth water. She felt faint from hunger, yet realized her plight.

Maybe I can work for a meal, she thought to herself. Surely there is a place somewhere that may need a little help just for this night. Tomorrow I can press on.

This thought cheered her only a little, for reality was all too clear. She had nowhere to go, no one to turn to and no coin in the pocket of her woolen skirt. She came to a crossroad and read the signs. One indicated the way into the heart of the village, the other merely read Merchant Street. Having no desire to enter the village where surely someone would notice her, or where Kenric might even be feasting, she chose the other road and continued her journey. The farther she went, the more she noticed her surroundings. The road, once hard-packed and smooth, was now unkempt and rutty. In the moonlight she noticed weeds growing tall within the small gardens, fences crooked and worn; even the passersby and their horses began to take on an uncared-for appearance. This was an older part of town, and she was thankful for the brightness of the moon lighting her way.

Unlike the new buildings Bekah had seen, with their bright facades and smooth portals, the structures here were as different as if she had entered another city. Gnarled wood, its grain brought out as distinctly as wrinkles in an ancient woman's face, had aged early from salt air and sun. Perhaps in daylight it would be a more cheerful place, but now, with darkened alleys and windows gaping at her, the neighborhood made her shiver. A heavy mist was coming in off the sea, creeping across the ground. Its wispy fingers encircled her ankles, driving her on. The memory of the lovely bedroom with its glowing candlelight came to mind. Why was she out here? What sense was there in this impulsive escape? Her goal was to be free of Kenric, but she had no desire to accomplish this through her own demise! She was being foolish. She should go back and wait until the morrow when sunlight and a full stomach could more comfortably guide her way. But suppose

Kenric had already discovered her departure—what would he do if she were to return now, frightened and humbled? The thought of his laughter and his teasing jibes made her set her jaw determinedly, her eyes straight ahead.

She was alarmed by a stirring in the bushes. She halted and stared into the underbrush. There was a deep growl that covered her with gooseflesh and she froze. Kenric had briefly told her that Jarlshof was not entirely civilized. What beast would emerge from the trees? she wondered. She had little time to think of it, for there was a rustling of branches and out stepped a large yellow dog, its fangs bared. The hair on its neck stood stiffly up, its nose wrinkled and its yellowed teeth glinted as it growled savagely.

Would that hoary beast lunge at her throat and rip out her life veins? Panic-stricken, Bekah realized it was she or the cur. Stooping down she brushed her fingers along the ground as the beast continued to snarl, advancing slowly towards her. She felt for the rock her toe was lodged against, clasping it in her hand and rising slowly. Its smooth, weighty assurance gave her confidence and she pulled back her hand, letting the stone fly with careful aim. A resounding whack sounded upon the dog's hip, causing it to yelp like a hurt pup. It turned back into the bushes, tail between its legs, and left without further argument. A half-hysterical laugh escaped Bekah's lips. She wrapped her arms around herself, shuddering with her victory. She could take care of herself and needed help from no one, especially Kenric of Kartney!

Her knees were weak, but she forced herself on, determined to reach some unknown goal. A shriek fell upon her ears and she jumped before realizing it was a distant peal of laughter which faded eerily into the night. Vague sounds could be heard; laughter, calling, loud and shrill voices. As she rounded the rough bend in the road, the houses growing sparse, she saw a building filled with light and noise, and she sighed in relief.

It was a large building, hewn of wood, the arched doorway spilling forth amber light which fell upon the brown roadway. Two small windows stood lopsidedly on either side of the entrance, curtained by yellowed fabric. An old stone well, its wall broken down, sat to one side, while a huge moss-covered oak hung its crooked tendrils over the building. One limb of the oak had grown through the eaves of the dwelling, and a hole had been cut to give sufficient room for the branch. Another large branch loomed near; a wooden sign hung on squeaking chains announced that this establishment was The Wild Boar.

The alehouse's atmosphere was jovial, the smells of sweat, salt and strong ale combined with the aroma of the large pig roasting over an open pit. Bekah passed by the doorway, going to the old well. There was a bucket filled with water and a tin ladle resting inside it. She drew out the ladle, wiping its edge before drinking, then used the rest of the water to rinse the dust from her hands and feet. The smell of roast ham was delicious, making her grow faint with the thought of food. Perhaps if she were to inquire politely within, they would allow her to work for her dinner.

She peered inside, seeing rough wooden tables and stools which supported a number of men and a few women. The women were dressed in a manner Bekah had never witnessed; they did not wear the clothing of those in the village, but rather immodest garb. One woman's blouse was extremely low-cut, barely concealing her bosom at all, while her red skirt was hiked up well above her knee, revealing her thigh. She was laughingly nuzzling the ear of a red-whiskered seaman who patted her backside affectionately.

A man who sat in one shadowy corner began playing upon a mouth harp, the lilting tune drifting through the air. The pig roasted over a crackling orange fire, the hearth the only light in the alehouse except for a single torch. Large barrels filled with ale lay behind a rough wooden bar. Behind this stood the proprietor, serving up tin mugs of the heady brew.

Bekah's common sense was washed away by hunger and she was lured by the salty aroma of roast meat. She must eat or she would faint from hunger. She took a deep breath and entered the din of the alehouse. The laughter and talking ceased, and the man who played the mouth harp set it down. He was a seaman; his skin was darkly tanned, his eyes a vibrant blue. He had a soft mane of blond hair, bleached white by the sun. He sported a light mustache and was clad in tight-fitting white breeches and a red and white striped seaman's blouse. His head was bare and his feet, planted in front of his stool, were naked. He was amply aware of the entrance of a singularly beautiful maiden, her face and form out of place in the bawdy Wild Boar.

Bekah strode forward, her jaw squared in determination as she walked to the counter, placing her hands delicately along the roughened edge. She was neither aware of nor concerned by the gawking stares she received or the hush in the conversation. The proprietor turned around, drawing back in amazement at the young woman who stood bravely before him.

He was a large man, his girth more muscle than fat. He had no hair on his head, but two large, bushy eyebrows, as well as a black mustache, dominated his face. His meaty fist set a mug of ale down upon the counter as he gazed at the maiden in a scrutinizing manner.

"And what might you want?" he asked brusquely, his deep voice booming down at her to wipe away her courage. She tried to find the words to speak but they would not come forth, and she gripped the edge of the counter until her fingers shone white.

Kenric was whistling softly as he moved down the half-dark corridor. Reaching Bekah's room, he opened the door, not noticing that it was no longer bolted. The room was nearly dark, the thick candle burned low, and he was very aware of the shapely form beneath the covers. Silently he set down the platter of food he had been carrying and moved towards the bed.

"Bekah," he called softly, placing his hand on her hip. She moved, reaching her arms up to him. His surprise was overcome by an even greater shock, and he stepped back, staring down in horror at Meg. He threw back the covers, thrusting the scantily clad Meg from the bed.

"Where is Bekah?"

"Why should you care, darling?" she cooed.

"Where is she?" he repeated cooly.

"Oh, Kenric! What is she to you anyway? Certainly not

your wife?" Meg asked in a worried voice. "She said she was, but I know she lies."

He stood glaring at her. "I have no time for games, Meg. Where is Bekah?"

She had never seen him like this, so possessed and determined. "I have no idea where the wench is. She just walked out of here hours ago."

Meg walked towards the door, smiling and swinging her hips. "Too bad, Kenric—at least I know how to please a man." She quickly slipped on her dress under his angry glance.

Just then they heard a commotion in the hall. Kenric brushed by Meg and out into the corridor where a red-bearded man met him.

"Lord Kenric, I've just come from the Wild Boar." He spoke breathlessly. "Your lady, sir, she's asking for employment there."

"What!" he exploded. "She's at the Wild Boar?"

"Yes, cap'n. I came as fast as I could. I knew you'd want to know," he said as Kenric bolted down the stairs and out the door. He leaped onto the sailor's horse and spurred the steed to a full gallop, leaving the seaman behind with mouth agape.

Bekah lifted a heavy platter of sliced ham, carried it to a nearby table and set it down. She felt no steadier on her feet than before; the proprietor had driven a hard bargain. She must put in a full night's work before she'd obtain her meal. She'd had little choice in the matter. She returned to the counter, collected the three mugs of pungent ale on a tray and took them to the appropriate tables. The gathering of coin, however, was left to the owner, and she ignored its dull glint on the rough wooden tables. The jovial sound of drinking and singing had long ago resumed, and there were boisterous shouts for her to bring ale or roast pig. Her name was bandied about and she soon became very adept at dodging both questions about her past and roving fingers.

The blond man in the corner, who had been playing a mouth harp for most of the time, was not handsome, but there was a ruggedness about him which was appealing. He signaled her for a draught of ale and she brought him the frothy mug. Before she could turn to leave he caught

73

her about the wrist and pulled her down onto a stool beside him.

"You should rest for a bit, miss. One as frail as yourself hardly makes a sturdy barmaid."

It was obvious as his fingers firmly encircled her wrist that he had no intention of releasing her. "Sir, I have work to do."

"Certainly you can spare a moment."

"I do not wish to lose this employment, meager though it is," she said, brushing the damp curls from her temples. She was not aware of his eyes following a trickle of perspiration as it traced a path down her throat, losing itself in the neck of her blouse.

"There is better employment than this for one such as yourself."

She looked up questioningly. His eyes smiled down into hers. "Better?" she asked.

"Indeed. You could have a place to stay, food to eat and enough coin to buy yourself a new dress—one more fitting to your appearance."

"Where would I find such work, and what would it be?"

"I could hire you," he said, caressing her inner wrist with his thumb.

"You? But you are a seaman."

"Yea, a sailor and a man, and there is need of a beautiful woman for a man. I would treat you well, Bekah, and you would be assured of a roof over your head at night." He smiled.

She drew back in shock. Did this man think her a common woman, no better than a strumpet to be found on any street corner? But then, what else could he think when she entered this lowly inn and asked for work? She wrenched her hand away, rising to go about her duties, but even as she worked his words burned in her mind. For what it was worth she could have stayed with Kenric and been his tainted woman as well as this seaman's! Was there no way for a woman alone to make her way in life? Nay, she thought miserably, there was no refuge for such as herself without family, friend or coin. Her situation was hopeless, and she felt herself to be sinking in a mire from which she could not escape.

Just as she returned to the bar for more ale the door slammed open and all turned to see Kenric, Lord of Kartney, enter. He had never frequented the Wild Boar before, and they looked in amazement as he strode forward, seating himself at a table in the center of the room. Bekah was filled with ghastly apprehension and anger. He had managed to find her! And her escape had not turned out as well as she had planned. She had done a great deal of hard work, and her belly was still empty. She thought of Kartney Manor and the hearty aroma that had come from the kitchen and felt a guilty pang of relief at the thought of returning there. She was startled from her thoughts when Kenric pounded a fist on the table and bellowed his demands in Nordic.

"You, there, barmaid, bring me some ale!"

Was he insane? What game was this he played, making her the brunt of his joke? She felt herself burn under the gaze of the inn's patrons. The owner shoved a cold mug of his best brew into her hands and sent her on her way. Reluctantly she walked towards him. The trek seemed to take forever. She finally reached his table, standing before him with the mug in her hands. He reached up, snapping his fingers in her face.

"Set it down, wench, or have you not the sense?" he said, provoking laughter from those who understood his words.

How dare he ridicule her as if she were an addled maid! She could not even speak, for her very words seemed to choke her. It was then that she set the tankard down, spilling its entire contents into his lap. He bolted out of the chair, curses on his lips, and he could not tell from her innocent expression whether she had done it on purpose or not. No one dared laugh at this Lord of Kartney for fear of facing his apparent wrath—though some were crimson with the effort.

The proprietor hurried forward, his face ashen, towel in hand. "Lord Kartney, forgive this foolish wench! I hired her only this evening and she is very clumsy. If it is your wish I shall release her of the hire, sir!"

"It is my wish," Kenric barked as he grabbed the towel, trying to sop the ale from his breeches.

"Very well, you foolish daughter of a mule, you can look for employment elsewhere!" the proprietor cried.

Bekah was aghast at the insult, and before she knew it she had ground her heel into the innkeeper's instep, making him cry out in pain and fill the air with curses, some of which she did not even understand. This was a great release for the onlookers and they roared with laughter.

"It was a mistake to look for hire in such a place," she said dejectedly in her mother's tongue.

"Obviously you have vented your frustrations, and you also speak Anglian," Kenric ground out as things fell into place.

"My mother was a well-bred Saxon, as am I."

"Well, Bekah, it seems you have lost your employment here. Where will you go?"

Their conversation was interrupted by the young seaman who appeared quite unruffled by Kenric's presence. "I have already offered the maid employment if she decides to take it."

Kenric raised an eyebrow questioningly. "You?"

"Yea, I. It appears the young lady does not care for you. Am I right, Bekah?"

Stunned, she nodded. Was it possible that this sailor might save her pride? But nay, she thought of his earlier offer and her heart sank.

"So you wish to offer her employment," Kenric said slowly. "And what, dare I question, might it be?"

"No doubt the same thing for which you want her," the sailor said, his eyes glinting like hard chips of blue ice.

"I see. Well, Bekah, there is someone who wants you. You may have your choice. Go with this seaman or return to the manor with me."

Bekah was silent for some moments as all eyes were on her. How she wanted to choose the sailor, how she wanted to wipe that smug look from Kenric's face! But if she went with the stranger, would he be worse to her than Kenric had been? If he were, could she endure it? She was very aware of both men studying her intently.

"Choose, Bekah. Which one of us will it be?"

"I do not know; I must think on it," she said.

Kenric's face was blank, giving her no enlightenment as

to his growing discomfort. Outwardly he appeared very calm, but inwardly a violent storm began to rage. Would she choose this sailor, thereby giving Kenric no chance to overcome her dislike of him? He had trapped himself, and if she chose the other then he was bound before these twenty witnesses.

"Listen, Bekah," the seaman said. "We would be good together; I know how to treat a wench like yourself. You warm my bed and I will offer you shelter, food and even buy you a nice new dress."

"Tell us your decision," Kenric said weakly, a light film of perspiration covering his forehead and upper lip.

She felt drained and without hope as she quietly said, "Very well, Kenric. You have won again, but you are not the victor."

Kenric felt his spirits soar. She had chosen him; he had not lost her! Still, her words did not settle softly on his ears. He pulled her out the door as the seaman watched, scowling.

Outside the fog was cold as the horse galloped through the mist and down the darkened road. Bekah grew chilled, even with the warmth of the heated horse beneath her and Kenric's arms about her. His wet breeches gave neither of them any comfort, and Kenric's mood was very sour.

"The Wild Boar! The worst den of vile lepers in all of Jarlshof island and you choose to go there. You lament your lost virtue, but you were extremely fortunate that you were not insulted by every man there. Can you not take care of yourself?"

"I was doing fine in my own homeland until you came along!"

"Oh, yea indeed, I remember! You were beaten by your brutish stepmother and doomed to wed her obnoxious son. By now you would be loathing his return each night."

"At least I would be legally wed!"

"Is marriage so important to you that you would wed an oaf fit for pulling plows? You disappoint me, my dear."

"There were many I could have wed, had I not been stolen away by a pompous rogue! But I now know that you know nothing about the decency of a sacred vow."

"Do not be so sure that you could choose so easily! With

your sharp tongue you would leave many suitors cut to the quick and bleeding. And should you be so lucky as to find someone to wed you, your icy heart would freeze him out of the bed."

This left her speechless with fury, but fortunately by this time they had reached the manor. He dismounted and she got off unaided on the other side. He cast open the doors, pulling her into the house and up the stairs. By the time they reached her room Bekah's last ounce of resistance had gone and she ceased struggling. The loveliness of the room reached out to her. The tray of food Kenric had brought in earlier was still on the table, and she could not resist choosing a piece of honeyed bread. She ate it hungrily and drank the apple juice which had grown warm.

"Do not tell me that for all your hard work there you never even got a meal?" he surmised with a chuckle in his voice.

She did not answer him but sat down, finishing off the food until she was no longer hungry.

"Well, it appears that you are not a very good businesswoman, Bekah. It even took you several minutes to decide you would return with me."

"I could not decide easily if I should go with him or with you."

He snorted angrily at this stab to his pride. "He would have been a cruel master in comparison to me. Why, I even give you my own room and do not demand that you share it with me."

"But here," she said, "I am a prisoner."

"Nay, no more, Bekah. You have seen Jarlshof and yet came away lucky. Even the very woods often present a danger. I will not bolt your door, for if you escape you will only be harming yourself. Perhaps next time I will not be there to rescue you. Here you are safe, and only a fool would run." He turned abruptly and left her, going to another bedroom down the hall.

The door would not be bolted, but still she was a prisoner, and she felt no joy in her small victory. She was tired to the bone. Every muscle ached and she took off her skirt. She crawled into the comfort of the bed, shutting her eyes. A heart of ice, did she have? He was blind to the ache she often felt.

There was no dealing with the heartless wench, he reckoned in the privacy of his own room. He stripped off his pants, casting himself across his bed. If there was any winning her, it would take patience—patience he did not have! If she did have a heart, then it would take much effort to chip away the tower of ice which surrounded it. If only he could have her willingly in his arms just once, then perhaps he would not be so possessed with these unearthly thoughts of her. If he could think with his mind, then he would know it would be best to be rid of her. It would have served her right if he had sent her with that common sailor—then she would have seen how fortunate she had been! There was no reason for a wench to get under his skin as this one had. Tomorrow he would put her in her place.

The morning sun pierced Bekah's room, along with the sound of chattering birds. She stretched and yawned, feeling rested after her night's sleep. It felt wonderful to be plagued by seasickness no longer and to have steady ground beneath her. The events of last night were fresh in her mind, and she grimaced as she reviewed them. She had been foolish to try to escape, especially when there was no place to run to. Perhaps it was best she had not worked at the Wild Boar all night, for there had been no bed to sleep in afterwards. She would bide her time, and someday she would escape. For now, however, it was best to let logic rule over emotion. Their angry words were not so intense in daylight, and she found herself hoping that Kenric was not too mad this morning. She had no desire to fight with him—especially when he so often came out the victor.

There was a knock at her door, and she pulled the covers about her, softly answering. In came a stout woman in a big white apron carrying a plate of food and drink. It was the cook Bekah had seen in the kitchen, and the woman smiled at her. Behind her were two girls rolling a large round tub, too heavy for them to carry. They glanced at her but said nothing. Instead they proceeded to fill the tub with huge buckets of water. It took many trips to fill the bath, and in the meantime Bekah hungrily ate the hot bread and the cooked ground wheat seasoned with milk and butter. There was a mug of tangy berry juice and a bowl of fruit. She felt she had never tasted a meal so delicious and ate until she could not take another bite.

As if the cook sensed that Bekah would prefer to bathe without any assistance, she shooed the girls from the room and then withdrew herself. Bekah sank into the big wooden tub that had been smoothly lined with pitch. She had never had a bath so wonderful, and she thrilled in squeezing the cloth of warm water over her skin, washing away the miseries of her voyage and the previous night. She washed her hair until it was squeaky clean with a marvelous soap which smelled of mint. It was all such a delight that she had no desire to leave the bath's soothing water. Finally it became too cool for comfort, and she rinsed herself off with the extra pitchers of water. She began drying off her hair and skin, then looked down at the heap of rough clothing with distaste. She could not bear to put those filthy rags on her clean skin, and instead wrapped a sheet about her. She combed her hair for a long time until it was nearly dry. How clean and golden it looked now, and she gazed in surprise into the metal mirror. She pinched her cheeks until they glowed and then stood back in admiration. She was beginning to lose the haunted look the illness had given her, and her cheeks were tinged with coral. As she stood looking at her reflection she was not aware of the door opening and Kenric's eyes looking at her with admiration.

"Now this Bekah pleases me," he said softly, and she jumped at the cool sound of his voice. A little cry escaped her. She grabbed the bed covers about her, her eyes wide with the horror of her disadvantage. How could she let him catch her like this, with only a sheet about her?

"Have you no courtesy?" she asked angrily in clear Anglian, the sound of his own language from her lips strange upon his ears. He was well aware that he looked roguishly handsome in doeskin breeches and leather boots. His white shirt was opened down the front, its light fabric doing little to conceal his muscular build. The crisp black hair on his chest contrasted with the white fabric, and his raven hair fell casually about his rugged face.

"Do you forget that I am quite accustomed to entering without knocking? There is little reason for you to be embarrassed."

She pulled the covers about her, saying nothing. She felt her anger rising, yet had no desire to continue last night's fight.

"Well, in any case," he said, "I brought you something else to wear besides those rags. Here."

He tossed a bundle of clothing onto the bed, and she gasped at the beauty of the finely woven cloth. How she wanted to wear something beautiful! But her pride would not allow her to reach out and take the clothing. "I cannot accept these," she said, looking into his eyes. "Not from you."

"And what is wrong with me?" he asked angrily. "Only last night a common sailor offered you a dress. Besides, I cannot let you go around in those rags." He seized her soiled clothing and tossed the bundle out of her reach and into the cold fireplace. "You are coming with me today, and if you prefer to come in a sheet it is of little consequence to me."

"You know I do not," she said with a lethal look. She could not discern if he spoke the truth or not, but she did not dare risk public embarrassment, so she conceded. Reaching out with her free hand she looked through the pile of clothing, so unlike her simple Nordic garments.

"If you would like some assistance . . . I know that the clothing of our countries is different . . ." He paused, her look withering the last of his words.

"Need I remind you again of my Saxon heritage? If you wait outside I will dress."

He stepped through the door, shutting it, and she heard him lean against the portal and saw the black of his hair through the grille.

She picked up the delicate clothing, fingering it before pulling on the undershift. Then she put on the light silk kirtle which was white, over which she added the soft cotton tunic. It was a pale shade of blue with an embroidered braid about the square neck and hem. Lastly she wound the soft leather thongs about her ankles.

"What takes you so long?" Kenric asked, peering

81

through the grille before he entered. He let out a low breath as he watched her wind the thickness of her hair into a soft curve at the nape of her neck and tie it with blue ribbons. It was not the tangled mass that had accumulated a dusty color aboard ship, but rather a silken gold. A few tendrils escaped to fall softly about her face, a face free of dirt and smudge and the pall of sickness. Her mouth was tenderly pink, her cheeks flushed, and the color of the gown heightened the hue of her eyes.

She looked in amazement at her reflection in the mirror and Kenric thought to himself that he was only now realizing her full beauty. She looked down at the gown falling softly about her and laughed in delight, displaying even, white teeth. This was no longer the child in poor Nordic clothing but a lovely woman. She caught his smiling image in the mirror and became more solemn, embarrassed that she had lost her reserve before him.

"I never thought that you could be more beautiful than on the first day I saw you, but you prove me wrong," he said.

I never thought you could look so handsome, you black devil, she thought to herself as her lips quivered with a smile. Looking down at the soft gown she wore she said, "I have never owned a dress this fine, I must admit."

"I hoped you would like it. I have ordered a number of others made up for you. They should be finished in a few days."

"Nay, Kenric! If I were to accept other clothing from you . . ."

He laughed, leaning against one of the tall posts of the bed and folding his arms, still inspecting her. "You would be my mistress. Now that is an interesting thought, but perhaps it is time you realize the truth of your situation. Did you know that by rights of the conqueror you lawfully are my slave?"

"Slave!"

"Yea, 'tis the law even in your homeland. After all, I did take you captive, and by the rules of battle you should accept your fate willingly."

She was so stunned by this preposterous idea that her

eyes widened in disbelief. "How dare you suggest such a thing?"

"Try to soften your icy heart. If you will accept your duty it will be more pleasant for us both."

"Very well," she answered sweetly, stepping near. She put her hands on his chest, running them up the soft fabric of his shift. "I see a job that needs my attention most urgently."

He smiled down at her, believing a kiss was coming, then stared at her in shocked surprise as she grabbed the cloth, ripping the buttons off.

"I cannot have my master going out in public like this, so you had better take it off."

Both of them cooled as she sat sewing the buttons back on. She threw the shirt at him and stalked out of the room. Quickly he pulled it on and asked, "Where are you going?"

"You said you would not lock me in any longer."

"Why should I?" he said as he easily kept by her side. "Perhaps you would rather brave the bite of a wolf's teeth or the claws of a bear."

She opened the front doors to reveal a gorgeous summer morning. Outside stood a large horse with silken muscles and a gracefully curved neck. The horse was auburn in color, with a long flowing mane. There was something in the masculine throw of its head that reminded Bekah of Kenric; master and horse, two individually strong stallions.

"What a beautiful animal! I have never seen any horse like it. I've seen only stocky farm animals, none like this beast." She stroked its neck, setting aside her anger for the moment, and it nuzzled her shoulder.

"Polo is of noble heritage. Here." Kenric grabbed her by the waist, swinging her onto the animal's back. Effortlessly he pulled himself up behind her, taking the reins and guiding the high-spirited animal away. "We are going to the village. I thought you might enjoy spending more time in the marketplace."

She said nothing in answer, but secretly anticipated seeing all she had only caught a glimpse of before. It was such a perfect summer day that it was impossible for either to long hold on to feelings of anger, and soon their previous harsh words were put from their minds.

Bekah felt as pretty as the day itself, and this time as they approached the village she was not embarrassed by her apparel. As she rode atop the large beast, sitting straight-backed in front of Kenric, the wind whipped the loose tendrils away from her face. Her eyes roved the pleasant hillsides and meadows, the cheerful little cottages with their yellow roofs, reminding her of her own house where she had lived as a child. A pang of homesickness stabbed at her as she thought of her father. Perhaps the land was more cultured here, the storms more gentle, and the sea not so violent, but still, she felt she did not belong here. Neither did she belong in the Nordic setting, and she felt once again as she had many times before that she was misplaced. Here the land was fertile and rich, not like the unyielding dry farmlands where she had been raised. Large trees lined the roadway, their green leaves vibrant against the azure sky; there were no twisted cedars here, scarred by vicious storms.

The destrier snorted and tossed its head as Bekah patted his silky neck.

"He likes your gentle touch," Kenric mused.

"He is a noble horse," she answered, reluctantly breaking the silence that had grown between them.

"He is well-trained. I rode him as a youth," Kenric stated. He let loose the reins, giving Polo his head. The obedient steed kept his pace, following the path into the village as Kenric guided him with his knees.

She was amazed at this and for the moment forgot her quietude. "How does he know where to go?"

"I guide him with my knees and legs, which is essential in jousting. Polo is trained well to it, leaving my hands free for other things." His hands encircled her waist and she visibly tensed under his touch. "Look!" he said in surprise. "I can hardly believe it! I can actually touch my fingers and thumbs, making a complete circle. Even women in Wessex are not so petite; how did such a frail flower blossom in the barren Nordic soil where only hardy plants can grow?"

She did not answer, and reluctantly he released his

hands, smiling to himself at how primly she sat. They neared the marketplace, the commotion ever-growing in the warmth of the summer morning. Kenric agilely dismounted from his steed; reaching up for Bekah, his hands encircling her waist, he easily lowered her to the ground. He tossed Polo's reins to a small boy who for a penny would care for the horse. There were so many things to see, and all the people appeared friendly and jovial. Many waved or spoke to Kenric, nodding their heads at the couple so opposite yet so attractive. Curious stares took in every detail of Bekah's countenance, yet she did not feel embarrassed, clothed in the lovely blue dress. Some of the people spoke a tongue which she could not understand and she looked at Kenric in puzzlement as he spoke a few words in Gaelic.

"Gaelic is the common language in this part of the world, and many of the old people speak it," he explained. "You see, my great-grandfather Alred was the younger twin son of Danric of Kartney, and because of his violent desires for the family lands he eventually was banished. He found his way here, and through a great deal of work and effort he settled in Jarlshof, claiming these lands. When he was forty he returned to Wessex, claiming the Kartney lands as his own, taking them from his elder twin brother. There was a great deal of bloodshed and battle, for Alred of Kartney was quite a warrior. He left his poor brother very little, even claiming his brother's young wife, Sabrina, quite a raven-haired beauty from what the family history tells."

"So," she said, "decadence is hereditary."

"Watch your tongue, miss. I am giving you a history lesson, and you'd best be courteous and listen. The lands were given to my grandfather Milton, who was Alred's only son, borne him by Sabrina. My grandfather, being a just man, and not wanting the battles that had happened between his father and uncle to be relived by his sons, divided the lands. My father Morely, being the eldest, inherited the lands in Wessex, except for one estate given to my uncle. Uncle Stanton, quite a nice man of whom I am fond, inherited the lands here on Jarlshof. My grandfather had enlarged the home here and also brought workers from Wessex. They have even built up the village here, with the help of my uncle and grandfather. We came here every summer when I was a child. My mother loved it. My fondest memories are of her in Jarlshof; she loved this simple life. I wish you could meet Uncle Stanton, but he has journeyed to Wessex to oversee his lands there. In any case, that is the reason that the majority of these people speak Anglian."

By now they had wandered into the hubbub of the village square, and Bekah enjoyed all that she saw. Kenric bought two peaches, huge, golden-orange fruits, the like of which Bekah had never seen or tasted. She ate hers daintily, and Kenric thought to himself that she was the epitome of all that a lady should be. Dressed in the soft blue frock, she spoke, ate and walked with the grace of a princess. He bought two mugs of cool apple juice, handing her one.

As they sat on a bench beneath the shade of a birch sipping their cool drinks they appeared to be like any young couple courting. No passerby could detect the indifferent resignation which the girl felt, or her guilt at enjoying anything in the presence of the man she had vowed to hate. At best a close observer might note Kenric's attempt to appear unruffled by her presence althought it was obvious that he was enamored. His free hand fingered the slightest fold of her skirt near him, his eyes glancing up at her flushed cheeks and pink mouth.

They resumed their tour of the marketplace. Bekah, forgetting herself, stopped to examine a table of mirrors and trinkets. Kenric purchased a beautiful wooden brush with bristles from the hide of a boar and a matching comb with a rose carved on the handles. He also bought a small oval mirror of highly polished metal edged in wood with a carved rosebud edge. They were beautiful, and Bekah very much enjoyed seeing them but was reluctant to accept them. Once out of earshot of the merchant she turned on Kenric.

"You must not buy me things, sir."

"Why not, for heaven's sake?"

"It makes me appear to be indebted to you. You cannot buy my favor."

"Oh, Bekah. Would you stop such efforts to be difficult?

You need a comb for your hair. I will not have you trying to comb it out with that crude piece of bone you brought with you."

"You will not?" she asked, her voice tainted with mockery. "Well, I do not care for the way people look at us together as if we were friends!"

"Friends? Oh, I assure you, we are not friends. We are more than that, fated for more than that! They think of us the same as every young man and woman in which the man buys the favor of his miss."

He threw his arm wide, pointing to other couples who strolled along gaily, or bent their heads together in some secret. "Do you see?"

Her face burned at his words, the pink flush only enhancing her looks. "I am not to be bought, as those foolish girls are. And it is foolish of you to buy me trinkets; it only labels me as a strumpet, and I will not allow it!"

Now it was his turn to be sarcastic. "You will not? We will see. Come along, miss!" he said, catching her by the wrist and guiding her along. He had not meant to buy her anything but her words spurred him on to alternative actions. He bought her a beautiful white lace shawl, casting it about her shoulders. He purchased a bracelet made of tiny white shells and another of braided copper, fastening them about her wrists. As well, he bought a beautifully carved maple box, filling it with trinkets, jewelry and glistening ribbons of every hue for her hair. If she cast her eyes in the direction of something, such as the scented lavender or rose soaps, or delicate silver rings, he purchased it, until finally she kept her gaze leveled at the hard-packed earth.

Kenric lifted up her chin, making her look at him. Her eyes were misty as she bravely blinked back tears, a few glinting like diamonds upon her black lashes. "What is wrong, Bekah?" he queried uncomfortably.

"Must you paint me as a common woman of easy virtue before the good people?" she asked, pulling her chin away.

"They do not think that. Why are you always such an innocent?"

"Do not ridicule me, sir."

"I do not ridicule you. The worst these people will think

87

is that we are in love, and although you might not warm to the idea, it is common here, especially in summertime. Everyone enjoys seeing those in love, and since we share different rooms at the manor, then word would be that we are friends, or betrothed. There are maids who flirt and coquette—take Meg for instance. She is quite a little minx, and all the men enjoy her pretty looks, even if she is a flirt."

"And do they think similarly of me? No doubt Dinnot and the other men from your ship have colored my past. Does everyone who looks at me know my story?" she asked sadly, her voice ringing harshly in her own ears.

"Nay, Bekah. For if I did not know better, I would guess you to be the purest virgin. Your very appearance cries out innocence, and in truth, since what happened was not by your consent, you are still a virtuous woman. There is no tarnish upon your heart, and I would venture to say it is virginal, for no man has gained it."

He guided her to a booth where a kindly lady with shining eyes smiled at them. "Why, Lord Kenric, 'tis good to see you! How many years has it been since you were cast upon these shores, or since we have seen you about? You were always such a mischievous youth, I must say you broke the heart of every maid on the island one time or another!"

"Oh, Lorna, you exaggerate."

"Nay, I do not! You were quite a wild blade in your youth, but it appears that you might be settling down," she said, her eyes resting on the girl at his side.

"This is Lorna, my dear. During winter she teaches the children; one time I was even her pupil." He smiled in a mischievous way that made him seem a boy. "And this is Bekah; I brought her with me and will take her back to Wessex when I go."

"Well, the village has been alive with news of her; even my own Violet has told us of her beauty. I must admit that you are lovely, young lady, and we are so glad that Kenric has decided to wed. He will leave a score of broken hearts in his wake, for he's a great conquest."

Kenric had said nothing of marriage, and inwardly Bekah quaked. She knew nothing of his plans for her future, and she suspected strongly that Kenric was undecided himself. To her great relief he said nothing of his plans but instead inquired after Lorna's husband, five sons and pretty daughter, Violet.

While they conversed Bekah found herself included less and less in their talk. She took the opportunity to look about her and form her own opinion of Jarlshof and its people. Surely everything here was more colorful and bright than at home, the people gay and hardly repressed. The wealth she had experienced on the farm on Norway would be considered poverty on this isle of abundance. Much of their riches depended largely on the fair weather and the black-brown earth, and Bekah had never seen many of the fruits they ate daily. Her mother had indeed been proud of her heritage, and Bekah was growing more and more to understand why. These people highly respected the Kartney name. She knew that should she find the chance to escape, none would give her aid if Kenric sought her. She did not know the land here, or what beasts might reside in the forests. The situation was impossible. She dreamed childishly of her father landing upon the shores of Jarlshof with a crew full of warriors from the village. She could see them battling their way to the Kartney manor and releasing her.

Admitting to herself that no such rescue would happen, she realized that if Kenric were to be brought to his knees, she must do it herself. She did not know how she would, for physically she was weaker than he, yet she reasoned that her greatest suffering had been within her mind and not her body. She sensed she had the power to humble this arrogant man, but how? What was it that made her father fight for her mother? What is it that keeps a man at one woman's side for years? The idea was beginning to dawn on her—but she could never have this type of power over Kenric!

She was startled from her thoughts by something being placed upon her head, and she realized that it was one of the garlands which Lorna sold. It was her most beautiful wreath, made of yellow rosebuds and dainty ferns. On either side of it hung blue and white ribbons, silky slender things that entwined in her hair. She put up her hands to remove it but Kenric stopped her.

"Nay, Bekah, leave it. It pleases me, even if your radiance does dim the beauty of the flowers."

"I ask you not to, sir," she said, embarrassed by this new gift.

"Why, miss!" Lorna exclaimed. "It is the loveliest garland I make and it looks enchanting on you. It is the custom here in our village that a young unwed girl can wear it as a symbol of her marriageable state. It means that the young men can look and court you. Once you are wed you will not be able to wear one again, for they are a symbol of an untouched maiden."

Inwardly both Bekah and Kenric flinched at these words, and he hurriedly looked at Bekah to see their effect on her. Her face remained calm although inwardly she ached. "It is too bad you do not have something she can wear to tell the other men to keep their eyes from her, for she is mine," he said softly with a smile.

"Once she is wed, then a flower behind the left ear, but for now it is the garland. It only means that you must keep on your toes, Kenric, so that another does not steal her from beneath your nose—and from the looks she has been receiving from the menfolk, you had best be wary," Lorna said, a twinkle in her bright eyes. She handed Bekah a single yellow rose to carry, and Bekah, realizing that each sale Lorna made was important to the nice woman, said nothing further about the garland.

Kenric, with his hand resting comfortably at the small of her back, guided Bekah along through the marketplace, stopping at a pastry shop. The aroma of hot breads engulfed them; he stepped in, returning in a few moments with two light confections. The pastries were made from very fine flour, which had been bleached, and were filled with cream whipped to a fluffy texture. Bekah thought she had never tasted anything so delicious, even venturing to say so.

"Yea, they make the best pastries in Jarlshof, or in Wessex for that matter. I loved the place as a boy, and when I was very young, my mother often took me here."

Finishing the desserts, they walked on past a sandal and

90

shoe shop where tanned hides were hung, the smell of leather strongly emanating from the little store. Next to it was a tool shop where a man pounded metal into useful objects, the din of his hammer ringing in their ears as they passed by. They saw a woman dipping candles again and again in the tallow, as each layer made tapered ecru candles. The craftsmen here were skilled in what they did, whether it was weaving, carving or smithing.

"I can see why my mother missed her homeland so," she sighed.

Kenric nodded. "What of you, Bekah? Do you miss your homeland?" he asked carefully.

"In many ways I do. The land was often rugged and stormy, but at times it was enchanting. I miss the cottage where my mother raised me, even though we did not live in it these past few years. I miss my father; I worry about him. Does he suffer because of his fear for me? Sometimes I cannot bear the thought of it. I loved him, the gentle man," she said, surprising Kenric with her openness.

He took her dainty hand, holding it in his own brown one, studying her tapering fingers. "I have realized my thoughtlessness and have sorrowed for my actions. Even once I wished that you had been born in this village, so that when I came to stay here I could have seen you in the marketplace, in a crowd, and been smitten by your beauty. Then I could have courted you and not found such disdain in your glance."

She drew back, stunned by the somber sound of his voice; looking into his eyes she saw no mockery. Slowly he stepped near, looking down into her face which was tilted up. His eyes seemed to speak of his repentance as he stood close, bending intimately near. She could not pull her eyes away from his gray ones, her sworn disapproval of him temporarily overcome like a forest by mist. His lips came close to hers and she was breathless. He did not take her into his arms; indeed, he did not even touch her at all. There was nothing forceful or dominant in his action as his soft lips barely brushed her own. The touch of them was electrifying, and she was lulled by an inner calm and a curiosity as to whether he would press closer.

There was a burst of loud laughter, a shout and the

sound of running feet. Instantly they pulled apart, as a buxom maid in full blue skirt and low-necked blouse was pursued by a husky youth in brown breeches and vest. They did not see Kenric or Bekah as the young man caught his girl, kissing her roguishly before they clasped hands, sauntering off in another direction.

The magical moment between Bekah and Kenric had been shattered, and she was once again the proper young woman with hands folded primly together. Without a word, Kenric guided her back to his horse, wondering at his own peculiar actions. He nodded at the towheaded boy who had cared for Polo and lifted Bekah atop the horse before mounting.

It was late afternoon as they headed back, each mutely observing the actions of the other. It was warm in the sun, and the smells of the sweating horse, pungent fields and ferns filled their nostrils. Bekah pulled off the shawl, folding it neatly in her lap. Sitting so close before him, she filled his senses and for a moment his head reeled. With a slap of his heels he spurred the horse on to a gallop, allowing him to grab her about the waist and hold her tightly against him. Faster Polo thundered down the path, and Bekah became frightened at such a high speed. Out of fear she turned, throwing her arms about Kenric's neck to keep from falling. The feel of her pressed against him, the touch of her flesh about his neck, the smell of her, all made a violent stirring within him, one which he had been suppressing all day. The horse, lathered and sides heaving, jerked to a halt before the doors of Kartney manor.

Bekah slid down from Polo's back, not waiting for Kenric's assistance. "How dare you!" she cried, stamping her foot as he dismounted. "You could have killed us!"

"Nonsense! I had complete control of Polo."

"You did that on purpose, so that I would have to cling to you for safety!"

"I did it to be here quickly and out of the heat of the day."

"You're hateful!" she cried out irrationally, for lack of a better statement.

"You are behaving like a child."

"And you are behaving like a fool," she said, her bosom heaving.

"Bekah!" he said stormily, a warning note in his voice.

She turned about, going to the doors, but they were stuck and she could not budge them. He stepped forward and with ease pulled the doors open, aggravating her all the more. She did not wait for him to enter but hurried up the stairs, down the hallway and into her room. She slammed the door shut, desiring to be out of his presence. The room was hot, and she pulled the curtains across the arched windows, darkening the interior a little. Wearily she tossed the garland upon the chest, the wilting roses filling the air with their pungent aroma. She took a drink from the pitcher, but the water had grown lukewarm, and she put it down. She cast off the blue tunic and kirtle, leaving on only her undershift as she removed her sandals, then wrung the water out of a cloth and wiped her face and hands with it, cooling her skin. She lay down on the bed, her eyes fluttering closed. She was no longer angry, only tired, and she pushed all thoughts from her head. As the sun began to set she was overcome by a light slumber.

Kenric, unable to analyze her reactions, shook his head. He went into the kitchen and the cook poured him a drink of cold ale. Her senseless chatter drove him back out to Polo. The horse snorted, nuzzling his master affectionately. Kenric patted his nose. Taking the packages from the horse's back, he led the steed to the stable, brushing him down and giving him water and oats.

"Polo, my fellow, your master is a fool. I swear that I will never understand the female mind! Women are not to be trusted, much less understood."

Returning to the house with the box he had bought for Bekah in his hands, he looked down at the finely carved lid with the picture of a swan on it. Once inside the house he took the stairs two at a time, arriving at her door. He was ready to walk in but remembered her dislike of his doing so and rapped lightly. There was no answer, and he wondered if she had left, knowing her penchant for escape. He pushed open the door, his eyes searching the dimly lit room.

She lay on the bed. He could see her small form covered

by a light sheet in the heat of the late afternoon. She seemed only a child to him when she lay in slumber. She had let herself be kissed by him today, and he wondered if she were coming around to him . . . or if she only pretended, waiting until the time she could escape. It would be so easy, so natural for him gently to let his heart take her as his marriage partner. Slowly he could teach her the pleasures of being a woman who is loved by a man. Her face was so innocent and trusting as she lay there, and he set down the box. The only ease for his emotion was her, he realized as he neared her. He bent over her, brushing her sweet lips with his own, tasting the nectar there. He wanted her, how he wanted her! His heart was pounding in his ears, his clothing clung to his muscular body and his lips trembled slightly as they touched hers. It was then that a flickering look of fear crossed her sleeping features, an inaudible sound of protest upon her lips.

Bekah found herself dreaming of Kenric, of his tender embrace as he held her. The tenderness they shared was overwhelming. In her dream she saw him come to her and saw herself accept him with ease and grace, finding joy in his love. Half awake, the thought of this surrender to Kenric so appalled her that she cried out, her eyes flying open. For a moment she could not distinguish between dream and reality as his face came into focus over her own.

"What is wrong, Bekah? Did you have a bad dream?"

She nodded her head. "I dreamed of us together," she whispered, the strangeness of it still clinging to her. She was horrified as she thought of that terrible acceptance of him and her desire for it. She could not comprehend such intense, alien, enticing feelings.

Kenric did not understand that the fear in her eyes was from her own desire, brought out in sleep. He assumed that it was from her memory of his ravishing her. He felt the strong rejection and, drawing up, turned away from her. He left the room, quietly shutting the door. Bekah felt a tiny pang of guilt at his departure, closing her eyes tightly as tears pushed their way through.

Kenric went down the stairs and out the door, turning to the stables. He felt such intense emotions that his pride flinched in shame. He could not stand to be by her. Neither could he live without her, and the thought of sending her away filled him with the blackest pain of loss.

He mounted Polo, riding the poor beast violently until he reached the widest part of a gushing stream. He quickly dismounted, pulled off his clothing and cast it upon a bush. He threw himself into the stream, letting it wash away his wants as it did his perspiration. Suddenly he had to laugh at himself, a grown man sitting in an icy stream because he could not get any response from the woman he so deeply desired. He shook his head sadly.

"What is becoming of you, Kenric?" he asked, splashing his face with cold water. "What is becoming of you!"

That evening a tray was brought up to Bekah, as usual, but she was able to eat very little, having lost her appetite. She was stunned by all that had happened. That unusual dream had been so haunting! Never before had she felt the vague stirrings of desire, and they had not been altogether unpleasant. This fact alone was the most disturbing to her. She pushed thoughts of the dream from her mind, rationalizing that it had been brought on by the heat and activity of the day. What ached at the back of her mind, however, was the expression on Kenric's face, like that of a small boy experiencing pain, before the mask of manliness slid into place. Over and over again the words she had spoken played in her mind. "I dreamed of us together."

Had he assumed she meant that day when he had taken her, never guessing the true meaning of her words? She had wanted to cause him pain, she had desired it greatly, but now, after seeing it, her victory was hollow. Revenge was not sweet. If anything it left a bitter taste in her mouth. Perhaps she could continue to cause him pain and make him suffer, but it did not appeal to her now. He must be punished, but she did not want to mete out the punishment. Her captor, the man who had defiled her, had in no way been as terrible as he could have been. What if Dinnot had found her that day instead? Her mind cringed from the very thought! After Kenric's first actions with her he had treated her with gentleness. He is a proud man, she realized, and it does not come easy.

She lay down again, trying to sleep, but sleep eluded her

95

for many hours. Often she replayed the scene in her mind, lingering upon the part where Kenric bent over her, the light fabric of his shirt clinging to the muscular lines of his body. Finally, when sleep did come, it was filled with dreams. Again she saw herself lying on the bed as he gently came to her. She lifted up her arms, slowly pulling Kenric to her. She was filled with excitement, and his lips teased hers. He bent to her ear, his breath tickling her as he spoke.

"You are mine, Bekah. You belong to no other, for only I have your virtue. It is mine. I love you, Bekah."

Could it be that her feelings for him were growing into the finer emotions of love? It piqued her pride that she could fall for a man who had been so disrespectful of her at their first meeting. She lay awake, staring at the ceiling. I am *not* falling in love with him! she thought. What cruel tricks is my mind playing on me that this man should haunt my dreams? It is only that there is no other for me here, and I turn to him out of loneliness. But if he had lived in my homeland would I have vied for his attentions or sought him out? She shook her head. I cannot love him, I forbid it!

She really did need to talk to someone but she had no friends here. She was alone. The heat of the night was so intense that her shift was soaked, clinging to her like a second skin. She pulled it off, casting it across a chair. She pulled back the heavy lace curtains, letting a breeze cool her off. It was dawn outside, the gray landscape tinged with growing pink and yellow. She lay back down on the bed, feeling tense and uncomfortable. It was as if she craved something which only Kenric could provide, and she was confused by her womanhood, blossoming now in this late springtime of her life.

In the dream he had spoken words, and she tried to remember them, but already they were growing fuzzy in her mind. In some sense he was right; she did belong to him. Who else could she go to? And even if they were to separate forever, they would still be bonded together.

The cool breeze comforted her, but she was afraid to sleep for fear the dream might return, causing in her such violent emotions and feelings. She did sleep, though, this time deep and untroubled, slumbering late. When she awoke she felt better, her mind functioning rationally in the daylight. She dressed quickly, venturing downstairs. She encountered the two girls who worked at the manor, Edlyn and Violet. Edlyn was busy polishing the Kartney crest while Violet dusted the furniture, a pink kerchief tied about her abundant brown locks. Annie, the cook, was in the kitchen, this time making pigeon pie, creamed peas and honey bread.

Bekah nodded her head in greeting to the girls. "Where is Kenric?" she questioned casually, not seeing him about.

Violet smiled, a little in awe of Bekah. "He was up bright and early, he was. Said he was going to the other side of the island."

"The other side of Jarlshof? Well, when will he return? Today?"

Violet shook her head. "Nay, miss. The journey is over one day, if he rides swiftly. He must be back by the day after tomorrow though, since it is the day before King Alfred's ship leaves and all the knights always come here as guests of Lord Kartney. Lord Kenric will stand in the stead of Lord Stanton Kartney as host."

"I see," Bekah said, feeling a little disappointed at Kenric's departure, then feeling annoyed at herself.

She went into the kitchen where Annie offered her some breakfast, but she had lost her appetite and settled for a cold mug of apple juice. Annie, who not only cooked for the manor but also ran the household, had gentle brown eyes and rosy cheeks. She was cheerful, her talkative manner pleasant, her ears always ready for tidbits of harmless gossip. She talked to Bekah for a while, chattering on about this or that, and Bekah could not help but like her. The entire manor was a pleasant place, and Bekah enjoyed it, for it made her feel closer to her mother's people. She helped Annie shell peas into a large bowl, the poor cook flustered by the young mistress's actions.

"Oh, miss! You mustn't do that; this is my work. Edlyn can help me."

"I enjoy it, Annie. I often worked at home."

This bit of information let Annie know that the maiden was not one of the royal folk. Lord Kenric had brought her

97

only for her beauty and not her family ties then. Well, she could understand that. In her younger days, men had flocked about her, until she had finally married Maynarde. She'd raised three young ones, Edlyn her baby, when Maynarde had been killed in a fishing accident. She had come to work at the manor after that, finding favor with the unwed Stanton, Lord of Kartney. As cook she had put on her extra pounds. Her culinary skills, her ability to organize and smoothly run a household, had endeared her to the manor, making her invaluable. Yea, indeed, she could understand what it was like for this pleasant young miss who was willing to lend a hand.

"But what will Lord Kenric say? Certainly he would not want you to work."

"He is not here, and I must do something; I feel more happy if my hands are busy."

Was the girl sad? Annie wondered.

"Besides," Bekah added, "it makes me think of my mother when I come into this kitchen."

"Where is your mother, dear?"

"She has been dead these past four years."

Annie's heart went out to the girl, and she put a comforting arm about her. This poor girl, without a mother's care all through the time in which she was becoming a woman! She thought of her own Edlyn and sorrowed anew at Bekah's loss. "Certainly you can help if you wish, miss."

Bekah smiled, her fingers adeptly shelling the peas.

To think she asks me to let her help! Most young girls, even Violet, beg not to work, desiring to be in the marketplace. The girl was remarkable. Annie would squelch any ugly rumors going about the village first chance she got!

Bekah donned a white apron, tied her hair behind her and threw herself into the chores. She helped to knead the bread with fingers strong from past bread-making. Later she went out to the garden, filling a basket with fresh lettuce, carrots and cucumbers. The chores done, the two girls Edlyn and Violet came to the kitchen and helped clean and cut vegetables. Seeing Bekah's guileless countenance they talked freely, laughing and sharing bits of gossip about the village. They discussed the situation of old Carver Donnic and his sixteen-year-old bride Hertha. They talked about the marriageable young men of the village, staying clear of any talk about Kenric or other topics that might embarrass Bekah.

The work done, Bekah strolled outside to the gardens. In addition to a huge vegetable and herb garden, there was a lovely flower garden in full bloom. She cut fresh blossoms and roses, bringing them in and arranging them in the vases, discarding the old blooms. After lunch she went through the house, looking into this room and that, enjoying all she saw. By evening she turned at every footstep she heard, hoping for some strange reason that Kenric had returned. She stayed up late, finally retiring exhausted.

She was afraid to sleep, fearing that she might dream again. However no dream pierced her peaceful slumber, and she awoke the next morning fresh and alive. She tossed back the covers, rising and washing herself with the cool water from the pitcher and drying herself as best she could. She dressed in the same blue frock, tying back her hair with a wide blue ribbon. She hurried downstairs, expecting to see Kenric, but he was not there. She became irritated at him; why had he gone? Because of what she had said to him? She had said many cruel things before, and they had not daunted him. If she were to run away, would he no longer care?

She continued helping in the kitchen, this time not so cheerful. She remained silent most of the time, nodding her head now and again at Annie's statements. After lunch she doffed her apron and strolled outside. It was a cool day, not hot and stifling as before. The clouds were gray and white, scuffling in the pale blue sky. She found herself nearing the stable, and she stepped inside.

A young lad, perhaps three years her junior, was brushing down a dainty mare with a shiny sorrel coat. There were only two other horses in the stable, the rest being out in the fields where they ran freely about. The young man, clad in coarse homespun shirt and trousers, his feet bare, glanced up as she entered. He knew her to be Lord Kenric's woman, and he grew flustered as she neared.

"What a lovely horse. Does she have a name?"

"Yea, ma'am, she does. It is Elyse."

Bekah stroked the horse's velvet nose as Elyse looked at

her with huge brown eyes. "May I ride her?" she heard herself say.

"She is for the guests of Kartney Manor and is gentle. I will ready her," he said, and she watched as he did so.

She did not know what had prompted her to ask, for she had very little experience with horses. She never would have been allowed to ride the workhorses at home. But riding on Polo the day before yesterday had not seemed so difficult, and the lad had said Elyse was gentle.

He led Elyse outside, put a box by the horse's side for Bekan to step on, then bashfully returned to the stable. Bekah stroked the horse's neck, talking softly to her before mounting. She could not ride sidesaddle, she decided, as she had on Polo. Instead she pulled up her skirts a bit, straddling the silky back of the horse, a blanket and leather pad the horse's only covering. She held the reins firmly, pressing her heels to the horse's sides as she had seen Kenric do. The horse took off at a friendly lope, and Bekah discovered it was not so difficult after all. She turned the horse down the road, the two ladies sauntering off together. After a quarter of an hour she felt more at ease, spurring the horse into a faster gait. As they wove between farmlands and meadows, past cottages and streams, Bekah felt her head clear. The wind felt good on her face and arms; she enjoyed the power of her mare beneath her.

Once again her thoughts turned to Kenric. She had made a violent vow to make him suffer, yet already in this short time she was losing her grasp on it. Men were so difficult to understand. Kenric had stated that it was she and her breed of female he did not understand. On the contrary, she understood herself quite well, finding that it was the male mind with its obstinate pride that was difficult to comprehend. Her mother had once told her that although a woman's state might be lesser in this life, she had the ability to rule over a man. Bekah thought on this now, wondering what Mary had meant. She thought of Lars. He had loved Mary beyond all reason; it had nearly killed him when she died. The only power her mother had held over her father was the power of love.

It was then that reason hit her with a strong blow. Love? Was that what could humble a man? If Kenric were to love her, then she could gain power over him, bending him to her will. Her bravery swayed as she thought of Kenric's love for no woman, least of all herself. He spoke kindly to her at times, even called her beautiful, but was that enough to make him love her? She did not know, for her experience was little in these matters. She thought of Meg. She could never be like her, a vivacious flirt. Nonetheless, she firmly accepted that if she were to humble Kenric it was to be done through his heart—though she had not the least knowledge of how to go about it. As the edge of the forest neared, she raised her jaw, setting it determinedly. If he were to love her, then he must never guess that it was her idea.

Kenric was weary. His mental exhaustion was greater than his physical fatigue, although he looked travel-worn. His shirt had become soiled, so he had removed it, letting the sun further bronze his naked chest and shoulders. He had headed towards the other side of Jarlshof but had never made it. Instead he had spent the night in the forest, doing a good deal of soul-searching. He wore a two-day growth of beard, and his black locks ruffled in the wind. His mind was weary, his soul totally explored. His decisions burned painfully and permanently, for he knew he could not change the past and establish a different relationship with Bekah, yet the present one of slave and master was not acceptable. As hard as it was going to be, Kenric knew that he must confront her and speak his thoughts. His anxiety grew as he anticipated the outcome. He was nearing the edge of the forest, which would soon yield to velvet green fields of young wheat. He could glimpse them through the dispersing trees, and Polo snorted, his nostrils flared, tossing his head.

As they came out of the woods there was a whinny, and a sorrell mare reared, frightened by their sudden appearance. Kenric was so near that he reached out, grabbing the reins and steadying the horse Elyse. It was then that he looked at the rider, clinging with handfuls of mane to the mare.

"Bekah!" he half-shouted. "What in the name of sanity are you doing out here on this horse?"

"I am riding her."

"I see. And who gave you permission to ride one of my mares?"

She dazzled him with a lovely smile, making him forget his anger. "The stable boy said she was for the guests to ride. Am I not a guest?"

"You do not know how to ride."

"I have been doing so for the past hour and had no trouble until your horse startled mine!"

"It could have been a snake or some other danger. Then what would have happened if I had not been here to keep Elyse from bolting? You could have been killed! Tell me," he added, his thoughts turning in another direction, "were you running away?"

"Nay, for as you pointed out, I have no place to go. I only wanted to ride; I grew tired of staying in the manor."

He nodded his head in acceptance of her answer, guiding their horses back in the general direction of the manor. They were silent for a moment, with only the sound of clopping hooves thudding on the ground.

"I missed you," he said quietly.

"I missed you, too," she said, "surprising as it seems."

He digested this information, gently reaching over to untie her ribbon, loosing her hair to the breeze. "I have spent this time by myself; I have done a good deal of reckoning."

She was astonished by the repentant note in his voice and looked up at him as the horses plodded along. She said nothing, and he continued. "I have come to a decision. If you wish to return home, then I will take you back." His eyes pierced her. "But before you answer, let me finish what I must tell you. If you decide to go back, then I will set you on the shore of the cove and you can return to your farm. It is best that you know what will happen. By the time we reach there, many weeks will have gone by, and your family will know that something must have happened to you. It will be impossible for you to hide what has happened, for no doubt your stepmother will guess it immediately. The Vikings place a great deal upon a woman being untried, so you may be given to whatever man will accept you. With your natural beauty, no doubt there will be some who will be willing to accept you. Perhaps your stepbrother. Do not interrupt me, Bekah. What I tell you certainly you must realize as truth, since we are both familiar with the customs of your father's people. I hope it is not so, but should you be with child your fate would be worse. You might be taken as a second or third wife, but you must be aware of the consequences to both you and the child should you have my baby."

She shivered at his words, realizing that he spoke the truth. She had desperately desired to return to her father, not wholly thinking out what her fate would be. Kenric was right, and they looked at one another as he continued.

"If you still want to go back, then I will take you. However, if you decide to stay with me, then I will protect you here. You will have the clothes you need, and food, and your room until we journey to Wessex. I will not force you to accept me. I will tell you now that I desire you greatly. I have not wished for a woman's attention as I have yours. Perhaps you do not realize how strongly a man's desires can drive him. You have not fully learned that yet. I will admit that on the day I first saw you I was so overcome by you that I thought you a vision, and did not truly comprehend my actions until it was too late." He stopped here, his pride overcoming him. He wanted her to stay, he wanted to court her as if he had just met her. But he must give her her freedom. He had decided during his night in the forest that he could keep her prisoner no longer. What a miserable night that had been! The torment of this decision to give her her freedom! When he brought her here he had assumed that she would come around to him as every maid in the past had done. It was not so, and his efforts to suppress his feelings were difficult beyond belief. If she left it would hurt him desperately. If she stayed it would be salt into his wounds.

"What is your decision?" he asked, riding along beside her, their horses so close that her dress brushed against his leg.

After a few moments of silence she spoke. "What you say is true. If I return there will only be pain and suffering," she whispered, her dream of rescue destroyed, making her very being smart with the pain of disillusionment.

103

"Then you will stay?" he asked, the slightest note of pleasure creeping into his deep voice.

"There is nowhere else for me to go," she said reluctantly. A small part of her was relieved, another part of her sore from the decision. She temporarily forgot her determination to humble him, to bring him to his knees through the sorcery of love. She was here to stay, and her soul made its last cry of homesickness before being replaced by the real blade of survival.

They reached the manor, the horses heading into the stable. They dismounted, handing the steeds over to the stable boy; Polo nuzzled Elyse affectionately, as he had throughout the entire jaunt.

They strolled towards the house, stopping in the flower garden. They stood for a moment there, smelling the sweet perfume of the roses, tulips, sweet peas and azaleas. Kenric bent down, plucking a deep red rose, its enormous petals like red velvet upon which a few diamond afternoon drops lay. He removed the thorns; stepping towards Bekah, looking down with his eyes a startling deep gray, he brushed her cheek with his hand as he reached across, placing the full-bloomed flower behind her left ear.

"It should be a garland of roses, sir."

Kenric smiled.

The next day Kenric appeared at her portal, this time knocking before opening the door. She had not finished dressing and bade him wait until she could pull on the light robe cast across the end of her bed. She was tying the sash about her waist as he entered. He was dressed in white, his black hair and boots in contrast to the snowy appearance of his clothing. His shirt, open at the throat, displayed his tanned chest and black hair. He wore white leather breeches, tucked into the black boot tops, and the material caught her glance.

"I have never seen white leather before!" she said. "Is it common on this island?"

"Only if you are Kenric, Lord of Kartney!" He smiled at her, flashing white teeth so in contrast to his tanned face. "Lovely day today! Are you ready to go for a ride?"

"Hardly," she said primly. She reached for her blue tunic trying to shake out the wrinkles of the past few days.

"Here, put this on instead," he said, holding up a package which he'd hidden behind his back.

Within lay a soft pink tunic of finest silk; it was woven through with ribbons of a wine hue contrasting against the pale pink. The sleeves fell in gathered folds wrought by the skill of a seamstress and the slender shift was fitted narrowly at the waist, falling in soft folds to her feet.

Thoughtfully he stepped outside, and within a moment she called him to come see. It fit perfectly, and with childish excitement she swirled around before him, watching the skirt billow. "Is it not lovely?" she laughed.

"Now, this is not one of your special dresses; they are still not ready. This one was for sale. And to think that I was concerned it might not fit! I should have known that you were tiny enough to wear it. Meg liked the material and had a seamstress sew it up for her."

Instantly the billowing skirt fell into place as Bekah looked at him in dismay. "This is Meg's dress?"

"It *was* hers. The seamstress made a mistake and cut it far too small. From what the poor lady tells, the honorable Meg was furious and refused to buy it since she could not fasten it even with the help of the two ladies who work at the shop. The store was left with the dress and no one in the village was small enough to wear it," he said and laughed. "I thought of you the moment I saw it."

She smiled at this. It *was* a funny tale. She finished brushing her hair, catching it back on either side. Out of the vase of white daisies she took a few flowers, arranging them in her hair. If she had thought the blue dress lovely, this pink one was doubly so, and she thanked him.

They went outside and found it to be another lovely day. The wind gently stirred the pale green tendrils of the huge willow. Polo was again saddled, and Kenric lightly lifted her onto the large horse's back.

"Why may I not ride Elyse?" she asked as Kenric mounted.

They were well on their way down the road before he answered. "First I must teach you to ride. When we have a free day I will take you out and show you all the pointers you will need to know. For now you must be content to share Polo's back with me."

The truth was that Kenric enjoyed having her sitting near him. When they rode together past tall wild plants and flowers it seemed as if she were his alone. He turned off the main road, following a wide path as it wove between fields and farmlands, shaded here and there by birch, oak, maple and pines. She sat straight-backed, aware of his large arms about her. The contact seemed like a warm glow between them.

"Where are we going?" she asked, laying her head back to gaze up at him, one of the daisies falling from her hair into his lap. He picked up the flower and fingered it tenderly. He could smell the clean sweetness of her hair and longed to bury his face in its golden thickness.

"To a spot by the stream."

Bekah sat straight and still.

"Is that any way for a betrothed to act?" he said near her ear.

"Betrothed?" she asked, glancing up at him.

"Well, you did tell Meg you were my wife. Really, it upset her." He chuckled.

Her face flushed warm, and inwardly she winced at the reminder. "What should I have said? That I was your evening's delight?" she said tersely, her eyes flashing. He threw back his head and laughed.

Why did she delight him so? he wondered. She often baffled him, and in truth was a mystery to him. Still, he cared for her more than for any woman he had ever known. Other women were shallow and predictable, but Bekah did totally different things than he expected of her. Not yet able to admit to himself that he loved her, he thought of his feelings for her as merely affection and a sense of responsibility. He honestly owed her a debt, and he was not one to be indebted to another. It was last night as he lay in his room alone that the light of a solution dawned in his mind. What did he want? It was obvious to him even now. He wanted her. He wanted to take her tenderly in his arms and love her in such a way that would forever make her his. What would it be like to have her willingly come to him? The very idea made his heart sing. But to receive this permission from her, he must give her what she wanted.

What did she want? This had puzzled him for a great

106

length of time, and he had not figured it out until early dawn. She no longer wanted to return to her home. Also, she was not some loose maid who would give herself to any man. He decided that it would be best for her if she could give herself to him without that ever-present cloak of guilt and shame she wore. To accomplish this, they must wed. Kenric had avoided marriage for years, finding the thought of bondage to one woman impossibly unbearable. Not so with Bekah, though. Actually, the thought of it teased and enticed his senses. He had decided to tell her that they would marry once they reached Wessex. Family tradition insisted that the Kartney heir be wed in the Wessex chapel in Kartney Castle. For now, they could be betrothed, and then no doubt she would be willing to love him.

"So, you fear what Meg, or any other, thinks. Very well, if you prefer being my wife, I do not mind."

"Mind? Well thank you, milord, but how could I ever be your wife, since I am your slave? Or do you consider the position one and the same?"

He was totally taken back. Any other woman would have jumped at such a proposal, and he felt his pride bristle. What a fool he had been that morning when he'd brought her the blue dress. Teasingly he'd told her she was his slave, and now she chose this exact moment to bring it up.

"Your sharp tongue will most likely reduce *me* to the position of slave. Have you no mercy on my beaten soul?"

She laughed, and although he found it enchanting, this was the least opportune moment for her to do so. "What beating your soul takes, Kenric, it deserves."

"Do you still hate me and consider me such a brute?"

"You cannot expect me to love you for your unkindly deed. Once I swore to hate you for what you did. What else did you expect, Kenric?"

He shrugged the question off, asking again in a calm voice which belied the knots in his stomach, "Do you still hate me?"

"Not really," she said, and he caught a glimpse of the child in her. "Hate is a strange thing. At times I have felt it strongly and other times not at all. I am smart enough to

107

realize that it could have been worse and you could have been cruel."

"Cruel?" he repeated.

Her eyes widened as she gazed up at him, and she could not help but notice what long eyelashes he had for a man; dark yet not unmasculine. "You have not beaten me."

"The occasion has not yet arisen." He grinned. Her eyes flashed angrily and she bridled at his words. "You need not worry," he said, touching her arm with his tanned fingers. "When you are my wife you shall have many things beyond your dreams." His hands tightened about her waist, sending a shiver through her.

"Wife? Why do you talk of marriage, Kenric?"

"There are some things you need to understand. My family is a noble one with position and wealth. I myself am a knight of King Alfred's realm as my father was a knight before me. My mother died when I was a child, and my father's second wife has given him nothing but daughters." She could envision a young boy growing up without a mother's touch, and for a moment her heart went out to him. "For many years now my father has been demanding my marriage so that I provide him with an heir. When we wed, on our return to Wessex, that will be your purpose, to provide me with children."

It was not until he finished speaking that she felt herself stunned by the impact of his words. He was actually serious about marriage. She had vowed to bring him to his knees, to have power over him, and marriage was indeed the first step. However, she felt as if she were a spider who, having spun its web over a stream and caught a minnow, did not have the least idea what to do with its prey. He appeared to be waiting for an answer.

"Well, Bekah, do you understand?"

"Are you insane?" she asked slowly.

"What?" he asked, stunned by her reaction.

"I will not marry you, you vain knave! First you say I will be your slave, and now this!"

He felt as if his chest were crushed under the weight of a huge stone, and he found her response hard to believe. She had scoffed at his marriage proposal and even insulted him! His pride prickled with indignation, and a stormy expression crossed his face.

"You will marry me, Bekah. We will not discuss it further," he said blackly.

"Do you suppose that you can force me to wed you? Even if you were to make me stand through the mockery of a wedding ceremony, never would I willingly give myself to you as wife! You expect me to be the carrier of your babies; you are sincerely wrong if you tell yourself that I will gladly bear your children." How dare he expect her to marry a man who did not love her?

"You will be my wife! Yet as for my partner I know of many a wench who will come willingly. I do not need you in that respect," he lied furiously.

She was crushed by this. "How dare you! You value your own freedom, yet no doubt would keep me prisoner as you did at first. How can you expect me to willingly come to my captor?"

His hands gripped her arms so tightly that she cried out. "Oh, Kenric, you are bruising my arms!"

"I could break them," he said bitingly, releasing her so swiftly that she would have fallen from the horse had he not caught her about the waist. "Indeed! Bear in mind that I still retain the power of the captor and can revoke your freedom at any time."

"You are spiteful!" she cried, struggling against him. "You value your freedom, yet rob me of mine! I will only bear the children of the man I love—and never in my whole life could I give myself to a man who does not love me!"

She fought back tears and Kenric turned her face towards him. As he viewed her closed eyes beneath highly arched brows, tears glistening unshed on her black lashes, he was overcome by the realization of her words. It was not he she fought against but the belief that he did not love her. If she only knew. If he were to woo her with gentle tenderness, if he were to love her, then she would come to him. A burden lifted from him, and he almost felt cheerful. She was not so different from other women after all. Let him say he loved her, let her learn to love him and that was the secret to success! It would take time, but now that he had guessed the truth he decided that the way to possess her would be to make her love him. He pulled her to him tenderly.

"Unkind words have no place between us, Bekah," he said softly, brushing a fallen tear from the gentle curve of her cheek.

She realized he was making peace, and that alone was enough to calm her. Perhaps the words he had said were prompted by pride, for he had a desire to stand unyielding. But now he had taken the first step towards making amends, and she acquiesced. The angry storm between them abated in the calm summer morning where shadows lay cool upon the bright lawns of wild grass.

They rode past fields of green wheat and through forests edged by quaking aspen. Kenric kicked Polo into a fast trot, holding Bekah to him lest she fall. She was very aware of his strong arm about her. However, she was not aware of Kenric's discomfort at having her so close to him, yet untouchable.

They rode along in silence, which gave her a moment to sit back and observe Kenric. His black hair and flashing gray eyes were truly appealing, as was his muscular body. But more than this it was his energetic manner, the love of living which surged through him. As she watched him talk and occasionally laugh, she thought about the words he'd spoken.

Did he actually consider that discourse to be a wedding proposal? Perhaps he wanted to marry her for other reasons than he'd stated, but his pride had not allowed him to say it. Was it possible that he was falling in love with her? If so, it was what she had desired, for in this way she planned to gain control over him. But now she began to see that it was more than she was prepared to handle. If only he would be totally honest with her! But then he would have to be totally honest with himself.

She had been upset—furious, in fact. He had insulted her, had brought her to tears. However, the more she thought about his actions and words, the more she became confused. She sincerely began to wonder if it were not simply his foolish pride that kept him from saying he loved her. If he wanted a wife to bear him an heir, wouldn't he choose someone of noble heritage, rather than herself, who sported Viking blood? Perhaps he dreaded rejection, and that was his reason for proposing to her in such a ridiculous manner.

She thought about marriage to him and what it would be like. He was ever-changing, but since his return from the other side of Jarlshof he had become gentle and pleasant to be with. Today's outburst was not like him. No doubt it was that foolish sore spot called pride. If they were to marry, would it be so terrible? After the dreams that had haunted her and her desire to humble him through access to his heart, she did not really know. No matter, she thought, strengthening her resolve. She must make whatever course they would travel difficult for him.

The destrier reached a shadowed spot by the stream and they dismounted.

"Oh, Kenric," she sighed, as she stood by the clear water's edge. "How lovely this is." Without waiting for him she removed her sandals and slid onto a low branch that overhung the water, placing her toes in the cool stream. Kenric joined her, and they watched the brook's swift passage between them, the water gurgling and splashing over smooth rocks.

The subject of marriage still nagged at Bekah, and she broached it carefully. "If you need a wife to bear an heir, you would choose wrongly with me. My mother was from a family of daughters and she bore no son that lived."

Her testing of the subject pleased Kenric, and his mood lightened. "Ah, I see! You wish to even the score by hearing me a daughter, is that the case? Well, I sorrow to disillusion you, but a daughter someday would suit me as well as a son. Although my father would prefer an heir, I only want a child. Many, for that matter. I think I should be a good father, in the far future."

"But you men always speak of sons as the most important."

"Sons! Only another burden to me. Sons are nothing but trouble, as my father will attest. I have hardly tamed my own wild will, while my sisters could not have been more docile or free of trouble. Except for one."

His last three words intrigued her, and she glanced at

111

him sideways. "What do you mean 'except for one'?" she asked.

He was quiet for a moment, looking down into the water, unsmiling. "When my father remarried, his wife brought with her a daughter two years my senior, from another marriage. Her name was Lizbet."

"Something in your voice makes me think that your memories of her are not fond," Bekah said.

"They are not. For although Lizbet appeared to be the epitome of sweetness to our parents, I saw a different side of her. Oftimes she coerced me into adventures which I later regretted, since it was solely I who felt the wrath of Father."

"There is often rivalry among siblings," Bekah added, thinking of Jorgen.

Kenric nodded his head. "When my first half-sister Emily was born, she was the apple of my father's eye, and I love her, too. She is a gentle maid, happily married and with two children of her own. I know she will like you as you will her."

"What of Lizbet? I would like to win her favor also."

His face clouded and she noted his expression. "That is impossible."

"Do not be too sure. I can win many hearts with my friendliness," she proudly said.

"That has little to do with it. When she was sixteen Lizbet found herself with child, for you see, my stepsister had very few morals. The father of her child was a servant who cared for the horses, and our parents would have been angered even more by this. The servant wisely disappeared when he realized what was coming. When Lizbet could hide the truth no more, she told them that the child was mine, much to my great shock. She played the part well, portraying an innocence which they could not see through. Instead of her receiving the punishment, it was I who bore the fury of our parents. No matter how I pleaded innocence my stepmother took the side of her daughter, and no matter how I begged Lizbet to reveal the truth she still portrayed her part of purity.

"My father sent me away to another's castle where I became a page. I missed my home very much but was not allowed to return for two years. While I was away, Lizbet slipped along the river bank and drowned. Her mother felt that it was the distress of carrying an unwanted child that made her cast herself into the river before the child was born. However, I knew her better than others did. Lizbet was far too selfish to take her own life, and I have always assumed it was an accident. Her mother always believed that the child was mine and that Lizbet's death was my fault, also. Things were never the same between my father and myself. I still, to this day, feel the hurt I felt as a youth, that my father did not believe my protestations of innocence."

She could feel the bitterness which he still held. No doubt it was this painful experience at such an early age which made him distrustful of women. She knew he often viewed them as deceptive or two-faced.

"That is past, though, and I have not recalled it for a long period of time, or felt that old anger at the ruination she brought on my family. I suppose it is foolish for me to feel that all women are like Lizbet. If it were not for the love of my other sisters, perhaps I would truly believe it so."

She felt an impulsive desire to erase the pain of his past and bring him a piece of comfort. She sat by the cool waters, placing the delicate flowers she had picked in a wreath around her hair. Turning to Kenric she asked innocently, trying to win him from his dour mood, "Do I please you, milord?"

"Yea, Bekah," he sighed. "You greatly please my eyes, but worse, leave me longing for your touch."

Her face flushed in embarrassment at his words and she tried to get off the branch which hung low over the gushing stream. She found her passage blocked by Kenric, who sat unmoving. "Sir, I cannot get down unless you do so first."

He raised an eyebrow. "You cannot? Then perhaps we will have to sit here until the moon comes out."

Worriedly studying his face, she did not know whether she should take him in earnest or not.

"Sir, I grow uncomfortable on this branch," she said, trying to turn her position to a more comfortable perch.

113

"I would be content to sit here for a while longer, Bekah," he said sternly, and she bristled at his rudeness. She had little patience with him now; all the pity which she had begun feeling for him vanished. It would have been best had she never mentioned his family, for his pleasant mood was entirely gone.

She did not want to lower herself to ask him to move again, but the perch grew more uncomfortable and she tried to adjust her position the second time. The narrow branch she had been holding on to snapped, throwing off her balance. She would have plunged into the water had he not caught her about the waist, pulling her close against him.

"Careful. I did not mind losing Lizbet in the depths of a river, but I would you." She sensed a mocking tone behind his voice which she had not heard for a while, and she pulled from him, sitting straight upon the branch, the feel of bark rough beneath her palms. He kept his arm about her, however, so that she might be more secure, and she tried not to notice the comfort it gave.

"I grow uncomfortable, sir. Would you get off the branch so that I may get down?"

"Certainly, miss. For a kiss."

"What?"

"For a kiss, I will let you pass."

"No," she said, shaking her head.

"Then we shall sit here a while longer, unless you wish to brave wading."

She grew angered at his lack of courtesy and pulled up her skirts, showing a lovely expanse of slender legs, ready to step into the rushing stream. Kenric grabbed her tightly around the waist, refusing to let her enter the water.

"Do not be foolish. Even if you do not drown you will certainly get wet."

"If you will not let me pass, then there is no other way," she said angrily.

"Very well," he laughed softly. "You have won this small match."

He slid off the branch, assisting her off, then bowing to her before leaning against the tree.

She felt a light thrill of elation at having bent him to her will, even in this small matter. She moved to Polo, stroking his silken mane as the horse nuzzled her shoulder.

"Noble destrier," she said, laying her head against his auburn neck.

"I would willingly trade places with you, Polo, for such affection from our lady," Kenric murmured so softly that she barely caught his words.

In time they again mounted the stallion, riding slowly towards the manor, each reluctant to return. A distant katydid gave off its high-pitched cry, and the summer warmth began in earnest.

The afternoon was hot and muggy. In her room, Bekah removed her tunic and wore only her undershift, resting from the heat. The manor was preparing itself for the evening feast, and Kenric was seeing to the care of house and stables.

As the sun lowered behind the hills and the cooler breezes of night came, Bekah began to ready herself for the night's festivities. Just as she had taken down the soft pink gown, Kenric came, hardly waiting between knocking and entering.

"Good eventide, Bekah."

She jumped at his entry, holding the dress before her. Kenric looked at her, with no intent of moving. She grew impatient, wondering if he would leave so that she might refreshen herself.

"Kenric, please."

"Please what?"

"Please leave! How can I dress while you watch me so intently?"

"You start by stepping into your tunic." He grinned.

"Milord, you make it greatly difficult for me to do so when you stare at me. I swear you make my face burn with the glare of your eyes!"

"It is not your face I am interested in at the moment," he said teasingly. "But since you protect your modesty I will force my eyes from you."

"Then turn your back."

He laughed, doing as she bade. Quickly she slipped into her underslip and washed herself with the urn of cool water, not realizing that his gaze fell on the copper mirror

115

reflecting her. She pulled on the tunic, unaware of Kenric's stares.

"I hope you are hungry," he said in a calm voice which masked his present feelings. "The feast will be huge tonight."

"Yea, I truly am. I seem to have regained my appetite since that difficult ocean voyage."

"Come then," he said with a smile. "Let us go."

He took her by the arm, leading her through the large house and into the great hall. Banners of the House of Kartney hung from the walls in blue, gold and crimson. Kenric was a full-blooded Kartney, both father and mother being of that house. They had been distant cousins, and the family traits of black hair and granite eyes had been apparent in both. These characteristics had been passed on to their son. Kenric, upon entering this hall where his mother had entertained so often, was very much aware of her memory. Although she had died when he was young, he could still remember her slight form and dark head. Her face, however, was not unlike Bekah's.

There were long wooden tables set out, along which were seated a number of people, all laughing and talking. Musicians strummed simple instruments, and torches sent flickering amber lights throughout the entire hall. A large side of beef roasted over an open brick pit, and two small boys turned it conscientiously.

As they entered the room the loud chatter ceased. After a few moments of silence it rose to a murmur, and Bekah felt as if all the eyes in the room were upon her. Furious glances filled the faces of many of the women as they recognized the pink tunic. How many of them had tried to squeeze into it, only to find that they were too fleshy for its narrow cut! Yet Kenric's woman fit into it with ease, the sheer fabric showing off her slender form.

Meg felt sick when she saw it, barely having the courage to remain seated as the couple approached the main table. Kenric led Bekah to the head of the table, seating her on his right. Jenica leaned over to Meg.

"Look, she wears the garment the seamstresses made for you!"

"I see, I am not blind!"

116

"She must have the smallest waist in all of Jarlshof, then, for even I could not wear it," Jenica said. She was a pretty girl, with straight black hair and golden eyes.

"She can only fit it because she has no bosom," Meg hissed.

"She has enough. I think she is beautiful, and I can see why Kenric loves her," she sighed.

The knights stood up, nodding their heads or bowing as Kenric seated Bekah, all struck by the beauty of the maid. The musicians resumed their playing, the hall filled with the lovely music of flute, lyre, drum and harp, and Meg resumed flirting with the men around her with even more ardor.

Conversation and laughter returned. The meat was taken up before Bekah had time to converse with Kenric, local hired women served it on huge platters. There were wild strawberries and blueberries with thick cream. Bowls of gravy and platters of bread with freshly churned butter topped the tables. Bowls of fruits and vegetables in season were placed before them, along with mugs of cool ale, milk or apple juice.

The feast was greater than any Bekah had ever attended, even more impressive than harvest festival in her own homeland. The meat was tender and delicious, and Bekah ate hungrily. The goblet of cider was pleasantly tangy, the vegetables firm.

The meal ended, music began and dancers came to the floor, Kenric pulled the reluctant Bekah to her feet, guiding her out into the great hall. A brave smile wavered on her lips. A dance had begun in which all joined, and Kenric took her hands, showing her the simple steps. She learned them with ease, and their fingers touched lightly. They wove their way about the circle, finally meeting again, their eyes steadfastly looking at one another. They danced for several hours, and Bekah's natural grace caught the glance of every man in the room. She dazzled Kenric with her smiles. It was late when the music ended.

They retired exhausted and laughing up the stairs. Kenric took her to her room. "Be careful, Bekah. I do not trust the other men, for there were many gazing at you with longing tonight."

117

"Oh, nay! They smiled in friendship."

" 'Twas more than friendship I saw in their eyes. My room is just down the hall, two doors away, should you need me," he said gravely, bringing a smile to her lips. He who had been so willing to take her in the past now desired to protect her.

Yellow sunlight imprisoning dust motes spun its way through latticed windows to dance merrily upon Bekah's face. The sweet scent of honeysuckle entwined itself about her, and a cool sea breeze caressed her. She felt at the moment as if the world were indeed good to her and as if she were at peace with life. She stretched and smiled to herself, recalling the events of the past night.

"It makes my heart light to see you so cheerful this morn, my lovely lady," a cool voice teased. Bekah started at its sound, a small cry escaping her lips. She pulled the covers up beneath her chin, her hair falling about her in disarray.

She did not know how long he had sat there in the finely carved chair of black wood, watching her while she slept. He smiled at her. She stretched her legs beneath the light cover. Did she have no privacy at all? Wherever she turned he was there! He was handsomely intriguing, a smile often on his lips even as an eyebrow was raised in a questioning glance.

How handsome he looked this morning! His eyes glinted darkly, reflecting his countenance. He wore a vest and breeches of finest doeskin and dark brown boots. A shirt of soft white linen did little to disguise the muscular curves of his chest and shoulders and the strength therein. His black hair was neatly in place, and his grin revealed perfect white teeth, which made him look wickedly handsome.

He lounged there, his long legs stretched out, totally at ease. He pointed to the bench. There lay several new gowns, and she took in a deep breath. "These will have to suffice until we reach Wessex. At that time I will provide you with much finer clothing; the looms of Jarlshof have little to offer."

She tried to reveal no excitement at the new gowns, and

keeping the covers still about her, she surveyed them, her eyes shining brightly. There were soft fabrics in several lovely hues, some silky and others crisp. There were also more shifts and underskirts of softest fabric, some white or pale pink and blue enhanced with tiny tucks, ribbons or embroidery. There were also several lightweight sleeping gowns and a soft robe of red velvety texture.

"I would love to stay and help you sort them out, but I must go and see the King's ship off. It is important that they deliver the papers I am sending to King Alfred as soon as possible. I would ask you to come along, but I fear the way those lusty knights look at you. I will be back in a few hours."

She nodded her head, watching him leave. The door closed behind him. Eagerly she hopped from the bed, sorting through her new dresses. They were lovely; how she enjoyed the thought of wearing them! She picked them up, putting them tenderly in the wooden closet. She folded the underclothing and gowns, putting them away.

Bekah brushed her hair thoroughly, piling it simply and softly upon her head, revealing the graceful curve of her neck. Kenric liked it this way, she remembered. She stood before the closet and drank in the beauty of the colorful fabrics before her. Never before had she seen such exquisite dresses, and they were hers! She felt pride at the thought. It seemed to her that the horror of her experiences was finally beginning to fade.

She chose one of the new dresses to wear. The kirtle was of the sheerest silk, scarlet in color. Over this she donned a tunic of bleached linen with wide square sleeves and a deep-cut bodice which revealed much of the bright silk. The tunic was embroidered in gold thread and belted with a gold-stitched girdle. The hem of the tunic was tucked into the belt at one side to reveal the expanse of red silk. She stepped into slippers of embroidered black velvet and checked her appearance in the copper mirror.

Bekah went downstairs, finding her way to the kitchen. Annie was busy from all that had happened the night before, just finishing with the last of cleaning up. As Bekah sipped a mug of milk and nibbled on some bread and honey-butter, she watched Annie's adept fingers working

119

the pie dough. The cook began to make tarts, skillfully crimping and fluting the edges that encased the raspberry filling.

"Dear me! I am left with all this crust and not enough raspberries to fill it! I guess I will just have to go pick more," she said, rubbing her aching back.

"I do not mind going," Bekah said.

"Nay, miss, I cannot ask you to. I will get Edlyn."

"She is busy cleaning the rooms of the gentlemen who stayed here last night," Bekah said over her shoulder as she picked up the straw basket and whisked out of the kitchen.

It was not as hot a day as Bekah had suspected; the sky had become overcast with soft gray clouds. The cool was a welcome relief, and she smiled to herself, thinking how pleasantly the previous night had turned out. All the gentlemen had treated her with respect, and Kenric had endeavored to be especially nice.

What a change had overtaken him! His stormy anger, his mocking attitude and devil-may-care way of life were all diminishing, being replaced by an actual sense of responsibility, sobriety and empathy. It was almost as if the man she had met on the beach were now a different being. No longer did she feel hatred when she looked at him, or even that strong desire for revenge. She enjoyed being with him at times, and it was amazing to her.

She walked past the garden, through the apple orchard and past pines with huge, bushy green needles. There were blue spruce, silver in the overcast light, and several large oak trees that obscured the view of the house, except its slanting roof and large chimney. She walked through tall emerald blades of grass and large wild clovers raising their lavender flowers up to her. A few stalks of wild wheat gently swept at her skirt, the wind slowly whirling about her as if it were her sweetest lover. The birds talked among themselves, chattering pleasantly as she neared the raspberry thickets.

It was wildly overgrown. Carefully she pulled back the branches, trying to avoid the thorns. She plucked off only the ripest berries that were reddish-purple, leaving the conical white centers on the vine. She began to fill the basket which hung on her arm.

Kenric returned to the house, striding in through the open doors. He went up the stairs, rapped lightly and entered Bekah's room to see it tidy and empty. He strolled downstairs, stopping Violet to inquire as to Bekah's whereabouts, but the flustered girl had not seen her. He looked through the house, ending up in the kitchen.

"Annie, where is Bekah?"

"She went outside. I ran out of tart raspberries and the dear girl offered to go fetch me some. She's so thoughtful," Annie concluded as he hurried out the door.

Bekah had always had such a desire to run away, and Kenric had the ever-present fear that she might again try to escape. If he did not find her in the raspberry patch, then he would mount Polo and search for her. He passed through the trees and overgrown meadow, sighing in relief as he saw her in the distance, conscientiously picking the berries.

"Bekah, what on earth are you doing out here?"

"Picking berries."

"There are servants to do this kind of work."

"There is nothing for me to do, besides sit in my room. I do not mind helping Annie. This is not work; it's pleasant out here and peaceful."

"It looks like rain," he said, stepping close behind her and helping her pick berries. He put a handful in her basket, leaning forward to do so, and kissing her lightly on the back of her neck. Chills ran up and down her spine, not an unpleasant sensation.

"Kenric, please."

"What, my love?" he whispered in her ear, his breath tickling her.

"I . . . I do not like the way it makes me feel."

"How is that?" he asked, his lips barely brushing against her neck.

"Funny inside, in my stomach," she finally said.

Did she enjoy it? He was both amazed and delighted! His hands held her arms, as his lips traced her neck and finally his teeth gently nibbled on her earlobe. She tried to pull away, but her skirt was caught in the thorns and she could

121

not get loose. She turned to him to entreat him to stop, but his mouth came down over hers, devouring the delicacies there. She felt weak, limp in his hands as his lips provoked her until she gathered all her strength to pull away. There was a rending sound as she pulled back, her hem ripping. She stumbled, dropping the basket, red berries flying everywhere. Instantly he was by her side, helping her up. She picked up her basket, blushing and flustered, and gathered the scattered raspberries as she knelt in the clover.

"Why do you fight it, Bekah?" he questioned. "You could never convince me that you did not enjoy that kiss. Tell me truthfully, did you despise it?"

She could not answer for a moment, then brazenly she decided to tell the truth. Her eyes downcast as she searched for the crimson drops of color in the meadow, she said, "I did not despise it, milord."

"Then why did you fight it?"

"What would I be if I were to accept the embraces of the same man who ravished me?"

He seriously mulled this bit of information over. "You did not pull away because you hate me?"

"Nay."

"Then may I take it that you no longer hate me?" he asked, suppressing a wild feeling of joy.

Wearily she shook her head. "I cannot lie, Kenric. I have lost my hatred for you, and I no longer have the will to bring it about."

"Then your only reason for resisting me is your sense of righteous punishment?"

"I do not wish to punish you, Kenric."

They gathered all the berries and she moved back to the bristly patch, determined to fill the straw basket. Kenric was quiet for a time, lost in some deep thought. It began to rain, large drops of water plopping onto the outspread leaves, a slowly rumbling chord of thunder overhead. For a moment they thought they might have to take flight, but the rain stopped, although the clouds still looked threatening.

"Bekah, let us play a game."

"A game?" she asked, looking up in surprise.

"Indeed. Did you never play games as a child?"

"Often. My favorite was to believe I was a woodland nymph who turned mean boys into mushrooms and toads."

He laughed. "Very well, then, let us play one now."

Her interest was piqued and she wondered what he had in mind. "What kind of game is it, Kenric?"

"One of pretend. I will be a prince who lives in yon manor, and you will be an enchanted princess who is doomed to this tower of raspberry thickets and who must pick the berries. Do you agree?"

She smiled, fascinated by this newest facet of Kenric's personality. He did not wait for an answer but disappeared behind the twin birch trees; she continued picking the berries. She heard him approach and looked up as he neared, waiting for him to speak.

"Fair damsel! I am the prince from yon Kartney Castle, out for a ride when I spied you."

"If you are a prince then where is your horse?"

"My noble steed bruised his foot on a stone and is tied in the trees. I have often looked at this tower from my castle roof and have been amazed by your beauty. I have come to free you from this thorny thicket and return you to your castle, if you will but direct me to it."

She pointed to a double row of large pine trees, totally secluded, their branches interweaving overhead. "That is my castle but, alas, I am a prisoner here and cannot return home. I am guarded by a mean ogre, and I am afraid that there is no escape for me." She smiled, and he bowed before her,

"For such a beautiful smile I will rescue you."

"Then you must be careful," she laughed. "The ogre especially loves knights for breakfast."

Kenric broke off a long branch of a sapling, pretending to do battle, fighting off imaginary ogres and dragons, describing his victories in full detail. She laughed again, clapping her hands. He could be so charming at times! Finally he reached the barriers of briars, rending them apart and setting her free.

"And now to return you safely home, my princess," he said, picking her up in his arms and rushing with her towards the pine trees she had indicated as her castle.

123

"Oh, Kenric! Put me down!" she laughed as they reached the enclosure of the trees. He did so, and they both laughed so hard that it echoed through the trees.

"Now," he said, pretending to grow serious. "I have saved you from the terrible berry ogre."

"Indeed you have! I am afraid that I have nothing with which to reward you, noble knight."

"Truthfully, you have one thing I very much desire."

"And what is that?" she asked, still smiling.

"A kiss from your lips, fairest princess."

"Certainly you have had kisses before, prince."

"Not one given freely and willingly from your lips," he sighed dejectedly. "To take a kiss or receive it as a gift are worlds apart."

"Very well," she said solemnly, yet still smiling. Nearing him, she encircled his neck with her arms. Their lips came together in a kiss so tender yet electrifying that when it was over each was shaken. Kenric was amazed at the deliciousness of it and of the skill born naturally from her lips. Bekah was startled by her own feelings, tumultuous, enticing, even inviting.

Kenric seated himself on a soft bed of fresh pine needles, pulling her down beside him. "Princess, there is something I must tell you."

The laughter was gone from them and she looked at him as he continued. "I love you. I have always loved you, even though I was foolish enough to never realize it. I want you to marry me. I know it is a difficult decision for you, but there will be no other woman for me. If I do not have your love in my life I will surely die as a leaf cast from a tree."

He leaned closer to her, his gray eyes melting her blue ones with the warmth of his love. Gently he laid her down, his arm supporting her head. He kissed her again and she returned it. She grew warm under his touch, his hands carefully unbuttoning the bodice of her dress. She tried to protest, but his lips covered her own, and as his fingers discovered the soft skin beneath her gown, desire filled her, overtaking her in waves of passion. Unleashed, her emotions overcame her and she felt terror at these new feelings, much more real than the sensations in her dreams had ever been.

"Nay, stop!" she cried, half-rising. Her chest was bare to his touch, and she pulled her bodice up to cover her. With a sickening feeling he realized that she had again remembered that day on the beach. He released her, desire ebbing from him. He had tried everything and lost.

"I am sorry, princess," he whispered, his face ashen.

Her breath was coming in wild pants until she finally calmed down. Her fingers fumbled with the buttons on her gown, and she could not fasten them. He pushed her hands aside, doing them himself. It began to rain, the drops falling in a soft pattering upon the ground and trees.

"I . . . I'm afraid," she said shakily.

"What do you fear, princess?" he asked, knowing the worst.

"The feelings inside me. My heart races so wildly that it thunders in my ears; what is it that makes me feel so warm and breathless?"

She was not frightened of him! With a wild leap of joy within his chest he realized that she was experiencing the first real pulses of passion. She was becoming a woman. He laughed happily as the rain began to soak them despite the protection of the trees.

"It is desire, princess."

"Desire!" she cried incredulously.

"You are beginning to crave that most beautiful jewel of love between man and woman." He took her into his arms, his mouth coming down to smother her protests.

His kisses were ardent, demanding the surrender of her lips. He laid her back on the soft bed of new pine needles, hovering over her. Her eyes were wide, and Kenric felt himself drowning in their liquid depths. His fervent mouth probed her own, then he closed her eyes with soft kisses of his lips. Bekah felt herself falling through the dark tunnel of desire. Her arms automatically traced a path along the corded muscles on his back. Her fingers kneaded the hard flesh, her nails sending sharp shivers through him. Her body was relaxing against him, and he took liberty in removing her clothing.

Her splendorous body was longing for his, and he knew now that she would not turn him away. He cradled her softly in his arms, treating her with reverence. This was the woman he would spend his life yearning for; only this love could fulfill his heart's passions. Bekah would be the only one to complete his puzzle and mold herself to him.

Bekah, the longing of her dreams now become real, was swept away by Kenric's caresses. Nothing had prepared her for this heat and dizziness, this ache that only Kenric's gentle strength could relieve. Instinctively she pressed her body into his, knowing only that she wanted him. They became one, and Kenric had never before experienced the utter fulfillment that this woman gave him.

In the quiet aftermath Kenric brushed her straying locks from her face and found tears glistening upon her cheeks.

"Bekah, why do you weep?"

She did not answer but pulled away from the warmth of his embrace. Quickly she brushed away the tears with the back of her hand as she stood up. She did not look at him as she hurriedly pulled on her clothes.

"Will you not speak to me?" he asked softly.

"It is not so much that you have betrayed me, but my own body also! You come after me at every turn and I have no willpower to send you away."

He rose too, straightening his attire. "It is nothing to be ashamed of. Oh, Bekah! You have not even tasted of the joys awaiting you. Do not fight it, for it is inevitable that you will partake of them sometime."

"I do not believe you!" she cried out, running from him towards the manor. What had he done to her? She tried to deny it, to ignore it, but he was speaking the truth and she despised herself for it. The grass and weeds that had seemed to be her friends only an hour before now grabbed at her ankles and skirt. She was totally rainsoaked by the time she entered the kitchen. She hurried through it, ignoring the stares of the girls and the cook, and ran up the stairs. Shortly thereafter Kenric entered through the door and set the basket of berries on the table.

"We were caught in a rainstorm. Have the men bring up the tub and then fill it with hot water before she catches a chill."

By the time she had made it upstairs and had shut the door he was close behind her and entered her room. They stood for a moment facing each other until she turned her back on him. "Do I never have any privacy?"

"Take off your clothing."

"What?"

"You will get a chill. Your hair is wet and you are drenched."

"It was my intention, but I will not do so with you here."

"Very well," he said as he opened the door. "I have ordered them to bring up the tub." As he shut the door she was left looking after him, a worried expression on her brow.

She peeled off the soaked dress and underclothing and removed her sandals, wrapping herself in a quilt. She shivered, pulling it tightly about her as there was a knock at the door. She answered, and Annie stuck her plump face around the door.

"Miss Bekah, the men are bringing in the tub."

She retreated to a shadowy corner as the two men entered, keeping their eyes respectfully down. They cast aside the rug, setting the large tub on the polished wooden floor. Then they filled the tub with buckets of water, two of which were boiling hot. The bath was pleasantly warm and Annie tested it before nodding her head as they all departed.

Bekah cast off the quilt, stepping into the large tub. With a sigh she let the warm water engulf her, leaning her head against the smooth edge of the tub and closing her eyes. It was wonderful to let the hot water soak away all her miseries and aches. She let her mind pass over what had happened earlier and the passion she had felt at his touch came quickly to mind. She chastised herself for that dark and pleasurable surrender which she had allowed, yea, even longed for! His touch brought about such a change in her, a change not unwanted. With an effort she told herself that it had been an accident, a mistake that must not come about again. Yet what had Kenric meant, that more awaited her?

She did not hear the door open, only its clicking shut, and her eyes flew open. Kenric stood before her, still in his wet clothing, ardently studying the gentle slope of her shoulders where the water teased him. With a groan she

127

sank lower until her alabaster shoulders were below the water, covering herself as best she could beneath the transparent surface of the water.

"Must you always enter my room without knocking?"

"I try to remember to knock, but if I do then it gives you the right to refuse me entry. Do not get angry, Bekah. Here," he said, tossing her an oval soap scented with crushed honeysuckle.

He took off his shirt, which had been clinging to his skin, revealing his muscular shoulders, his crisply curling black hair adorning his chest and stomach. In stunned silence she watched as he stripped off his breeches, exposing his nakedness to her shocked gaze. She averted her eyes to the window where rain lashed against the closed shutters.

"Have you no decency?" she chided.

"None at all." He smiled casually, standing totally at ease before her wavering gaze which was drawn to him like a moth to a torch.

"What are you doing?" she cried as he stepped into the tub, easing into the water. She rose up to take a quick exit but that exposed her to his devouring gaze. She sank back into the tub, hiding beneath the protection of the water.

"Look away, sir, so that I might get out and leave you to your bath."

"Nay. You depart and I shall feast." He smiled.

"Kenric, please! Why do you do this? To punish me?"

"Oh, Bekah," he said, shaking his head. "Why must you fight me at every turn? This tub was meant to accommodate two and it is the only one up here. Would you have me stand without in my damp clothes and die of the ague? Do you begrudge me a little of your water?"

"It is not the water I begrudge but myself. Already you have taken more than I should give."

"Why do you disdain passion?" he asked softly.

Her face burned at the memory of what had passed between them. "Do not talk to me of passion!" she said, her bosom heaving in indignation as he watched the rippling water. Angrily she covered herself with her arms, glaring at him.

"What is wrong in passion if there is love between a man and woman?"

"If there is love, then nothing."

"That is right. Did I not tell you that I love you, princess?"

"This is not a game now, Kenric."

"It was not a game then, either. I love you. How else can I say it? I love you!"

She was so startled by this that she gazed at him in mute silence. There was no mocking in his voice, no sarcasm, only sincerity. It was what she had wanted. If she could make him love her then she would have power over him. She felt no power; there was no victory now. He loved her, and it was not what she had thought it would be!

"I want us to marry. I swear to you that once we set foot on Kartney soil—within the month—we will be wed."

She felt stunned. "I do not know what to say."

"Say that you will marry me. Did you not desire a man to love you? And I know that your lips told me in kisses what they will not tell me in words. No man will love you as I do, sweet love. Forgive me for my past actions and give me your consent!"

"I must think about it. How can I give my acceptance when I am filled with these feelings I do not understand? I felt more secure when I could hate you."

He smiled, satisfied for the moment. "Very well, I will wait upon your answer. Whether you answer yea or nay I will love you still."

He was extremely pleased by the confused look that rested on her lovely features. She had not called him a fool or glared at him in disdain. He had a foot in the door, and he would soon be inside and in her heart. There was no insincerity in his words, and he was amazed that he could so calmly accept the fact of his own growing love. Why not? She was beautiful, more beautiful than any woman he had ever seen. She was good, pure in an innocent way that delighted and provoked him. Though he had never felt that women could be trusted, somehow he felt that his trust was safe with her. She was the fairest flower in all this corner of the world, and he thought of the pride he would feel upon showing off such a lovely wife.

The soap slipped from her grasp, sliding beneath them,

and Kenric dove for it, his hand brushing against her thigh.

"Kenric!"

"I am sorry, Bekah, I only try to get the soap!" It kept evading his fingers, and he followed it around the tub and behind her, his fingers invariably brushing against her skin in a manner that sent chills through her.

"Will you stop!" she cried, trying for the soap and slipping beneath him, coming in full contact with his steely frame. She rose up, accidentally brushing against him; then groaned and pulled away as he leaned back with a smile coming to his face.

"I got it!" he cried, holding up the dripping bar of soap. He began to lather his head, shoulders and chest, humming a tune to himself. He tried to reach his back, not very successfully.

"Will you lather my back?" he questioned, and she caught a glimpse of the boy in him as he turned his back to her. He rested his arms on the sides of the tub as she lathered his back. His muscles felt smooth beneath her touch and she enjoyed it. He caught her hands, pulling them around to his chest.

"Let me see the soap," he said as she pulled away. She was afraid to drop it, remembering what had happened before, and she handed it to him. He turned around and she crossed her arms in front of herself. "Turn around and I shall do your back."

"It is not necessary."

"Few things are. But you have not lived until you have experienced the delight I just did."

She sighed, turning her back to him, feeling it was some protection from him. Not true. He piled the wet ribbons of her hair onto her head and ambitiously began lathering her back. She kept her arms tightly to her sides as he ran his roughened hands over her soft skin, the touch a unique sensation. He ran his fingers over her shoulders and down her arms, massaging, touching, finally resting them on her shoulders. His hands slid over her shoulders and she took in a sharp breath as he lathered her flesh.

"Stop, Sir Dragon!"

"I am lathering you."

"You do not know the back of a maid from the front," she said, pushing away his playful hands.

"I assure you I do, princess."

Finally she sank beneath the water and away from his grasp. He rinsed off his hair and shoulders, rising up in all his splendor and reaching for a towel. He wrapped a linen about his waist, bidding her to stand up.

"The water grows cold. Rise up."

"Nay, rogue! Not until you look away."

"We have bathed together and I have known you," he said quietly.

"I shall not be gazed upon."

"Bekah, you are the woman I love. Now rise up before you get chilled!"

Reluctantly she did so, snatching up the towel and stepping out of the water under the towel's protection. She wrapped it about herself, still dripping wet.

"Can you do nothing for yourself?" he asked playfully, whisking her towel from her and proceeding to dry her despite her protests and laughing attempts at escape. Quickly she seized a gown that was pale blue, slipping it on. She felt strangely light-headed, unlike her usual self. He tied the slender ribbons at her throat, the oval cutout beneath it edged in the same dark ribbon. It fell in a cascade of blue, embracing her body and doing little to disguise the bounties beneath it. She sat down on the edge of the bed and he sat down too, taking a dry linen and rubbing her hair with it. He grabbed the rose-handled brush, running it along the length of her hair. They sat in silence as he brushed it dry, each lost in private thoughts. She felt tired, warmed by the bath and his attentions. He laid her back across the bed, lying beside her, leaning up on his elbow and turning her face towards him.

"I have declared my love and you still hold out. My heart aches for your words of acceptance."

She wanted those words to come, to declare that their lovemaking of an hour ago had been what she had wanted and that she longed for more. To lie in his arms as his wife would be the sweetest pleasure of all. But it was difficult to find the words to tell him.

"You cannot be indifferent or you would not allow my attentions. Do you love me?"

"I do not know," she said, her blue eyes staring up at him.

"Sometimes you are such a child. Perhaps it is because I treat you as such."

"You can think of me as a child after all we have been through?" she asked.

"Oh, nay. I see you as a woman who tempts my very soul—which, my dear, is not nearly as virtuous as yours. I have cast aside my pride and turned to you with an honest desire to love you. Does this great effort mean nothing at all to you?"

"It does mean very much to me, and I hear the sincerity in your voice. It is just such a shock to see that you do love me—you who I feared and called enemy. You have changed before my very eyes, yet am I to believe the warning of my heart or the gentle persuasion of your words?"

"Does my gallant behavior these many weeks prove nothing? How many times have I wanted to take you and mold you to my ways, but you would not bend. And now I offer you that which I have given to no other, and you do not want it."

"I did not say that, only that I must have time to think," she said shakily.

He nodded. "Very well. I understand your hesitancy and have no right to push you to a decision. But you must come to me. I will ask no more."

She felt her heart stir at his words. She had caused him pain . . . but there was no joy in it, only a terrible sorrowing ache! How could she hurt this man who loved her? He was no longer the man who had ravaged her. She must try to overcome her fears. There was no other for her, either, for only he had her virtue which he tenderly held to him like a precious jewel. She had not lost it, only given it to him for safekeeping. She would turn to him and give herself to him. As her decision came to mind, he rose and, without looking back, left the room.

What had she done to him and to herself? Did she love this man? She had said she did not know, and yet she did have intense feelings, for even now her heart pounded a strange rhythm in her breast. She thought of Kenric as she had just seen him, tender and earnest in his desire to win her. There was a tingling pleasure at this thought, for he loved her and there was never so good a feeling as that.

There was a rap at the door. She answered, expecting to see Kenric. Instead Edlyn peeped in, informing Bekah that dinner was laid out in the main hall. Quickly Bekah rose, straightening the wrinkles from her dress. She stood before the mirror, pinching her cheeks. She rubbed her lips together to give them the rosy hue of her cheeks and ran her brush down her golden tresses. She felt pleased with her appearance and could not wait to greet Kenric as the new Bekah.

He was not there. He did not come to the meal that night, and none of the servants would tell her where he was. She waited for him to return to his room, her needlework becoming a bother when his footsteps were not heard. Finally she decided she would have to wait until morning to present to him her exciting new self. She lay in her bed hugging her knees to her as she thought of the game that she was going to play with Kenric tomorrow. It would be pure pleasure to watch his face as she showed off her newfound feminine wiles.

When she awoke the next morning, the weather was no longer stormy but again the tender summer day to which she had grown accustomed. She thought of Kenric and smiled to herself. He loved her. He loved her! What was the past? Nothing of worth, and at that moment she cast it aside. She sat up, and saw that at the foot of her bed lay twenty beautiful roses, yellow, pink and red. They were beautiful, the dew still upon them, and they took her breath away. Kenric must have put them there while she slept. She picked one up, kissing it tenderly.

She rose quickly, dressing in the white kirtle and blue tunic. She braided her hair, letting it hang down her back, and tucked a yellow rose behind her left ear. She hurried downstairs and looked for Kenric, but he was not there. Edlyn told her that he had risen early and had left. She felt bitter disappointment, but it was nothing compared to what she would experience.

She did not see him for nearly a week. No matter how

early she arose, he had already departed and did not return home until well after dark. He spent his days riding about his uncle's lands, visiting or attending to business. Sometimes he frequented the marketplace, but he could not stand to see happy couples together. Once in a while he would go to an alehouse, but there was little comfort there. Now that he had declared his love for Bekah she invaded his thoughts every waking moment and haunted his dreams. He had lost her without even having had her, and he could not bear it.

Sometimes when he arose early in the morning he would quietly enter her room, watching her sleep. In this way he possessed her and could love her without fear of rejection. He left her gifts: a beautiful necklace of black stones, a tiny bluebird in a pretty cage, a beautiful conch shell with a pink heart and a bleached white exterior that he'd found on the beach. He bought a set of combs for her hair, made of polished black wood with insets of rainbow shell. One time as he watched her sleep he left a fragrant sprig of lilacs beside her pillow.

She rejoiced with each thing he left her, yet grew terribly frustrated at never seeing him. She tried to help in the kitchen but was useless. She picked raspberries, but there were such tremendous memories there that she could not stand it. Did she love Kenric? Logic reeled and she could not think clearly. Could they love each other and put the past behind them? As each day passed his absence made her thirst for his presence. She was coming to see that she really did love him and want him. Like thunder and lightning, they belonged together. She was experiencing new worries of losing this bond with him, yet was fearful of going to him with full truth. He began to haunt her dreams making her stir with memories. I think more of him each day, she realized. Have I no control over my heart? She did not. It was as if it had a will of its own. Her heart would love him despite her attempts to feel otherwise.

She began to gain courage and her resolve crystallized. She must tell him, must accept his proposal of love and marriage.

But what if she had pushed him too far? She remembered the pain in his face, the pain she had caused him. She lay down on the bed, her head throbbing. What should she do? She did not know. It had been seven days since he had professed his love for her, and she could stand it no longer. Sleep was hours coming. She wanted to cry but could not. Her mind soared with ideas, with worries and plans, and finally she fell into an exhausted sleep like tumbling into a black pit. A dream formed before her eyes in which she saw Kenric lying still in the embrace of death. No light flickered in his gray eyes, no smile on his lips. She was filled with desperation to save him and awoke with a cry.

She found herself in the center of her room, her heart racing wildly, her face wet with the tears she had not been able to shed before. It was dark in the room, neither night nor morning, and she could hear restless winds outside. Her bare feet swished across the floor, and she pulled open the door, the draft in the hall encircling her. She hurried down the hall in the direction her mind had taken so many times before.

Kenric lay on his back, his hands beneath his head. He stared at the ceiling, awaiting the sleep which always came only hours before dawn. He would leave Jarlshof and return to Wessex, to Kartney Castle. It was home there, and it would be a balm upon his aching heart. He could not stand to be around her yet not possess her. And she could not be around him, for he always brought doubt into her eyes. For the rest of his life he would hate himself for what he had done to her that first day. If he had wanted her so badly, why had he not just stolen her away, then wooed her here at Jarlshof? She had tried to come around to him, but it was impossible for her. He would leave, and she could stay here. He would make sure that she was cared for with a cottage of her own. She would have plenty of sustenance and perhaps some man would court her and she could go to him willingly. He knew she had experienced desire, but she could not acknowledge it because of their past. If only they could put that past and those memories behind them! How he hated and despised himself for ruining their future together. He must leave and never see her again. Even as he thought of it he knew he would never be the same.

The door to his room banged open, the draft sweeping in.

She stood there, the wind whipping the white of her gown about her. Her hair swirled forward about her face. He shuddered, fearing for his sanity. Now he was dreaming her in visions! Would he go mad? The door closed. Her gown fell in straight folds about her as the wind died, leaving her as still as one of the statues at Kartney. She stepped forward into the shaft of moonlight which milkily entered the room, turning her hair into spun silver. He half-rose, seeing her as she was. Real, and beautiful, with love in her eyes. Her fingers reached her throat in a moment of hesitation. Her eyes were shining with unshed tears as she came to him. No words were spoken. None were needed. He was overwhelmed and unsure. What if he drove her from him? The thought of this so terrified him that he could do nothing. She leaned over him and her lips tenderly tasted his. She lay down beside him then, putting her head on his chest. He felt such violent emotion that he quaked from it.

"Kenric, I love you. I want you and I am yours. Twice before we have come together, but this shall be different, for this time all the giving is mine. It is my gift to you to prove that the hurt of our past is ended."

He tightened his arms about her, dizzied by the warmth of holding her, willingly, for the first time. "Are you sure?" he asked hoarsely.

Bekah nodded, brushing her lips against his. Gently he rolled her over, his hands touching her as if she were the most fragile flower. For all his bravado, he felt like a frightened youth. The time on the beach had been miles and years ago, a faded stain upon the past. And the second, in the trees, had still held no commitment. But this would be the time that would forge them as one, and he would rather be cast down to hell than have this end in tears from her.

He let his fingers explore this woman whom he loved and she shuddered, amazed at how easily she could accept this man. Her gown slipped away to lie discarded, as useless as the fabric of her pride. Her silken limbs were entwined with his as they came together, all thoughts swept away by the tide of passion that washed over her. His mouth sought her eyes and throat, her face and hair, and she held him to her. Desire grew to wild heights and she

136

cried out, gasping as she drowned in him. It was as if the heat of passion forged their beings together.

As a bird that had strained its wings to soar into the heavens, expending its last bit of strength, she glided slowly downward on the currents, circling back to earth.

So this was love. No wonder poets spoke of it and singers sang of it! There was no poem now, no song or tapestry. This was the art in itself, at its finest. They fairly shook with the violent feelings they had experienced; all time was lost, all thought. Wind whistled through the shutters, entwining her hair about them as they lay together. The intense explosion of feeling had died away to become only the beginning. Kenric had been right.

The wind sighed softly down as if in tired agreement, the moonlight wavering as the orb moved behind midnight clouds. In time the sun began to rise, the edges of color a signal of the dawn.

The morning sky was a dusty rose color, the clouds neither red nor brown but some indescribable color. It was a stormy sky, yet not unfriendly. It sent shafts of gray morning light to lie upon the floor of their chamber.

A single meadowlark unleashed its lilting melody in joyous refrain of a storm passed by. Outside the manor, morning awoke with its usual excited expectations.

When Bekah awoke the memories of the previous night filled her senses. She was happy, happier than she had even been in her whole life. She and this splendid man had spent the night together, reforging bonds of love. There had been little sleep for them, but she felt better now than she had for months. At some early morning hour he had carried her back to her room, putting her in her own bed and pulling the quilt about her. This act had been the kindest thing she had ever seen from the Anglian warrior. He was aware of her sensitivity and had taken a kind caution with her reputation. He did care about her and how she felt. Suddenly she realized that it did not matter in the least to her if the entire world knew of them together. She was Kenric's woman now.

She loved him and he would make her very happy. They would go to Wessex and be wed, and she would bear him sons and they would be so content. There would be things to overcome in that new land, too, but with Kenric by her side she was afraid of nothing!

She realized that she was just beginning to experience the joys of loving this great man, and with this she lamented the waste of the time behind them. But having earned her, would he not hold her dearer to him? Few things in life easily obtained were tightly cherished. And there were many years that stretched out ahead of them like an endless road. They would grow old together, she thought, and the time would only bond them closer. She lay relishing her happiness before rising, letting the deliciousness of love engulf her before allowing daily activities to start. She remembered how tenderly he had returned her to her room last night, the light touch of his kiss still fresh in her mind.

She dragged herself from the bed and quickly washed. Standing in front of the closet, indecision seized her. She had never had such lovely dresses to choose from before and finally she selected a tunic which was fawn-colored, brown ribbons sewn in a decorative pattern across the bodice and along the wide sleeves. It was a short tunic, the hem coming to her calves, and beneath this she wore a long ivory kirtle.

Bekah donned brown kid slippers, then at the mirror began to brush her hair. She caught her hair up weaving through it ribbons identical to those in her dress. She then wound it atop her head as a few silken tendrils escaped to caress her neck and face.

She waited a few minutes for Kenric to come and then decided to seek him out. She went down the hall to his room, tapping on his door. His deep voice bade her enter and she hesitantly opened the door. He stood near the washbasin, pulling on a silk shirt. He glanced up and smiled broadly, spreading his arm wide, "Come into my humble abode. Anyone as fair as yourself is welcome."

She smiled and stepped inside, for the first time taking a good look at the room as he came near and kissed her gently. "You call this humble?" She laughed, looking about a room resplendent with black wood furniture. A huge four-poster bed, draped with dark green velvet, dominated the room.

"Since you took my room they removed me to the servant's quarters," he teased.

"Well in that case, the latchet on my slipper has come undone. Be a good servant and do it up for me," she said as she lifted up the hem on her gown.

He dropped to his knees, examining first one slipper and then the other. "But neither of these is undone."

"Oh? Well, they felt loose. Never mind then," she said, stepping back.

His eyes narrowed and he nodded. "Hmmm."

He pulled on his boots and she walked around the room, examining things. A huge carved box sat atop a writing desk where there were neat stacks of paper, a quill and an ink blotter. An ornate closet was on the south side of the room, its door slightly ajar, and she saw many rows of clothing hanging within. A large oak chest was at the foot of the bed, and upon it was a leather-bound book which she remembered was his ship's log. The fireplace mantel held thick white candles in carved stone holders. Kenric took her arm, and they went downstairs together. The house was filled with their laughter.

They ate a breakfast of melons, bread and honey, and oat cereal with milk. The sun, coming out to dry up the fields, fell in heated streamers through the windows. He held her slender hand within the confines of his tanned fingers, reluctant that she should be very far from him at any time. They laughed and teased one another with simple jests until the meal was done. Then Kenric pulled her to her feet, and they walked to the stable together. He saddled Polo. "Tomorrow or the next day I will teach you to ride Elyse. But for today, let us go together because we must be back in a few hours. Tonight is the summer festival and a portion of it is to be held at the manor."

"The festival so soon?" Bekah said. "I did not realize how far into the summer we are! But I must admit that I have looked forward to seeing the festival, for my mother talked of it." He lifted her onto the horse's back, mounting behind her.

The horse sauntered off through familiar fields and down well-worn paths as a breeze cooled them from the heat. She leaned back against him, resting her head on his shoulder as she looked up at him. "Had I been told a month ago that I would willingly use you for a rest I would not have believed it."

"You do not know how many times I wanted you to, and how often my arms ached for the feel of you," he said, smiling. "But you were always very prim, your back straight as an arrow. Last night, when you came to me . . ." He shook his head. "I thought you were a vision. In truth, when I awoke this morning I feared I had dreamed all that happened last night. Will you tell me what convinced you to bend that iron will of yours?"

"I think 'twas your absence. The more we were apart the more I thought of you."

"Had I known that I would have departed long ago! I had given up hope of you."

"Indeed?" She looked up questioningly and he bent down, brushing his lips against hers.

He pulled back and looked at her. "Do you know how long I've wanted to claim you as mine? The ocean voyage may have seemed a jumble to you, but to me it was torturously long. I chastised myself often for bringing you with me."

"Then why did you?"

"Because I could not stand the thought of leaving you behind . . . for some other man. What I did to you! When I see how innocent you are and what you have gone through, most of it my fault, I despise myself."

"Kenric, that is the past."

"Let me finish. You have indicated that you have forgiven me but I will never forgive myself. A hundred times over I have thought that I should have stolen you away and never touched you so that this wooing of you would have been easier on us both. But what I did was done in a trance and there is no erasing that memory for either of us."

"Then talk not of the past. Is it not enough that I have acknowledged my love of you?"

"Yea, 'tis enough." He tightened his strong arms securely about her as they rode through fields of wet clover and grass.

As the morning passed into afternoon, the air became

muggy, thick with the scents of flowers and spices, and Polo snorted his worry. It smelled dusty and the wind stirred the long fronds of the willow. They watched as clouds gathered thick and dark until the whole eastern sky was black, yet the sun still shone in the sky. There were three rumbling claps of thunder, and suddenly the rain came down in a thin veil. It turned the earth from brown to black, and the green wheat bowed under its force.

They dismounted and stood in the shelter of the willow tree, but soon became soaked despite their attempts to keep dry. Still, she was warm in the protection of his arms. The rain, after washing the earth clean a second time, slowed and then stopped. Honeysuckle, wet earth and wild spices sent out their fragrances tinged with the sour-sweet smell of rhubarb. A few birds timidly chirped the departure of the storm, and the sun streaked the clouds with yellow and red. Before them was a perfect rainbow, a total arc in its symmetrical spectrum of colors. "It is beautiful," she breathed.

"Yea, but it cannot compare with your perfect face. You are the sweetest thing I have ever seen. I have a friend who is quite the philosopher, and he says that the rainbow is a symbol of a good future."

"Your friend is wise," she said, thinking of the future which had appeared so bleak to her only a while ago. She thought about being his wife and bearing him children. Even now she wondered if she carried his child. She had pushed the thought from her mind, but now it emerged again. Once she had dreaded the idea, yet now she held it closely to her as if it were a precious jewel. A child, a creation of their own! What would Kenric really feel if she were with child? Their love was new and very tender, a fragile thing not yet ready to rise from its cocoon.

The thought of telling him she might be with child plagued her and she worried about it. He talked of an heir, but what if his child had already been conceived? She shivered a little, and he took it to mean she was chilled. He lifted her atop Polo and swung himself up behind. He headed the horse in a homeward direction, the destrier quickening his stride. Kenric kissed the tender nape of Bekah's neck, and she relaxed against him as they rode in silence. The sun was still high above all the purple hills as they reached the manor. He swung her down from the horse and led her inside where there was a fire in the hearth. They warmed by the fire and then went to their rooms to change out of their wet clothing.

She put on a gown of red, simply cut with narrow sleeves that reached her wrist in a point and were edged in white lace that ran up the sleeves several inches. It fit her well, clinging to her and hanging straight to the floor. She adjusted the neck that was cut square and had a lace inset which encircled her throat. A slender chain fit around her waist, and she was just fastening it when there was a knock at the door. She looked up to see Kenric peering in through the wrought iron grille.

"Come in, sir," she smiled, sitting down and putting on red slippers. She picked up a brush and ran it through her hair until her tresses hung down her back in a silky cascade. As Kenric watched she caught it back with the two combs he had given her. He was wearing black leather breeches and boots and a red velvet jerkin much the same color as her dress. "You look most handsome tonight, milord," Bekah said slyly.

He lit a candle as the light in the room began to fade. "Thank you," he said, stepping near and looking at her. "And you are beautiful as always. Why don't we stay here and enjoy one another's company?"

"But the guests are already gathering downstairs, I can hear them!"

"The dinner will not commence for a while yet," he said, taking up the brush and smoothing out a tangle she had missed in the back of her hair.

"But you are the master of the manor and should be there to greet your guests, should you not?"

"Rotten festivals," he grumbled, setting the brush aside. "I think you are beginning to like them."

"Indeed, ever since you taught me to dance."

She reached out to extinguish the candle, and without a word he stopped her, handing her a small wooden box. Looking at him questioningly she lifted the lid, pulling back the bit of velvet cloth within. She took in her breath as she looked down at a lovely ring of beautiful sapphires

142

and diamonds in a flower setting. She suddenly thought of that first day on the beach when she had compared her virtue to a precious gem and she realized that she had not lost it after all. Kenric became perturbed by the tears he saw in her eyes.

"What is wrong, my love?"

"Oh, Kenric, 'tis beautiful!"

"It belonged to my mother and is one of the Kartney jewels. When I thought of the sapphires the same color as your eyes I knew that you needed to be its owner. Here, put it on. See, it fits perfectly! Come now, no more tears, you silly girl. As you said, the guests are gathering downstairs."

He was right. They could hear the strains made by the musicians' instruments and the sound of mingled voices. They went downstairs, everyone turning to see this unusual couple. There were rumors that she was a Viking's daughter, yet as they looked at her some whispered that the rumors were ridiculous. There was nothing about her which depicted such ancestry. An older man leaned over to his wife and said, "If any descent is seen upon that brow, then it is Anglian royalty," he said with a knowing nod.

Kenric seated her, then took his place at the head of the table. There were foods of every kind, and each person who came had brought a dish. They filled their plates and ate among the chatter and gaiety. The merrymakers had hardly finished eating before music started up and the ladies began to participate. Bekah moved to a secluded corner, preferring to watch, and Kenric followed her. He slipped his arm about her and they watched together.

The festival left the manor, Kenric and Bekah going too, and traveled through the village and to other hearths. As the merrymaking grew less rambunctious, Bekah found that she could hardly keep her eyes open, and Kenric led her home again. Home, she thought. Is this home? She shook out her dress and carefully laid it away before crawling into bed. Home is wherever Kenric is.

The days passed swiftly, endless ribbons of time, as the summer's brief warmth began to fade. Bekah sat upon the cliff top, her knees tucked under her chin. She thought of the boat down on the shore, a sleek monster of black wood with flapping sails and a very tall mast. It was long, bigger

143

than the small vessel that had tossed about on the seas when she had been Kenric's prisoner. This ship, sent by King Alfred and of a new design, had more room, and there was a large bed aboard, as well as a good larder of food and several big chests to hold her clothes. This journey would be a hundredfold better, he had assured her, with everything for her comfort. Still, she did not look forward to leaving. She had become accustomed to the spacious manor and the freedom of riding on horseback. She thought of the hours to pass on board ship. She had gathered materials and yarns, having learned the art of embroidery from Violet, but that was little enough to take up time. She remembered, too, how ill she had been on that journey between Norway and Jarlshof. But, then, she'd had reason to be sick.

Goudwin stood not far behind her, watching her gaze out to sea. He could certainly understand Kenric's reverence for her, and silently he was happy. The sorrow he had felt on Bekah's behalf had diminished when he saw her joy. The cap'n had come around and openly admitted his love for the missy. They would be wed upon reaching Wessex, and Goudwin had beamed happily when Kenric had told him the news. If anyone deserved security, honor and happiness, it was Bekah. Often Goudwin would reflect that Kenric deserved little because of his past actions but was indeed a lucky man to have gained the love of such a gentle maid.

She wore a delicate dress of plain yellow edged with amber threads, her head crowned with that thick, sun-colored hair that was so lovely, interwoven with amber and yellow ribbons. The Norse child had been replaced by a woman now, one who seemed to hold her own with quiet strength.

He approached her and she looked up. "Why, Goudwin, 'tis good to see you," she cried, rising.

"I have heard tell that ye will be marrying the cap'n. I would like to offer ye my congratulations," he said, embarrassedly kicking at a pebble.

She smiled at him, her fingers playing with the folds of her dress. "Thank you, Goudwin. Kenric and I have come a long way. I marvel every day that I now love the man whom I once hated."

"It is best this way, miss. The cap'n loves ye, and I can tell ye that he is happier now than ever before. He has never loved any woman 'til now."

She smiled, clasping her hands as the sea breeze blew her skirts back from her. "It is for the best, you are right. It is good we will be wed, especially now."

He scrutinized her face. Did the miss mean something by this? His eyes glanced down at the gentle curves of her still childlike form and his eyes widened. His face grew ruddy and he stammered, "Miss, may I ask, are ye in the delicate way?"

She looked at him for a moment, then nodded her head, a worried expression on her delicate features. " 'Tis so, Goudwin. I have denied it for a while, but the truth is evident even to you."

"And what does the cap'n say, missy?"

"He does not know, and oh, Goudwin, I beg you to be discreet! You are in my confidence."

"I cannot believe he does not know, Bekah."

"Perhaps he does not see what he does not want to see. He only thinks that I have gained a little weight from the food I have been so eagerly eating."

It was true. She looked as if she had gained only a few pounds, her form still very slender. Goudwin was amazed that he himself had guessed. It had not been her form, but rather something in her face. He had recognized the same in the dainty face of his beloved wife, so long ago that his memories had dimmed. His darling Erilla had died before their son had been able to catch the first breath of life, and he inwardly vowed to protect Bekah to the best of his ability.

"Ye can rest easy, for I'll not tell Cap'n Kenric. I might advise ye to tell him soon, afore he discovers it on his own."

"Very well," she sighed resignedly. " 'Tis best, but I worry about how the truth of it will fall upon his ears."

"He loves ye, miss," Goudwin said. "Ye can rest assured that it is in your hands, and since the voyage will be long, there will be plenty of time to tell him afore we land on Wessex shore. All will be well," he said comfortingly, patting her hand.

"Thank you, Goudwin."

145

"We will be leaving soon, and the cap'n has already ordered your things aboard. I better be helping them ready the ship." He left her to her solitude. He hoped everything would go well for the young lady and his captain. He would ask God to bless their future union, and allow none to come between them. Even so, he could not push the unhappy thought from his mind that such happiness as theirs was not meant to last forever, as he knew from experience.

Goudwin moved back towards the ship, hoping they would make it swiftly back to Wessex so that the marriage would be soon. It was best for Bekah, the baby and the captain.

As Bekah sat upon the sea cliffs, she wished that this tranquility would not end and that they could stay on Jarlshof forever. She stared out at the smooth gray sea, the color of Kenric's eyes, as beneath her the men prepared the ship. Soon they would come to Wessex, where they would find Kenric's family and his home. Even though she would be wed there, she could not be content to leave this green and rocky island.

She looked down at the slight curve of her belly, well hidden by the folds of her yellow dress. How swiftly time had passed since her first meeting with Kenric and the conception of their child. She thought tenderly of her father, hoping that he had not suffered too much with her disappearance. There was no returning there now, and she turned her thoughts from Norway. There were other, more pressing matters here.

How she longed to tell Kenric of the child! She was haunted, however, by something bidding her not to spoil their remaining day here. There would be time enough once they were aboard the ship.

Kenric was busy, and she used this as another excuse to keep the secret. She did not want too many problems to dwell within his mind.

She caught her lower lip between her teeth for a minute and then said to herself aloud, "Nevertheless I must tell him."

"Tell him what, my sweet ensnarer?" she heard Kenric's masculine voice ask.

"Oh! You startled me. I did not hear you come up the path. You walk as stealthily as a cat, I think." She smiled.

"I learned to do so as a page, an important part of any knight's training. Now tell me," he said as he handed her a bouquet of wild flowers, "who must you tell what to?"

"You, milord. I only thought to be sure to tell you . . . that I love you," she said, breathing in the fragrance of the flowers. He knelt beside her, nuzzling her hair. He loved her more each day. He liked spending time with her and never tired of talking to her and gazing at her. She looked so pretty now, with the rosy hue of health upon her cheeks, and he hoped that she would fare much better on this journey across the seas than on the previous one. He was anxious to return to Kartney, more so than ever before, so he could marry her and have her completely.

He pulled her to her feet, holding her against him for a moment before guiding her down the path which ended at the shore. Here the boat lay anchored.

"Is she not a lovely ship, my heather-eyed lady? One of the best of King Alred's ships. I find myself wondering why neither Saxons nor Angles ever took to the sea as the Norsemen have. However, it looks as if we will finally have a fleet—which only seems reasonable, since we are an island."

She watched her trunks being pulled on board by sweat-slick backs and stowed below deck. Men worked to pull the hemp cords taut, finally fastening them to steel tie bars. The sails overhead crackled as the stiff canvas caught the pull of a northern wind. The surge of water foamed about the ship in an effort to tear it from its mooring, and she thought how small this large ship was when compared with the force of a huge ocean.

Kenric left her. He rowed out to the ship and pulled himself up by a rope that hung down the side. Bekah watched him give instructions to his men. She admired the handsome man so in charge, the wind stirring his black hair as he strode about the deck of his ship. His capable hands retied a rope before he turned and made the short trip back to her side.

"Everything is ready." He smiled.

"Then we leave soon?"

"Yea. She is seaworthy, this new Anglian ship—nothing like the vessel in which I brought you here."

"You act like a little boy with a new toy," she teased.

"You are not far wrong. The sea is special to me, enchanting, somehow. The only thing I like better is a fast race on a horse."

She laughed and looked into his face. "Then we must be sure to have a race, you and I, once we are in Wessex."

"We have many horses there, and you can have your pick of mares. Maybe we can find you one like Elyse. But no use talking about it unless we plan on leaving. Are you ready?"

She looked towards the ship again, becoming very still. A cold wind blew over her, making her spine tingle with strange apprehension. As she stood there, gazing out over the incoming green waves, fear seemed to overcome her senses. She watched the wild, crashing waves, so capable of covering her face, cutting off her breath. Icy winds seemed to encircle her, and she leaned against Kenric.

"What is wrong? Your face is so pale."

"It is just that I feel cold."

"Cold? But it is a warm day; look at that blue sky. I fear it is one of the last before summer is gone."

"Yea, 'tis a beautiful day," she breathed quietly, shivering in spite of her words. "Kenric, do we have to leave Jarlshof? After all, we have everything we need here. I do not want to leave it."

"But Bekah, you will love Wessex, and Wessex will love you. You are only uncertain of the future, but I promise you that everything will be as good there as here."

"I . . . I cannot explain this feeling of foreboding which I have, like a sudden shadow casting itself across the sun's path. I feel fear, Kenric."

He took her chin by his fingers, tenderly kissing her lips. "You are only frightened because of the last unpleasant sea voyage. This will be a pleasant journey. There are no more cramped quarters, and we will travel mostly along the shore with several stops for our enjoyment. You have nothing to fear. After all, I will be there to protect you. Now, I do not care to see that frown upon such a lovely

148

face. Come now, smile." She gave him her most entrancing smile, and her cheeks regained some of their color.

"I suppose you are right, Kenric. I do not know what came over me."

"Come, look closely at the ship. It's truly a masterpiece of workmanship." He pointed out its features, and as she studied it, she did agree that it was much finer than any of the Nordic ships she had seen.

Some of the villagers were there to see the ship off, giving gifts of cheese, nut breads and jugs of apple juice to their departing friends. After everything was ready, Kenric carried Bekah aboard and into the comfortably furnished cabin. There was room to move about, and the soft bed was covered with pelts. Trunks of her clothing sat against one wall, the copper mirror she had admired above them. There was a wooden chair nailed to the floor, its seat and back padded by cushions covered with blue and green needlework. There were thick quilts to wrap about her legs when it got cold, a shawl and a fur wrap. Tapered white candles to light the room were secured in carved wall sconces.

As the day waned they were soon on their way, the craft being tossed upon the depths of the waves. Bekah was not overcome with seasickness as she had been before.

She thought about her baby. Kenric's child. She was hardly aware of that tiny life within her, made known only by the rounder curve of her chest and belly. As she pressed her hands to her temples she realized that she must tell Kenric before she grew much larger and he guessed on his own. The time would be right soon.

She slipped up on deck to watch the activities, standing out of the way. Goudwin deftly secured the ropes again as a younger crewman scaled on up the mast. Kenric directed his men with an easy demeanor, and she derived pleasure from watching him in his authoritative role.

Cool sea breezes caressed her face and whipped her hair. She watched his dark head nod in approval as the crewmen followed his orders. This ship would be secure against the great force of the sea. In time she watched Jarlshof disappear behind them. The sun was like a golden orb slipping into the ocean as she returned to her room. She undid

149

her hair, brushing it out slowly. Soon she stretched out on the warm fur pelts, letting the motion of the ship rock her into sleep. She knew not how much later it was when she felt hands touching her, covering her up with a quilt. She stretched and opened her eyes, looking into granite-colored ones.

"I did not mean to wake you."

"You did not," she murmured. "I was half-awake."

"How do you feel? Any seasickness this time?"

"Nay." She yawned, blinking her eyes. "I feel quite well so far."

"Good," he said. "I brought dinner if you are hungry."

She sat up, and he handed her a tray with fruit and cheese. He studied her as she ate. "I grow more anxious each day to wed you and I hope that this journey goes by swiftly."

"But we have our whole life together."

"Still, I long to have you as my wife and start a deep love." He smiled knowingly at her.

"I, also, long to call you husband, but you have said that the journey will not be long. And I am happy for each moment we have together before we reach Kartney Castle."

"Are you anxious about going there?"

She nodded. "What if your father does not approve of me and forbids the marriage?"

He laughed at this. "How can he help but approve of you? He is a great appreciator of beauty and charm, and I must admit he will be relieved to see that I have finally decided to marry."

She almost took that opportunity to tell him of the child, but he continued, "The more he knows you the more he will come to like you, just as everyone does. And in a year or so when you give him a grandchild, the heir to Kartney for which he has begged me, then he will love you as much as a daughter."

Bekah flinched, but said nothing. After their meal she lay with her head on his shoulder. Content for the moment in the soft rocking movement of the ship, she felt herself overcome with weariness. There was always tomorrow, and if not then, perhaps the next day to tell him.

Jarlshof was left behind, and the tiny ship was its own

island among the gray-green waves. Later, Bekah could hardly remember the several days which passed, each a mixture of sleep, quietude, and the sea wind on her face and gulls circling overhead. All these memories were interlaced with the sunlit moments of Kenric's presence. Kenric commanding the ship, or showing her the skills of reading the stars and the waters. Kenric laughing, his lips in a smile which she knew so well and which made her love him more. At times when he was working she could study him; he looked so young and carefree, and she could see some of the reckless spirit in him then.

It was hard to say if he was handsome, for certainly he did not have the flawless features of some youths she had seen. His well-tanned skin and shaggy black mane only enhanced his wild appearance, and his granite features made him look rugged. Still, there was something in the flash of his eyes and the quizzical slant of his lips which could quicken any maid's pulse, she thought. Even his long, thick lashes were not feminine. Nothing about him was anything but masculine; perhaps it was this which made him so irresistible to her.

As with the first sea voyage she soon lost track of time, sometimes sleeping during the day or sitting on deck studying the stars at night. One morning she awoke in the darkness to find the ship strangely peaceful and she rose, quickly dressing. She found her way to the deck where the first morning light appeared on the horizon. No wind filled the sail, and a shiver ran down her spine as she noticed the exceedingly quiet and glassy surface of the water.

"Is it not too cool for ye here, milady?" a rusty voice queried, and she turned to find herself looking into Goudwin's weathered face.

"Nay, I only shiver because it is so quiet here. Not even the seabirds are screaming their usual calls. I cannot recall seeing the sea like this before."

"Yea, 'tis so, miss. I fear we will be in for some wind."

"But it is so still and quiet."

"Look yonder to the east, Bekah. Only ye are brighter than the dawn."

She looked upon the eastern horizon, where a deep red glow began to fill the heavens. It came slowly at first, growing deeper and with a bloodier glow than she had ever seen before. "It is beautiful," she breathed.

"Not to me, lady. Not to me."

"Bekah, you are up early," Kenric said, admiring her golden hair which caught the lights of the red sky.

"I could not sleep. It is so quiet that it haunts me. Indeed, I swear I have never seen the sea in such a strange manner."

"You do not worry again, do you? Goudwin here keeps a tight ship and we shall weather any storm."

"Storm?" she echoed. " 'Tis hard to believe. It is so quiet, and there is no sign of storm on the horizon."

"Yea, the cap'n is right; I smell a storm, though ye need not worry," Goudwin said, binding together the last length of a coiled rope. "The sea is a strange woman. One minute she is calmly deceptive, and the next—!" He shrugged his shoulders.

Kenric, resting his hands on Bekah's shoulders, looked down at the young woman who had come to be so important to him. He reined in his usually incautious nature, concluding that he would not risk this most precious cargo.

"Turn the bow and head towards land, Goudwin. We will not outrun the storm, I am sure, but if we reach land soon enough perhaps we can weather it there. Bekah, you look pale," he said, watching his orders being given by Goudwin. "I thought you were faring better this voyage. Do not tell me you are afraid of a storm?"

"Nay," she said, as he pulled her into an embrace. He held her, and it was a comfort, but still she sensed that strange foreboding. She felt haunted, as she had the day on the shore before they left Jarlshof.

A slight wind arose, ruffling the sail and almost imperceptibly stirring the water about the ship. Kenric guided her below and into their chamber, laying her upon the thick pelts.

"It is still early and you could use rest after our late hours last night," he grinned, and she smiled at the memory of their lovemaking. She couldn't sleep, though, the foreboding still upon her like a mist reluctant to leave. She picked up some of her needlework, working the blue

152

thread through the white fabric to make some flowers. Kenric brought down some cheese and bread and slices of raw salted potato, eating in silence with her before slipping back on board.

After the repast she became sleepy. She seemed to sleep more and more now that she carried the baby. She stretched drowsily on the warm pelts, pulling the quilt about her. She thought of Kenric and smiled to herself, the memory of him still in her mind as the rocking of the ship lulled her into a light slumber.

She was troubled by an unpleasant dream in which shadows slowly danced about her, and there were strange, half-chanting voices, voices that sobbed and moaned and rose to a shrill cry. She jerked suddenly awake, her eyes wide with fright as the moaning banshee still haunted her. With a sigh she lay back, shutting her eyes. It was only the wind, shrouding the ship, trying to enter through any crack or hole. In time the craft began to move violently, its boards creaking and groaning, waves beating against the sides.

Time passed, and no longer could she sleep, for the ship rocked and swayed brutally, the forces of the sea beating at the outside to gain entrance. Finally she couldn't stand it, and she grabbed Kenric's large cloak and pulled it about her. She tried to ascend the ladder, but with the pitching of the boat it was difficult. She succeeded after three tries, finally making it onto the deck. The ship rocked about on the waves as if it were only a leaf riding on the wind. The sky had blackened to darkness like that of midnight, roiling blue-black clouds threatening overhead. Spray stung her face; its salty smell assaulted her nose.

The clouds broke open, sending spears of rain down upon her and making the deck slippery. As in a horrid, frightening dream, seconds crept by, the wind at a roaring pitch, deafening her. What had once been a frightening shadow had turned into a very real blood-seeking ocean. A black ocean.

The cloak which had first offered protection had now become drenched in the torrent, trapping her and making it impossible to move. With shaking fingers she struggled with the clasp, finally forcing the slippery metal apart. The sodden cape fell from her, granting her more freedom, but the sharp needles of rain nearly burned her skin. She hardly felt it at all now, and her eyes tried to focus through the rain, her fear intense.

Kenric! she thought wildly; she must find Kenric! The ship seemed to wrench itself from beneath her feet, several times making her crawl on her hands and knees until she found a rope she could hold on to. She was drenched and cold, but this discomfort was nothing to the panic she felt rising within her. She tried to scream his name, yet the wind whipped the words away as if they'd never been spoken. A streak of lightning hit the water far off in the distance, sizzling and cracking into the water. The thunder was deafening above the cold force of the waves crashing about them and washing over the deck.

One crewman was swept overboard by the force of a wave, another crushed beneath a fallen timber, his blood reddening the deck only momentarily before being washed away. Bekah froze, the horror of what she saw making her unable to move.

Then Kenric was there, suddenly by her side, holding tightly to her as the rain began to pour down on them in a renewed burst of stinging needles. She must tell him that she carried his child! She didn't know why it was important now, even as their very lives were at stake.

"I carry your child!" she screamed, but her words were swept away from her, and a horrid lurching of the ship threw them apart. She grabbed a rope, holding on to it tightly, even as it burned her fingers and blistered her hands.

"Kenric!" she screamed again, watching him struggle against the violence of the storm to reach her. The ship's mast cracked, sending splinters of wood flying everywhere. A piece cut into the flesh just above Kenric's left eye, crimson blood spurting from the wound. She watched in horror as one of the falling timbers crashed into Kenric, flipping him over the edge and into the engulfing waters. She did not see him rise again. She screamed his name in terror and pain, her hands frozen to the rope. The ship seemed as if it were retching and shuddering, giving a

154

final shrieking sob as a bolt of lightning struck its timbers. She felt herself thrust into the relative calm of icy waters. Down she was going, rising now for air which cut into her lungs. She was able to grab on to a piece of timber which struck her, bruising her side, and she fought for each breath.

Goudwin struggled against the gagging salt water, his wiry frame working to keep afloat. The ship was going down, all his doubts about the new craft proven. He knew he was going to die, and he felt quite calm in the knowledge, hoping to cling to this meager thread of life for as long as possible. A large piece of mast floated near, and he grabbed hold, his bleary vision focusing on a figure clinging limply to it. The face looked up, and happily he saw that it was his beloved Erilla, just as she had been all those years ago. As he looked at her his vision cleared, and instead he saw Bekah. It was as if the two were one, and he thought sadly that she carried a baby, she herself a child. He had been helpless those many years ago to save Erilla and their son, but he was not so helpless now. He worked his way around the mast, coming near her just as her hands slipped away and she slid into the watery blackness. He grabbed her arm, buoying her back up as she gasped for breath, the salty air rasping in her throat and lungs. His hands and arms, sinewy with the strength of years of pulling ropes, secured her tightly about the waist, holding them both to the mast.

She was barely aware of clutching hands giving her support. The numbing cold left no thought in her brain except the primitive fight for breath.

She was half-concious, yet in the back of her mind was a tiny thread of desperation urging her on. Oh, Kenric! her mind cried again and again, and then, Our baby!

"Please, dear God," she prayed aloud, sobbing. "Save Kenric and our baby!"

The icy wind surrounded her. Her fingers around the timber were scraped raw. The victorious ocean would not relent, even stealing Kenric's ring from her finger. The rain abated some, the roiling water still thrusting them about. Subdued slightly, the ocean still had little capacity

155

for mercy, leaving the question of life or death hanging unanswered. Was there any chance to survive this violence and fury? she wondered before sliding into unconsciousness.

The morning dawn would tell.

PART III
WESSEX

THE OCEAN WAVES CAUGHT THE GRAY OVER-cast of early morning sky, crashing on the hard sand to dissolve in lacy foam. The hills of coastal Northumbria were carpeted in the heather that gave the landscape a violet cast, the harsh shoreline coldly rugged yet beautiful. Overhead the sky was like watered silk of a pearly gray hue and gulls of darker gray spiraled above Bekah's head.

She pulled her shawl tighter about her, standing and looking out to sea as she had a hundred times before in the many months she had stayed here. Time had elapsed, time that had found her cast upon the debris-strewn shore in the grasp of death. She had come very close to dying before Desmond had found her and carried her to the manor. Lady Devona, a kindly lady who had lost her daughter, took Bekah in to try to bring her back to life. It had been a difficult struggle, for she had been very ill, and when she awakened she had remembered little.

Bekah still recalled with pain Kenric's death. This same sea that she now stared at had taken him from her, and she cursed it. She herself had survived by some strange twist of fate that had cast her on the shore where the young servant Desmond had discovered her. But although the manor's serfs had searched the coastline for miles, the only other body found was that of old Goudwin who had helped save her life. Bekah did not even have the small comfort of seeing Kenric interred.

At first she had nearly lost her mind with grief, but Lady Devona had guided her through the awful time, and although she felt the tinge of continual sorrow there was one bright spot in her life. That was her tiny, black-haired baby girl. Kendra Ember had been born under the helping hand of the manor's lady, and she had caught them all in her spell. With her mother's bright blue eyes and her father's black crown, she filled the ache in Bekah's breast.

Barely two months in age now, she had brought Bekah comfort in the mothering that was required of her. Though Ember was a continual reminder of her father, to Bekah she was a balm to ease the hurt in her heart.

The pain had been terrible. How many times had Bekah cried out for him, had awful dreams of his being taken from her by the sea? It was a rending of her soul, her deepest inner self, and she knew she would never be the same. At first she had lain in the tight hold of death, waiting gratefully for its claim. But that tiny seed, planted deep inside her, was the last of Kenric. She loved him still and could not let this part of him die. For this one reason she had lived, to nurture the child, their daughter. But she had become a shell, hollow in its empty ache. She had learned to love Kenric, then she had lost him, her daughter the only tie left between them. Would she ever love again? She could not imagine it. She knew that she must forget the past, but that there could never be forgetting. How often she had cursed the cruel fate that had separated her and the child from their Anglian warrior.

After the hollow aching had ebbed, she had sought for survival. By starting at dawn and working until dark, she had managed that. But there was no joy in her life, only the comfort that numbness brings after the pain of a terrible wound.

She had grown comfortable with these people in the many months that she had lived in this rugged countryside. The folk were simple, living about and in the manorhouse in a fashion that made life easy. She worked with them, weaving a piece of bright plaid on the loom, helping in the herb garden or with the sewing. Her life had become a somber tapestry of common routine, yet that was what had helped her keep her sanity. And there were friends in Northumbria. Lady Devona was a kind and concerned woman; Alodie, Desmond's sister, was a sisterly friend. And Desmond felt nothing but concern for her. She frowned a bit as she thought of him. Desmond was in love with her, but there was no love in her heart for him. Friendship, yea; concern, indeed! But having known Kenric, no mere youth could take her heart. Desmond had offered to wed her, to give her child his name, but she had refused as gently as possible. There had been only one for her, and she would have been content to go on with his memory wrapped about her and to raise their child in this simple country place. But once again fate had intervened.

Her heart hardened as she thought of Lord Radburn. She would curse the vile rogue until the end! He was the lord who owned a great deal of the lands hereabout, and he came every two years to collect his duties from the manor. Bekah had been upstairs when he had arrived, and the commotion had been great at his coming, with everything in an uproar. There had been a small troop of soldiers with him, clad in dark chausses. Some had cast off their weapons and mail, others had thrown themselves down on benches or straw. They had quenched their thirst with ale, and the strong odor had filled the manor.

Bekah had come downstairs to see the excitement, and the noise had come to a halt when the soldiers took in her appearance. Though she was clothed in a simple frock of gray wool run through with orange threads, her hair pulled back severely, nonetheless her beauty had struck them. It had been at that exact moment that the doors had flung open and Lord Radburn had strode in.

He was richly dressed, wearing an embroidered mantle of royal blue that was cast up over his shoulder. He had been speaking to Lady Devona. "Yea, I can see that the land is not doing as well this year. I will ride out to inspect, but if it has done too poorly to pay the taxes, then my trip shall hardly have been worth the effort and expense."

He had black hair and a sharply pointed beard. Bekah had watched as he cast off his mantle and sank into the comfort of Lady Devona's chair. There was something striking about the man, yet it was more in his carriage than in his face, which bore a scar on the left cheek. His eyes were long and narrow, resembling those of a fox, his nose strongly dominant. There was something about his trenchant appearance that Bekah did not like. It would be best to stay out from under the spread of this bird of prey's wing, she decided. As she had turned to depart, his piercing eyes lighted on her.

"Hold!" his voice had struck out, catching her before she

161

could leave. "Why, Devona, what maid is this? Why have you kept such fairness from our presence?"

He had stepped forward to Bekah and lifted her chin up with the crook of his finger. "What is your name?"

"Bekah," she had replied.

He had smiled, inviting her to join him for dinner. She had done so reluctantly and had not enjoyed his company. He had stayed for a few days, and she had been relieved when he was ready to take leave—until he told her of his plans to take her with him.

At first she had thought it some peculiar jest, but there was no glint of humor in the noble's eye. And suddenly she had found that there was nowhere to turn, no place to hide, for this man was law in Northumbria, and despite Lady Devona's pleas he intended to take Bekah back with him to Wessex. She had been horrified, and had told him that, should he try to lay one hand on her, she would destroy herself. To her amazement he had laughed.

"Fear not for your virtue! I do not want your flesh."

"Then why should you wish to take me from these people? I do not understand your motives!"

"I am a man of business, and my taxes here have been poor. I take you as a means of payment, for you are of value to me."

"But I have no wealth!"

"Wealth more than you know! Have you not seen your reflection? Yours is a face that could win a fortune. Men have traded their souls, or their inheritances, for such beauty as yours. The courts of Wessex, and not this forsaken land, are the place for your loveliness. Though I have no interest in men's souls, their fortunes intrigue me. And you shall be my means of gaining them."

She had been impassioned, pleading for her own release, but it had been of no use. The lord was determined. It was then that he had discovered her child. He had instructed Lady Devona to keep it, for it would be an encumbrance to him.

Bekah had become distraught. No words could persuade the demon until she stood with knifepoint to her breast. She had threatened to use the blade unless she be allowed to keep the child. Lord Radburn had not taken her seriously until the point had drawn blood, the crimson circle spreading on her gown. He had acquiesced upon her word to go willingly with him.

She turned now, and went to the manor to collect her things. After embracing Lady Devona and Alodie, she wrapped her tiny baby in her blanket before leaving. They went to the ship that rocked gently on the incoming waves, and she and her infant were carried aboard. As the ship drifted out to sea, she looked back at the craggy shoreline that spoke of the last of her memories of Kenric. She felt terribly alone.

She took Ember below to their small room. The baby grew fussy and Bekah unbuttoned her frock, watching as the child eagerly sought her breast. She stroked the silky black down as the baby nursed until slumber finally overcame her, and then Bekah laid her on some soft blankets, tucking the baby's quilt about her.

This journey at least contained neither passion nor adventure, for Radburn, true to his word, did not seek to use her for himself, and the voyage was mild. Bekah's greatest worry was what would become of her and Ember. What fate awaited her in Wessex?

"Will fate never let me be my own mistress?" she sighed, lying down beside her baby, Ember.

The days were long, and time crept by slowly. Lord Radburn, whom Bekah had feared, was not even to be seen, and her meals were brought in by the servant Quill. Bekah tried to be unobtrusive, keeping to herself and making sure that Ember's cry was not a disturbance, for if the child grew burdensome in any way she felt there would be nothing to stop cruel Radburn from tossing her into the sea. Time seemed like an endless ribbon as they sailed past Danelaw and around the isle to Wessex.

The thought of landing here brought a surge of pain to Bekah, for it was here that Kenric had lived, and here that they were to have been wed. She consoled herself that there would be some comfort in seeing the land of which Kenric had spoken so fondly, and which was in the wide area under King Alfred's rule. This land was rightfully Kendra Ember's inheritance.

With these thoughts in mind, Bekah awoke one morning

aware of a soft lapping of waves rather than the usual tossing. She dressed hurriedly in a plain brown frock, then
dressed Ember, and had barely finished when her door was
flung open and Quill announced that they would be eating
ashore. Bekah eagerly ascended the ladder, thrilled that
she could once again feel the morning sunlight and see a
blue sky. It was warmer here than at Devona's manor, and
she cast off her cloak, letting the warm sun rays fall upon
herself and the baby.

She was helped ashore and led to a cottage of good size
that was clean and orderly. The hearth was cold this morning, since the spring weather brought an unusually pleasant sky. The furnishings were stark and few, the main
piece being a long table with benches on either side. Windows, once shuttered, were cast open to allow the sunlight
to enter. Here Bekah enjoyed a good breakfast of fruits and
a warm pot pie, even though she was forced to share company with the detested Radburn. An elderly couple, showing excessive respect for this honored guest, flitted around
Radburn and his men like two nervous hummingbirds. Bekah rightly assumed that they were the proprietors of this
inn, observing that other people, not of Radburn's ship,
were eating there as well.

She ate in silence, barely answering Radburn's questions and avoiding the polite conversation. As he gazed at
the graceful girl beside him, he thought that should she
not prove useful as he had planned, then he certainly
would not mind keeping her for himself. However, that
was neither here nor now, and since she seemed reluctant
to converse, he finished his meal in silence, chastising
himself for his moment's weakness. It was best not to become enamored of the wench, lest she become like a tick
beneath the skin, impossible to be rid of without getting
burned.

Since she was the object of many curious gazes, Bekah
was relieved to depart. She was aware of her things being
placed securely upon a pack horse, and realized that she
would be traveling on horseback. This excited her, for she
felt happy to be on horseback again, reveling in this freedom. Quill assured her that the horse was a good-tempered
creature which had been chosen especially for her. Indeed

the beast did look safe enough, and Bekah smiled inwardly to herself as she thought of the many rides she had taken with Kenric. They mounted their steeds, and Bekah was grateful that the day was warm and pleasant. Bekah bound Ember tightly to her with her shawl, knowing that the steady rhythm of the horse and the combined warmth and beating of her own breast would lull the baby into sleeping most of the day. The arrangement was also convenient for nursing and kept her baby safe while it freed her own hands.

The sky was bright periwinkle, and the day smelled of new blossoms and honeysuckle. The sun felt wonderful upon them. Bekah's hair seemed like spun sunlight, capturing the admiring glances of Lord Radburn's men. They traveled past fields of wild poppies and yellow gorse, and other fields where yellow-green wheat appeared as smooth as velvet from afar. After several hours they stopped and rested. All too soon, however, she was again told to mount the gentle steed and move along.

They traveled past thatched crofter's cottages with their sloping yellow roofs so near the ground and two strange chimneys. On they went, stopping at noon for a slight repast, then again traveling on as sunlight flitted across the green meadows. They passed through moors and then farmlands and forests.

Just as Bekah felt their travels would never end, a shout went up and they hurried their pace through a light forest filled with colorful pheasant and quail. As they ascended one last hill, the castle came into view and nearly took her breath away. It was the castle called Briarwood.

Surrounded by a natural fortress of blue water, the castle's jagged towers thrust skyward. It was constructed of weathered wood and stone, with a high stone wall surrounding it. Upon the wall grew a wild profusion of an ebony thistle with long, sharp thorns, which served as a beautiful, natural protective shield. The keep was in a large courtyard, guarded by small lookout towers in each of the corners.

It was certainly not one of the greater castles on the isle, but to Bekah, who noted the rough castle stones overgrown by deep green moss and black briars and the evening sun glinting off the battlements, it was beautiful. Wild swans swam on the clear blue-green water. Goldenrod, lilacs and roses grew in profusion down the mossy banks. It was all as Bekah would have thought it to be, all as her mother and Kenric had described their homeland. Her heart throbbed with excitement, even in her weary state, and she watched as Radburn slowed his horse until it was even with her own.

"We are approaching our destination now. This is Briarwood Castle, so named because of the black briar which grows so protectively about the walls."

She nodded at this bit of information. Radburn seemed proud of the game-rich estates, and she found herself amazed that he could be connected with any place so beautiful. She thought of Kenric, wondering if Kartney Castle was similar to Briarwood.

It was still a quarter hour more before they reached the entrance, where there was a great commotion in which Bekah felt lost. Quill touched her elbow, guiding her unnoticed through the excitement to a flight of circular stairs. They went up these, then through a narrow corridor. She soon found herself in a small chamber and was able to lay the baby on a comfortable little cot. Ember, finally able to stretch out, almost instantly quieted her fussing and slept. After Quill's departure Bekah, too, had barely removed her cloak and dress before collapsing upon her own bed. Every part of her ached, and her back felt nearly broken. The comfort of the bed felt so wonderful that she was asleep before she had even finished murmuring a thankful prayer.

Morning light, softly pale, entered the dark chamber, edging things with fuzzy lace and dancing on Bekah's face. She stretched and yawned, feeling gloriously refreshed. It was Ember's sweet, fussy sounds that had awakened her, and she realized that they had both slept late.

She changed the baby, then snuggled her close as Ember searched hungrily for the warm milk. Bekah sang softly to her daughter, who grasped her mother's shift in her little hand, as if afraid to lose her. "Little Kendra, do you think I should lose you, or let anyone harm you? Nay, sweet Ember, I should never let that happen," Bekah murmured. She glanced around the chamber. It was square, with a stone floor and a heavy wooden door. Opposite her was a large window which in winter would be tightly shuttered but which now stood open to reveal a small court which contained a garden surrounded by a high stone wall. This Bekah hoped to view better when she finished with Ember. The only thing to break the severity of her room was a heavy brown and ecru tapestry which covered some inner passageway. It depicted a dull landscape and was dusty with age.

As she was studying the tapestry she noticed it move and instinctively covered herself. From behind it stepped a small tawny-haired boy. He was followed by an even smaller boy and she guessed their ages to be three and two. They shyly peered at her and she smiled at them. As they tiptoed forward, in rushed a young woman, hastily shooing them out.

"I am most sorry," she apologized. "I can hardly keep up with my boys!"

"Are they yours? I should never have guessed, for you look too young to be their mother." Bekah was quite right, for the girl was even more slender than herself. Her large green eyes, set in a perfect oval face framed by a wild mane of chestnut-colored hair, gave her an innocent air. This was checked only by the lively sparkle in her eyes.

"Well, I must confess, I am not terribly old," she replied. "Jaycen, my elder, was born when I was only sixteen, and Chad thirteen months later. How old is your baby?"

"She will be almost three months. Her name is Ember, and I am Bekah."

"I am Pamela," she smiled, "and I am in the next room with my two boys. I stay here part-time and serve Lady Mildred, and my husband is the gamekeeper. Tell me, are you hungry? Good, come have breakfast with me. Lay your baby down. She certainly is petite, and so darling!" Pamela chattered idly as Bekah quickly dressed, smiling to herself at this new, enjoyable friendship. Suddenly she realized how lonely she had been since she had left Lady Devona's manor. She liked Pamela immediately, and felt as if they had always been friends. It was so unusual, yet a

167

natural friendship. Bekah felt no fear, as she often had with others, that her words would be judged critically. With Pamela there was a gentle acceptance, as if she kept only those important words Bekah spoke, casting the unnecessary chaff to the wind.

As they ate fruits and bread, watching the two boys play, they talked. Bekah learned much about Pamela, who was wildly in love with her husband Charles and gaily told about their courtship. Pamela's story swept Bekah off into another world until she actually found herself laughing. Charles, it seemed, was a handsome, shy man with curling blond hair who had fallen in love with his wife at a tender age. They had been wed early and now lived in a pleasant little cottage in the woods, not far from the castle. When Charles was off about other work, Pamela and her sons stayed within the castle as protection, her work bringing in extra goods such as cloth, spices, salt or leather. Pamela's husband had the important task of scouting game for the castle within Briarwood's realm and protecting the hunter's prey from poachers.

As the two women talked, with interruptions made only by their children, Bekah began to feel more at ease than she would have had she been pressured by questions. She learned much from Pamela's open discussions and listened earnestly to the friendly gossip.

Lady Mildred, Bekah learned, was Lord Radburn's sister, and she had gone to celebrate her brother's homecoming. However, Bekah was surprised to hear that Radburn was not lord of the castle, but actually a guest and cousin to Lord Garth, the castle's baron.

"The way he spoke, I assumed that Briarwood was his!"

"I have no doubt that he wishes greatly that it were, but he has little claim to it, and he is here only at the generosity of Lord Garth, who is a kindly gentleman. Everyone here is fond of him."

She learned that Radburn's sister, Lady Mildred, was also a guest of Lord Garth's. Pamela hastily informed Bekah that she was a shrewish woman who was difficult to get along with. Lady Mildred, it appeared, was one of those women determined to keep a youthful appearance despite the fact that she would be much more becoming if she would accept the attractive garment of mature womanhood. As clearly as Bekah could understand, she herself was to be only one more servant here to wait upon Lady Mildred. However, the afternoon passed undisturbed, with Ember napping most of the day. After a light evening meal Bekah retired before dark, finding that the journey of the previous day had tired her.

She awoke early the next morning, looking much prettier now that the dark shadows beneath her eyes were gone. Lady Mildred had returned late the night before and had again departed. Bekah was in no hurry to meet the castle's mistress, and was prepared to enjoy one more day of freedom with her new friend. She had learned that since Lord Garth's wife was long ago dead, and he had not remarried, Lady Mildred acted as mistress of the castle. Especially since she and her brother had no castle of their own, it had been a friendly gesture by Lord Garth.

This second day of Bekah's stay at the castle was much the same as the first, except that she helped Pamela make up Mildred's large bed and clean the dust from the elegantly carved furniture. Bekah began to feel akin to Pamela in a way she'd felt toward only one other—her mother, Mary. She confessed this to her new friend.

"Yea, indeed, it is truthfully strange. It seems as if I have known you before, and I never have talked so freely with anyone, except my own mother, who lives not far from here. Perhaps it is because I have longed so dearly for a friend. There are even things which one cannot always discuss with a mother. However, though I spent most of yesterday telling you about my own history, I feel you have talked very little about yourself. Do you realize that I know nothing but your name?" She smiled.

"If you are interested," Bekah said slowly, "I will tell you of my past, for it is a strange one which I have confided to only one other. My mother was a Saxon, and her name was Mary. When she was a young girl, exceedingly fair and light-spirited, she lived in a small coastal village. However, it was during a time when there were many raids by the Norsemen, and her people were terrified by the barbarians. She told me often how they would hide in the hills at warnings of their attacks. One day she was roaming through the forest near her home, singing softly to herself as she picked wild flowers for her mother and father. She had a lovely voice, and often she would sing to me. As she was walking back, she was spied by a band of Vikings who by force took her with them aboard their sea vessel. They ran into stormy weather and blamed her presence for their troubles. They were about to offer her as a sacrifice to the sea god when Lars, my father, stopped them. He was very much in love with her, and took her as his woman, defying the others and staving off their challenges. He was a very brave warrior, his strength holding the others in awe. He made my mother a special home, and soon afterwards I was born in Norseland. My mother missed her home and family very much and often told me about them. How I longed to come here—to the wonderful, enchanted land I had dreamed of seeing since childhood!" She shook her head sadly. "However, I did not foresee my dreams being realized in the manner in which they were."

"How did you come here then?" Pamela asked, deeply fascinated.

"Well, it is an incredible tale, even to myself. After my mother died, I was terribly unhappy, and missed her warmth and tender love. She was so frail and delicate that when she came down with a fever she was easily taken. My father remarried a woman who resented and hated me because she was very unlike my mother, whom my father still loved."

"Why did your father marry her then?"

Bekah sighed. "I do not know exactly, for I thought her dull and unattractive in both manner and appearance. She owned a great lot of land and was very wealthy, however, and perhaps that was an attraction for him.

"She had a son, much like his mother in appearance, who would have forced me to wed him had I stayed there. He had small eyes, like a ferret, and stiff yellow hair. He was domineering and coarse, and I disliked him. It was all a hostile circle, for Helg hated me and Jorgen was determined he and I should marry. One day Helg beat me with a rod, and my father caught her. How clearly I remember that day! He told me to go for a walk, and I did so, not real-

170

izing that it would be the last time I laid eyes on my father."

"You never saw him again? What happened?"

"I walked down to the beach happy to be free for a while. There was a secret cove I loved that was sheltered on either side by cliffs. It was a hot day, and I bathed in the tidal pools there. Suddenly I looked up to see a man standing over me. He was as dark and as wicked-looking as Satan himself. He was handsomely terrifying, and at first I hardly believed him to be real at all." She paused, remembering the moment clearly.

"And you without one thread of clothing?" Pamela cried in shocked amazement.

Bekah nodded. "I have never felt such gripping fear. I tried desperately to escape him, but it was useless! He was very strong, and then I fainted. He took me against my will. I remember that it began to rain, and he took me up into the cliff where there was a small cave behind a ledge. I can still see the storm raging without and hear the waves crashing beneath us. I was so afraid of him." -

"How could he have done that to you? It fills me with pain to even think of it!"

"Do not condemn him yet, Pamela, until you have heard the entire tale."

"Do not tell me that you feel no anger for what he did! No woman could be that forgiving."

"I assure you that I hated him. He would not even allow me freedom, and took me with him on his ship back to Jarlshof. I fought him, but to little avail, and he took me to his manor."

"In Jarlshof? Is that not a northernmost isle?"

"Yea, craggy and beautiful. He took me to live in his manor, and in time my hate waned. It is difficult to tell you of Kenric, for he was a hard man, even upon himself. He came to hate himself for what he had done to me as he came to love me. He protected me and had the greatest patience and tenderness for me, bearing many rebukes and insults. He repented of his cruel acts and eventually pulled me into his realm of love. Finally I found myself fighting not only his love but my own also, and then, as truly in-

171

credible as it may seem, we fell in love. If only you could have known Kenric, perhaps you could understand."

"Where is this Kenric now, if he cared so greatly about you?" Pamela asked skeptically.

Bekah was quiet for a while, then said, "He is dead, Pamela. We left Jarlshof for his home, Kartney Castle, here in Wessex. There was a terrible storm, and I saw him die before my eyes, cast into those freezing depths by a jagged timber. I never had the chance to tell him of our child, Kendra Ember; he did not know that I carried his baby."

Pamela blinked back a mist of stinging tears, turning away. Finally she asked, "What of you, Bekah?"

"I, too, was cast into the ocean, then thrown upon the shore. I was found by a servant from a nearby manor, where they cared for me until I was well. Lady Devona loved me and helped me throughout my confinement and the birth of my baby. The pain I felt over the loss of Kenric eventually abated a little in the joy of our daughter.

"Then Radburn came," Bekah said, her voice hardening. "He decided to take me with him, for what reason I am still uncertain. He threatened to make me leave Ember, and I held a knife at my breast and told him I should kill myself if he made me leave her. He let me keep her then only if I promised to come peacefully with him. And that is how I came to be here."

"I have never heard a more tragic tale than yours, Bekah! Oh, if I were a man I would thrash that Radburn! He is so vile!"

"He is worse than most I have met, for his passion is greed, his heart frozen. How deceptive his smiling ways and polite words are."

" 'Tis so, but you must speak only graciously about him here. Only we will know the truth."

Bekah nodded. "Yea, he is a powerful man, and I do not wish to anger him. The past needs to be put behind me now."

"You can trust me to keep your story secret in my heart, for I understand you as much as if I had lived through it myself," Pamela said, blinking back the annoying mist of tears.

Pamela asked many questions which Bekah answered,

until every scene in Bekah's past was recalled. Pamela was so receptive that it was an easing for Bekah to tell the depths of her feelings to her, in a way she had never been able to with Devona or Alodie. The bond of friendship was firmly forged, and Pamela vowed to herself that a day would not go by that she would not remember her new friend in her prayers.

They sat in the garden, the stone wall moss-covered in the darkened corners where shadows often fell. Fruit trees hung their graceful limbs over the wall, their emerald leaves cupping various blossoms of pink or white. Clover and moss covered some of the spongy grounds, and rose bushes grew about the walls. Some of the ground was covered by well-trodden stones between which violets and clover pushed through, widening the cracks. There were flowers starting to bud: iris, morning glory, hyacinth, tulip and daisy. Purple and gold pansies raised their velvet faces here and there among the grounds, as did fluffy yellow dandelions. They were enjoying the warmth of sunlight on a patch of clover, when a pebble clattered to the ground, breaking the solitude of the moment. Pamela jumped up with excitement.

"My husband has come, and if I hurry I can be with him for a short while!"

"But how will you get out? The wall is too high to scale."

"I will show you, and then you will have the same freedom as I—only do not let Mildred see you!"

"Very well," Bekah smiled. "I will watch your boys and account for you should Lady Mildred return."

Pamela smiled in thanks, and Bekah watched as she hurried to a corner of the wall which was thickly overgrown with vines. Pamela brushed these aside, uncovering an old wooden door which Bekah had never noticed before. It was easily unlatched and swung open. Pamela quickly disappeared through it.

Bekah laughed softly to herself, then looked in on the trio of children, all in various poses of sleep. Ember stirred once but fell back into slumber, and as Bekah studied the peaceful face crowned in blackness that reminded her of Kenric's own black hair, her heart filled with pleasure and love for her daughter. That sweet, sleeping baby with dimpled hands quietly curled in sleep, whose lips uttered a sleeping sigh, filled her also with pride.

Kenric would have been well pleased had he been able to see their lovely child.

An hour passed slowly as Bekah waited, and finally Pamela returned with shining eyes and bright color in her cheeks and lips.

"Mildred has not returned?" she questioned, glancing around.

"Nay, I have yet to meet her."

"It will be soon enough," Pamela sighed in relief as she put away her shawl and cap. "Thank you for watching the boys. It was so good to see my husband and spend time alone with him. Soon we will move into our cottage permanently, and I will not need to spend so much time here. His job is an important one, but I miss him during his time away from us. I can hardly wait until he can spend more time home each night."

Pamela had returned none too soon, for Lady Mildred came into the private chambers. She had barely stepped into her wing of the castle when she began demanding a cool drink of water and that her heavy formal dress be removed. She would do nothing for herself but stood in the center of her elegant room demanding care, for she was tired and the day had been long. Mildred was older than she pretended, and there was much resemblance to her brother, Lord Radburn. Unfortunately, the sharp, narrow features which he wore so elegantly were too harsh for a woman's face. However, while her brother's hair was black, Lady Mildred's was red and worn braided about her head. She was taller than either Pamela or Bekah, her posture as rigid and as queenly as she could make it. Bekah fetched her a lightweight gown, under Pamela's direction, and watched as her friend combed out the fine red hair. Mildred spoke harshly to Pamela for catching a snarl in the comb, but Bekah realized that although she scolded Pamela she actually liked her, for no one disliked the young mother.

Mildred's glance, however, fell sharply upon Bekah, as if noticing her for the first time. "Who is this?"

"This is Bekah, milady," Pamela said, putting the brush and comb away.

"Oh? Is this the girl that my brother brought from Northumbria to serve as a handmaiden here?" Without waiting for a reply she continued, "My brother sometimes is possessed by foolish notions. Bringing you here is one of them. Do as you are told, and remember that there is no room in our castle for idleness. You will do well to learn from Pamela that laziness is a scourge and will be punished. Tomorrow she will show you the clothing that I need washed and how to do it with care. Also, this floor needs sweeping. Pamela will show you where the reeds are and how it is to be done. Can you use a needle?"

"Yes, ma'am."

"Address me as milady, or Lady Mildred, from now on. Here, mend this by tonight, and take care to keep your stitches small." She tossed a light brocade scarf of silvery blue at Bekah. "That is all for tonight. I have a painful headache and desire a rest. You are dismissed for now. Oh, and Pamela, try to keep your children quiet. This is no place for children."

With that she lay down upon the soft comfort of her bed, dismissing Bekah with a scornful glance and Pamela with a wave of her hand. Pamela raised her eyebrows meaningfully, and Bekah nodded, fully aware that her friend had been too kind in her description of the acting mistress of Briarwood.

Pamela fetched Bekah a needle and thread, and Bekah carefully mended a hole in the scarf, hoping that Mildred would not judge her needlework too harshly. The light-heartedness that Bekah and Pamela had felt before was now shadowed by Mildred's presence. Once her mending was done and she was assured that Lady Mildred was fully retired, Bekah took the opportunity to don a cloak and escape through the hidden door for a short evening walk, leaving Ember in Pamela's care.

The fading summer light danced through the forest, and as Bekah strolled about she began to lose the mounting tension which had so painfully controlled her throughout this last fortnight. It was so beautifully pleasant, that glorious time of new, budding summer, barely out of its youth of springtime. If she could escape for these times by herself, and continue in Pamela's friendship, and indulge her baby's love, then life would be tolerable, despite Mildred's presence. Bekah returned for the night, her heart feeling much less oppressed, and a slight feeling of optimism about her.

Three days passed, uneventfully, with little change except for Bekah's total loss of optimism. Lady Mildred's antagonism toward her had increased, and she spent much of her time cleaning, mending and caring for the mistress's things. She had spent most of her waking hours this day sewing a lovely gold and white kirtle. She had kept her stitches small, her work some of the finest Pamela had ever seen, and yet Mildred found fault. It was too small in the waist, and puckered, and the hem was not wide enough. And atop that, she criticized not only Bekah's efforts but her appearance. Lady Mildred felt it was a sin to wear one's hair loose about the shoulders and made Bekah bind her tresses tightly back. Once she even insisted that Bekah wipe the rouge from her lips, which was impossible, for Bekah wore none, unlike Mildred. It was quite unfitting for a serving maid to look in appearance as the queen of the castle was privileged to.

Bekah learned that Lady Mildred had two other handmaidens who served her when they were not involved in weaving or sewing in other parts of the castle. They were older than Pamela and Bekah, but kindly and friendly to both. They were sisters, Hadlene and Ellena, and though they were respectful of their mistress, it was apparent that they did not like her.

Mildred, upon discovering Bekah's baby, openly displayed her shock. She declared that Ember must be declared a child of sin, even ridiculing the child's name. She felt it her duty, she explained to Hadlene and Ellena, to chastise Bekah for her wicked past. Little did Mildred realize that her harsh judgment of Bekah only made the sisters form a fiercer friendship for the new serving maid.

Several times Bekah had been very close to tears, yet Pamela had given her courage and taken her part as much as she dared. "Do not let the old shrew bother you," she whispered once. "She is only jealous because of her long face and sharp nose."

Bekah smiled weakly at this, trying not to disappoint Pamela by feeling sorry for herself. It was surprising how soon she grew accustomed to the rebukes, ignoring the sharp pricks of pain. Ellena came forward quietly, telling Bekah that Ember was a lovely baby, while Hadlene brought her a special sugarloaf from the kitchen once. Perhaps there was reason to feel sorry for Lady Mildred, who never experienced care or concern from others, driving away with her sharp tongue every loyalty she might have possessed.

Early afternoon on the third day after her return, Lady Mildred was getting ready to go riding in a quail hunt. She wore a lovely outfit of dark green velvet, a nice complement to her red hair. Lord Marchis had come for a brief stay at the manor, and Mildred fancied he had an affection for her.

Pamela was painstakingly trying to build a lovely structure of braids, but Mildred's straight, fine hair was giving her difficulty. Nothing Pamela could do was right, and Mildred grew testy. Even when the structure was finally completed, Mildred was still not pleased.

"Well, it will simply have to do, Pamela, but it is not what I had in mind!" With that she strolled from the room and spied Bekah, who, having completed her chores, was busy combing her own hair.

Mildred eyed her coldly. "Is that how you occupy yourself? One of your position should not waste time giving herself airs. Vanity is a sinful and foolish habit, Bekah."

"I am not vain, milady, only removing the tangles from my hair," she said, putting the comb aside. "I was often taught that orderliness and cleanliness were virtues."

"*You* speak to *me* of virtue?" Lady Mildred scoffed harshly. "Your idleness disgusts me, as does your vanity!"

Mildred's eyes lit upon a pair of sewing shears, and she picked them up, slapping them into her palm, her eyes narrowing. "Perhaps if you did not have that expanse of hair you would not waste your time so wickedly."

Bekah eyed Mildred suspiciously, noticing how much she looked like her brother. "I will mend that frock now," she said, reaching for the blue dress Mildred had just discarded in a heap on the floor.

"In a moment, Bekah. First come sit here, so that I can trim the excess off those unruly locks."

"I keep them bound back, as you instruct me to."

"They are not so now," Mildred said coldly, bringing the shears menacingly close, her intent obvious. It would be more than just a little trim, and Bekah recoiled from the idea. She backed away, holding the garment to be mended tight in her fists.

"I cannot allow you to cut my hair, milady," she protested. Mildred's face flushed at this insolence.

"You dare to disobey my orders? Perhaps it would be best if you had no locks at all, so that you might gain your much-needed humility."

A heavy voice interceded in the conversation. "Do you intimidate the poor girl, my sister?"

They both turned to find Radburn leaning in the doorway.

"I am only trying to show this serf her proper place," Mildred said.

"By cutting off her hair?"

"She is vain and idle, my brother."

"And you are jealous. I have seen it before, Mildred; it wears ugly upon you. I do not want you defacing the girl. I am keeping her here with you until she is of use to us. Surely, my sister, you realize that the beauty you so despise can also be turned to our advantage?"

Mildred tossed the shears to the floor, where they fell with a clatter. Her brother was intelligent in one aspect, that of monetary affairs, and she saw the reason in his words. She would leave the girl alone—for now. No doubt the wench would get her just rewards. Mildred shrugged.

"I have no time for this. Albert—or rather, Lord Marchis —is expecting me. We are going for a hunt."

Without a backwards glance she left, swooping up her riding crop. Radburn, still leaning against the door, kept his eyes on Bekah, the tableau holding for a few indeterminable seconds. He stepped slowly towards her, catching her chin in his lean fingers; bending over, he brushed his lips against hers. She turned her head as if he had burned her. She was astonished at his actions, and even more so at his words.

"If I cannot use you to fulfill my plans for you, then I would not mind taking you as my own mistress, Bekah," he said casually. "However, that is in the future, and I detect that you dislike me for now."

"Actually, I despise you, and I am not likely to change," Bekah said stiffly.

He laughed at this, a hollow sound; turning on his heel, he left. The memory of her lingered sharply in his brain. She was clothed in a frock of brown, rust-hued wool, its skirt falling away in soft folds from the square bodice. It sported sleeves pulled in below the elbow; beneath this was a kirtle of soft cream color, high about her throat and with long, slender sleeves. The hem of the brown frock sloped up in front to reveal the kirtle's skirt.

Her garb was simple, with no braid or embroidery to enhance it, and yet that was the great appeal of it, giving her an innocent air. He thought again that she was like a lovely jewel wrapped in rough cloth, enhancing her beauty all the more. If he were more a lover than a businessman, he would have very much wanted her for himself. Even now he restrained himself, pushing from his mind the memory of her lips. If she affected his own logical self this way, in what manner would she affect other, more willing men? The thought intrigued him. A woman such as Bekah was an asset to his power. He was not sure how, but he knew that if he worked things correctly, he would be able to raise himself in both position and power. It was a shame that Mildred had not been born with such poise, not to mention beauty.

Bekah hurriedly found Pamela. "I must leave for a while, before I scream! Ember should sleep for another hour or more, but would you listen just in case she should wake?"

"I could not help but overhear their words, Bekah."

"Radburn and his sister are more than I can tolerate. If it were not for your friendship I do not know how I could survive here."

"Go, then. A walk will do you much good."

Bekah nodded her head. "I shall not be long," she said,

179

donning a delicate brown wool cap which tied with narrow ribbons beneath her chin. The cap was only a long, slender oval covering her head from ear to ear, leaving her hair to cascade freely down her back.

She pushed back the wooden door, slipping into the mist-shrouded forest. The sunny days had been interrupted by this one gray, cloudy day that threatened rain. The forest seemed unusually quiet; the dripping of damp underbrush and the stray call of a single bird were all that she could hear. She wandered deep into the woods through patches of mist where steam rose from the warm ground. The solitude and peacefulness of the moment began to change her mood, and she found herself almost happy. She came upon a stream where the water laughingly rushed towards the sea. It was very clear, with a mossy bank and a floor of smooth stones and sand. She knelt and scooped a drink from it, finding the water cooly refreshing.

She gazed into her own wavering reflection and then at another from across the stream on the opposite bank. Her startled gaze shot up at the sight of the man across the brook. Perhaps it was her surprise which blazed this moment clearly into her memory.

He stood akimbo, looking at her with piercing hazel eyes deeply set in a face of finely chiseled features that made him irresistibly handsome. Thick chestnut hair, sun-lightened to a fairer shade, fell softly about his face. He wore a doeskin hat, chausses of finest leather and an azure jerkin with tied sleeves over a fine linen shirt. His summer mantle was cast over one shoulder as if he always carried such a casual air about him. She noted his very handsome appearance, and as she rose to her feet her face became lightly flushed. Disconcertingly, he smiled at her. She turned to go, but he called out to her, stopping her departure.

"Fairest maid! Would you leave me so unanswered?"

She lifted her eyes to his, the words he spoke touching her curiosity. "Unanswered?"

"Yea, unanswered! Never have I seen a woman so fair to have simply come through the forest mist as you have just done. I might be inspired to think you are the goddess of woodland creatures dwelling here, so dressed in brown. Who are you and whence have you come?"

The musical tone of his voice was pleasant, and his words filled her with an excitement which she did not understand. She must return to the castle, lest this unusual pounding of her heart betray her! Leaving the stranger's questions unanswered, she turned to flee, finding that the hem of her kirtle had become ensnared in the thorns of a small branch growing up between rock and stream. Try as she might, she could not loosen it. The trembling of her fingers caused her actions to be awkward.

"Here, let me assist you!"

"Oh, nay!" she cried out.

The frightened innocence of her eyes stabbed him to the very heart, and he felt his pulse quicken. There was more to this young woman than perfection of feature; there was some tinge of sorrow about her that added to her beauty and guileless air.

"I only mean to help you," he called out, braving the water of the stream without thought. However, as he forded the swift current with steady assurance, his foot struck a stone slick with moss. Without a moment's notice he plunged into the water, then sat there sputtering and cursing angrily at this mishap.

It was all so humorous that quiet laughter escaped Bekah's lips, and the young man looked up at her. "You naughty wench, did you cast some spell upon this water?"

"I cannot be held to blame if you are not capable of crossing a stream without falling in," she laughed.

"You shall soon learn who has the last laugh!" he said, rising up out of the chilling water. "And I will be your teacher!"

A cry escaped her and she tugged frantically at her skirt. Just as he was almost close enough to touch her, her skirt came loose with a rending sound. She turned and ran frantically, a desperation about her as if she feared the consequences should he catch her.

"Wait!" he cried out, bounding out of the stream, but the banks were slick clay, and by the time he had emerged she had disappeared into the mists. He tried to follow her trail, but the thick underbrush was deceiving. He searched through glades and along trails which ended in underbrush or at the castle walls.

It grew dark, and finally he returned to the castle, a bit of cream-colored wool in his hand. He was in a black cloud of anger at himself and at the turn of events, continually berating both. He was accompanied on his homeward journey by the sound of squelching, wet leather, and he promised himself he would find the girl no matter where she was! He only hoped intensely that she did not already belong to some other, more fortunate man.

Bekah nearly stumbled over a large tree root in her haste, and as she stopped to catch her breath she was angry with herself. She had acted childishly, but she was not a child! She was a woman, perhaps too much of a woman. She felt shaken by the incident. What was there about that young man that had been so startling, so somehow attractive to her? Perhaps Kenric had taught her too well.

She pushed these thoughts away, hurrying through the rustling underbrush, catching her skirts up and running through the forest. She caught the familiar trail that returned her to the hidden door in the castle wall. As she reached it, she tried to straighten her hair and dress, smoothing the folds and examining the tear in her kirtle. Taking a deep breath, she entered the court without incident.

That night she lay awake in her bed, unable to sleep. She stirred restlessly, staring into the darkness which surrounded her. She was unable to drive the picture of the handsome young man, looking so inquisitively at her, from her mind.

Aidan moodily studied the twig with its two leaves as he rolled it between his fingers. He cast it aside and ran his hands through his hair, his brow knit in an unhappy expression.

He, who was always in such excellent control of each situation, and whose outlook was always brightly optimistic, was in a storm of moodiness. His servants and friends were baffled, and even his father heard of his son's strange atti-

182

tude. It was this that made him storm into the room where Aidan sat.

"Well?" he asked, casting his portly, comfortably dressed frame down across from his son. "No need to look so surprised, Aidan. You need not pretend there is nothing wrong. You have been barging around the castle, upsetting the servants and, from all I have heard, you have been impossible to please."

"Impossible! I cannot be blamed if the servants are bumbling dimwits!"

Aidan's father shook his head. "Son, you have never spoken so. What is wrong? Do not tell me some young maid has pricked your heart and you are lovesick again?" He chuckled.

"What do you take me for? Certainly you do not think I am one of the young lackeys who fall in love with every skirt that swishes by!"

His father laughed. "Oh, son! I am not accustomed to such bitterness from my usually witty and pleasant-tempered offspring. You are my only son, and whatever illness troubles you, I hope it is cured quickly," he said, cajoling him.

"It is no illness."

"Then perhaps what you need is a wife. Too long you have been the fair romancer of this castle. It is time you settled into the role of husband and father. Perhaps it would somewhat steady your present disposition." Lord Garth thought for a moment. "What about your cousin Mildred?"

"What about her?"

"Well, I realize that she is not the most beautiful damsel in this land, but she is of a good family."

"She is old enough to be my mother!"

"Certainly not! For your own sake I should hope that you never say that within Mildred's hearing."

"Indeed, she has a serpent's tongue and should poison me, no doubt."

"Then if you are dissatisfied with her, there are dozens of maidens both here and in the surrounding villages that would be not only pretty but quite agreeable wives. It matters little to me if she is peasant or royalty, as long as she is capable of bearing sons. Mildred looks sturdy enough and is no doubt willing. If I were to choose for you, son, she would be a likely choice."

"When I take a wife she will be one of my own choosing!"

"Very well, but I must suggest that you find one soon. I have been far too patient, and I want grandsons to carry on our name and the inheritance of the castle. I have asked very little of you before. Where are you going?"

"Out to get a wife. Where else?"

"With a bow and quiver?"

"You did not say how you wished me to get her," he said, and after donning a cloak over his light wool tunic, and fastening it on the shoulder with a brooch, he departed.

His father, adeptly hiding his pride in observing his only son, laughed out loud. The thought of his handsome, agile son partnered with Mildred made him roar. Nonetheless, the threat of wedding Aidan and Mildred was a useful one.

With this little problem of Aidan's moodiness temporarily solved, he left Aidan's chambers, finding his way into the kitchen to see what tasty treat he might scrounge up. That was the problem with being a castle baron. The greatest part of his time was spent straightening out others' affairs.

Lord Garth was one to come straight to the heart of a matter, no bumbling around with polite conversation. It was this ability which enabled him to handle the problems of his kingdom. True to form, he dismissed the matter with his son from his mind and made a quick inventory of his other problems. The most pressing was the feast to be prepared for King Alfred's visit.

Little did he realize just how close he had come to guessing the root of Aidan's problem. His son, who was currectly stalking angrily through the surrounding forest, felt as if he were a different man, possessed by burning ambition. He felt certain he had changed a great deal in the last seven days.

It had begun on that day a week ago, within the very moment he had laid eyes upon the young woman in the forest. It was as if she were some special force which had entered his life, changing his perception and his goals. That evening he had returned to the castle unable to rid her from his thoughts even if he had wanted to. He spoke of her to no one and was out early the next morning to inquire about her at the closest village, confident he would find her. But his hunt proved useless, for all the maids and married women he saw were not she. He was intensely frustrated by the fact that no one had even heard of a woman fitting her description. His optimism at finding her began to wane.

One of his castle's own serfs had seen such a woman as he described, but when asked, Baldor told all that he could recall about her. It had been two fortnights ago. She had been on horseback with a number of men and rode by the side of one of the traveling noblemen. But he did not recall who. Neither did he remember the direction in which they traveled, for his glimpse of her had been slight. All he could recall was a crown of golden hair and the face of a saint or a spellcaster, one could never be sure which.

At the end of a fruitless day Aidan was disillusioned and at a loss as to where to search next. He and his tired destrier, Chauncey, returned. Many times in the days that followed he returned to the place where he had seen her, waiting, hoping that she would reappear. She never did.

She began to haunt his dreams, and often he would see her in these dreams in the misted forest. He would pursue her, then just as he was about to catch her in his grasp she would evade him and he would awaken with a start. He began to believe she was not real, that he had imagined her. If only he had not frightened her, if only she had not fled! He became so possessed that he felt as if fire surged through his veins.

Now he held his slender, well-crafted bow firmly in his grasp, determined to forget the maiden and begin his hunt. He was skillful with the long bow and had often supplied the castle with venison. The day was cool and clear, sunlight splattering across the yellow-green underbrush. There were feathery ferns and tall clovers with huge, papery-thin leaves. Delicate shafts of light speared through the layers of leaves overhead, and the forest was alive with sounds. Brown paths snaked their way through the underbrush, marked by wandering, twisted roots and rabbit burrows.

He was nearing the castle wall around one of the lesser known courtyards when he suddenly heard the flapping of wings overhead. Aidan caught sight of the largest raven he had ever seen. As he watched, it landed in a tree next to the wall. He set his bow with steady aim and let the arrow fly. At that exact moment the raven took flight with a loud screech and Aidan's arrow landed firmly in an upper branch of the tree.

Aidan cursed softly, for that was his straightest arrow and he had already lost one today. He must retrieve it, and henceforth would have to lessen the waste of his arrows. He laid down his two ring-necked pheasants, then lithely scaled the tree. Maneuvering to the appropriate limb he managed to work the arrow from the bark. From his position in the tree he could easily see over the garden wall and into the courtyard below, realizing it was a section of the castle that he was not at all familiar with; it was the quarters where Mildred and her ladies stayed, he assumed.

After one glance he was ready to return to the hunt, when the sound of a sweet voice arrested his attention. The clear notes were being sung in an unusual melody; he glanced around but was still unable to locate the singer. In a few swift movements he was on the wall, and looking down he sucked in his breath.

For a moment he could hardly believe his eyes, wondering if they deceived him and his dreams had taken the shape of reality. But the vision did not fade, and with a jolt he knew for certain that it was she—right within the walls of his own castle. He had looked everywhere but here, the closest place to him! The irony of the situation struck him and he smiled to himself, the jest upon no other.

He looked down on her, her beauty clearly visible in the sharp sunlight. She was even more lovely than his mind had remembered, and he drank in her beauty. But as he looked at her a battle of mixed feelings raged in the pit of his stomach.

In her arms she held a black-haired baby which nursed sleepily at the white swell of her breast. He felt a sinking feeling within as he realized she was probably one of the ladies who worked for the castle under Mildred's direction.

No doubt she was wed to one of the men who serviced the castle grounds. Unhappily he thought of an adoring husband.

Despair filled him as he turned to leave, but he could not tear his gaze from her and stayed for a minute longer. He watched as she buttoned the bodice of her dress; it was a simple frock of fawn color, edged with amber braid. Her hair was in a thick braid wound at the nape of her neck. She wrapped the sleeping baby in a cloth and laid her in a strong basket lined with a soft quilt.

He shifted his position atop the wall, sending down a scraping of crumbling pebbles. Aidan's movement startled Bekah, and she glanced up with a little cry.

"You!" she gasped a pink flush coloring her cheeks.

He smiled down at her, not at all embarrassed by his unlikely position atop the garden wall. "At last I find you, fair lady!" he said, his eyes shining. "It was cruel of you to leave me so, thrashing about in that deep current."

She could not keep a smile from her lips, and he felt encouraged. He sat down on the wall, palms down.

"I have searched this forest broad and far and asked about you in the village. It was as if you had never existed, and I began to doubt my sanity. I am much relieved to see that you do exist."

She looked about, and once assured that they were alone she smiled again. "I assure you that I do exist."

"Then if you are real, will you tell me, beautiful lady, what is your name?"

"It is Bekah," she said, turning to go.

"Would you leave me again, Bekah? I would not think that one so fair could be cruel to leave me wanting!"

"What more can I give you?" she asked.

"Only some of your time and a few words." He smiled, jumping down from the wall.

"You must not! Should Lady Mildred find you here I would be in great trouble. It is most fortunate that she has taken a rest for this hour and does not demand service."

"Mildred is no threat," he said catching her hand and seating her beside him on the bench. He did not immediately release her hand, but she did not appear to mind the warm touch of his fingers on her own. He bent towards the basket, brushing a finger against the soft cheek of the sleeping baby.

"This is a pretty baby," he said.

"Thank you. Her name is Ember."

It was now that the question came, as both of them knew it would, and Aidan tried to ask it lightly, although the words troubled him, sticking in his throat. "She is yours." It was not a question, and he continued on. "Are you married to another man, Bekah?"

The answer took forever in coming, and the air grew uncomfortable between them. "Will you tell me please?"

He was not prepared for the answer when it came, bracing himself against her words. "Nay, sir, I am not."

He nodded his head once in resignation before looking up. "Did you say you are not?"

She shook her head, expecting the usual look of accusation. Instead a smile burst upon his handsome features. "Oh, blessed words! For a moment I feared that my ears deceived me! How pitiful I should have been, vowed never to wed another." He pressed her hand to his lips, placing a tender kiss upon it, and she looked at him, bewildered.

"Certainly you will think me mad, but I assure you, I do not always act so rashly. I have been frantic in my search for you, and when I could not find you I became desperate in the extreme! I began to dream of you, and finally I believed that I had imagined you, that you were not real. It plunged me into a black mood, relieved only now by your presence."

She was amazed at his words, remembering her persistent thoughts of him. "Perhaps I should have stayed, but I have had experience with a man's force, and I was overcome with fear."

"I have berated myself over and over again for my foolishness and beg your forgiveness. I hope you do not think me too bold, for I am not so under most conditions. But I feel as if I know you, since my thoughts have dwelt almost exclusively on you. May I ask how I have lived in Wessex my entire life, without ever seeing you? How has Mildred managed to hide you away from all the young men?"

"I have been here only a short while."

"Where have you come from, to grace our land?"

"I was born and raised in Norseland."

"But you speak Anglian so beautifully."

"My mother was Saxon, captured by a Norse raider. She raised me much as her own people would have, but I grew up along the coast of Norway."

"But how did you come to be here? Did your father bring you and your mother back?"

"Nay." She paused for a minute. "Once as I roamed along the seashore I was captured by an Anglian raider. He took me with him on his ship against my will. It appears that the women of my family have little control over their fate. I hope that my daughter will have greater control of her life."

"She is a pretty child. I cannot believe that her father would willingly give up two such lovely ladies."

"He did not do so by will of his own. He died before he knew that she had even been created."

"I hear some pain behind your words, and I sorrow that I brought it about by my careless inquiries. I had no right to question you."

"I do not mind," she said, lifting her eyes up to his. Seldom had she been so at ease with a man, but he seemed to demand nothing of her. Although a stranger, he was kind and concerned. Perhaps it was this which made her enjoy his presence.

"I enjoyed the song you sang, Bekah. Is it one your mother taught you?"

"Nay, 'tis one I composed to sing to my daughter."

"We enjoy the same art, I see. I myself enjoy creating verse. There is one which I worked on in the hours when you invaded my sleep, and now it is well learned upon my memory."

"Tell me, then, for I very much would like to hear it. I have never had one written for me and am honored," Bekah smiled, unable to keep her eyes from his sincere face.

Aidan cleared his throat and recited "To My Woodland Nymph."

His woodland nymph? Bekah thought. His rhyme was not terribly good, but she was thrilled nonetheless.

189

He stopped. Almost embarrassed, he said, "If I knew you better, I could have written better."

Her heart was thudding steadily within her breast; this handsome young man was in love with her! It was not just the desire she saw in men's eyes. Nay, this was gentle caring. She was touched by his poem and the sincerity within his eyes.

" 'Twas a beautiful poem, sir. You are indeed a poet of skill, and I admire your talent."

He smiled broadly at this compliment, extremely pleased with himself that he had found favor in her eyes. "I am happy that you like it, milady."

Heaven and earth, she was beautiful! He was struck by it again and he could not stop himself from reaching over and taking her hand in his. He looked at her slender fingers, relaxed in his own, the nails shortened by hard work, the skin soft despite the small calluses. He felt a brief surge of anger that one such as herself was forced to do scrubbing and cleaning for his cousin Mildred. He said nothing, however, not wanting to break the quiet.

There was a wordless communication of comfort between them, and it was the first time since Kenric's death that the hollow ache in Bekah's heart was stilled.

Finally Aidan spoke. "I would like to be your friend. You need not fear me."

"I know that," she smiled. "Yea, I would like to be your friend." It occurred to her that she did not know this amiable stranger's name. She was just about to ask him when there came the distant sound of approaching voices. Bekah rose to her feet.

"Quickly, you must go! Should they find you here they would be very angry!"

"We have nothing to fear." He smiled, thinking of Mildred's puckered face should she catch him here courting one of her maids.

"You do not understand. Lady Mildred hates me, and should she find you here she would make my life miserable!"

An angry expression crossed his face, as if he would not want anyone to make Bekah unhappy. Perhaps he should stay and face his cousin, but he could not resist the plead-

190

ing in Bekah's eyes. Besides, it was pleasant to play the wayfaring stranger, for obviously she did not know his true identity.

"Very well," he said, pulling himself atop the wall, "but when will I see you again?"

"I do not know," she answered hastily, looking behind her to see if anyone spied them.

"Would you sentence me to such an unhappy exclusion? We must meet again, tomorrow."

"I cannot tomorrow, for it is King Alfred's coming and there will be little time for me with my duties here."

"Paugh! I forgot old Alf is coming. Then the day after?"

"You must go hastily sir. I hear their voices near!"

"I shall not go until I get an answer. Can you get out the day after?"

"Yea, there is a door hidden in the garden wall," she whispered fiercely, her hands clasped tightly to her breast. "At noon I will be by the stream. Now go quickly!"

"It shall be forever, my fair love, and I shall count every moment." He easily scaled the wall.

"They are coming; you must go!" she pleaded, wringing her hands.

"Very well," he said, plucking a blossom from a tree outside the wall and tossing it to her. The sweeping gesture of his arm threw him off balance, and he wobbled precariously before falling backwards. There was a loud thud, then rustling in the thick foliage and the sound of soft cursing.

Bekah could not hold back her laughter. Aidan, realizing that this was the second time he had caused her mirth, brushed the nettles from his chausses.

Despite his embarrassment, he could not help but take delight in the sound of her voice. As he walked away he made a vow to himself that he would wed that fairest blossom who had taken pride in his poem. The forest never looked more lovely! The goldenrain tree was in bloom with its multitude of tiny orange blossoms. The small, white sweet orange blossoms with orange-dotted centers were nestled in emerald leaves. The fragrances were sweet, and he plucked one of the orange blossoms to carry, similar to the flower he had tossed to Bekah.

Bekah held the soft whiteness of the flower in her hands as Mildred and her brother stepped into the courtyard. Bekah's face was flushed, her heart beating wildly. She hoped that they would not notice, but Radburn's eyes were sharp. He lifted her chin with his finger, an annoying habit she disliked, and she pulled away, walking to the bench near where Ember slept. She sat down, folding her hands in her lap and looking at her baby.

He questioned, "Did I not hear laughter?"

"What would she have to laugh about?" Mildred said.

Radburn dismissed his sister's comment, clearly noting Bekah's disturbed state. He strolled over to the bench, seating himself beside her.

Bekah's mind was racing as she retraced the afternoon's interlude. The young stranger, whoever he might be, was a delightful intervention in her tedious situation. His kindness and caring were most pleasant, and she felt a happy excitement as she recalled his free manner. She was amazed at the freedom she had displayed—she, who could love no other than Kenric. But she was young, too young to mourn for the rest of her life. She needed the special friendship of a young man, and Ember needed a father. Ember! He had spoken kindly of her daughter, and this pleased her very much. Again she was happily amazed at his acceptance of her and her past. There was no condemnation in his voice, no self-righteous vindictiveness or cruel curiosity. All that she witnessed in his demeanor was friendship and sincerity.

Suddenly her thoughts were interrupted by Radburn's sharp voice. "Bekah! I do not believe you have heard a word I have spoken."

"I am sorry, Lord Radburn, but I have had my mind on other things today," she murmured.

"So I see. What is wrong?"

"Nothing at all, sir."

"Well, then I expect you to be ready on the morrow for the greeting of King Alfred. It is not every day that he stops here on his way to Wantage."

"I cannot possibly go," she said, alarmed, and now giving her full attention to him.

"And why not?"

She was at a temporary loss, yet she tried to think of some excuse. She certainly did not want to attend the banquet to be displayed by the detested Radburn. "You would not wish me to appear too bold, would you sir? I have never even attended a banquet here, and I have no proper clothes to wear."

" 'Tis so," Mildred said. "She would stand out as a peasant among royalty."

"Not if she were clothed in one of your dresses, sister dear."

"Not one of mine!" she cried in horror.

"A fitting dress would not be hard to come by."

"I do not want to go, Radburn," Bekah said coldly, drawing their shocked looks. Mildred, amazed at the girl's foolishness, was well aware of the distraction Bekah would bring at the feast.

"Do not bring her to the feast, brother. It would be inappropriate and she would do better later on."

"Very well, but I do expect you to make a show sometime—though perhaps the opening banquet would be too crowded to do you well, Bekah."

She nodded her head, relieved, smelling the blossom still in her hand.

"Well, I shall leave now, ladies; I have other things to attend to."

They both seemed relieved by his departure, and Mildred returned to her rooms after turning a scorching stare upon Bekah. Left alone again, Bekah packed up her baby and retired to her own chambers, where she busied herself with embroidering small yellow flowers on one of Mildred's new dresses. The work was tedious, and her thoughts returned at once to the young stranger. Once again she realized that she did not know his name. She wondered what it might be, and imagined several names which might be worn by him, but none was exactly right. Perhaps he would be just the person to help her, to take her away from this prison. Pamela was her only happiness here, and soon even she would be leaving the castle for good. If Bekah could only manage to further evade Radburn's plans, then she could meet the young man on the day after tomorrow. However, she had the unhappy feeling that Radburn would not be so easily dissuaded next time.

She retired early that night, her dreams full of hope. The night was peaceful, but she was awakened early by much commotion. The castle had been readied the day before, but today there was the preparing of the feast. The forerunner had arrived yesterday to announce the approach of King Alfred and his entourage.

"I cannot believe you do not wish to attend the feast. I would enjoy going and participating in the exceptional banquet," Pamela said.

"You do not understand, my friend. Radburn wishes only to peddle my wares to the highest buyer he can find. I have no desire to meet the fate which he greedily plans."

Bekah hurriedly finished the green leaves she was embroidering about the flowers on the dress Mildred was anxious to wear, and Pamela was finishing an undershift. Both were strangely quiet, listening to the idle talk of Ellena and her sister.

Aidan of Briarwood strode through the halls and through one of the archways which led into his father's comfortable study. The windows, cast open to the new summer light, overlooked a spacious view of surrounding water and land. A large oaken table, oval and shining smooth, was surrounded by sturdy, intricately carved chairs. These had high, straight backs and padded leather seats. A wall of tall and narrow double shelves held rolls of tied parchment, ink quills and wooden boxes. There were journals bound in leather, of Aidan's father and grandfather. On the north wall hung three narrow white banners embroidered with pictures of Briarwood, the lake and swans, and the black briar thorns which grew in abundance about the castle. Aidan liked his father's study; it was as familiar to him as any other room in the castle.

His father, Lord Garth, and his cousin, Radburn, were deeply involved in a discussion about King Alfred. Garth was an old friend of the King's, and once, when Garth had been younger, they had fought side by side. Often Garth had related to his son the tale of battle in which they staved off hordes of Danish battle-axes and swords. The story was so well known to Aidan that he could clearly envision the stain of crimson on the battlefield and hear the clang of metal.

"It is my opinion," Garth was saying, "that Alfred's journey to Wantage is more than just a mere summer trek. I believe that he intends to claim London as ours, and rightfully it is!"

"Do you not think that it would be dangerous, for no doubt a battle will ensue with the heathens."

"Alfred has never been one to fear a skirmish, as you should know!"

"The more one has to risk, the more one has to lose."

Garth snorted. "You never were one to do battle or brave a fight, sir."

"Neither have I been one to foolishly charge into war," Radburn said, turning the attention away from himself and towards the map which lay spread before them on the table, its yellowed edges curling up. "Where are the King and his company now?"

"The messenger said here," Garth said, using a thick finger to indicate a point by a river, marked on the paper. "Accounting for traveling time, I think we can expect him this afternoon. I hope there will be little delay, for I long for the presence of a true fighting knight!"

Radburn ignored the barb and nodded his head sagely. "I suppose he is bringing most of his knights."

"Yea. That is why I follow the theory that he will lay claim to London."

Aidan, caught up in the conversation, strode into the room. "Good morning, Father! A most beautiful day, is it not? I hope you are right about King Alf, for it is time that London again belonged to us. Will you lend him some of our knights?" he asked, his face lit up in a smile. "And how are you, Radburn, my good fellow?"

Garth and Radburn turned their amazed stares on Aidan, and he picked out a red apple from the bowl of fruit, crisp from the cold cellar. Radburn had had the distinct impression that his cousin did not like him, and never had he referred to him as a "good fellow."

"Aidan, may I ask what gives you this morning's boundless good cheer?" Radburn inquired.

"I would certainly like to know, too!" Lord Garth said, watching his son bite into the crisp apple. "I swear, I am not certain whether I have raised a mad son or not. Yesterday you were in the depths of unhappiness, and I suppose that on the morrow it will return."

"Nay, Father, never again. For I have taken your wise council and selected a bride."

"What?" Garth exclaimed, wrinkling his brow in perplexity. "When was this?"

"Days ago. I accidentally stumbled upon her in the forest." He chuckled at his choice of words. "Unfortunately she escaped me. Then yesterday I found her again. There will be no other for me, for I am in love with her! She is fair above all others. She has the face of an angel and hair like purest sunlight."

It was this last statement which fully caught Radburn's attention, and he keenly pricked up his senses.

"Her name is Bekah. You must meet her soon, Father. You also, Radburn."

"I must confess," Radburn said cooly, delighted by this opportunity, "I already know of her."

"Oh, of course. She stays in the same quarters as your sister."

"Indeed. I brought her here from Northumbria. She had been shipwrecked on one of my family's distant shores, and my tenants found her and cared for her. When I saw her, I brought her here."

"What!" Aidan said, tossing the apple core out the window to the courtyard below, startling a flock of geese. "I cannot believe that you have kept her so, without ever letting us even see her!"

"Can you blame me? As you yourself have since discovered, she is most desirable, and I should very much like her as my own wife."

"She said she belongs to no man!"

"And indeed 'tis true. The one thing which has kept me from wedding her is that she does not love me. After all, what value is a gem without the polish of love?" Radburn was thinking rapidly.

"Well spoken!" Lord Garth said, delighted with the turn of events. He knew all too well that if Radburn wanted this maid for himself, he would neither marry her nor wait for the turn of her affection. If his son had found a girl to marry and give the castle an heir, then saints be praised. But if his son had to earn her, then he knew that she would be dearer to Aidan's heart.

"Perhaps well spoken," Aidan said. "But you have no use for her, and I am in need of a wife."

"This particular one?" Radburn questioned, resting a long finger against the side of his temple as he sat at the table.

"Yea, and no other!"

"Hold on now, son. She is Radburn's rightfully by first claim, and you cannot ask him to simply give up such an asset as this fair maid obviously is."

"If only you could see her, Father. She is the most delicate flower in all of Wessex!"

"It seems as if the flower has bitten the bee," Garth chuckled. "Besides, perhaps she would prefer your cousin's company."

"Nay, never!" Aidan said, too late realizing his tactlessness.

"Aidan!" Garth said in mock horror, holding back his mirth with difficulty.

Radburn said cautiously, "She feels that in bringing her from Northumbria I was hasty, but often we resent what is done for our own benefit."

"If you are so concerned with her care, then why not let her decide who she wishes to wed?" Aidan asked forthrightly.

"Aidan, obviously Radburn feels that to give her up would be a loss. Perhaps we could make a trade."

"What do you propose?" Radburn said, placing his fingertips together, elbows on the table.

"Well, how about if we give you two of our handmaidens in exchange? What about those twin sisters, Constance and Celia?"

"The girls with the round faces and straight brown hair?" Radburn chuckled humorlessly. "Bekah is worth ten serving girls. I suppose I will just have to keep her for myself."

"Nay!" Aidan said in horror at the thought of losing his newfound love, as Radburn pretended to rise to leave. "Certainly there must be something to offer him!" he said, turning to his father for help.

"Well, there is one thing . . . nay, you would not be interested in that," Garth said slowly.

"What?" both Aidan and Radburn questioned.

"Well, you have long jested of your want for my land and manor in the south of Mercia, since you have no manor of your own except for land in Northumbria. But I realize that it was only a jest, and that it would not be desirous to you."

"I might consider it, with some thought."

"It's a great piece of land," Aidan interjected, "and you know that when I do wed, Mildred will no longer be comfortable serving as lady of the castle."

"True," Radburn said, prolonging his acceptance of the offer. How he had wanted that parcel of land! Had his grandfather been eldest, all this should have been his! Yea, he had known that Bekah should prove good for him as long as he was patient, but he had not anticipated how good! Garth was a fool to give up that lot of land in Mercia, but certainly he himself deserved it! He was startled from his thoughts by Garth's voice.

"Well, Radburn, what do you say?"

"Understanding Aidan's professed love for her, what can I say? I hate to give her to another, but since she does not love me, and you, Aidan, are my cousin, then I am pleased with the outcome."

Aidan gave an exclamation of pleasure, clasping his cousin tightly on the shoulder and shaking him with friendly acceptance. Garth let his humor loose and could not help but laugh at Radburn's self-imposed tolerance.

"Very well, my fortunate son. When shall you wed her?"

"The sooner the better! What about tomorrow? King Alfred will be all settled, and it will be a very appropriate time to have a wedding feast."

"That is true," Garth said, rubbing his chin. "Will she think it rash and object?"

"Nay," Radburn said. "I am sure she will agree. In truth I can guarantee it. I will go tell her."

"I wish to be the one to do so," Aidan said.

"Do you forget that custom forbids it?" his father said. "The peasants hold firmly to it, and there is no reason to break it. Tomorrow will be soon enough, for you will both need the time for preparation."

"But I was hoping to see her again."

"We must use the time to turn our attention to the wedding plans. Alfred will be delighted. He has admired you from the time you were a youth. Go prepare her, Radburn, and in the meantime I will draw up the deed in your name."

Radburn nodded, a rare smile on his lean features. "I will tell her the happy news," he said, departing.

They watched him leave, and Aidan threw himself down in one of the chairs. "Thank you, Father. I cannot wait for you to see my future wife! It will be a hundred years until tomorrow. But there is one thing which plagues me," he said, leaning forward. "How can I allow you to give up your land in Mercia to Radburn for my sake?"

"Despite his denial, Radburn has envied that land even as his father did before him. I know that you are satisfied with these lands here, and little does Radburn know that I should have given him the Mercia land soon, anyway. Radburn and Mildred cannot stay here forever, and the servants dislike them. Besides, that land in Mercia was becoming a burden; it is too close to Danelaw and I care not for constant defense of it against the Vikings of Guthrum. Our cousin will have his hands full."

Aidan laughed. "Poor Radburn. But tell me, why did you agree to the marriage when you have not even seen my betrothed?"

"I have long trusted your judgment, my son. I have also long awaited your marriage. You are my only son, and it has seemed as if I have waited forever for an heir. Besides, I will see her tomorrow at your wedding. Tell me, do you think her capable of being mistress of the castle?"

"Indeed, I think her capable of organizing the stars! She has a natural gentleness which no doubt will be much appreciated by our servants, and I shall help her in the learning of her responsibilities."

Garth nodded, watching as his son reached for another apple and polished it on his sleeve until it was shiny. Suddenly from the rooftop a trumpet heralded the approach of King Alfred.

The whole keep literally buzzed with excitement, which reverberated in the courtyard. The anticipation was high, and even Bekah and Pamela sensed it within the confines of their own quarters. The King and his accompanying troupe arrived in time for the main meal of the day, much earlier than Garth had guessed. An excellent feast was nonetheless ready; Alfred would be well pleased.

Mildred was wearing a green dress of lovely material, edged in white lace. Pamela finished doing Mildred's hair just as Radburn entered the room, and his sister rose to be surveyed.

"Very nice, my sister. Alfred is here and the feast will begin soon, for his knights are hungry and all is prepared. Are you ready to go?"

"Soon," she said, fastening a gold and silver bracelet.

Radburn turned his gaze on Bekah. "Bekah, I have come here for the express purpose of talking to you. I have some excellent news for you."

"And what might that be?" Mildred inquired.

"The long journey here has at last proved worthwhile." He paused for a moment, allowing Bekah's curiosity to build before continuing. "I have managed to procure a husband for you."

"What?" Bekah gasped, unbelieving.

"You should be pleased."

"What serf have you managed to buy off?" Mildred asked casually, preening in front of a polished oval of copper.

"Aidan, son of Garth, who is baron of this castle, is to be your husband," he said to Bekah.

Mildred turned and gaped at her brother. "What!" she cried, echoing Bekah's earlier word. "Are you mad? Do you think he would marry one such as she?"

"Of a certainty. It is all agreed upon and shall take place on the morrow."

"What have you done! Why did you not arrange that marriage for me, your own sister? What are you to gain by talking the young fool into a marriage with her?"

"Hold your sharp tongue, sister. Lord Garth has given us the manor and lands in Mercia. At least we will have our own land!"

"Land that should have been ours, and would have been, had Aidan and I wed," Mildred said bitterly.

"Aidan would not have wed you, Mildred, and now we will no longer need to depend on our cousins' generosity."

"What on earth made Lord Garth agree to such an outrageous arrangement?" she asked, both of them temporarily unaware of Bekah, who was aghast, and Pamela.

"He is old and most anxious to have grandsons. He has often said he wished his son would marry."

All this time Bekah had been shocked into silence. Finally she said, "I cannot believe you! You cannot sell me for a parcel of land."

Both of them turned barely tolerant gazes upon her.

"What a little fool you are," Mildred stated coldly. "I do not understand how Radburn has managed to sell your wares so successfully, but he has always been a good bargainer. You should be grateful that he has managed to arrange a marriage at all for someone as lowly as yourself."

"Mildred, your bitter tongue is least appealing. We have little time to talk about the marriage now; King Alfred has arrived and the feast is about to begin. I will talk to you later of this, Bekah. Come, sister." With that they departed, and Bekah stood staring after them, amazed.

"Pamela, did you hear?"

"Yea, and I must admit that this is the most surprising news I have yet heard! Here you are a serving girl one day and to be married to Aidan on the next. You will be the envy of every woman in the castle."

"But I do not want to marry someone I do not know or love! Perhaps Radburn managed to paint to this Lord Aidan a lovely picture, but he cannot know me, or that I have a child!"

A puzzled expression rested on Pamela's face. "You are right. It is difficult even to guess what will happen in this strange situation."

"Oh, Pamela! Why do these horrid things happen to me? What shall I do?"

"What can you do? There is no foxing Radburn, for he is far too powerful. You will marry Aidan. Do not be so distressed, Bekah, for Aidan is the most enviable match in half of Wessex."

"Perhaps I could simply leave through the garden door and hide in the woods."

"Nay, that would be foolish. You cannot risk Ember to such a cool night. I could give you shelter in my cottage, but Radburn would be sure to find you and punish you."

"And you as well, I am sure," Bekah said, her brow knit in concern. "Perhaps Radburn is only jesting, satisfying his streak of cruelty. It is impossible to tell with him, or even to guess what he is thinking. If I am to be wed tomorrow then certainly I will meet this Aidan."

"Nay, 'tis the custom here that the bride be kept in seclusion for three days," Pamela said.

"What on earth for?"

"It was because of Elthelwood, Lord Garth's great ancestor, who started to build Briarwood. He was betrothed to Lady Ann, who was most fair. As the tale goes, three days before their wedding, the woodland fairies stole her away."

"Woodland fairies?"

"Many of the folk believe in myth and lore. Anyway, as the story goes, he learned of it and was furious. Elthelwood went in search of Lady Ann, a fair woman as ethereal as the wood nymphs. The legend is that the fairies had taken her to celebrate the upcoming wedding and to give her special gifts and talents.

"When Elthelwood found them he slew the fairy king and took Lady Ann back. The fairies were so furious that they hid their presence from all mortals henceforth and put a curse on all who see their betrothed three days before the wedding. The curse is that one or both will die within three years, as Lady Ann did while riding after a year of marriage."

"Certainly you do not believe that story!"

"Of course I do not, but many of the people do. It is the

custom; the people love tradition and Lord Garth likes to humor his people, for they love him so."

"Well, if that is the tradition, then what shall I do, Pamela?"

"I do not know, for I have no power against Radburn. Did you ever think that it might be wise to accept this marriage? Being wed to Aidan would make you lady of Briarwood, and Mildred would no longer be mistress over you. In fact, if what Radburn says is true, then Radburn and Mildred will leave for Mercia. You will become mistress of the castle, and a much better one than Mildred. Think how pleasant it would be with servants to wait on you and many new clothes to wear! You would attend the feasts and have more free time than you could imagine."

"I do not desire to be waited on by servants, and I do not know this Aidan. How can I wed a stranger?"

Pamela sighed. "I have seen him, Bekah, and he is most handsome, and never has he been crude or mean." She felt it would all turn out for the best, once her friend met him. He had such a winning way about him that even her strict friend could not resist him, she was certain. Bekah did not look sure at all, but Pamela had no time to reassure her. She heard the light knocking outside the garden door and with hurrying footsteps ran to it, pulling it open. She cast herself into her husband's waiting arms, warm in that secure embrace. It was something Bekah needed, and Pamela felt sure that Aidan would be good for her.

The day crept by slowly, like a caterpillar inching along a branch. Bekah spent time playing with Ember, who cooed and smiled at her, waving her dimpled hands in excitement. The child was growing more beautiful with each passing day; her hair still remained black, as did her long eyelashes. Bekah found much joy in cuddling the chubby little baby; there was something pure, so sweetly calming about motherhood. No matter what happened, she had her little Kendra Ember.

As evening approached, Mildred returned in a bitter mood, and as soon as she spied Bekah, her feelings found vent.

"Well, here you are. No doubt you are eagerly awaiting your marriage. Finally you will have a name and a place. I cannot believe how skillful my brother is. Certainly Aidan cannot know of your past.''

She paused, but, getting no rise from Bekah, she went on. "What would he think if he were to find out that you are no better than any street wench who sells her wares?''

"Then why do you not tell him, Mildred? I am certain your tongue has enough of a blade to do so.''

Mildred ignored this insolence. "Not I! It is a great piece of land Radburn has taken from Garth, and I would not ruin my chances by saving Aidan from you. Yet when he finds out he has been cheated he will be furious. Once you are wed, however, it is done, and Aidan will be stuck with you. I guess he will have no choice but to keep you and get rid of your brat.''

"What do you mean?'' Bekah asked, trying to keep her voice calm.

Mildred sat down before her mirror, reapplying her lip rouge made from mulberries and rosewater. "He cannot allow his wife to keep another man's unnamed brat. No doubt he will be quick with the sword or cast it off to some peasant. Once he sees how he has been duped, he will no doubt beat you often until you learn your place.''

Mildred, satisfied with Bekah's pale lips, smiled to herself. Once freshened she left to find better company. Albert was always anxious for her company, if King Alfred's knights were not.

Despite Pamela's reassuring words, Bekah felt helpless and drained. "What if her words are true?'' she asked herself aloud. "I must find this Aidan and tell him of my past before it is too late!''

She hurried through the doorway, leaving Ember sleeping comfortably on a cot. Bekah had never been in the depths of Briarwood, but she had heard much talk of it. She hurried down the hall and past the well and the storage areas, winding her way around to the front entrance that held a flight of stairs leading down into the spacious courtyard. Close to the entrance was a spiral staircase leading up, and as she hurried up the flight of stairs she touched the cold stone for support. They wound past an open, arched window, and as she climbed she found herself at the large room that served as kitchen and garrison.

Since the largest meal of the day was now long past, the room was deserted except for a few tending serfs. She climbed up past the great hall and found it filled with King Alfred's soldiers, laughing and drinking or sleeping. She climbed higher, feeling an empty darkness in the pit of her stomach. She should not be here; what if someone should find her?

Bekah found herself looking into a long, dimly lit hallway, and since from here the stairs only led up to the pigeon house and battlements, she entered it, walking down part of its length. As she looked about the hall and through several doorways, she realized with a start that she was on the floor where the bed chambers were. It would never do for her to be found here! She turned quickly, ready to descend the stairs, when she heard boisterous voices floating up to her.

Someone was coming! She stood frozen for a moment, unable to decide what she must do. If only she had not been so foolish as to come here in the first place! They were getting closer, and she could hear their laughter and see the flicker of an approaching torch. At the last moment she found herself fleeing through a partially opened door. She was greatly relieved to see that she was not in a bed chamber but in some sort of office with a beautiful oval table and chairs. On the table sat three fine books, the likes of which she had never seen before.

She had little time to notice her surroundings, for the voices were close outside the door. She could hear one mellow voice say, "In truth, the cowherd's wife did scold me most severely when the cakes burned, and actually called me a sot!"

There were barks of laughter at this, and the door suddenly flew open to reveal Bekah standing there pale and still as a statue.

"What is this!" roared Garth, staring angrily at Bekah. "Wench, what are you doing here? Have you come to steal my books?"

"Nay," she stammered. "I was lost . . ."

"And you came here?" he said skeptically.

"Garth!" said the tall, fair man with burning blue eyes. "Do not be so harsh. Tell me, maid, what is your name?"

205

" 'Tis Bekah, sir," she said, slightly lifting her chin.

"Bekah! Why this is the one Aidan is to wed on the morrow. I was going to see her today before I gave my final consent to the marriage, and here she has saved me the trouble." The rotund man who had frightened her at first was not so intimidating now.

"Garth," said the other, stroking his clean-shaven face, "Does she remind you of anyone?"

"Indeed, there is something about her . . . but I cannot remember who."

"I shall tell you. Do you remember when we were youths and took that journey that lasted well over two months? It was then that I met the Saxon girl with the somber gray eyes, the one named Mary."

"Yea, there is a great likeness, only if I recall correctly, Mary's hair was of a darker hue," said Garth.

"Mary was my mother's name," Bekah said, studying them both seriously with her large eyes.

"Then could it be the same Mary?" Garth asked.

"I returned soon after" said the other man, "and was told she had been killed in a Norseman's raid. Her parents were terribly distraught and in mourning."

"Then 'tis not my mother. She was captured by one of the Norsemen; they were wed and I was born after they reached Norseland."

"What!" cried Garth. "Radburn did not tell me you were of Norse blood! Would he deceive me in this matter? I cannot allow my son to wed a daughter of Nordic descent, for they are our enemies to the death! Certainly he knows my feelings on this."

At that precise moment Radburn appeared and stepped through the door. "Your Majesty," he said, bowing to the fairer man. Bekah gasped as she realized that this tall, comely man was King Alfred. "Lord Garth, I did not mean to deceive you. I only thought that since Kind Alfred's own ancestor called Sceaf the Scyld, a corn king who had floated alone in a mysterious boat to our island, was well known to the Norsemen . . ."

"I mean no disrespect, and certainly King Alfred know this," Garth said, giving Radburn a scorching look.

"Of a certainty," Radburn said smoothly, "But our liege

is descended of Ine, who as everyone knows traced his descent from Odin. Is this not so, Your Majesty?"

"So 'tis said," the King replied, turning his attention to the girl. "Tell me, Bekah, why are you here?"

"Why, I was looking for Aidan."

Alfred laughed softly. "Are you so anxious to see your betrothed?"

"I must speak with him," she said, casting her eyes down at the wooden floor.

"What? And disregard Elthelwood's law? That would mean disaster of a certainty, if we are to believe the legend of Briarwood. Tomorrow will be soon enough," the King said and smiled, his winning way putting both Bekah and Radburn at ease. "Radburn, since she is in your charge, you had better take her back to where she resides. Before you go, Bekah, will you tell me, for the sake of curiosity, what became of your mother Mary?"

Bekah paused before turning to leave. "She died of a fever when I was young." The king nodded his head, seeming satisfied at this answer. Garth, still furious, glared at Radburn.

Radburn guided Bekah roughly out of the room and down the stairs, through the large hall. Bekah caught the attention of the soldiers, all eyes turning towards her. The men quieted some, watching the maiden pass through them. Murmuring came behind her like waves rushing together.

The soldiers wore heavy underclothing and trousers cross-gartered to the knees. They wore knee-length tunics, belted at the waist; their leather girdles carried knife, sword and often a pouch. Some wore cloaks of blue or purple caught on the left shoulder with a brooch of semiprecious stones or carved metal.

The hall held hunting equipment, weapons, harnesses and four wolfhounds which stirred restlessly. Hawks with sharp eyes and curved beaks sat on perches, narrow chains about one leg keeping them in place.

Bekah passed high-arched windows and in the distance could view serfs wearing unlined pilches of wolf and sheepskin, some caught with a stout leather belt. They worked in rhythmic unison in the fields, driving the oxen. Those with furs dyed red seemed like drops of blood against the brown earth they toiled.

Radburn hurried her on and soon they were back in the quietude of the sunny garden.

"What did you think you were doing!" Radburn shouted at her, pacing agitatedly. This was the first time she had ever seen him flustered and angry. "You may have ruined everything!"

"I am sorry. I only wished to see Aidan, to explain . . ."

He gave her no time to continue. "No doubt you have not only lost me my new wealth of lands but have ruined your hopes of having a husband of worth. Do you not see that what I did would have been of good benefit for you also? No longer am I in good standing with Lord Garth and King Alfred. You have made me appear the fool!" he cried, raising his hand to strike her. She put up her hands in defense.

When the blow did not come, she glanced up, seeing his hand still in midair. He appeared to give it a second thought. What good would it do to mar her face with a bruise? He brought his hand down swiftly, slapping it against his tunic. He regained control of his anger, reining in the fury he felt.

"Perhaps I can find some serf who toils the ground or an old soldier to take you off my hands. You have become a burden to me. Now I must go to pacify Garth, if that is possible."

She watched Radburn stalk out of the room and smiled to herself. Well, at least her child was safe, and herself as well, for the moment.

She picked up Ember, changed her soiled clothing and then fed her. Pamela came in, watching the mother and baby in comfortable union.

Bekah told her what had happened and that she had met King Alfred. "He appeared to know my mother, though I am not certain it was she. He said that I looked much like a girl he knew whose name was Mary. It was perhaps not she, but indeed a most strange coincidence."

"In truth! Do you think it was your mother he knew?"

Bekah shook her head. "I will never know, for I cannot ask her. It is an interesting thought."

Evening came upon her sooner than expected and she retired early. In time she slipped into a deep sleep that lasted well into the morning. Yet if she had known the conversation that had ensued between Lord Garth and King Alfred, she would not have slept at all.

"I do not think," said King Alfred, "That you should make a hasty decision concerning this matter, despite your convictions."

"But I could never accept a wife or grandchild with Norse blood," he said testily. "They are blood-thirsty barbarians. Oh, I can well understand your pact with Guthrum, what with the Arabs, Bulgars, Magyars, Franks and Slavs all causing trouble. A treaty giving Guthrum and his Danes Danelaw was the only smart thing to do. But does that first acceptance of them into our land mean that we must let them wed into our families?"

"Nay, of course not. I would agree with you, were the maid of Norse descent. But she is not."

"What? Her mother may have been Saxon, but her father was a Viking; she said so herself."

"Listen to this story, first, my friend, and then judge the maid. Do you remember my wedding to Ealswith?"

Garth nodded, leaning forward to better hear everything his King had to say. "What I tell you is in strictest confidence. No other must ever know of it."

"It will be so, milord. Please continue; what of your wedding day?"

"I was afflicted of a great pain."

"Yea, I do remember!"

"I must tell you, through these many years Ealswith has been a gentle wife, always patient and understanding. Yet in the years before our marriage, I suffered much at the memory of young Mary. She had not just beauty, but innocence and trust. I can still see her running through the meadow near her homeland, her dark golden hair flowing away behind her; she had a countenance of inner happiness. My memory of her has not faded one whit.

"Mary became my first love, and I, hers. That tender bud grew full-bloomed and I vowed to wed her. How was I to know that my elder brothers would each depart this earth and leave me the throne? At that time it was not of

209

any consequence who I, the youngest brother, loved or wed. It was my plan to marry her; when we were forced to return home, I gave her my pendant, telling her to send word if she needed me. A short time later I received the pendant back, and within it was a note."

He paused for a moment, freshly overcome by these memories long ago buried away.

"May I ask the contents of the note?"

"It was brief, telling me that she carried my child."

Garth stared at his old friend with renewed awe. "I never knew, sir."

"I should have left that very moment and gone to her. But I was young and very foolish. I stayed at my father's house nearly a fortnight until he gave me release to take leave. When I arrived, her grieving family told me of the Norsemen's raid; they assumed her captured and killed. I never told them of our child, not wanting to add to their sorrow. I mourned after that, and in some slight part of me I still mourn." He stood in quiet solitude for a moment. "Bekah was born shortly after Mary's arrival in Norseland. Apparently the Viking who took her was as smitten by her as I and either accepted the child as his own or assumed it to be his. No barbaric blood of a thick-skulled Viking courses through that maid's veins. There is grace in her walk; royalty is upon her brow, as is my own fair hair."

He paused for a moment, nodding sagely. The realization of this previously unknown daughter took a momentary toll. "The death of Mary and our unborn child nearly drove me insane. Mary haunted my dreams, and when I finally wed Ealswith, I was filled with such great suffering at the knowledge that it should have been Mary in her place that the pain became physical. Unknown to the physicians, only I knew its real cause."

"I remember the strange malady which plagued you at your marriage. Are you recovered from the pain?"

"I thought so, only yesterday. Now, after all these years, I have found my firstborn and I cannot even embrace her. She has no mother, even as I. My own mother died when I was young. She was a noble woman of fine stature. She often read to me from *Beowulf*. I should have read the story to Bekah when she was a child, but there is no retrieving the past."

"Yea, your mother was a kindly woman. But what of Judith? Your father, Ethelwulf, seemed to care for her."

"Indeed, but she was no mother to me. And now she has gone off and remarried."

"Baldwin, is it not?"

"Yea, a vain little man I do not care for." King Alfred should have been even more appalled if he were to know that in the future his own legal daughter, Ethelfleda, would marry Judith and Baldwin's son.

"Well, enough of this talk of the past," the King said. "It has left me weaker than I care to admit. My soldiers no doubt await instructions."

"Wait," Garth said. "I shall keep the secrets you have revealed to me, but what of Bekah?"

"That is up to you, sir—but I should not wish to find her at the mercy of your ambitious cousin."

"Nor I! Then let them marry. I should be most honored if your daughter should wed my son."

Alfred smiled, clasping an arm about the shorter man's shoulders. "It would ease my pain to know that after all these years the child I mourned for will be safely kept."

They journeyed to the main hall where the men were drinking ale to quench their thirst and telling tales of the tattooed Picts of Scotland. The talk turned to the emperor of Constantinople, and Alfred told of a chariot race he had once seen Michael III win.

"He won it right off and afterwards collapsed in a heap. He was out for three days!" There were rumblings of laughter at this. "He was not called The Drunkard for little reason!" Alfred added, and there were renewed guffaws. His men listened to every word with admiration. Their fair-haired sturdy leader was a fighting hero, and they loved him.

The morning sun brought welcome warmth, and Bekah stretched. Ember was fussing, so she changed the baby, then brought her into the warmth of the bed where she hungrily nursed. Bekah sang a soft song and talked to Kendra Ember about Mary and the stories she'd told. In half an hour she laid the baby down on a blanket on the floor where Ember cooed and smiled, looking at all the wonders around her.

Bekah bathed quickly, donning a slender white undershift and combing her hair into a long silken flow. She was pulling on a plain gray dress when Pamela came in hurriedly. She wore a bright blue dress edged in white. Bekah noted how petite and fragile her friend looked, her hair in a beautiful brown caress about that perfect oval face.

"Bekah, Radburn is here!" she whispered hurriedly only moments before he strode in.

Bekah turned her back quickly, buttoning the bodice hastily. "Have you no decency, Radburn?"

"We do not have time for your righteousness, Bekah. You had better hurry with your hair. After all, you are being wed within the hour."

"But how, after yesterday—?"

"I am hard pressed to understand it myself! After I left here I was so angry with you that I could have broken your pretty neck," he said harshly, standing akimbo and eyeing her rudely. "However, after some ale and a rather obliging wench, I sought out Garth to see if I could reason with him. His attitude was most changed; King Alfred had spoken wisely to him, for the King saw your potential."

"I cannot go through with this!" Bekah protested.

"Do not burden us with such hollow airs," he said testily. "Young Aidan is most anxious to see his bride."

"I will not be part of your scheme, and I will not wed Aidan for your sake. You cannot use me like this!"

"Yesterday I almost was glad of Garth's decision. I thought how nice it would be to have you for myself. If you refuse to wed Aidan, then I will be glad to keep you for myself. I do not think it would be terribly difficult to tame a sparrow such as yourself."

"You do not frighten me by your pretense, Radburn. I know the extent of your greed and that of your sister. I cannot assist you in your scheme."

"You cannot?" he said, raising an eyebrow and looming before her. "You have no choice! You will do as I say or you will never see that brat of yours again."

212

He reached Ember before Bekah, picking up the startled baby whose face formed a pout before she burst into tears. He held her away from the worried Bekah.

"My sister would surely like to have a child to raise as a servant," he mused.

"She hates the child! She is jealous of me and would be jealous of the baby as she grew older. How could my child exist in such a life?"

"She might survive."

"Your sister might even kill the baby! Would your greed carry you so far as to permit murder?"

He shrugged, and Ember's wail grew louder as Radburn carelessly held the infant in a precarious grasp. "Then it is up to you, is it not? I will keep the brat until such a time that Aidan tells me by his own voice that he is well pleased with his new bride. Then, with his consent, you may have the child back."

Bekah's face was ashen, and Pamela stood by with clenched fists, hating Radburn for his cruelty. Bekah reached for the baby, but he would not release the crying child, and it was torture for Bekah.

"She is dependent on me for her very food; she will starve!" Bekah cried, broken by her helplessness.

"Then I suggest that you make the wedding chamber most pleasant. I do not think that should be too difficult a task for one such as yourself. Come, come. It is not as if you were an innocent virgin, unaware of a man's pleasure! Do you consent?"

The tears which rimmed Bekah's eyes threatened to spill over, and she shut her eyes. She nodded, and Radburn released the baby to her. She saw the red marks on Ember's arm where he had held the child too tightly. She pulled her baby close against her, shushing the child, who quieted within the tender circle of her mother's arms.

Radburn grabbed Bekah tightly about the arm, guiding her into Mildred's empty chamber. Laid out on the bed was an exquisite dress.

"This is your wedding dress."

"Mildred will not allow me to wear it, for she highly values all her gowns."

" 'Tis not hers. It belonged to Aidan's mother; in fact she

213

wore it when she wed Garth. It will be most suitable; Garth was happy to supply it. I suggest that you dress quickly. You might help her," he said, addressing Pamela. His eyes quickly scanned the young girl. "Unless, of course, you care to walk in the garden with me."

"Bekah needs me here," she said, the loathing in her voice apparent.

He shrugged and departed, casting a few words over his shoulder. "I will be back soon to fetch you."

"What are you going to do?" Pamela questioned, trying to calm her own frustration.

"I am going to do exactly what Radburn has told me to do." She looked down at Ember, tears still at the corners of her eyes; the child looked up questioningly, as if wondering why she had been forced to endure pain. Almost immediately she closed her eyes, squirming down into the comfort of her mother's arms. She sighed, a jagged tearful sigh, and slept.

Bekah held her a moment longer, reluctant to lay the baby down. Finally she did, and then looking up at Pamela she said, "If I am to be this Aidan's wife then I will become the lady of the manor, and I will gain enough power so that no one will ever hurt me or my baby again! By these means I will obtain my freedom from Radburn and his sister. Please, will you help me with my hair?" She forcibly stilled the trembling of her hands by clasping them tightly together.

Pamela plaited Bekah's hair into soft, silken braids with dark velvet ribbons running through them. These she wound about Bekah's head, much like a crown. Strands of hair fell loose like silk ribbons resting lightly about her cheeks and neck. "I have outdone myself," Pamela said. Bekah was unusually pale, and Pamela applied a light coat of Mildred's rouge to Bekah's cheeks and mouth, determined that Aidan should be pleased with her.

Then Bekah pulled on the lightweight slip and the dress. It was as if it had been made for her. Of softest wine-colored velvet, it fit closely over the bodice, then fell away in folds which trapped many shades of light. It was edged with narrow braids and pearls. A delicate gold chain with entwining pearls fit about her slender waist.

"Oh, Bekah!" Pamela exclaimed, momentarily forgetting their plight. "I have never seen anyone look so perfect."

Bekah looked up at her sadly. "What of my baby, Pamela?"

"Do not worry. I shall take Ember to Jana, a friend of mine who feeds a healthy baby boy of her own. She has more than enough milk and will gladly feed Ember."

Bekah nodded, eased a little by this. "Give her my thanks. You are sure she will care for her well?"

"Yea, do not worry. Here, do not forget the velvet slippers. You look beautiful. You cannot help but steal Aidan's heart."

"That is the best I can hope for. Should he find fault with me, then my baby's life will be at stake."

"I wish that I could be there to see you wed," Pamela sighed.

"Then you shall. If I am to be the mistress, perhaps for only a short time, I need at least one friend at this wedding. But what of the children?"

"Hadlene and Ellena are here. Perhaps they will tend them." Pamela hurried out into the garden where the sisters sat mending. They were pleased to do a favor for the new mistress and agreed readily. Pamela ran back inside and told Bekah, then brushed her hair until it fell in a soft mane about her face. There was something enticing about Pamela. Clothed in the soft blue fabric which so skillfully outlined her slender curves she should have appeared meek, but this was not the case. There was an aura of excitement about her, though she was little aware of it, often surprised by the reaction of men who observed her. Bekah realized, as she looked at her friend, that while many women tried very hard to learn the skill of coquetry, Pamela was naturally born to it.

Radburn strode through the doorway just as Pamela stood up. "I am pleased to see that you are ready, Bekah."

"I have little choice, unless you have come to some sense of decency and will release me from this." Bekah went into the garden and took a deep breath of air.

"I am no fool," he said as he followed her. "Let us go."

"Pamela goes with me, for I need a friend."

"Ah! Well, if you wish, Pamela, you may join me at my table."

"I come for Bekah's sake, sir," she answered cooly.

He shrugged, signaling them to follow him from the garden. Pamela picked a pretty bouquet of white lilacs, handing them to Bekah. They walked through winding passageways as Radburn hurried them along. In time they found themselves at an arched doorway which led into the great hall. Bekah was amazed at the transformation of the place. Where once had been an ale hall now was a wedding festival. The floor was cleanly swept, and where straw had once been strewn now there were flower petals. Bright banners hung about the walls and from the high, vaulted ceiling. Garlands of apple blossoms were delicately curved over archways and draped along windowsills. Honeysuckle, ivy, marigolds and myriad other blossoms were centered down the long shiny tables which had been coated with beeswax.

The people were dressed in their brightest apparel. Women wore lovely dresses, many with white caps on their heads. The men were comfortably dressed, free of chain mail and swords. They all murmured among themselves, speculating, not aware for the moment of the bride's presence.

In one corner musicians played. Nimble fingers stroked the Celtic harp, the chords it produced interlaced by the strains of several flutes, a lyre and a drum. It was all so beautifully pleasant that under other circumstances both Pamela and Bekah should have been delighted. It was a perfect day for a wedding, the warmth of the new day budding in the first of July.

But the convivial spirit and heat of the day did little to warm Bekah. Fear for her baby and their future plagued her. She must succeed in this for Ember's sake! Foremost in her mind was the difficulty of her situation, and she hardly noticed as the musicians stilled their instruments and the crowd ceased their conversations; heads turned to stare at her.

After a moment's silence the music began again. Radburn, elegant in a dark purple tunic and breeches, circled his arm through hers, smiling pleasantly. Only Pamela knew of the dislike and hostility between the two. He led her through the congregation, which formed a pathway for them to pass through. She could not see Lord Garth or his son at the other end of the long, crowded hall. With surprise she realized that Radburn was to escort her to the bridegroom and give her to him. Because this was traditionally an act of love, the irony of the strange situation mocked her.

It was an effort to appear calm, and she stepped forward at a cruelly slow pace, placing one foot before the other. Her hands trembled slightly and she clasped them tightly about the white lilacs, watching as a few of the shaken blossoms fell slowly to the floor. She kept her eyes cast down, this wedding trek seeming to take far too long. For one bleary second, Kenric's face appeared clearly before her own, a look of sorrow engraved upon his features, and she faltered in her step. Radburn steadied her with his iron grip and she continued on as the crowd parted further.

The vivid memory of Kenric left her weak, and she was filled with a sudden remorse as she realized the meanness of her fate. Kenric haunted her now, flooding her with guilt and sorrow. She had no control over this mock wedding. She found that her feet had stopped, and looking up she saw Lord Garth and King Alfred standing proudly side by side. On the other side was Mildred, trying to look pleasant, and a circle of knights around all. But these people she barely noticed, for before her stood the young stranger whom she should have been meeting by the stream this very noon.

Her eyes deceived her and she closed them for a moment, bewildered. Why did her confused mind place him before her eyes at this exact moment? She opened her eyes to see his image still perfectly clear before her. A shaft of light from a high window fell upon him, outlining every feature.

His chestnut-colored hair fell softly about his handsome face. His eyes were piercing, and sunlight enhanced his features. He wore a short tunic of white velvet trimmed with bright green of the same fabric. His chausses were the same bright green, his boots a soft gray doeskin. Stepping forward, he took her hand in his.

She was most confused. What was the stranger doing

217

here, guiding her forward? He released her, and they stood away from each other. Perhaps he played some role as attendant in the ceremony? He was dressed more as a knight; perhaps that was his position. She looked about, feeling lost, a leaf fallen to a rushing stream, carried to unknown destinations.

A friar, very short in stature and wearing a long brown tunic, stepped forward, instructing her to kneel. She did so. Then he told Aidan to kneel, and Bekah watched as her young stranger stepped forward, kneeling close by her side. The bouquet of lilacs fell from her hand.

She turned her head towards him, looking up inquiringly at the stranger who knelt so closely by. Aidan!

Garth stepped forward, symbolically placing Bekah's hand in Aidan's. Her fingers were icily cold on this warm day, and his hand securely encircled hers, resting between them. Where was the Aidan whom she had expected to be vain, or plump like Garth, or cruel like his cousin Radburn?

Her mind was racing wildly, her cheeks flushed as warmth reached her fingers. Aidan smiled down reassuringly at her, and it was not until the friar spoke her name that she looked up, speaking assent to his question of avowal. Aidan did the same, and the bonds of marriage were forged.

King Alfred handed Aidan a ring of exquisitely carved gold with diamonds and sapphires woven into the auric circle. This Aidan placed on Bekah's finger. The friar, fingers together in a holy manner, nodded his round head, and Aidan turned towards her. With the gentlest touch of his fingers, he lifted her mouth to his own. Slowly their lips came together, and all held their breath as they awaited the touch. As Bekah and Aidan met in what appeared to be a ceremonial kiss of purity, a heated glow spread between them. It was more than a perfunctory kiss and lasted almost longer than appropriate. Once it was completed, an exhalation of breath filled the hall, and King Alfred stepped forward, assisting the couple up.

A shout of festive joy filled the castle, and the musicians again took up their instruments, the clarsach, that valued Celtic harp of golden wood, singing out. Alfred stepped forward, kissing Bekah upon the forehead in such a gentle manner that she looked up, pleased by his kindness. Little did she understand that look, so profound, which lingered upon his face and in the depths of his eyes. Nor would she ever understand the truth of their relationship.

"Aidan, you have the most beautiful bride in all my kingdom, and I bless this union."

"Thank you, Your Majesty." Aidan beamed. "I am happier today than I can ever remember!"

Alfred smiled at them both as if they were children whom he loved, and Garth stepped forward, taking Bekah's hand. He harumphed, then leaned forward and kissed her cheek, saying, "Welcome to our family, my dear. I am most pleased that my wayward son has finally been snared."

She smiled at this, a sense of intense relief still flooding her as she realized that her new husband was the special friend she had made in the garden. Her relief was followed closely by happiness she felt at having foiled Radburn's plans of cruelty. However, realizing that the stranger she had grown fond of was Aidan of Briarwood, she felt a moment of awe.

She was led about the circle of knights and introduced to all, remembering none. Mildred avoided her, refusing to meet Bekah on her new level. The people of Briarwood had begun dancing, and Aidan and Bekah found themselves separated by ambitious merrymakers.

As the pace of the music slowed, Aidan became annoyed that he was unable to see his bride. Bekah, too, felt lost as she danced with every knight. They fairly fought among themselves for her attentions. Colors whirled about her as she moved among varied partners, blurs of faces and unremembered names. When she felt almost too weary to dance another step, she felt her hand tightly clasped, another dancer pulling her away. She turned in exasperation, only to see it was Aidan.

She felt great relief at this, and he led her to a quiet alcove hidden by a huge red and blue tapestry. Soft golden light surrounded them as they caught their breath, free of the clamor about them.

"You look angry, milord. Does anything trouble you?" she asked, a smile trembling on her lips.

"Nay, I am only angry that you are my wife and yet I have not had one chance even to speak with you."

" 'Tis so; your people have a great capacity for enthusiasm."

"I realize that perhaps all this seems strange and even frightening to you. We have only met twice, and I noted surprise in your eyes as we knelt together."

"I did not expect this all to happen as it did, Aidan," she said, tasting his true name for the first time with pleasure upon her tongue. "I must admit I am most bewildered as to how this has all come about, and so quickly."

"Things should have been done differently. I realize that I should have taken time to come see you, but there are legends . . ."

"I have heard of them."

"Not that I believe them, but it is custom here. Also, when I learned that Radburn wanted your hand, I made all haste to remove you from him."

"I am glad to be free of him, for I found his manner unkind." She thought of Ember, whose fate rested in Radburn's cruel hands. She hoped beyond hope that Aidan might be kind enough to help her in this plight. But she must please him first, as his cruel cousin had demanded. She could not risk her baby by the hastiness of foolish words.

"I was right when I assumed that you care little for my cousin?"

"Yea, 'tis the truth."

"I knew you would not wish to marry him and I told him so," he declared, pleased with his own perception.

"He sought to exchange me for a better prize, such as the land he will receive."

"There is no better prize than thee, my bride. The jest is on him, anywise. He would have received the land in time, for you see, my father cares little for it." He braced himself with one arm against the wall and leaned near her. "There are many troubles in Mercia with the serfs and raids by the Danes."

She smiled at this and he leaned nearer. "Oh, you please me when you smile!" He looked down at her, placing his free arm about her slender waist. Slowly he drew near, bending forward. She lifted her face up to his, receiving a kiss so sweetly tender that honey was sour in comparison. Time held still, as did the noisy merrymaking and music without, to them. The kiss endured until each slowly drew back, the physical bond broken, the unseen bond created.

The perfection of the moment was shattered by the tapestry being flung back and Lord Garth striding in. "Here you are! A party proceeds in your honor and the two honored guests are not to be found!"

"Am I allowed no privacy with my wife, Father?"

"There will be time enough for privacy, yet, son," Garth laughed, wrinkles coming to the corners of his eyes. "Are you not aware that the feast is beginning? How can we start without you?"

In the hall there were long trestle tables, and the food was being brought out in a line from the kitchen. For the first time Bekah was able to view the great hall at ease. It had a large open hearth that would keep it warm during the dark winter months. There was a small room near, called the armory. She could see through the archway the barrels of sand and vinegar with swords and crossbows. The treasury was in the keep, too. It held the best wines, which were now being brought out. There was also the wardrobe in which were kept the spices grown in the herb garden.

The windows of the great hall were covered with oiled parchment, and in the corner was the wellhead. The walls were solid, built by skilled hands.

The main meal, always served late in the morning, was beginning, and Bekah found herself seated between Aidan and King Alfred. There was beef, mutton, pork, chicken and dried herring, with a large assortment of vegetables, fruits and breads, both dark and light. There were many wines, red and purple both. Large pitchers of ale and mead sat along the tabletops. There were bowls for washing the hands, and finely carved horn spoons. The people ate their food on trenchers, thick slices of day-old bread which served as plates.

In spite of the gala feast, Bekah found it difficult to eat, excitement tightening the emptiness in her stomach. She

221

again felt relief as she looked at her new husband, who laughed and talked to those around them. This man, whose hand held hers beneath the trestle table, was so amiably pleasant that she felt caught up in his happiness.

She looked down at her hand, seeing the beautiful gold ring which fit perfectly. She remembered the flower-shaped betrothal ring which Kenric had given her, and which the sea had taken from her. She closed her eyes until the vision disappeared and the sharp feeling of remorse stopped washing over her. There was a chance here, in this newly forged marriage, if only she could be promised Ember's safety and if thoughts of Kenric would stop haunting her.

She would try very hard to make Aidan a good wife, loyal and true, and knew it would not be too difficult a task.

King Alfred smiled at her, talking pleasantly to them both. She found herself returning the smile and listening eagerly to his anecdotes. Farther down the table she could see Pamela in the uncomfortable predicament of having two handsome young knights vie for her attention. They were talking animatedly, smiling deftly to cover the fierce competition between them. Bekah smiled, realizing that if anyone could handle a difficult situation it was Pamela. In a way she envied her friend, so secure in the love of one man. And she hoped that this man who had brought her from handmaiden to mistress of Briarwood in one quick step would be that one man for her.

After the feast they all gathered outside for the mock battles and tournaments. The soldiers and knights put on a fine show of parading their prancing destriers through obstacles and leaping over embankments.

There were games and competitions using the crossbow, lance and sword, and all the men competed in the archery games. Aidan did exceedingly well, and she noted the way he rode his horse with total command and ease. While he was involved in these games, Bekah hurriedly slipped away to her old rooms where Ember fussed hungrily in Ellena's arms. She fed her daughter, taking this precious moment to caress her infant, before reluctantly returning to the festivities. She felt more at ease now, knowing her daughter would sleep well.

Aidan, finding nothing amiss, dismounted from his fine steed, Chauncey, and approached his waiting bride. "Come. Let us leave these games. They are nearly finished."

He led her back through the castle, cool in the heat of the day, and past the nearly deserted hall. They climbed up the spiral steps until they arrived at the fourth floor. He took her into a large chamber to the right, and she realized that this must be his room. It was beautifully furnished with a desk and bed of dark wood. The room was large and hung with exquisite tapestries. A portion of the room was divided by one beautifully woven in green and blue; it depicted hills surrounding a valley and lake, upon which swans trailed streaks in the water. Fluffy white clouds rested in the sky, and yellow flowers dotted the imaginary hillsides.

There was a sturdy stone hearth which would be greatly appreciated in winter but which now lay cold, holding instead a large bucket of water. The bed was large, with sides and headboard carved with a sunburst design. The mattress was filled with feathers and down, as were the large pillows, covered with blue quilted slips. Huge fur pelts lay atop it, and one lay upon the floor near the edge of the bed. Lightweight fabric, tied back for the moment, hung about the bed from ceiling to floor. A large trunk at the foot of the bed and an upright chest with carved doors held Aidan's possessions.

Bekah felt the comfort here; the room was every inch like its master, and she enjoyed its uniqueness.

"It is beautiful here. Not just in the castle, but this room especially," she exclaimed, throwing her arms wide.

"I think of it as my haven. This has been my one place of privacy since I was a youth," he said, casting off his mantle. "Tomorrow I will show you all about the castle and its grounds, as you have never seen it before. I imagine you saw very little of it, being held almost in a prison as you were."

"It would be lovely to see all that Briarwood has to offer. As a child I used to dream of being wed to a castle baron. Little did I realize that I would be," she said, picking up a carved wooden horse and fingering its delicate lines.

"But Bekah, did you not understand from that day in your garden that I love you?" he asked, looking at her with earnest eyes.

She put the horse back in its place, raising her eyes to his. "I thought so, as you told me your poem."

"Did you not think that I would wish to wed you?"

"Indeed, I hoped so. But I did not know you to be Aidan. Do you not remember that you did not tell me your name?"

"What a fool I have been!" he slapped his hand to his forehead. "I thought it was great fun that you knew not who I was. My poor Bekah!"

"I was most concerned about wedding some man I did not know, and even more unhappily I thought I should never see you again. I did not understand who you were until the friar had us kneel."

"I am so sorry to have caused you such worry. In my anxiety to have you here as my wife I have not thought clearly these past days."

She wondered if she should ask him about Ember but realized that her baby would be safe with Pamela and that this time belonged to her new husband and herself.

He looked at her, taking a deep breath. "I realize that our marriage is not starting off on the best footing. Perhaps you would feel more at ease if I tell you that I do not wish to demand of you what would be difficult for you. What I mean to say is that I know I must still seem very much a stranger to you. I do not want to do anything now that would frighten you or cause you embarrassment. Time will bind us together as man and wife should be."

"There is nothing about you which would frighten me."

The fabric of sunlight wove its way into the room, illuminating the area in a pale glow. She studied Aidan. His hands, strong yet expressive, reached down to her hair. "May I?" he asked, carefully unbinding the braid of her hair until it fell loosely about her face.

"You are so beautiful. I have always been fascinated by long hair, and yours is of such a golden color. It feels like silk," he said, letting his fingers thread through it. "My mother had beautiful long hair."

"Your mother? I did not meet her at the wedding."

"She died two years past."

"I'm sorry. I have lost mine also."

He nodded. "My memories of her are special. I regret that you two could not meet; she would have loved you."

"This is your mother's wedding dress, did you know?"

"You look most beautiful in it, my wife."

He took this time to familiarize himself to her and put her at ease, delighting her with tales from his childhood. He talked of Christmases and hunting festivals. She sat down on the bed, listening intently. She laughed and added stories of her own.

"Do you know that I broke my arm?"

Her eyes widened. "Nay!"

"Right here. My father set it."

"How did you break it?"

"I was knocked off the back of my galloping steed."

"Were you in battle?"

"Ah . . . nay. 'Twas during a fox hunt when I was caught by a low branch. I was but a youth. The pain was very intense and my mother stayed up the whole night to comfort me."

"Tell me more of your experiences," she urged.

"Well, there was the time when I was very little and we went out on the lake. The boat overturned and I nearly drowned. The next day my father took me out and taught me to swim. I soon became proficient at it. I even helped the tutors at it when I was a page under old Applehead."

"You were a page? In this castle?"

"Nay, in another on the far side of Wessex. Before a youth can ever think of becoming a knight he must learn the basics of manners and etiquette so that he may appear at King Alfred's court and try for knighthood. We also learn fighting with the sword and crossbow, the lance and jousting pole. After that time I became a knight. I was in the court of King Alfred for a while after that before coming home to help my father run Briarwood. But here I have been talking only about myself. Tell me about yourself, Bekah of Briarwood."

"There is not a great deal to tell about me," she began. She told of her childhood in Norway and of the fond memories of her mother, who she told him had been a Saxon lady. He asked questions about her family and homeland. She told about her father's remarriage and Helg's treatment of her, and he sympathized. She paused for a moment, realizing how simple her problems had been in comparison to the complexity of those she had recently experienced. "My special place was a cove with warm tidal pools where I went to bathe. You cannot imagine my horror as I looked up from my bath to see a man standing there."

He put his fingers to her lips. "Wait. Do not go on. It is done and it is past. It has no meaning to our lives now."

"He is dead now, Aidan." She looked at him earnestly. "You know of my child, yet you have looked for the good in me. That means so much to me."

He broke the spell of the moment, desiring to make her earlier happiness return.

"Come," he said, guiding her to a table where there sat a board of inlaid squares and delicately carved pieces. "Do you play chess?"

She shook her head. "Is it a game?"

"Yea, and these are the pieces. These two are the queens, most powerful. And these are the kings, definitely men who are dependent upon their wives. These are knights and bishops."

"And these are the castles. What are all these little pieces?"

"Pawns. They are small but can by very useful in a game. Would you like to learn to play?"

"I would, very much. Will you teach me?"

"Sit down," he said, seating her in a chair near the table and pulling one up for himself. He explained the rules of chess to her.

"Then 'tis a game of war."

"Exactly! Shall we begin?" They did so and the game proceeded slowly while she paused to ask questions. He was more interested in watching his new young wife than in playing the game, and he laughed at her great delight in capturing a pawn and her obvious frustration at losing a bishop. It was not long until her king was taken and she rose abruptly.

"I do not think that I care for this game." She did not let on that she saw his real reason for playing the game, which was to put her at ease.

"It is only because you lost. Tomorrow you will be eager to try it again. You played quite well for your first game and after all," he pretended to jest, "you cannot expect to win over someone as experienced as I."

The afternoon light was fading, its soft amber rays mellowly announcing the ending of the day. Aidan stifled a yawn and pretended to stretch. "It has been a long day, with all the feasting and tournaments, and night is nearly upon us," he observed.

She reached out and touched his sleeve. "Aidan, I have nothing to wear but this dress."

"Oh, I have taken care of everything. Here," he said, opening the chest. "I have purchased a few things for you." He pulled out a long silky ivory-colored gown, an exquisite thing edged in brown lace and ribbons.

"It is lovely," she said, smiling as he handed it to her. She fingered the material gently. She had not had anything this fine since . . . a long time ago. "There are other things also, and I had your own things brought up. It grows dark," he said, lighting a few tapered yellow candles.

Bekah slipped into the small alcove off the bed chamber, hidden by a tapestry. She stepped out of her dress, carefully laying it aside, then pulled off her slip and undershift and quickly pulled on the silky nightgown which fell about her in soft folds. With trembling fingers she tied the ribbons at the bodice. The stone floor was cold beneath her feet and still she stood, waiting for what, she did not know.

Aidan pulled off the green velvet jerkin and removed his chausses and boots. He pulled back the coverlets and pelts on the bed, slipping beneath them. He leaned his head back on the pillows, his hands beneath his head. His eyes glanced frequently over to the covered chamber behind which his bride stood. He could detect no movement or sound behind the heavy tapestry. She was taking a very long time, it seemed, yet perhaps he had just undressed more quickly than usual. He smiled to himself and kept his burning gaze upon the tapestry which divided them.

It was parted from the side and she stepped through. Now that the sun had set, a chill breeze swept through the chamber, rustling the silk of her gown. He saw the slender, graceful curves of her form, the gown modestly enticing, her hair falling past her waist. She shivered a little, whether from cold or apprehension Aidan did not know. He held his hand out to her and timidly she came near, holding her own hand out until the two came together. He pulled back the covers, silently inviting her to enter, and she slipped beneath them, lying within their warmth.

She lay quietly in the dusk of coming evening, waiting for what she knew would come. Apprehension flickered across her features as she listened to every footfall beyond the chamber door and to the calls and shouts without the castle walls as the tournaments came to an end. She looked up into Aidan's golden eyes, and he smiled at her in appreciation, brushing back her tresses and taking her face into his hands, kissing her lips tenderly. She looked at his handsome face, framed by wheat-brown hair, and realized what a special man he was. 'Twould be easy to love this man, she thought. Tonight she would take that first step.

The touch of this beautiful man seared her very being, and the full remembrance of being a woman was brought home to her. It had been so very long since she had known the touch of a man, the giving of being a lover. Sweet sensations were created anew with this man, this golden stranger who had been meant for her. She began to feel that Aidan was the mate her soul longed for, and she shuddered within his embrace. There was a shower of sparks and the hammer of his desire was brought full force against the metal of her being. She said his name, tasting of it as she tasted of his passion. The desire between them was as quicksilver, sought but unfathomable. This consummation forged, Bekah fluttered dreamlike back to earth, lying cradled in her new husband's arms.

Aidan ran his fingers through the gold-spun hair that

fell in a tangled mass about them. This woman had been more than he had imagined possible, and he sought one last kiss from those soft lips. Never had he tasted of such tender fare, and he realized that he had never enjoyed any woman as he had his bride. No virgin had ever been so innocent, he thought, and for the first time in his life he was truly happy and fulfilled.

The warmth of slumber surrounded them as evening came and turned into night. Bekah awoke to find herself securely held in her husband's arms. The long hours she had gone since feeding her baby left her feeling full and very uncomfortable. She knew that Pamela would care for her baby, and that Jana would not let the child go hungry, but still she wished to hold Ember and see for herself that the child was still well.

She arose as quietly as she could, not wishing to disturb Aidan's sleep. How young he seemed, and how handsome. It was as if for the first time she might be given the chance to live a normal life—as wife to this castle baron. How gentle he had been, and how concerned for her. But more than that, he had stirred up the fires of passion in her that had nearly died out. He had made her a woman again, teaching her the delights of love that had faded from her memory. To be held in his arms, to experience those pleasures so longed for yet denied, was wonderful to her.

Things would be very different for her now. She would have a place in life, and no unkind person could harm her with barbs of gossip. She would have a position here, one which even Mildred must respect. If only she could have her baby back!

A chill swept over her and she gathered up a shawl which lay on a nearby chair, wrapping it about her and turning to gaze out the window at the midnight dark.

"Bekah," Aidan's voice called out sleepily as he reached for her. Then suddenly, "Bekah, where are you?"

"Here, Aidan," she said, turning from the window.

"Oh," he moaned, falling back into the thick pillows. "I dreamed I had lost you again. What are you doing up at this early hour?"

"I am troubled, Aidan. I must ask you something."

"What?"

"Have I pleased you?"

"Why, Bekah! Did you not know?" he asked with wonder.

"In truth, I felt that I had done so. Then will you tell Radburn," she said, an unusual pleading creeping into her voice.

"Radburn! What in the devil does he have to do with anything?"

"He told me that I was to please you and he must hear it from your own lips."

"The scoundrel! I shall have words with him!" he cried, half-rising.

"I only wish him to return Ember to me. It is not since yesterday that I have fed her, and I am most uncomfortable and concerned for her safety."

"He keeps her from you? I thought you were just having her taken care of for the night. Would he harm her?" he asked incredulously.

"I do not know what he is capable of. He said that if I do not please you then I should never see the baby again. He said he would give her to Mildred."

Aidan leaped from the bed, angrily pulling on his breeches and shirt. He stalked from the room so quickly that she had no time even to question his actions. He paced through the hall and down the stairs, then barged into Mildred's room.

"Mildred, where is the child?" he said sternly, his face stormy.

Mildred, aroused from sleep, pulled the coverlets closer about her throat and let out a frightened squawk. "The child?" she repeated, sleep still thick upon her tongue.

"Bekah's baby. Our baby. Certainly you have not let her come to harm? I would hope for your sake, dear cousin, that the child is all right."

"Just a minute," she stammered, calling out to Ellena to fetch Pamela. Pamela soon entered with Ember, who had slept fitfully and was now awake.

"I have taken care of her all night and she is fine," Pamela said, happy at this good turn of events as Aidan took the fussing baby from her arms.

"You are very lucky, Mildred, that this baby's only problem is a missed mother. Where does your brother reside this night?"

"I do not know. It is not my concern where he beds down for the night."

"Then I will talk to him in the morning." Aidan returned to his chamber as quickly as possible. He was very glad to turn Ember over to her mother, who wiped away tears of gratitude.

"I cannot thank you enough, Aidan. You are kinder to me than anyone in my life has been these past years." She slipped her arms about his neck, kissing him in thanks.

"Why did you not tell me of this last night? I would have gladly sent for Ember."

"Radburn thought that if you knew I had a baby you would never have accepted me, lest I pleased you well. In truth, I feared also for my baby, until our wedding ceremony when I knew who you were."

"But the jest was upon Radburn, for I knew of the baby after our meeting in the garden."

He lay close to Bekah, watching as she nursed the eager baby. She looked up at him and smiled. "I am glad to have her back in the safety of my arms, but last night belongs to us."

"She is a small child. I have had little experience with babies."

"She is dainty as a girl should be. Our sons shall be strong like their father," she said.

"They will have to be, if they carry their mother's beauty," he chuckled. "Father will like grandchildren. And all our sons will need a sister to protect."

"I cannot tell you how happy it makes me that you like Ember. Poor little waif, she has never known a father's love. You do not mind that she is my first child?"

"She is much like you, and who am I to resist two such lovely ladies?"

Bekah gave him a sweet smile and laid the sleeping baby on a warm bed of furs, wrapping her tightly against the morning cold. Aidan watched her graceful movements, his eyes alive with liquid lights, like a lightning storm over a green sea.

Did she think often of this other man? Jealousy plagued

him. He wondered if she had ever loved him. He knew that this villain had taken her by force and perhaps she had hated him; however Bekah's love was a prize worth all a man's patience. Perhaps he had taken time to convince her to love him. And if she had? The thought was tormenting, the only comfort lying in the knowledge that the kidnapper was dead. He did not ask, for he did not want to face the truth of an answer.

He could not know that Kenric would no longer haunt Bekah's dreams nor would she feel empty inside. This past year she had missed him terribly and longed for him. But Aidan would fill that loneliness in a different way, and she was happy.

This cool summer morning when they found themselves holding each other close for warmth, it was as if a silent vow were taken, a vow of love and friendship that was bonded by the physical union. A desire never to hurt the other brought peace to them, and trust. In time they would come to know each other very well. The lights in his eyes, his handsome brow, his strong hands, were all things she would come to know and love.

As they lay still, his breath the only sound she could hear, she looked at a tapestry covering a wall near her. What fingers had woven with such beautiful workmanship the tapestry that must have taken from youth to old age? she wondered. There were wild horses, black, white and silver, running with their manes flying, the muscles in their necks taut. Upon one rode a maid, barely clothed in a pale green tunic, her red-gold tresses flying. She held a spear in one hand, a shield in the other, a look of defiance on her face as she viewed her opponent. Wolves snarled at the horse's hooves, and by the side of a large wolf stood a splendid man with bronzed skin and golden hair. More powerful than the girl, still he was not the victor.

Bekah wondered what it would be like to live as the woman in the picture. How she longed to be defiant, strong and victorious! It occurred to her, the more that she looked at the picture, that the woman was the victor because she was a woman. Yea, a woman had many strengths. She looked at Aidan asleep by her, his arm across her, his fingers resting on her shoulder, and Bekah began to feel her inner strengths.

The late morning meal was a farewell feast to King Alfred and his knights, who would leave Briarwood shortly. Bekah prepared for the occasion. She had been given many lovely clothes and accessories as a new bride and mistress of Briarwood. Aidan had left two hours ago to take care of certain matters about the castle. Bekah did not know that he intended a discussion with Radburn. Aidan still felt an angry flush upon finding the man. He looked at his cousin coldly and requested that he leave that day and take Mildred with him.

Radburn, hearing the menacing quiet of Aidan's voice, found himself at a disadvantage. He felt uncomfortable under his cousin's harsh glare and consented to make plans to leave with King Alfred's entourage. He left Aidan and sought out the king, noticing briefly that for his victory he felt a compelling sense of failure. It appeared that his young cousin was really in love with the girl.

Bekah knew nothing of the incident. She bathed in scented lilac water, washing and drying her hair until it was, as Aidan described it, "a floating cobweb of purest gold." Her face had regained its youthful radiance, making her seem younger than her years. She chattered happily to Pamela, who spent much time with her.

She explained to her friend about having met Aidan twice before, and her happiness at the situation pleased Pamela very much. Pamela herself had gained a new status among the castle dwellers and she was happy both for herself and for Bekah. She thought it like an enchanted tale of the little peasant girl whose beauty and goodness ensnared the heart of a prince.

They looked through the trunks of clothing, exclaiming at this and that until Bekah finally decided on a tunic of dark green over a kirtle of a lighter hue. Both were sewn with silver braid and the tunic's hem was tucked into a wide belt heavily embroidered with silver thread. There were dresses Bekah said were wrong for herself, but suited Pamela perfectly.

They looked through chests in which many garments

233

lay. They sorted through them, neatly folding and putting away the undershifts, slips, kirtles and sashes. There were also a variety of sandals and slippers. Bekah lifted out two mantles. One was lightweight, of indigo color. She folded it and put it carefully away. The other was of warm sorrel wool lined hood and all with sable. She stroked the fur.

"Did you ever think that you would have beautiful clothes like these?"

"I did have many . . . once."

"Kenric gave you many nice clothes?"

"Yea, for I had only the one skirt and blouse I was wearing when brought from my home. I was happy to have those lovely things, and yet I fought accepting them. He was very stubborn, though." She had been stroking the fur against her face and reluctantly folded the cloak and put it away. "That seems like years ago, another time and place. And now Aidan loves me and cares not about my past. He is a good man, I think."

"Yea, he is. I thought that when you met him and saw what he was like that you would not protest the marriage so. And then when he came down early this morning to get Ember I knew that all was well for you."

Bekah held up several nightgowns, examining their fine workmanship before placing the last of them away. "It was so remarkable! He went and brought Ember back to me. He accepts the child and is willing to forget my past, indeed not even wanting to know of it. It is a great easing of worry for me."

"Can you put the past away, though?"

"I must. I have been handed a future as precious as a sparkling gem and all that happened to me is but a memory. Ember is the last remnant of my past; everything else of it is gone. But I know that to talk of that past would hurt Aidan, for he loves me, and I cannot bring this man pain. I will not talk of Kenric, or of those other days, again."

Pamela nodded. " 'Tis wise of you."

Aidan stepped through the chamber door, coming to his wife.

"You look beautiful in that new dress, Bekah!" he exclaimed, smiling into her eyes. "The color suits you well."

"Thank you for the clothing, Aidan."

234

"They were the clothes that my mother saved for the bride that I would choose."

"Then I am doubly pleased."

Aidan and Bekah walked down the stairs, heading towards the main hall. A window in the stairwell let in a beam of sunlight, turning dark stones to dull gold. The two paused for a moment, looking at each other. There was a silence between them, an unspoken avowal. Aidan slipped his arms about her, pulling her into him. Her hands rested against the fabric of his shirt, smooth over powerful muscles. His brown head bent to her golden one, his mouth seeking hers. There was heat in his kiss, passion and strength in his hands as they slid up her back. The heat of his kiss proclaimed that she was his, that no other could touch which was declared Aidan's.

When at last he pulled away, still she leaned against him. Bekah looked up into his face, the light that edged their features adding flecks of gold to his hazel eyes. A slow smile came to his lips and he took her hand, leading her down the stairs. Even though they left the solitude of the sunlit place, still his kiss lingered with her.

Few did not notice Bekah's flushed cheeks and shining eyes or Aidan's cheerful manner. All decided that it had gone extremely well for the wedding night, and the hall became even more cheerful.

The feast was soon begun and Bekah ate more heartily than she had the day before, the food especially tantalizing. Once again she was seated near King Alfred, who paid her kindly attention, talking about many subjects which she found interesting and to which she added her own comments.

The salt merchant from Cheshire had arrived, and with him a band of traveling minstrels who entertained with their songs and poetry and humorous wit. Bekah found them and their music enjoyable, remembering that her mother had often talked of such entertainment. By noon the feast was over and the king and his knights were ready to depart—along with Radburn and Mildred.

Before leaving, King Alfred gave Aidan a wedding gift. It was a delicately carved horning lantern of wood and white oxhorn. He had designed it himself and was quite proud of it; a number of candles inside the basic structure would burn at four-hour intervals; in such a manner time could be closely estimated by its use. Until now all that Briarwood had had was a sundial in the main garden, but it became useless on cloudy days. King Alfred demonstrated the lantern as everyone listened in awe, Garth especially pleased.

As they stood without the wall of Briarwood, ready to depart, Alfred's eyes fell upon Bekah, as beautiful as her mother had been, if not more so.

"You have brought back my youth, daughter," he said fondly, his blue eyes meeting her own. "May God and kind lady Saint Mary bless you, Bekah."

He seemed to sense that within all the years of his reign, he would never be so touched by any maid as by her. He gave one last glance at his unacknowledged daughter before mounting his large brown steed.

"He seems quite fond of you, my wife," Aidan said, encircling her waist with his arm.

"Indeed," Garth murmured, smiling sagely.

As the kindly king and his entourage departed, all at the Castle Briarwood watched, then each went to his own task or diversion. Aidan, on a stroke of inspiration, decided to take her with him on his rounds and to show her all over which he ruled. They strolled to the stables not too far from the castle.

She had never been here before, and was amazed to see the many lovely beasts of different colors and breeds. They mostly roamed free in the near meadows adjoining the stables. She chose to ride with her husband, which pleased Aidan, for he could not be close enough to his new bride. He lifted her upon his destrier Chauncey and they rode off, each pleasantly aware of the other.

They skirted the many farmlands where men in breeches and wooden sandals, tanned by the summer sun, toiled at weeding, tending and irrigating the long rows of abundant produce. The lands owned about the castle stretched far and long, and often they passed tenant houses where fat naked children came out to wave until rosy-cheeked mothers shooed them away with their aprons.

Fields were green with clover or gold with hay, and the

236

day's warmth brought all nature within view of the two lovers. Butterflies danced from poppy to sunflower, and the aroma of life was richly inviting. Never had Bekah felt so accepted by life, and so at peace.

Let it always be so, she prayed fervently within.

There were cattle, pigs, goats and an assortment of fowls here in their land and all manner of wild game roaming freely through the forests. Bekah liked the woods best, for it was in the forest that she and Aidan had first met. The woods bordered on the clear blue lake, the Castle Briarwood on its edge. It was not a large lake, and Aidan explained how it was slowly drying up, and in perhaps a century or so it would be gone. This saddened Bekah, for she hated to think of this beautiful handiwork of nature disappearing.

There were small boats which could go out on the lake, and Aidan took her out in one of these. She was thrilled at the depths of the water as she gazed down, trailing her hand in it. Small silvery fish darted beneath them, and a cool wind sent ripples across the lake's surface.

Beautiful white swans with gracefully curved necks glided by, followed by the babies in a straight line behind their parents.

"They are beautiful birds, Aidan, and I have not seen such before."

"We are proud of the wild swans which choose to inhabit our lake. They are a bird that our people respect, for they figure prominently in our legends."

"How?"

"I believe it is the haunting song that they sing upon their death. It is said that when they die their last breath is a melody eerie beyond all else. I have never heard it, but then, I have never been in the presence of a dying swan."

"Oh, Aidan." She laughed at his serious expression. "I should like to hear this strange swan song."

"Oh, nay, my dear wife! It is legend that he who hears the sad call experiences tragedy."

"I take little stock in your legends. For instance, that one about us seeing each other before our wedding."

"Indeed! Our people take it seriously you know."

"But we saw each other before the three days' separation."

His brow puckered in concern for a moment, and then he smiled broadly, throwing his arms wide and rocking the boat. "There is no fear in a union blessed by King Alfred himself!"

"Take heed not to rock the boat lest we drown!" she cried as the boat continued to tip.

Back inside the castle, Aidan gave her a view of his home she had never before seen, hidden away as she had been. They visited the gardens first, where a sundial of carved stone stood beautifully in the center. There were fuchsias, asters, marigolds and lilacs. Roses in yellow, red, pink and white grew about the walk. Then they went into the sunny herb garden, where the pungent, spicy scents were combined in a tangy aroma which wafted to them in the summer heat. There were saffron, thyme, rosemary, basil, mint, sage, mustard, parsley and other herbs which Bekah could not identify.

They went through the lovely orchard of fruit trees and sculpted yews, and Bekah marveled at the beauty of budding fruit and jade-green leaves.

Then he took her through the castle, starting with the dungeon, which was unoccupied in this time of peace. Aidan pulled back the heavy wooden door and guided her down the twenty-seven narrow steps which led into the dank hole. Even with his arm about her she shuddered, wanting to withdraw. He pushed back another door of crossed metal bars, and as her eyes became accustomed to the darkness she could see the small, crowded room carved out of earth. One small hole gave ventilation and light.

"This is a dreadful place, Aidan. I never dreamed that this beautiful castle could have such an unholy place!"

"Yea, it is not pleasant here, as those who have occupied it will say. But there is no need to fear while I am near you."

"It is not used anymore, is it?"

"Once in a while. Mostly it has been used for those captured while warring against us. However, there are many tenants whom we rule over. Most of the serfs are happy enough and do not wish to cause trouble, only to live under

238

Briarwood's protection. There are sometimes poachers, or those who steal and will not right the wrong. My father is a good judge, and most fair in the minor squabbles that arise."

"Still, do you put troublesome serfs in here?" she asked, her eyes wide with interest.

Aidan laughed, his pleasant voice dispelling the gloom a little. "Nay, the last time was nearly a decade ago. One of the serfs found his wife in the arms of another man and killed both the woman and her lover. He was brought here for safekeeping until judgment could be passed. However, before his trial he killed himself, and those of a more superstitious nature say he haunts the dungeon now."

"I do not believe in ghosts."

"Neither do I, but what would our people do if they had nothing of interest to talk about here? The dungeon is seldom used now," he said, guiding her from the darkness of the place. "It was occupied more in my ancestors' time, for theirs was seldom a time of peace. It is said, however, that one of my great-uncles had a better use for it."

"What better use?"

"Well, he was married early to a rich noble's daughter who as time passed became much of a shrew. When he could take it no more he would cast her into the dungeon until she would promise to cease her nagging."

"How dreadful! I should hate to be held in this musty place. Is that a warning to me not to become a nagging wife?" she asked, her face dimpling into a smile.

He laughed at this, shaking his finger at her. "You are very perceptive, my love."

They found themselves in the storeroom eventually. The shelves held food supplies of every kind, and there was even a section for materials of many weaves and varied threads. There were coarse cloths by yards, while the finer materials were locked away. Spinning wheels, looms, bales of carded wool and rounds of cotton weaving threads were stored here also. There were huge rows of salted, smoked or cured hams, bacon, beefs and other meats. Barrels of unknown items exuded enticing odors and there were bins which held goose down feathers. Bekah found it all fascinating, and Aidan practically had to drag her away.

Next there was the kitchen with its huge open hearth and a large iron caldron for soups and stews. There were large tables where pleasant ladies in varicolored dresses worked, stopping to curtsy as the couple entered. There were delicious smells, and busy, cheerful sounds. Aidan gathered up two rolls, coating them with pale, creamy butter.

This floor also held the garrison; there were rows of mail tunics, conical metal helmets, swords, crossbows, spears and scramasaxes. She met the armorer who kept the weapons in order and who appeared very much the good soldier. Though short and stocky, he had a courageous look about him, and carried scars of battle.

Bekah was introduced to Portney, who was steward of the castle, managing and controlling the constant flow of the people and supplies belonging to Briarwood. He bowed deeply to honor the new lady, glancing around anxiously to see if all was in order. He hurried a lazy serf with a piercing stare, and smiled at his new mistress.

The treasury was here also, and Bekah was allowed to tour it. The best wines and spices, materials and metals were kept here, and she met the wardrober, Crant, who was also the treasurer. He was a gaunt man with small flashing eyes that were pale and seemed to count and recount each penny and piece of gold. A penny was one of thirty parts which equaled a mancus, which was the price of an ox. These, and each item with which he was entrusted, were secure in his miserly care.

She noted with humor the obvious friction between Portney and Crant, who in truth despised each other. Crant thought that Portney was an extravagant spender, while he thought himself the most frugal of persons. Portney, on the other hand, though by no means a gracious spender, thought the castle treasurer the miserliest of persons ever born. They battled constantly: Portney wished for the most appropriate things for Briarwood, and Crant desperately tried to hoard all for the hard times which inevitably came to the castle.

Caught between the two was the chaplain, who was also

the cleric, and who kept records of each item and activity.
Both Crant and Portney were in need of his services, so he
was constantly exposed to their minor battles which he
tried to rule over with justness, honor and help from the
Almighty.

The marshal in charge of horses arranged all traveling
procedures. Bekah also met the maingate porter, Wes-
gally, a plump man with only a fringe of red hair who
carried a ring of keys importantly upon his wide leather
belt.

In the great hall were knights, whom Bekah had already
met, and servants who at night slept here on benches or on
rushes wrapped in cloaks. There were also sewing ladies
who produced the clothing. There were over a hundred people here at Briarwood and Bekah was amazed to learn of
its intricacy and method of survival.

They ascended to the bedrooms and Lord Garth's study.
This was the room she had wandered into when she had
met King Alfred. Here she was able to see books and many
other things, including maps.

Aidan showed her a map of Angland and she marveled
at it, for it appeared so small on the paper. He showed her
where she had come from and she could hardly believe that
her long journeys could appear so insignificant.

He pointed out York and Mercia, Cambridge, Wales and
Northumbria. He showed her Danelaw which Guthrum
ruled. There was Wessex, too. How small it seemed on
the map, yet how huge and all-encompassing in life. He
showed her Appledore; not far from there was the castle
where he had served as a youth.

Aidan told her thrilling tales of tournaments, of track-
ing wild boar and taming his pet hawk, Soran. She was en-
thralled by his stories of wild rides at dawn and pranks on
old Applehead, their teacher. Aidan spoke of his best
friend, Jouster, so called because he never lost a jousting
tournament. Aidan himself had excelled in horse jumping
and the crossbow. Perhaps the fact that the two youths had
been superior in the physical skills of the knighthood, if
not in manners, had caused them to be the envy and the
admiration of the other pages. They became as close as any
two brothers, although Aidan, more the poet and philoso-

pher, had sometimes clashed with Jouster's sarcastic view
of a paradoxical life.

"Have you seen him often, since then?"

"Indeed, for we served in King Alfred's army together.
But I have not seen my friend for these past two years, and
I am most anxious to show him my beautiful young wife."

"And I should be most anxious to meet any friend so
dear to you, my husband," she smiled, noting again his
handsome features.

He finished the tour by showing her the pigeon house
where plump blue-gray and white pigeons cooed and called
to each other. These were a good investment for the winter
months, when they would often have pigeon pies, and the
young birds, not ready to fly, were turned into delicious
dinners. This was Aidan's favorite food, and as he described the dark, salty meat to her, Bekah made a mental
note to have it for a special occasion.

He took her up to the battlements, where in times of
peace the tenants still kept watch, in partial payment toward the rent of their land. She could see the farmlands
and forests, stretching to the horizon, appearing to be a
lovely piece of cloth cast at her feet. The lake was a shimmering aqua jewel upon which floated the wild swans and
domestic geese, barely specks of white from this height.
The setting sun spread its golden-pink aura over the land,
dancing upon the water, while the pale orb of the moon sat
patiently awaiting its reign.

Aidan pointed out the granaries, the tanning and smok-
ing houses, the horses running through the meadows.

"It is all so splendid and so plentiful—as if I should never
worry or be hurt again," Bekah murmured half to herself,
leaning her head back against his chest. "Do you not view
this and wonder at its beauty, Aidan?"

"Indeed, for it is my home and my heart is here, no matter where I travel. Yet you have become my life in this
short time. As I love viewing my lands from here through
each season and in different hours of the day, so it is with
you, my love."

He caught her chin in the crook of his finger, lifting her
face up. "There is a boundless joy within me as I gaze at
your beauty, ever changing with the emotions that depict

themselves upon your features. My greatest happiness has become my study of you, gazing at your fairness in different lights and varied places. It is enough to know that you are mine."

She reached up and stroked his cheek with a single finger. He bent towards her, heedless of the gawking serfs, their lips coming together in a warm touch. They descended to the main hall where a great goose had been cooked and was being served.

The meal over, they escaped to their chamber, now drenched with the silver glow of twilight. While others enjoyed idle talk and played draughts or chess, Bekah and Aidan pursued a more tender and fulfilling use of their hours. It was not enough merely to know each other's physical attributes, but more important still to search into the depths of soul and mind.

The evening ended with them clasped in love, and this was followed by sleep, their pleasant dreams interrupted only by the song of the nightingale or the copper threads of morning sunlight.

The lands of Briarwood began to become part of Bekah and she became a part of Aidan. It was a magical time for them.

Bekah began to just have fun. It was an incredible, small thing, but it was something which she had not experienced before. She and Aidan did things together. Impetuous or hilarious, they were things of sheer enjoyment. Bekah's relationship with Kenric had been a deeply passionate one, but it had also been stormy. Aidan was very different from Kenric, and so their relationship was different.

Aidan took her out for a ride on a sultry day when Ember was asleep under Pamela's care. They sauntered through fields of willowy wheat and riotous wild flowers. Then Bekah sat before Aidan on Chauncey, leaning against her husband, relaxed and happy even in the oppressive heat of the day. She had never felt this at ease with any man, for there was nothing about which Aidan tested her or pressed her.

They found themselves by a stream which wound its way into a steep gully well hidden by trees and bushy foliage surrounding its mossy banks.

"Come, my wife, let's ease the heat by a swim."

"Oh, Aidan, should we? What if someone should come by?"

"It is very secluded here. I have come to this spot before," he smiled, his arms encircling her and hugging her to him.

"Oh? And who have you brought here before me?"

"Do I detect a small worry of jealousy?"

"Certainly not," she said, slipping off the horse.

"Then why are you walking away?" he called teasingly after her, throwing himself off Chauncey. The animal snorted and wandered off to chew on some tender blades.

"There was someone I brought here, I remember now," he said thoughtfully.

She turned and looked up at him. "Oh?" she said, pretending disinterest.

"Hmmm," he affirmed, walking off to look at the cool stream. "It was in my early youth; I was but fourteen or so."

"And what did you do here?"

"We went swimming, of course. It was a hot day much like this. We ran into mishap, however. Foolishly we had put all our clothes in the saddlebag on the horse and it wandered off. We had not a single stitch on, either of us!"

"I see!" she said, her lips pursed.

"We were afraid that we would have to go home with nothing on if we did not find that blasted steed. It is quite humorous now to think upon it, but at the time I was worried."

"I think you deserved what you got."

"It all worked out fine, for we found the horse and next time were smart enough to toss our clothing over some bushes."

"You came more than once here, swimming?"

"We came here all summer long." He nodded, standing on the water's edge and peering down into it. "After all, Jouster stayed for the summer, and there was little else to do."

"Jouster!"

"Yea, who did you think I meant?" He grinned.

"Oh!" she groaned, pushing him with a quick thrust

that made him slip on the mossy bank and fall with a resounding splash. He came up sputtering water and surged
out of its depths.

"You'll not leave me floundering in a stream this time!"
he said, grabbing hold of her to bring her in with him. She
darted quickly away, but he climbed out and caught her.
He tightened his grasp about her, getting her wet. "Now
either come in swimming with me or I shall toss you in."

"All right." She smiled as he stripped off his wet clothes,
tossing them into the sun to dry. She took off her tunic and
kirtle, leaving on her shift for modesty's sake, and then
took to the cool refreshment of the stream.

Aidan dove into the water, splashing her and rising up
out of the stream in a shimmering spray of water droplets.
They splashed and squealed like children at play. She
thought how handsome he was, the muscles in his chest
and shoulders strong and silkily fluid, his belly flat. His
thighs were strong, his body agile, and he swam about the
deepest part of the stream with strong strokes.

He surged up out of the water before her, his hair dripping and a happy grin upon his face. He spent some time
showing her the rudiments of swimming, finally giving up
at this endeavor. She lay back in the water, letting her
hair float like wet silk about her.

"You are so beautiful, Bekah."

"I am?"

"Have you not been told often?"

"By my mother."

He laughed. "What of men? Certainly many have sung
your praises."

"A few, but I assure you that it has been nothing but a
problem to me. Look at your cousin Radburn. He took me
away from a place of kindness, as good as my own family,
and I had to threaten to take my own life in order to make
him let me keep Ember."

"The blackguard! I have never liked him or his sister."

"That is past now, and I am here with you."

"Even I am at fault, though. I wanted you for myself.
But I do not love you because of your beauty, but rather for
the quiet, tender girl behind your appearance." He pulled

245

her close against him, holding her in a warm embrace as the gurgling water rushed between them.

They splashed in the water, soaking each other, and Aidan dove under the water again, tickling her legs and pretending to nip her calves or feet as she squealed and tried to dodge him. Finally when they were chilled they climbed onto a large flat rock, hot in the sun, to dry themselves. Later on they lay on a grassy bank, making love as newlywed husband and wife.

They arrived home just as Ember was more than ready to eat, and Aidan watched quietly as his wife nursed his new daughter. He tickled the baby's foot and watched her curl her toes.

That night there was a festive affair with a good meal of cold foods and drinks. As the evening brought coolness, there began to come together the light strains of Celtic harp, flute and drum. Some people began to dance, and soon Bekah and Aidan found themselves joining in. They followed the traditional steps, his right arm around her waist, her back to him, their left hands together, fingers entwined. She smiled up at Aidan as she quickly caught on to the steps, thinking how handsome he was, his eyes flecked with gold, picking up the candlelight. He returned her smile, thinking for all the world that he was the luckiest man alive.

Cool breezes caressed the dancers, making the candles cast darting shadows about the old walls. Lord Garth, watching his son and his son's wife dancing happily together, smiled to himself. His son was in love, and he could understand it all too well. With satisfaction he noted that Bekah returned the feeling. He also noticed that they retired early, their desire to be alone apparent.

A week passed. Early one morning, while the light that seeped in through the window was yet a flat gray, indicating that neither sun nor serf had arisen, Aidan aroused Bekah. She yawned and stretched, muttering his name before slipping back into slumber.

"Get up, wife," he said, softly shaking her shoulders. "Would you sleep the day away?"

She pried her eyes open, pulling the covers about her. "What are you doing up, Aidan? It is still night."

"Nay, it is not!" he said, pulling off the covers. "Cast off that gown and put these on." He tossed her some clothes and pushed her to her feet.

He helped her dress, ignoring her inquiries and hurrying her along. "Do not worry about your hair."

After she had hastily dressed he grabbed her hand, pulling her out of the room and down the hallway. They hurried down the circular stairwell until they found themselves outside in the black-gray of early morning, the air crisp in summer dawn, a puff of white breath visible. They went to the stables, the animals pricking up their ears as the master neared. Chauncey snorted as if in disgust at the rude hour of awakening, and at having a bit placed in his mouth before grain.

"Aidan, we are going for a ride this early?"

"Indeed, this is the best time!"

"I doubt that Chauncey thinks so, or desires to carry us both at this hour."

"Ah, but he shan't. I have a surprise for you!" Aidan brought out a slender little mare. She was a dappled gray, with a shiny pearl-gray coat and a silky mane and tail.

"This mare is for you. I brought her back yesterday, so that you could ride whenever you wish."

Bekah took in a deep breath. "Oh, Aidan! She is lovely! She is for me, my own horse?"

"At my word, she is."

She laughed, happily clapping her hands, then running to him and kissing him. "Thank you!" she said, tears misting her eyes.

"Do not cry," he warned, embarrassed that his simple action should bring about such gratitude. "The lady of Briarwood needs a horse, and when I thought of you riding and saw this little mare, I knew you would like her. You do like her, do you not?"

"I do, indeed, and never have I had such a thoughtful gift! What is her name?"

"She hasn't one. You can name her whatever you wish," he said, putting the appropriate tack and fleece saddles on the steeds. "But for now we must hurry. I had planned to give her to you this afternoon, but I could not wait. Let's ride out."

"Where are we going?"

"It is a surprise, so let us be on our way," he said, helping her mount, then lightly casting himself atop the snorting, indignant Chauncey.

They galloped off at a fast pace, the feel of freedom and of the surging, muscular steeds exhilarating beneath them. The brisk wind whistled past them, tingling their skin and wiping their words away. Aidan pointed towards an eastward hill and Bekah nodded. She spurred her horse on, faster and with a thrilling speed. The thudding sound of hooves upon sod was a steady drumbeat as Aidan realized that they raced, and that his wife was pulling ahead. The wild mane of her hair, silver in this early light, flew back like a cape, the features of her face intense in the concentration of the race. For a single moment he thought of her as a Norse goddess deserving of a splendid piece of poetry, before he realized that she might beat him to the top of the hill. He spurred his destrier forward, determined that no mere sylph should win the chase and tarnish his manly prowess. The hill grew steep, the ride labored, as his horse pulled barely ahead of the dappled gray to win the race.

The horses' sides were heaving, steam rising from their sweaty coats and shooting out in white plumes from their flared nostrils. Bekah's cheeks and Aidan's own were brightly flushed from the ride, their eyes shining.

"Where did you learn to ride like that? You must have had an excellent teacher," he surmised, catching his breath.

Suddenly a memory of Kenric astride Polo, herself on Elyse, filled Bekah's mind. Nay, she steadied herself against it, determined that Aidan should see no sign of a memory upon her face. Deftly she changed the subject.

"Why did you bring me to this hill? I see no surprise, Aidan."

"But look," he said, pointing eastward, where the gray light was being dispelled by a thin silvery-orange line traced along the horizon. They watched as it widened and grew into a multitude of hues. Yellow, pink and gold emerged in varying shades, turning the gray to violet in a perfect blend which only nature could cause to melt together without conflict.

"Let us go," he said, turning the prancing horse about.

"Where now?" she asked, looking into his handsome face.

"Home, of course."

He did not give her time for questions but headed his horse rapidly down the hill. She pressed her heels into the mare and followed him down, racing swiftly towards the stables. They thudded to a halt, slinging mud, and jumped down from their horses. A sleepy stable youth stifled a yawn and came foward to tend to the animals.

Aidan caught Bekah's hand in his and they ran through the wallgate and courtyards into the main castle. She muffled her laughter as they hurried up the stairs to the rooftop. The cold stone battlements were darkly gray in the new morning, and Aidan put his hands on her shoulders, turning her eastward.

The sun was just beginning to rise to view at Briarwood. Streaks of white rays shone like heavenly pillars through the blue clouds. It was a different sunrise; still, the sky had the exact same gray as her new mare. She decided to call her Sunrise.

"There," Aidan declared proudly. "What do you think of that?"

"The sunrise, Aidan?"

"Not just the sunrise! Do you not understand that we are probably the only two people in the world to see a sunrise twice in one morning?" He looked at her in surprise as if this moment should be as special to her as it was to him.

She laughed, reaching up and kissing him. He pulled her closely against him, passionately possessing her lips. The dawn matured and they descended the flight of stairs to their own room, arms about each other. As the morning light wafted through the window like silk through a loom, they once again proved to each other their deep commitment.

Bekah was elated with Sunrise, and she often went riding with Aidan. Once again she found the exhilaration of a brisk ride exciting. Her skill as an equestrienne returned, and she felt happier than she had ever been.

She wanted to give Aidan a gift in return, preferably

something made by her own hand. She secured some finely woven muslin, then bleached it in the sun until it was a lighter color. Then she laid it out on the floor, puzzling over cutting it. With Pamela's help she cut the fabric into the pieces of a shirt. Needle in hand, she sewed it together, keeping her stitches as small as possible. She hid it from Aidan whenever he was near until it was completed. Then she laid it neatly folded at the foot of the bed. That night when they retired, he noticed it.

"What is this, a new shirt?" he asked, holding it up. It had long sleeves and a collar which opened down the front. Around the collar and edges were tiny rows of embroidered braid, in multiple colors.

"I made it for you from the muslin in the storehouse," she said.

"Why, Bekah, I am most pleased that you would take the time to make me something special," he said, pulling off his other shirt and putting this one on. "It is a perfect fit! Our seamstresses seldom do such fine needlework."

"I am happy that you like it."

"How did you get the size so right?"

She ran her hands lightly over his chest, smoothing the fabric. "Your form is well emblazoned on my memory, milord."

He smiled at this, kissing her.

August came warm and sultry, its heat lessened by the cool stone walls. The newlywed couple often went riding in the cool evening or morning hours. They also frequented Pamela's cottage. Aidan and Charles had known each other from youth, and when the men went hunting game, Pamela and Bekah spent their time together.

Bekah's new position in the castle was slow to change her routine. Although she now had the freedom of the entire castle and resided in Aidan's quarters, she still lived much the same. She cared for Ember and washed her baby's soiled clothing herself, although she could have had others do it. She had several maids to wait upon her, but she preferred to do most things for herself.

The castle's people were busy from dawn to dusk. There were gardens to weed and protect from birds and small animals. Water was averted down the rows, and little boys could be seen floating leaf and twig boats down the rivulets.

The abundant harvest produced grains, vegetables, fruits and berries. Young boys continually herded flocks of fowl, numbers increased by what had been fuzzy goslings and ducklings only months before. These days the backs of serfs were continually bent in toil and harvest, reaping from the bounteous earth what could be gained before winter. The abundance at Briarwood often brought Jarlshof to mind.

In the raspberry thickets, the burdened fruit trees and well-tended gardens, Bekah saw the island revisited in her mind. Had it been only one year since the summer on Jarlshof, only one twelve-month span? It felt as if it were a millennium ago that she had lived and loved there. Kenric was still emblazoned on her mind, yet so unreal at times it was as if that past segment of her life had been but an extended dream. Other times, however, when she looked up to see a familiar scene of tree and meadow, she was transported back. She became careful to guard against such intrusion, so that it never became obvious to her husband, often pushing the memories of Kenric and Jarlshof from her mind. She knew that Kenric's people were nearby in Wessex, and in time perhaps she would meet them. Baby Ember would grow up knowing of her real father, but her place, and her mother's, was with Aidan now.

Aidan spent much of the month of August supervising the building of the new mill, putting his own work into it. The old one had burned down during the winter months, becoming a mass of charred timber and fallen stones. This had been a hardship for the people, who had to grind the flour slowly by hand. The people looked forward to its completion, and long hours were spent finishing it.

In the evenings Aidan had many chess games with his wife, laughing on the evening she finally checkmated him triumphantly. Then he taught her draughts and showed her the castle books and histories. He eased her into the role of Briarwood's mistress, and she learned much under his guidance.

The first week in September was still hot as granaries

251

became filled with precious wheat and the last of sliced fruits and drying vegetables were dehydrated under the hot sun. Later they would be stored beneath the keep along with cheesecloth sacks filled with dried corn. Dried herring and salmon brought from the ocean were also put away against the hard times. Salt was a precious commodity, and was used in preserving meat.

By the end of the month Ember was crawling, much to Bekah's delight. Aidan took pleasure in the baby, often holding her and playing with her. The baby would laugh and smile impishly at her new father, nestling her head comfortably in the crook of his arm. Eventually she would fall asleep and Aidan would turn her over to her mother, who would put the baby down for the night.

With his arm about her, Aidan and Bekah strolled up to the rooftop of Briarwood, deserted for the moment. Always amazed at the beauty of the view, they looked out over the expanse of their kingdom. The sun had disappeared in a muted blaze, for there had been a cloudless sky for most of the day.

As the blue darkened to black, pinpoints of light appeared in unique configurations in the sky. The couple studied the different arrangements of the stars, and Aidan pointed out what appeared to be a square ladle.

He soon lost interest in the stars, though, focusing his attention on his young wife. "Someday, my love, I hope you will bear my child."

She looked up at his handsome face. "Sweet Aidan. I love you!"

"Oh, Bekah! Do you know how I have longed to hear those few words?"

"But, sir! Certainly my love for you has been apparent."

"Indeed it has, but still there was an empty space which your words just now filled. Remember that you were made to enter into this marriage by force."

Bekah stood on tiptoe, kissing his lips, and he responded warmly. They left the battlements, returning to the solitude of their room.

Autumn brought with it a briskness that was refreshing after the summer's heat. Huge golden pumpkins and squash fell from the vines; cobs of cooked corn were rolled in plates of butter. Baskets of gleaming red apples were placed in cold cellars, and stubby orange carrots were buried in sand to retain their sweetness. Potato mounds were dug and filled with enough potatoes to carry the castle through winter, and last crops of late peas were harvested and served with almost every meal.

Briarwood received another visit from the salt merchant before winter, and in his company was an explorer of sorts, whom Bekah was glad to meet. Ivan was from her homeland and spoke her tongue, and he also conversed fluently in Anglian. He, too, was most pleased to meet the fair maid. After the morning meal she talked to him, inquiring about her homeland. He did not know her people, but was aware of the village in Sogn near the farmhouse.

"In truth I know of it," Ivan said. "I shall be traveling back there within the year."

"Within the year! I have not thought of my homeland these many months, or of my father. Would it be too great a favor to ask you to deliver a message to my people?"

"For one such as yourself, fair mistress of Briarwood, it would be an honor."

"My father is Lars, who dwells upon the Helgsdatter farm southwest of the village. I know that he will be most anxious for word of me, for he has had none for over a year."

"Does he not know where you are?"

"Nay, he does not. I was taken from the coastline of my homeland against my will by an Anglian raider," she confided in a half-whisper. "Will you tell him that Bekah fares well and has come to Wessex, where she is mistress at the Castle Briarwood, and that she has a daughter? Tell him that I am happily married and not to worry anymore for my safety. Also . . ." she paused for moment. "Tell him I love him."

"I will do so, milady."

"And one more thing. You must tell only Lars. No one else on the farm."

"It is done. We leave within the hour, and should I return this way I shall bring you news of him."

She smiled her gratitude, giving him a mancus, much to

the observing Crant's horror. A part of the old ache of hidden homesickness lessened within her as she watched the young red-haired Ivan mount along with the salt merchant, and leave.

The Christmas festivities were wonderful. A crisp layer of snow covered the ground and completely coated the prickly black briars that surrounded Briarwood Castle. The cold weather brought energy and excitement to the holiday.

The food was abundant, with many sweetbreads, nuts brought from the storehouse in rough sacks, honeyed snow lumps and dried fruits. Pine boughs and scattered dried mint leaves filled the air with sweet Christmas smells.

Bekah thought of her Christmas in Lady Devona's manor, and arranged to send word to her distant friends that she was well and happy. She extended an invitation to Lady Devona, hoping to have the good woman come for a visit to Briarwood in the spring.

Bekah's Christmas at Briarwood was joyous. The festive air fairly crackled, as did the fire in the huge stone hearth. Darting orange flames flickered constantly, licking at pine and cedar logs, sending warmth out to all the celebrators.

Christmas Eve there was a beautiful pageant reenacting the Savior's birth. Bekah loved watching the children in bright costumes playing parts of shepherds, kings, Mary and Joseph. Afterwards the chaplain read scriptural passages as everyone gathered around to listen. Later the children were given honeycomb and nuts, and the older people sipped hot spiced apple juice.

Christmas morning all serfs gathered at the castle and were given special gifts of pence, their own fowl or salt. Children with shining eyes stood in an eager crowd around Lord Garth, happily receiving maple cakes. The servants received gifts of herbs, salt, and their annual pay in pence and mancus. Bekah gave Aidan a pair of expertly crafted boots of soft leather, which she had had made especially for him. He in turn gave her a gold chain to fit about her waist, to which was attached a small, sheathed knife, a flat leather pouch, a pair of delicate little scissors and the castle keys. This was the symbol of her special place as mistress of Briarwood, and she wore it proudly.

Pamela gave Bekah some lovely bars of soap, scented in honeysuckle, lilac and rose. She had also made her some small satin bags filled with crushed dried rose petals, for sweetening her clothes trunks. Bekah gave her friend a small silver wrist chain, and they were both very pleased with their gifts.

Bekah made Garth a shirt similar to the one she had made for Aidan. She made her daughter a doll from cloth scraps and also sewed a little red wool frock, which she put on Ember on Christmas morn.

The January weather, true to form, was crisp and cold. On this particular day it was beautiful, with a clear sky and a yellow-white sun. For two previous days the castle and its surrounding lands had been shrouded in cold fog, which had finally departed, but only after everything became frozen. Each tree branch, twig and weed was covered in hoarfrost, smothering everything with unique, feathery beauty. It transfigured even the ugliest weeds into lacy masterpieces, and all at Briarwood were held spellbound.

It had been more than half a year since Bekah and Aidan's marriage, and in that time the castle had truly become Bekah's home. She oversaw the kitchen and what foods were prepared and instructed about the workings of the looms. In the winter months a great deal of weaving, mending, sewing and embroidering was done. The constant sound of clicking loom combs and swishing shuttles filled the main halls; a gathering of ladies with needles in hand was a common sight about the hearth. In her free time Bekah worked with needle and thread, becoming more adept at stitchery.

Often she worked closely with Portney and enjoyed his admiration. He was prompt to follow her instructions, giving her helpful hints about the books or helping her manage servant problems. She wisely followed his advice, winning him over with an approving smile. It did not take long until she had learned the managing of Briarwood's problems, important or small, and the servants always found her fair in her judgments.

She learned the skill of bargaining with the merchants and even achieved a better price from the salt merchant. Those who had dealings with her found her beguiling manners and honesty most appealing. Her frugalness was pleasing to Crant, too, and the chaplain commented that she had truly been brought to Briarwood by God's gracious hand.

Lord Garth, when he had first learned of Ember, had felt deceived and shamed. Other barons' sons had wed widows, but they had always been rich and of noble families. Bekah certainly was of a noble family if she was the daughter of King Alfred, but that news was known to no one but himself and the King. Still, even the King had not known that she already had a child. In time, however, Garth learned the whole story of Bekah's past, and became sympathetic. What brought him around completely, however, was Bekah's extreme competence.

By February Bekah had Briarwood running smoothly. Dinner meals were on time, foods were prepared with more cleansing procedures, and there was no room for the lazy servant or serf. She was always kind to her father-in-law and her genuine concern for his health was ever present.

She had a natural skill at healing the sick and a knowledge of herbs and root cures taught her by both her mother and Lady Devona that made her indispensable to the people. Pamela taught Bekah the skill of midwifery and she helped deliver three babies at the castle, something about which she was pleased and proud.

Both Crant and Portney came to inform Garth of her frugal use of supplies and her talent as a bargainer with the traveling merchants. Soon Garth was aware that petty problems and squabbles, which had greatly annoyed him, were no longer being brought before him but were instead being handled by Bekah. He was relieved that he could spend his time on important matters and useful undertakings. He realized, too, that the burden had lessened for Aidan.

Bekah had Garth's home running more smoothly than Mildred had ever done. In truth, his cousin had caused nothing but upsets. The last time Garth had seen the castle so controlled was when his own wife had it in her capable hands. Adelle would have liked Bekah, he realized suddenly. The familiarity of things as they should be was very comforting to Lord Garth.

At night, when he could not sleep and paced his room and the hall, Bekah would have a warm concoction flavored with ale sent to him, and he found himself sleeping better than ever. In time he found it impossible to resist her winning smile and gentle manners. The baby was innocent and had her mother's smile. Even if the child was darkhaired, she did have her mother's blue-violet eyes.

He was aware, too, of how much fuller Aidan's life had become. He seemed to enjoy Ember, whom he would hold and smile at as if she were his own. Bekah loved her little daughter, and Aidan came to care for Ember, too.

Bekah liked Garth, loved Aidan and found Ember to be a continual source of enjoyment as the baby learned to crawl swiftly and then to toddle about with help. There was completeness in life.

Finally Bekah had a womanly sense of fulfillment, and her once yearning heart was now filled with love. There was no bitterness tinging the cloth of her life. Briarwood was everything which her mother had talked of, and more. This was the life she was meant for.

She tried to envision the future. She had grown into a woman here, and her daughter would grow here also. There would be sons for Aidan. A new heir to Briarwood, who possessed his father's winning way and her own golden hair, would gain Lord Garth's heart and forge the links of their family lines together.

The days in Wessex glided by, silken threads run through the loom of history.

EPILOGUE

THE GLOWING COALS OF THE DYING FIRE LAY nestled in white ash and charred black wood. Outside, the howling wind had died down. Bekah's memories had been like the storm, raging, tormenting and now calm, very calm, like the soft patter of the rain washing down outside. Remembering had brought pain, but that was now washed away.

Bekah realized that the twisting of fate had brought her to this point, but she would never be able to solve the puzzle of why. Why had Kenric stormed into her life, changing it so? Why, once he had won her heart, had he been taken from her so cruelly? She could not regret him or his coming, for without it she would never have known him, never have had her little Ember, never have known her beloved Aidan. Kenric was a part of her life that would always be there, a part that had made her grow into the woman she was. But she must let go of him.

"He is gone from me," she said to herself. "And forever is a very long time. We were star-crossed. We were not meant to be. This life now is what was meant for me, and I love it. I am happy now. I love my husband, and this is the life that I want. I loved Kenric, but I must let him go from me."

She set her embroidery down, for it had grown too dark to see the stitches, and she had done little of it as her mind had roamed the halls of remembering. She looked down at her child who had fallen asleep on the floor while playing with the leather horse Aidan had made her. She knew nothing of pain, only of love, and that was as it should be.

Aidan entered the chamber and looked at his beautiful young wife. It struck him again just how much he loved her and how fortunate he was to have her. Always sensitive to her needs, he felt the quiet of the moment and said nothing. Instead he picked up his little daughter, placing her in her bed and pulling her warm coverlet about her. Then he came and sat down beside his wife and they both gazed into the fire.

He loves me so, she thought, and my love for him is doublefold.

Aidan put his arm about her, leaning his cheek against her hair in thoughtful quiet.

Bekah's memories were as ivory parchment, and in her mind she placed them upon the hot coals. Their edges seemed to brown and curl before they burst into sparks, dying away to become the last embers of the winter flame.